Bennie didn't know what prompted her.

Whatever the reason, when she turned to get the sugar and found herself standing only a few tiny inches from

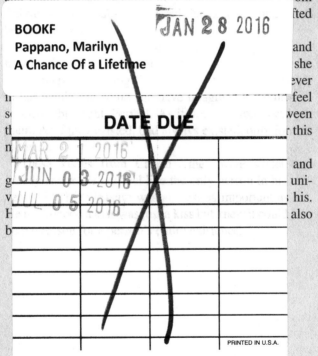

...fted

...and

...she

...ever

...feel

...ween

...r this

...and

...uni-

...his.

...also

Acclaim for the Tallgrass Novels

A Promise of Forever

"Heartbreaking and heartwarming...Pappano blends a realistic vision of returning soldiers with a tender love story."
—***Publishers Weekly***

"A good military romance with strong characters that will truly touch your heart."
—**HarlequinJunkie.com**

"A heartfelt read... With beautifully honest storytelling, Pappano expresses the vulnerable hearts of Ben and Avi."
—***RT Book Reviews***

A Love to Call Her Own

"Deeply satisfying...Pappano's characters are achingly real and flawed, and readers will commiserate with and root for the couple... This deeply moving tale will remind everyone who reads it of the great sacrifices made by those who serve and the families they leave behind."
—***Publishers Weekly*** **(starred review)**

"A solid, tender plot, well-developed, vulnerable characters and smart, modern banter are the highlights of this heartwarming story."

—*RT Book Reviews*

A Man to Hold On To

"4 1/2 stars! Through her beautiful storytelling, Pappano deftly expresses the emotions that come with love and loss. The genuine love that grows between Therese and Keegan melts the heart. Pappano's latest packs a powerful punch."

—*RT Book Reviews*

"A powerful and welcome return to Tallgrass...Pappano excels at depicting deep emotion . . . including plenty of humor."

—*Publishers Weekly* (starred review)

A Hero to Come Home To

"Pappano shines in this poignant tale of love, loss, and learning to love again...[She] creates achingly real characters whose struggles will bring readers to tears."

—*Publishers Weekly* (starred review)

A Chance
of a Lifetime

A Chance of a Lifetime

Marilyn Pappano

FOREVER

NEW YORK BOSTON

Forever
Hachette Book Group
1290 Avenue of the Americas
New York, NY 10104

www.HachetteBookGroup.com

Printed in the United States of America

First Edition: December 2015
10 9 8 7 6 5 4 3 2 1

OPM

Forever is an imprint of Grand Central Publishing.
The Forever name and logo are trademarks of Hachette Book Group, Inc.

The Hachette Speakers Bureau provides a wide range of authors for speaking events. To find out more, go to www.hachettespeakersbureau.com or call (866) 376-6591.

The publisher is not responsible for websites (or their content) that are not owned by the publisher.

For all the combat medics and corpsmen who rush into danger to save not just their buddies but anyone who needs their help. You guys are the bravest, the toughest, the heroes responsible for giving a second chance at life to so many of our troops.

And as always, for my favorite "Devil Doc," my husband, Robert. Your Marines and I are lucky to have you!

The soldier, above all other people, prays for peace, for he must suffer and bear the deepest wounds and scars of war.

—General Douglas MacArthur

It has been said, "time heals all wounds." I do not agree. The wounds remain. In time, the mind, protecting its sanity, covers them with scar tissue and the pain lessens. But they are never gone.

—Rose Kennedy

A Chance
of a Lifetime

Chapter 1

You can't go home again, someone had famously said.

Someone else had added, *But that's okay, because you can't ever really leave home in the first place.*

Calvin Sweet was home. If he tried real hard, he could close his eyes and recall every building lining the blocks, the sound of the afternoon train, the smells coming from the restaurants. He could recognize the feel of the sun on his face, the breeze blowing across his skin, the very scent of the air he breathed. It smelled of prairie and woodland and livestock and sandstone and oil and history and home.

There were times he'd wanted to be here so badly that he'd grieved for it. Times he'd thought he would never see it again. Times he'd wanted never to see it—or anything else—again. Ironically enough, it was trying to ensure that he would never come back except in a box that had brought him home, alive and unwell.

He didn't close his eyes. Didn't need a moment to take it all in. Didn't want to see reminders of the streets where he'd grown up, where he'd laughed and played and lived and learned with an innocence that was difficult to remember. He just stared out the windows, letting nothing register but disquiet. Shame. Bone-deep weariness. It wasn't that he didn't want to be in Tallgrass. He didn't want to be anywhere.

"You have family in the area," the driver said, glancing his way.

It was the first time the corporal had spoken in twenty miles. He'd tried to start a couple of conversations at the airport in Tulsa and in the first half of the trip, but Calvin hadn't had anything to say. He still didn't, but he dredged up a response. "Yeah. Right here in town."

When the Army sent troops to the Warrior Transition Units, they tried to send them to the one closest to home so the family could be part of the soldier's recovery. Calvin's mama, his daddy, his grandma and aunties and uncles and cousins—they were all dedicated to being there for him. Whether he wanted them or not.

"How long you been away?"

"Eleven years." Sometimes it seemed impossible that it could have been so long. He remembered being ten and fourteen and eighteen like it was just weeks ago. Riding his bike with J'Myel and Bennie. Going fishing. Dressing up in a white shirt and trousers every Sunday for church—black in winter, khaki in summer. Playing baseball and basketball. Going to the drive-in movie, graduating from elementary school to middle school to high school with J'Myel and Bennie. The Three Musketeers. The Three Stooges.

The best memories of his life. He'd never thought it possible that *All for one and one for all!* could become *two against one*, then *one and one*. J'Myel had turned against him. Had married Bennie. Had gotten his own damn self killed. He hadn't spoken to Calvin for three years before he died, and Bennie, forced to choose, had cut him off, too. He hadn't been invited to the wedding. Hadn't been welcome at the funeral.

With a grimace, he rubbed the ache in his forehead. Remembering hurt. If the docs could give him a magic pill that wiped his memory clean, he'd take it. All the good memories in his head weren't worth even one of the bad ones.

At the last stoplight on the way out of town, the corporal shifted into the left lane, then turned onto the road that led to the main gates of Fort Murphy. Sandstone arches stood on each side, as impressive now as they'd been when he was a little kid outside looking in. Just past the guard shack stood a statue of the post's namesake, Audie Murphy, the embodiment of two things Oklahomans valued greatly: cowboys and war heroes. Despite being scrawny black kids and not knowing a damn thing about horses, he and J'Myel had wanted to be Audie when they grew up.

At least they'd managed the war hero part, according to the awards they'd been given. They'd both earned a chestful of them on their tours in Iraq and Afghanistan.

With a deep breath, he fixed his gaze outside the windows, forcing himself to concentrate on nothing that wasn't right there in front of him. They were passing a housing area now, the houses cookie cutter in size and floor plan, the lawns neatly mowed and yellowed now.

October, and already Oklahoma had had two snows, with another predicted in the next few days. Most of the trees still bore their autumn leaves, though, in vivid reds and yellows and rusts and golds, and yellow and purple pansies bloomed in the beds marking the entrances to each neighborhood.

They passed signs for the gym, the commissary, the exchange, barracks and offices, and the Warrior Transition Unit. Their destination was the hospital, where he would be checked in and checked out to make sure nothing had changed since he'd left the hospital at Joint Base Lewis-McChord in Washington that morning. He tried to figure out how he felt about leaving there, about coming here—psychiatrists were big on feelings—but the truth was, he didn't care one way or the other.

His career was pretty much over. No matter how good a soldier he'd been, the Army didn't have a lot of use for a captain who'd tried to kill himself. They'd diagnosed him with post-traumatic stress disorder, the most common injury suffered by military personnel in the war on terror, and they'd started him in counseling while arranging a transfer to Fort Murphy. Soon he would be separated from the Army, but they would make a stab at putting him back together before they let him go.

But when some things were broken, they stayed broken. Nothing could change that.

Within an hour, Calvin was settled in his room. He hated the way people had looked at his medical record, hated the way they'd looked at him. *He's a nut job, a weak one. Killed the enemy in the war but couldn't even manage to kill himself. What a loser.*

More likely, those were his thoughts, not the staff's.

He sat on the bed, then slowly lay back. He could function on virtually no sleep—he'd done it too many times to count—but sometimes his body craved it. Not in the normal way, not eight or nine hours a night, but twenty-hour stretches of near unconsciousness. It was his brain's way of shutting down, he guessed, of keeping away things he couldn't deal with. He could go to sleep right now, but it wouldn't last long, because his parents were coming to see him, and Elizabeth Sweet wouldn't let a little thing like sleep deter her from hugging and kissing her only son.

Slowly he sat up again. His hands shook at the thought of facing his parents, and his gut tightened. Elizabeth and Justice hadn't raised a coward. They'd taught him to honor God, country, and family, to stand up for himself and others, to be strong and capable, and he'd failed. He'd tried to kill himself. He knew that sentence was repeating endlessly, disbelievingly, not just in his head but also in theirs.

He was ashamed of himself for such poor planning. He'd never once seen anyone at that public park in all the times he'd been there, and he certainly hadn't counted on some misguided punk to intervene. After "saving" Calvin's life, the kid, named Diez, had stolen his wallet and car and disappeared. Some people got the Good Samaritan. He got the thieving one.

Announcements sounded over the intercom, calling staff here or there, and footsteps moved quickly up and down the hall, checking patients. Calvin sat in the bed and listened, hearing everything and nothing, screening out all the extraneous noises until he heard the one he was listening for: the slow, heavy tread of his father's work-booted feet. Justice had a limp—arthritis in knees punished by years laying floor tile—and the resulting imbalance in his steps was as familiar to Calvin as his father's voice.

The steps stopped outside his door. Calvin's heart pounded in his chest, so he took a deep breath to slow it, to prepare himself, and imagined his parents doing the same. He slid to his feet as the door slowly swung open and his mom and dad just as slowly came inside. For a moment, they stared at him, and he stared back, until Elizabeth gave a cry and rushed across the room to wrap her arms around him.

She was shorter, rounder, and he had to duck his head to rest his cheek against her head, but he felt just as small and vulnerable as he ever had. There'd never been a thing in his life that Mom couldn't make better with a hug— until now—and that just about broke his heart.

It seemed forever before she lifted her head and released him enough to get a good look at him. Tears glistened in her eyes, and her smile wobbled as she cupped her hand to his jaw. "Oh, son, it's good to see you." Her gaze met his, darted away, then came back with a feeble attempt at humor. "Or would you prefer that I call you sweet baby boy of mine?"

He managed to phony up a smile, or at least a loosening of his facial muscles, at the memory of her response when he'd complained about being called *son* in front of his friends. "Son is fine." His voice was gravelly, his throat tight.

"You know, I can come up with something even worse." But there was no promise behind her words, none of that smart mouth that she lived up to quite nicely most of the time. She was shooting for normal, but he and she could both see there was nothing normal about this situation. He hadn't known normal for so long that he was wearied by it.

Justice stepped forward. "Move on over a bit, Lizzie. Let a man give his only boy a welcome-home hug." His voice was gravelly, too, but it always had been, rough-edged and perfect for booming out *Amen*s in church or controlling small boys with no more than a sharp-edged word.

Elizabeth stepped aside, and Justice took his turn. His hug was strong and enveloping and smelled of fabric softener and the musky aftershave he'd worn longer than Calvin had been alive. It was so familiar, one of those memories that never faded, and it reminded Calvin of the person he used to be, the one who could do anything, be anything, survive anything, and prosper.

The one who had disappointed the hell out of his mother, his father, and himself.

After his dad released him, they all stared at each other again. Calvin had never seen them looking so uncomfortable, shifting their weight, wanting to smile but not sure they should or could. The psychiatrist in Washington had tried to prepare him for this initial meeting, for the embarrassment and awkwardness and guilt. For no one knowing what to say or how to say it. For the need to be honest and open and accepting and forgiving.

Calvin had been too lost in his misery—and too angry at Diez—to pay attention.

Should he point out the elephant sitting in the middle of the room? Just set his parents down and blurt it out? *Sorry, Mom and Dad, I tried to kill myself, but it wasn't you, it was me, all my fault. Sorry for any distress I caused. Now that we've talked about it, we don't ever need to do it again. So...how's that high school football coach working out?*

And as an aside: *Oh, yeah...I'm getting help and I haven't tried anything since. We're cool, right?*

Unless—his gut tightened—he did try again. He didn't want to, swore he didn't, but the fear haunted him: that the docs would help, the meds would help, he'd find a reason to live, and then something in his screwed-up brain would put a gun in his hand again.

His throat worked hard on a swallow, his jaw muscles clenched, and his stomach was tossing about like a leaf in a storm, but he managed to force air into his lungs, to force words out of his mouth. "So...it was cold outside when I got here."

"Dropped to about thirty-eight degrees." There was relief in Justice's voice for a conversation he could embrace. "Wind chill's down in the twenties. The weather guys are saying an early winter and a hard one."

"What's Gran say?"

Elizabeth's smile was shaky. "She says every winter's hard when you're seventy-six and have the arthritis in your joints."

"She wanted to come with us, but..." Justice finished with a wave of his hands. "You know Emmeline."

That Calvin did. Emmeline would have cried. Would have knelt on the cold tile and said a prayer of homecoming. Would have demanded he bend so she could give him a proper hug, and then she would have grabbed his ear in her tightest grip and asked him what in tarnation he'd been thinking. She would have reminded him of all the switchings she'd given him and would have promised to snatch his hair right out of his scalp if he ever even thought about such a wasteful thing again.

He loved her. He wanted to see her. But gratitude washed over him that it didn't have to be tonight.

"Your auntie Sarah was asking after you," Elizabeth said. "She and her boys are coming up from Oklahoma City for Thanksgiving. Hannah and her family's coming from Norman, and Auntie Mae said all three of her kids would be here, plus her nine grandbabies. They're all just so anxious to see you."

Calvin hoped he was keeping his face pleasantly blank, but a glimpse of his reflection in the window proved otherwise. He looked like his eyes might just pop out of his head. He'd known he would see family—more than he wanted and more quickly than he wanted—but Thanksgiving was only a month away. Way too soon for a family reunion.

His mother went on, still naming names, adding the special potluck dishes various relatives were known for, throwing in a few tidbits about marriages and divorces and new babies, talking faster and cheerier until Justice laid his hand over hers just as her voice ran out of steam. "I don't think he needs to hear about all that right now. You know, it took me a long time to build up the courage—" His gaze flashed to Calvin's, then away. "To get used to your family. All those people, all that noise. Calvin's been away awhile. He might need some time to adjust to being back before you spring that three-ring circus on him."

Elizabeth's face darkened with discomfort. "Of course. I mean, it's a month off. And it'll be at Auntie Mae's house so there will be plenty of places to get away for a while. Whatever you want, son, that's what we'll do."

They chatted a few more minutes, then took their leave, hugging Calvin again, telling him they missed him and loved him, Justice thanking God he was home. Her hand on the door frame, Elizabeth turned back. "I don't suppose...church tomorrow, family dinner after...It would just be you and me and your daddy and Gran..."

Calvin swallowed hard, looking away from the hopefulness on her face. "I, uh, don't think I can leave here yet. Being a weekend, they're a little slow getting things settled."

Disappointment shadowed her caramel eyes, but she hid it with a smile. "Of course. Maybe next time."

Calvin listened to the door close behind them, to his father's heavy tread walking away, and his mother's earlier words echoed inside his head. *Whatever you want, son, that's what we'll do.*

The problem was, what did a man do when he didn't want anything at all? How did he survive? Was there any conceivable destination that made the journey worthwhile? Or was he going to suffer until the day he finally died?

* * *

Lifting as many reusable shopping bags from the trunk as her two hands could carry, Benita Ford hurried along the path to the back door of the house she shared with her grandmother. Lights shone through the windows, and the central heat and air system hunkered against the house on the back side was rumbling, meaning it would be warm and cozy inside. Why in the world had she worn a dress, tights, and her new black boots to go shopping today? She'd lost contact with her toes a long time ago, and every time the prairie wind had blown, it seemed the cold had headed straight up her skirt for a *woo-hoo* of the sort she didn't need. Jeans, wool socks, leather running shoes, a T-shirt or sweater, and the gorgeous wool coat that reached almost to her ankles—*those* were shopping clothes.

"*Brr!* At least I know my ice cream didn't melt on the way home." Mama Maudene Pickering was waiting in the kitchen, ready to unpack the bags while Bennie went after the rest. The old lady wore black sweatpants that puddled over her shearling-lined house shoes, along with an orange, black, and purple Halloween sweater that was scarier than anything else Bennie had seen throughout the day.

"I don't remember ice cream being on the shopping list," Bennie teased.

Mama shook a finger at her. "You don't want to give an old woman palpitations. But if you do, be sure to ask for the good-looking firemen when you call 911."

"And you do the same for me if I ever need it." Ducking her head, Bennie rushed out into the cold again. She had another six or eight bags, along with four cases of bottled water that she had to haul in or risk finding her trunk covered in icicles the next day.

By the time she made her last dash, she was finally warm, sweating inside her clothes. She took off the cardigan that was a cute match to the dress, tossed it on the back of a chair, and began helping her grandmother.

"See anyone interesting at the grocery store?"

"Just people hoping to get home before they froze."

"You young kids. In my day, we didn't have all the nice clothes and gloves and central heat and a grocery store just down the street."

"No, you had a sandy warm beach just down the street." Mama had grown up on the barrier islands of South Carolina, soaking in lazy breezes and running barefoot in the sand and living—at least, to hear her tell it—an idyllic life. Bennie knew it hadn't been all sunshine and roses, especially after her marriage ended. Still, it had been sweet.

"It got cold there, too, missy. I remember one time it snowed twice in one month. Almost covered the ground both times." Mama burst into laughter. "I have to admit, if I'd known more about Oklahoma weather, I might have kept on traveling a little farther west. But when I got here, the sun was shining, the air was crisp and clean, and the leaves were the most wonderful shades of yellow, orange, and red. I knew this was where I wanted to be." Her brow furrowed in thought. "That was in October, too."

"And this is its evil twin, Octobrrr." Bennie emptied the last of the canvas bags, rolled each one, and stuck them inside the largest bag to return to her car in the morning. "But warm weather will be back again soon."

"Most likely. I've worn shorts in January and a sweater in June." Mama shuffled to the refrigerator, arms filled with milk and yogurt. On her way to the small pantry, Bennie opened the door for her. Grocery shopping was a regular Saturday activity for her, and October was always her overstocking time. She'd been forced to trudge to the grocery store once years ago when snow and ice had kept their neighborhood impassable for days. She had learned her lesson. If the streets froze now, they had enough food to feed themselves and the neighbors. If the pipes froze, there was plenty of bottled water, and if the power went off, they had a huge supply of candles and batteries for flashlights, and firewood stretched the length of the house two ricks deep.

Bennie was prepared for anything.

"—reheat the leftover pot roast," Mama was saying when Bennie stepped back into the kitchen. "Chop everything up, mix it all up with gravy, and serve it with some thick slices of fresh white bread. Hm-*hmm*, that sounds good."

"It certainly does." Bennie put away the last of the groceries, then gave her grandmother a hug. "You know, your good cooking is the reason you and I are both on the round side."

Mama snorted. "I've been a size twelve my whole grown-up life. I should know, since I'm the one cutting the size tags out of my old clothes and sewing them into my new, bigger ones." Her hearty laugh emphasized the roundness of her face, filled with lines and haloed by gray hair and as beautiful as a face could be.

Gratitude surged in Bennie, tightening her chest. Her mother might have run off before Bennie saw her fifth birthday, and her father might have died before her tenth. She might have lost her husband, J'Myel, in the war, but she'd always had her grandmother. Mama's love was boundless and forgiving and warmed a girl's heart.

"Did you get all your shopping done?" Mama asked as she pulled the leftovers from the refrigerator, then gathered a knife, a cutting board, and a large cast-iron pot. Bennie had once given her a much lighter stainless pot, and Mama had proclaimed it just what she needed before putting it away and continuing to use her cast-iron, even when picking up a full pan required a grunt of effort.

"I bought a few things," Bennie replied as she wiped down the oilcloth that covered the kitchen table, then began setting it for dinner.

"I finished my Christmas shopping in July."

"Braggart."

"If you'd use the Internet, you could've finished yours already, too."

Bennie rolled her eyes, careful not to let Mama see. When the neighbor kid had shown her grandmother how to get online, Bennie had thought it would be a passing curiosity. Then the first purchase had arrived and proven her wrong. Since then, the UPS and FedEx drivers had become Mama's newest BFFs.

"Aw, you know me. I like to do my shopping in person. I want to touch stuff, see it, smell it."

Mama made a dismissive gesture with the knife. "I touch it, see it, and smell it when it gets here, and if I don't like it, I send it right back for something else."

Bennie wasn't an avid shopper, not like her friend Jessy, but she enjoyed the experience, especially when the Christmas decorations were up but the holiday was still far enough off that people weren't yet frantic. It reminded her of her childhood, of trips to Tulsa for the parade, of driving around the neighborhoods looking at extravagant lighting displays and visiting Santa Claus at Utica Square.

It reminded her of different times—not better, just innocent. She hadn't known about death and loss then. Yes, her mother had abandoned her, but her father and Mama

had filled that void. Back when Christmas was still magical, she hadn't known her father would die. She'd never
dreamed that her two best friends in the entire world
would grow so far apart. She'd certainly never guessed
that she would marry one of them, then lose him before
their second anniversary, or that the other wouldn't even
call her to say he was sorry.

Moisture seeped into her eyes. She could handle thinking about J'Myel or Calvin one at a time, but having them
both on her mind saddened her. Them losing their bond
still seemed impossible, as unlikely as Bennie deciding
she no longer loved Mama. It just couldn't happen.

But it had.

And she'd been oh, so sorry ever since.

Forcing the thoughts and the loss away, she poured
two glasses of iced tea, heavily sweetened the way
Mama had taught her to like it, then went to her room
to slip out of her boots and into a disreputable pair of
loafers. Her toes wiggled in relief, her arches reveling
in comfort, after a whole day in the heels. She would
put herself through a lot to look good in public, but at
home, comfort reigned.

By the time she returned to the kitchen, sleet was spitting against the windows, not much, the sort that said
Mother Nature hadn't decided whether she was just playing with them or intended to give them a storm. Every
tropic-loving cell in her body hoped for the former while
every realistic one prepared to accept the worst.

Mama had filled two steaming bowls with roasted
beef, potatoes, carrots, and celery and placed a loaf of
warm bread between them on the table. They joined
hands and said grace, a short prayer that had survived at

least four generations in the Pickering family, then dug into their food. It tasted even better than it had sounded.

They chatted about nothing: the weather, the gifts she'd bought for her friend Ilena's baby boy, John, the presents they would ship to family back in South Carolina, the Halloween decorations that were spookifying the house before coming down next week. The room was so cozy, the food so comforting, that Bennie was slowly being lulled into lazy, hazy contentment. Then Mama pushed her empty bowl away, folded her arms on the tabletop, and leaned toward Bennie. "I talked to Emmeline Sweet just before you got back."

So much for contentment. All it took was one mention of Calvin's family and, poof, the turmoil returned. She tried to hide it, to act casually as she picked up her own empty bowl and carried it, along with Mama's, to the sink. "How is Miss Emmeline?"

Mama didn't answer but went straight to the point. "Her grandson's back in town."

* * *

Joe Cadore stood in front of the refrigerator, bent at the waist, searching for something worth eating for dinner, and had no more luck than the last two times he'd looked. There was yogurt, protein drinks, eggs, fruit, milk, and cheese—all perfectly fine in their place, but their place was not on a dreary, freezing Saturday night. This was a time for comfort foods like his mom's homemade macaroni and cheese, or Dad's chili and jalapeño corn bread, or Grandma's pasta Bolognese.

This was a time for his neighbor Lucy's home cooking.

He looked out the window over the kitchen sink and watched the ice where it glistened on tree branches and fence wires. Lucy could have plans that didn't include a self-invited guest. She could even be on a date. Everyone had grown so used to her single status that when she'd started dating the doctor jerk from Tulsa last summer, none of them was as shocked as she was, not even Joe. Thank God, the doc had hooked up with Avi Grant and moved out of state with her last month.

Just because the doc was gone, though, didn't mean there weren't plenty of other guys out there waiting for their shot at Lucy. She'd be the type to meet cute—someone changing a flat for her, helping her out of a tough spot, or reaching for the same loaf of bread she did—and *boom*.

Joe's feet had grown cold on the wood floor, and the reflection looking back at him in the window wore a scowl. Grabbing a protein drink and an orange, he returned to the living room, sliding over the back of the couch, landing on the cushions just as his phone rang. What his nieces called his grouchy face disappeared the instant he checked Caller ID, a grin taking its place. "Hey, Luce."

"Have you had dinner yet?"

He set the fruit and drink on the coffee table. "Nope. I looked in the refrigerator three times, and there was nothing to eat in there."

"You know, there are times when protein drinks and fruit just don't make the grade."

"Yeah, I know."

She laughed, and he thought it was one of the best sounds in the world. She hadn't laughed a lot in the beginning, still mourning her husband, trying to figure out how her perfect life had come to such a screeching halt. But eventually the laughs had returned, and the smiles and the grins, and they'd grown a topflight friendship. She was the easiest woman to be with that he'd ever known—the sweetest, funniest, most giving. The time spent with her was the highlight of his life. Well, along with the time spent on the football field. And with his family. But, yeah, Luce definitely ranked in the top three.

Her voice interrupted his thoughts. "...beef and cabbage stew and a loaf of peasant bread still warm from the oven, if you want to join me."

He definitely wanted. But he kept his tone casual. "And all I have to do is...What? Persuade Norton to go out in the sleet and do his business?"

"You think I would bribe you with food to take care of our dog?" she asked sweetly. "Besides, you're from Alaska. This weather is supposed to be like a mild fall evening to you."

He snorted as he pulled on the socks and shoes he'd left on the floor earlier. "Ice is cold no matter where you're from, Luce. Do you need anything?"

"I'm from San Diego, land of warm sandy beaches. I always stock up for times like these, so all I need is you and your appetite. See you in five."

He hung up, put the drink and orange back in the fridge, then headed for the back door, where his heavy coats hung on a rack. After a minute, he pivoted and went to his room, throwing his T-shirt toward the hamper in one corner, pulling a clean shirt from a hanger, and tugging it on. He sprayed on cologne, then combed his hair.

Back in the kitchen, he slid into a down jacket, a black

knit cap bearing the OSU Cowboys logo, gloves, and a scarf before ducking out the back door. The ice on his patio crunched beneath his feet, taking on a different pitch when he reached the grass separating his house from Lucy's, then another crunch across her patio. Welcoming light shone through the fixture over her door, scattered and prismed by layers of glass.

Norton's bark was just as welcoming, a loud *woof* accompanied by frantic scratching. An instant later, Lucy opened the door and Joe gratefully stepped inside.

Her house was laid out just like his, but his never felt like hers. Incredible smells filled the air, there were homey touches everywhere, and he swore the house had a personality all its own. But maybe that was because Lucy had so much personality that it spilled over, filling the space around her.

"Hey, Luce." He crouched to rub behind the dog's ears, earning a grunt and a few thumps of tail against cabinet. "You need to go out, buddy?"

Usually, anytime was the right time for Norton to sniff the backyard and renew his own scents, but tonight the dog backed away from him and the doorway, not stopping until his butt hit the opposite wall. There he slid down, chin on his paws, and kept a cautious watch on both Joe and Lucy.

"You know his last encounter with ice wasn't much fun," Lucy said as she dished up two bowls of stew.

"Not for him, though as I recall, you got a good laugh from it." It had been last winter, and Norton had gone bounding out the door, unaware of the two inches of sleet covering everything. When he'd hit it, his feet had slid out from under him and he'd sailed halfway across the yard before an oak tree stopped him. He'd struggled to his feet, peed, and inched his way back to the house, body intact, dignity totally disintegrated.

Joe stripped off his outdoor clothes, tossing them on the kitchen table, then filled two glasses from a pitcher of water with lemon slices floating in it. He carried them to the coffee table, went back for napkins and silverware and a basket filled with thick slices of sweet, yeasty bread. The crust was golden and buttery, dotted with flakes of sea salt and rubbed with roasted garlic. It was in the running for one of his favorite foods ever.

They sat on the floor between the couch and the coffee table, shoulders bumping as they settled. In all the hundreds of meals he'd eaten here, not once had they ever used the kitchen or dining table. On the couch, on the floor, outside on a pretty day…they always chose best-buds comfort over propriety. It was just one of the things he liked about Lucy.

One of about seventeen million and counting.

Chapter 2

Lucy lay on her side on the sofa, her stomach full, the heavenly tastes of butter, salt, and garlic lingering on her tongue. If she put one more bite in her mouth, she would get that achy, shame-inducing discomfort that she'd become so familiar with in the last seven years, but her brain still followed the rules it had learned when she was a child: After dinner, you offered a guest dessert. "You want dessert?"

Joe lay on the love seat, head resting on his bent arm, legs hanging off the other end. He'd kicked off his size fourteen shoes at some point, and his left big toe poked through a hole in its white cotton sock. She'd suggested to him once that he throw away all his athletic socks that had worn toes or heels, and he'd looked genuinely puzzled because *the sock still works fine.* "What've you got?"

Mike's reasoning had gone along those lines, which was why she'd tossed out so many ragged jeans and shirts when she'd finally found the courage to clean out his closet.

Feeling the squeeze of her heart that always accompanied thought of Mike, she smiled. "Cupcakes in every flavor you can imagine, coffee cake, or sweet little tarts. Apple, cherry, lemon, or chocolate." She was already getting to her feet because Joe always liked dessert and had the muscle-to-fat ratio that allowed him to eat it without worrying where the calories went.

She didn't worry, either. She knew every excess calorie in her body went to her butt and boobage.

Instead of heading toward the kitchen, she went down the hall to the guest bedroom, opening the door carefully so Norton couldn't push his way inside. The furniture that had filled the room, hand-me-downs from both her and Mike's grandparents, had been moved into storage in her friend Marti's garage. Now five-foot-long tables ran the length of the room, with narrow aisles for squeezing through, and every table was filled with luscious, beautiful pastries, secured in clear plastic containers to keep them fresh.

Sugar and butter and flavoring—vanilla, almond, hazelnut—perfumed the air with a sweet, heavy aroma. Six months ago, if she had baked this many desserts, she would have eaten enough of them to make herself sick. Now all it took was a whiff of the scents to give her stomach a queasy tumble.

"Jeez, Luce, you should take pictures," Joe said over her shoulder.

"For what?"

"Your website. If you're going to start a business, you're going to need a website."

"They are pretty, aren't they?" she said with satisfaction even as his words—*a business*—sent flutters through her, both the anticipatory kind and the scared-out-of-her-wits kind. What did she know about starting or running a business? More than she had four weeks ago, she admitted. In the past month, she'd read endlessly, talked to small business owners and small business advisors. At the last three Tuesday night dinners with her best-friend margarita girls, they'd discussed nothing else. Therese's stepdaughter Abby had even come up with a name that Lucy loved: Prairie Harts. Abby had sketched a logo, too, a spring prairie scene with wildflowers, each of their blossoms heart-shaped.

"What are these for?"

"The singles and seniors Sunday school classes, plus a reception the colonel's having Monday."

"Paid or donation?"

"Free to the church. The colonel insisted on paying." Her boss wouldn't even accept the discount she'd offered. The reception was official Army business, and if they paid full price to anyone else for catering the sweets, he said, they would pay full price to her. "It's my first real event."

Grinning, Joe bumped her shoulder. "It's official then. Prairie Harts is in business."

She grinned, too, even as a tiny shiver rippled through her. She pretended she didn't know where it came from, but of course she did. It was from margarita girl Jessy, who'd innocently suggested last month that Joe deliver a hug and a kiss to Lucy, and from the morning of Mike's birthday when she hadn't been able to drag herself out of bed, so Joe had joined her there, offering sweet words of encouragement and a sweeter touch. Holding hands. So simple. So innocent. And exactly what she'd needed.

And since then...She stole a glance at him from the corner of her eye. Tall, lean, solid, his hair blond, his skin golden, and his eyes the prettiest blue. He was twenty-eight going on sixteen, irreverent, immature, and totally lacking in seriousness except when it came to his beloved football. The high school kids he coached revered him, the students he taught respected him, and women lusted after him. Every one of the margarita girls admired him, even the ones who hated sports.

Lucy had loved him from the moment they'd met. He was her best guy friend. But lately...

Remembering Ben Noble, the gorgeous surgeon she'd crushed on over the summer, she sighed. When had she started falling for guys so far out of her league?

But she'd gotten Ben, the woman inside her whispered. He just hadn't turned out to be what she needed. There had been plenty of affection and love, just no spark. She *wanted* a spark. Heavens, she wanted a whole wildfire.

Joe picked up a mini caramel-frosted cupcake and popped it in his mouth, closing his eyes for a moment. "Damn, Luce, that's good."

"Thank you. And thanks to you and your team for being my taste testers."

"What happens if the weather cancels church or the reception?"

"I will put on my coat and boots and personally deliver them to every parishioner. As for the reception, neither rain nor sleet..."

Plastic crackled as he removed a glazed tart from one of the containers. "That's the post office."

"Well, it applies to the Army, too. Hospital staff has to be there, no matter what, to take care of the patients. I may have to walk all the way with the food on my back, but I'll get it there."

Behind her, Norton whined before trotting down the hall to the living room. Lucy watched him disappear around the corner, tail curled in the air, then turned back to Joe. "I believe the baby is calling your name."

He popped the rest of the tart into his mouth, took a second for good measure, and squeezed past her. "I'm coming, buddy."

She breathed in the scents of fabric softener, shampoo, and man—eau de Joe—and smiled as she flipped off the light. Lord, she missed man smells: shaving cream, cologne, sweat, funky running shoes, and even the engine oil that had migrated under Mike's fingernails. Her house always smelled great, but these days it was distinctly feminine. She wanted the male fragrances back, both good and bad.

Just one of many things she wanted back.

When she returned to the living room, Joe and Norton were there. The man was standing in the doorway to the kitchen, swinging Norton's leash to tempt him to follow, but the dog was hunkered at the front door, frantically sniffing the bottom of it, his head down, his butt wiggling in the air, and agitated whines coming from his mouth. "What's up with him?" she asked. Norton rarely went out the front door, and he never got this anxious to potty. He was well known, in fact, for peeing in the middle of the kitchen floor whenever he felt like it.

"I don't know." Joe came closer, waving the leash. "C'mon, buddy, let's go out."

Norton didn't even spare him a glance. With a shrug, Joe went to the door, grabbed the dog's collar with one hand, flipped on the porch light, and opened the door. Norton's feet scrabbled on the wood floor as he lunged toward the small stoop, putting so much power into it that Lucy would have been tumbling down the steps about now, but Joe managed to restrain him.

"Damn, Lucy, get a towel, will you?"

She hurried down the hall to the bathroom and grabbed a large towel. When she got back to the living room, the door still stood open, but Joe had hooked the leash onto Norton's collar and pulled him to the couch. He traded the leash for the towel, and she braced her feet against the dog's straining while Joe stepped outside.

Norton's whimpers rose to a howl in the seconds Joe was out of sight. He stopped mid-*erooo* when Joe came back inside, holding the towel bunched in his hands. Sleet dotted his hair and shoulders, but he was grinning as he opened the towel to reveal the tiniest, scrawniest, wettest creature she'd ever seen, encrusted in ice and shivering violently. As she stared, the kitten lifted its little orange head, opened its little pink mouth, and pitifully meowed.

"Look, Luce, Norton found you a new baby," Joe said, as if the thing she wanted most in life was another animal. "Good boy, Norton, good boy."

* * *

Calvin dressed early Sunday morning and left his room to find a decent cup of coffee. What he got from the RN at the nursing station was a heavy mug, filled half with hot coffee, half hot milk, and smelling like his mom's cinnamon cookies. *My specialty,* the nurse had said with a wink before tucking the Thermos back into a cabinet. Warming his fingers on the hot pottery, he returned to his room, breathing deeply of the aroma, and took a seat in the chair next to the large window. The coffee smelled so good that it seemed a shame to drink it, but once the steam dissipated to occasional wisps, he took a sip. Damn, it was as good as it smelled.

"Good morning." A medic let himself into the room, carrying a tray. "Normally, our ambulatory patients eat in the dining hall down on the second floor, but you're getting a special delivery. You want to move to the warmer side of the room for breakfast? Granted, I'm just guessing that this side is warmer based on the fact that at least there's no ice formed on the walls over here."

Calvin glanced at the window behind him, traces of frost etched on the inside of the glass. When he was a kid, in the few minutes before his mom rousted him from the bed on winter mornings, he'd drawn all kinds of scenes on his windows, using his fingernail to scrape off the frost. "No, thanks. I'll be okay here."

The medic set the tray on the bed table, wheeled it over, and adjusted it to the proper height. He lifted the lid. "Looks like you got the I'd-rather-have-MREs special. Lucky you." He scanned the tray, then met Calvin's gaze. "Can you think of anything I forgot besides the flavor?"

Calvin shook his head.

"Okay, then, I'll be back in a while to pick up your tray. Enjoy your breakfast."

Calvin took another sip of coffee while inventorying the tray. There were scrambled eggs, their color so pale that they must be egg substitute. The toast could have used another minute or two in the toaster, and the jelly was strawberry instead of his favorite, grape. A piece of gray sausage, probably substitute meat, and half an orange rounded the plate, while circling the plate was a single-serving box of cereal, a carton of low-fat milk, a four-ounce carton of grape juice—he'd rather have orange—and a cup of cold coffee. No sugar, no cream, and the little package of salt was fake.

If he were a few miles away at his parents' house, his mom would be fixing sourdough pancakes, eggs over easy, fried potatoes, homemade sausage, biscuits, and thick cream gravy. But she would expect something in exchange for that breakfast: some hint, some reminder of the son who used to be. She would want conversation— deep and painful or lighthearted and fake—and he wasn't yet up to either.

Picking up a plastic fork, he poked at the eggs, cutting them into chunks that held their shape. Not sure whether the movement of his mouth was a rueful smile or a grimace, he laid the fork down and picked up the cinnamon coffee again. He knew for sure it was a smile when he tilted his head back, closed his eyes, and savored every drop of it.

The air pressure changed as the door opened. He'd already learned that there was no such thing as privacy in a hospital, but he kept his eyes shut as footsteps approached, until the bed creaked.

"Coffee may be the drink of the gods, but it doesn't count as breakfast." It was Valentina, the nurse responsible for the cinnamon brew. She leaned against the foot of the bed, hands pushed into the pockets of the jacket that covered her scrub top.

"I'm not hungry."

"Hm. I've never had that problem in my life. But you have to eat something. If you don't, the dietitians find out, and they come and rag on me, and then I have to pull rank on you."

"Which is hard since I outrank you." Barely. She was a lieutenant, one paygrade below his own rank.

She smiled as she straightened. "You're on my turf now, Captain. Those bars don't mean a thing here."

A few years ago he would have made some joking remark—would have checked to see if there was a wedding band on her left hand and then flirted with her whether there was or wasn't. This morning, he couldn't quite remember what that was like, joking and flirting with a pretty woman. There was a part of him, though, that damn wanted to.

"I understand that home is somewhere near here." She gestured toward the tray, and he automatically picked up the fork.

"The northwest part of Tallgrass. Neighborhood called the Flats." He lifted a chunk of egg to his mouth. He still wasn't hungry, and it was as tasteless as he'd expected, but if he ever wanted to escape the close scrutiny brought on by his suicide attempt, Chaplain Reed back in Washington had told him, he had to try. He could never quit trying.

It sounded like a life sentence.

But better than a death sentence.

"The Flats?" the nurse echoed. "I've only been here at Fort Murphy a few months, but from what I've seen, the entire county is pretty much flat."

"Aw, don't say that. The elevation of West Main Street

is a good fifty feet higher than East Main." That was kind of joking, wasn't it? She did laugh. "There's plenty of hills outside of town. They just come on so gradually that you don't really notice them." Along with a lot of trees, wide-open spaces, and gullies cut deep by heavy rain and hard winds. Minus the trees, it didn't sound so different from the deserts of Iraq and Afghanistan. "Where'd you come from?"

"Fort Stewart. Winn Army Community Hospital. Before that I was in school at UCSD. I grew up in Southern California." She shivered, pulling her jacket tighter. "I joined the Army so I could experience life outside of San Diego County. I never stopped to think that might mean twenty degrees and ice in October."

He had joined up for the same reason. He'd seen far more than he'd bargained for. "It'll warm up again. We get occasional days in the seventies and eighties to get us through winter."

"And frequent summer days of a hundred degrees plus all summer long to make you long for it again."

He swallowed the last bite of eggs, cut the sausage patty in half, and ate one piece. It wasn't as bland as the eggs, with at least a hint of sausage flavor. The orange was good—not much the hospital kitchen could do to a piece of fruit—and the toast was dry. When he finished, he looked at Valentina. "Satisfied?"

Her laughter as she pushed away from the bed was warm and cheery and reminded him of better times. "It takes more than a clean plate to satisfy me. Keep your cereal. Waste not, and all that."

"Want not," he finished the saying for her, even as he took the sealed plastic cup from the tray.

"Want the milk?"

"Who puts milk on cereal?" That was teasing, too. Twice in one conversation must be some kind of record for him.

"Yeah, I don't, either." She carried the tray from the room, calling from the door, "I'll be back..."

He looked out the window and grimly murmured, "I'll be here."

Picking up the coffee again, he turned to stare outside. The sun reflected off the ice that coated everything, bright enough to blind even though it wasn't far above the horizon yet. He remembered going out to play after a heavy snow or, yeah, even just sleet, bundled in layers, two of everything except shoes and gloves. He would stagger down the steps and into the sun, baseball cap under knit cap, brim pulled low to block the glare. Most times, by the time he'd made it to the street, J'Myel was sliding out to meet him. They'd made snowmen and snow caves, ambushed other neighborhood kids with well-aimed snowballs, and tried to leave no patch of white untouched before frozen feet or hunger drove them back inside.

Good times, J'Myel had always said when they reminisced about childhood stuff. He'd accompanied the words with an ear-to-ear grin.

Calvin's chest grew tight, his next few breaths hard to pull out. His fingers gripped the coffee mug so tightly that the tips turned pale, and a strangled sound escaped his throat before he clamped down hard on it. He wanted some good times again, God help him, he did. Because he couldn't go on like this forever.

* * *

In the twenty years Bennie had lived with Mama Maudene, she could count on one hand the number of times they'd missed church on Sunday morning that weren't weather related: three trips back home to South Carolina to visit family and the two Sundays following J'Myel's death. It averaged out to once every four years, not a bad record. She knew a few pastors who couldn't claim such diligent attendance.

This cold bright morning, she dressed in fleece pants, an OU Sooners sweatshirt, and fuzzy house shoes over woolen socks. The shirt actually belonged to Mama, a gift from one of her numerous nieces, but being an unwavering OSU Cowboys fan, Mama had passed the shirt on to Bennie. Someone should get some use from it, she'd declared, but it wasn't going to be her. Cold-natured Bennie couldn't care less what logo was on the front as long as it kept her warm.

The instant she opened the bedroom door, she smelled coffee and cinnamon rolls. Good for her soul, not so much for her hips. "Morning, Mama," she greeted when she shuffled into the kitchen. "Isn't it beautiful outside?"

"It would be more beautiful if our yellow grass was showing." Mama handed her a cup of coffee, fresh from the Keurig.

Bennie blew gently across the top of the mug. "Smells wonderful. What is it today?"

"A Salvadoran medium-roast with notes of almond, honeysuckle, and pipe tobacco." Mama's smile wreathed her face. "Listen to me. I've become a coffee connoisseur. Oh, and the packaging is ninety-seven percent recyclable. Saving the world one K-cup at a time."

The aroma alone was enough to make Bennie happy

she'd gotten out of bed. Settling at the table, she tested it with a tiny sip, and when it didn't scald her tongue, she took a larger drink, then mmm-ed her appreciation. Since Mama had discovered Internet shopping, they hadn't had a single cup of regular old supermarket coffee, and Bennie, for one, was grateful.

"I'm trying a new recipe today," Mama said from the stove. "Hashbrown potatoes, onions, peppers, eggs, cheese, and chorizo. That's Mexican sausage. While it finishes up in the oven, why don't you see if the newspaper boy managed to get through this morning."

Obediently, Bennie went to the front door, opening it to an ice-covered world. Though it was thirty degrees south of bearable, the air wasn't as frigid as she'd expected. With any luck, most of this mess would be gone tomorrow and she'd never, ever see sleet again. She crossed two fingers on both hands and squeezed her eyes shut, making a wish of the thought, then bent to pick up the paper in its plastic sleeve.

The newspaper boy, a retired rural mail carrier, had indeed made it. He was as reliable as the sun coming up every morning. His secret, he claimed, was his seventies-era Volkswagen Beetle. Where other cars gave up, ol' Bess just kept on chugging, and if she slid into a ditch or a fence post, well, what was another ding?

Bennie was about to close the storm door when she stopped, her gaze traveling across and down the street. The Sweet home was barely visible through the ice-laden tree branches, a tidy place set back from the road. Justice would have already gone to the small cabin on the other side, probably along with Calvin, to help Miss Emmeline make a safe crossing to their house, and they would be sitting down to breakfast about now. Bennie smiled at the thought of the spread Elizabeth would have cooked, all delicious and fattening and filled with love.

Had Calvin's first night home been a good one? Had he felt warm and secure in his old room that had once been an attic? Had he stretched out in bed and thought, *Thank God I'm home*?

Probably. Had he thought about J'Myel? About the way things had ended between them? Had he regretted the way he'd treated Bennie, missing their wedding, not showing up for J'Myel's funeral, never saying a word to her about the worst time in her life?

Her jaw tightened, tension twisting through her gut. Probably not. Her best friend forever hadn't turned out to be such a great friend, and he'd sure never lasted close to forever.

"You're letting the outside in," Mama called from the kitchen doorway. "Get on in here, let's say the blessing, and see how this new dish tastes."

Forcing a calming breath, Bennie did as she said, stripping off the plastic sleeve and laying the paper next to Mama's recliner on her way past. After discarding the dripping sleeve in the waste basket, she sat, bowed her head, and while Mama prayed, Bennie mouthed her own prayer that Calvin's visit would be short, that she wouldn't see him, that he would go away again and let her return to her hard-won life without him.

After taking a few bites of the casserole and praising the recipe as a keeper, she remarked casually—she hoped, "It would be nice for his folks if Calvin can stay through Thanksgiving."

"Christmas would be even nicer, but I doubt the Army

can afford to let him be gone that long. You know he's the best, toughest, most gung-ho soldier in the history of armies anywhere. So says Emmeline." Mama's eyes gleamed. "It's hard to believe. Him and J'Myel were two of the orneriest boys I ever saw. We never knew what the three of you would get into next. Though I gotta say, you never made me really whomp you."

There had been no shortages of spankings and swattings from Mama, all of them well deserved, but her *whompins* were the stuff of legend. When they visited family, there was usually a cousin or uncle there who'd gotten whomped. All they would say was it scared the crooked straight out of 'em and was the closest a person could come to meeting Jesus while still breathing.

Mama's smile was happy and sad, present and distant at the same time. "Them boys and you was like pieces of a braid. Take one out, and it all falls apart."

"We surely did fall apart," Bennie agreed, grimly wondering if the memories they had were enough to make up for the ones they'd never gotten to make. "I don't suppose Miss Emmeline mentioned how long Calvin *will* be here."

"Nope. You know Emmeline. All she said was he had arrived and Justice and Elizabeth were on their way to see him."

Bennie dished another small serving of casserole onto her plate, then pondered that. So Calvin wasn't staying with his mom and dad. And the reason for that would be...he'd brought someone home with him. Maybe a woman. Maybe a wife. The marriage would have been a last-minute thing, or the whole neighborhood surely would have heard about it, and the trip could be their honeymoon, and they would require privacy for, oh, you know, *this and that*.

How would Bennie feel about running into a brand-new Mrs. Calvin Sweet?

It didn't seem possible that there could be a Mrs. Sweet without her knowing all about it. But if there was, well, it wouldn't be the Mrs. who needed to keep a distance. It was Mr. Sweet—*Captain* Sweet—who poked at the sore spot in Bennie, who wanted to grab him by one ear and ask him just one question: *Where the hell were you? What happened between you and J'Myel? Why didn't I hear from you when your best friend in the entire universe died?*

 Okay, more than one question.

She sighed heavily. Did it matter now? J'Myel was dead. So was her friendship with Calvin, and her life was going on. She was as happy as a woman could be when she'd been widowed before thirty. She had her health, a home, a good family, and good friends—all the things that mattered in life. She was *satisfied*, and had put the past in the past. *Or thought I had.*

"You want any more casserole or coffee?"

Blinking, she focused on Mama, standing next to her, hand extended toward her plate. "No to the food, but I'll take another cup of that excellent coffee. I'll make it, though."

Mama snorted. "Set yourself back down. I'll take care of it for you. I do it better than you anyway."

Bennie resettled in her chair. When she'd come to live with Mama, her grandmother hadn't hesitated to assign chores to her. She'd taught Bennie to cook, clean, do laundry and housework, to make her bed first thing in the morning and to leave the kitchen spotless after one meal and ready to cook the next one. When they'd both worked full-time, they'd done an equal share of the chores, but when Mama had retired six years ago—finally old enough, she'd decided, at seventy-five—she'd taken command again. Bennie had tried to wrest back her fair share of the work, but when she was at the hospital for eight-hour shifts five days a week, it was hard to stop a headstrong woman from doing what she pleased.

And what pleased Mama was keeping her house shining, taking care of her granddaughter, shopping on the Internet, and making the best cup of coffee in the house.

"Too bad you can't take advantage of our morning off to visit with your friends," Mama remarked as she set a steaming cup of coffee on the table, then carried away the rest of the casserole.

"Isn't that always the way. You get a bad-weather day, and the weather keeps you from enjoying it. When are they going to give us a day off because it's unusually sunny and warm?"

Mama's laugh warmed her even more than the coffee. Rising from her chair, Bennie gave her a fervent hug. "I'm so lucky to have you for a grandmother."

"Not lucky," Mama reminded her, and together they said, "Blessed." Then Mama added, "And you've been twice the blessing to me. Now if you'd just give me some great-grandbabies while I'm still young enough to play with them..."

"Let me get right on that. You can help me put an ad on the Internet. 'Single black female looking for good provider and father material. Only marriage-minded men should apply.' Think that will get me a few takers?"

One of Mama's rare somber expressions crossed her face. "You know, as much as we wish otherwise, J'Myel isn't coming back."

Bennie's throat tightened, her chest squeezing. She barely found the air to force out a pained reply. "I know."

"You're too young to live the rest of your life alone, with nobody but me for company. You know, I'm not going to be around a whole lot longer. I probably don't have more than ten, maybe twenty years left in me."

"Oh, only ten or twenty, huh?" As Mama's trademark grin broke free, Bennie pretended to swat her. "Let's get this kitchen cleaned up so you can read your paper and I can get a head start on my studying." She took classes two nights a week, working toward an associate's degree in nursing. She'd always had an interest in pediatrics and, she added with a sidelong look at Mama—geriatrics.

"If you need any research done, you just let me know." Mama winked. "My laptop and I are ready."

Chapter 3

Treating Calvin like any other patient when he was discharged on Tuesday morning, Valentina pushed him to the front entrance of the hospital, where water puddled from the vehicles driving beneath the portico to pick up patients. He'd insisted back on the floor that he could walk, but she'd said no. He hadn't even suggested that she didn't have to wait for him. Someone was coming over from the Warrior Transition Unit to pick him up and deliver him to his new command. One of these days, he supposed, he should think about replacing the car that had been stolen in Tacoma. In an Army town, it was always easy to get around, but in the last year he hadn't been very good at asking favors from others.

"I have to say, Captain, I wish all my patients were as compliant as you," Valentina said. "You're very good at taking orders."

"I'm a soldier, ma'am. They kind of teach that," he said dryly.

She wheeled the chair to the nearest empty seat and sat down to face him. "You'll do good at the WTU. They've got a relatively new facility, and the staff over there is great. There's a class of third-graders from the post school who visits every week, and Sarge...aw, man." She grinned like an adolescent girl who'd just found out the football captain was her lab partner. "I'd take Sarge home with me if I could. Everybody loves Sarge."

"Doesn't sound like any sergeant I've ever known. Not even me when I was one."

"Trust me." She grinned, then her gaze slid past him to a sedan stopping under the portico. "There's your chauffeur. I'll introduce you." She pushed the wheelchair through the double sets of doors. At the car, she opened the front passenger door, then ducked down so she could see the driver. "They haven't pried you out from behind the wheel yet, huh?"

"Nope, and they're not going to. If they try, I'm just gonna drive away."

"Captain Sweet, meet Corporal Stephens. Take him on the scenic route, will you, Justin, and put it on my tab."

"Will do, Val."

The nurse stepped back, locked the wheels on the chair, and folded up the footrests. As Calvin settled in the front seat of the car, she flashed that brilliant smile again. "Take care of yourself, Captain. If you get a craving for cinnamon coffee, you know where to find me." She squeezed his hand briefly before closing the car door.

Calvin flexed the fingers she'd gripped. Of course her skin was softer than his, and it smelled of antiseptic foam and lotion. Hospital odors aside, though, everything about her was soft, sweet, tantalizing. He'd missed those things, damn, so long. They'd come along in short spurts: the girl he'd dated senior year for three months; the girl he'd met at basic training; the new neighbor when he'd returned from his first tour of Iraq; the red-haired doctor, brand new to Afghanistan and in need of comfort when the bombs hit too close. Little bits of happiness that dotted years grown darker and harder.

"You need to make any stops?" the corporal asked as he pulled away. "We're not far from the PX and the commissary."

"No," Calvin replied, then belatedly added, "Thanks, though."

"Val's great, isn't she? She was one of my nurses last time I was in the hospital. Smart and funny, and she ain't hard to look at, either."

Calvin took a covert look at him. He appeared healthy and whole, and his morale was certainly upbeat. He hadn't stopped grinning yet, though Valentina was probably the reason for that.

Then Calvin noticed the crutches stowed between the driver's and passenger's seats, and the hand controls on the steering column. Corporal Stephens was healthy and upbeat but apparently not whole. Guilt seeped into Calvin's brain, kicking his own mood down a notch. What did he have to complain about? He was alive. He'd come home with both arms, both legs, all body parts intact and exactly the way they'd been when he'd left. So he needed medication to counteract the depression. So he had trouble sleeping, thinking, trusting, relaxing. So he couldn't always avoid the dark, cluttered places in his brain.

He was alive.

He was physically whole.

He had so damn much to be grateful for, and he wanted to be grateful for it, if he could just figure out how.

"Cool car, huh?" Stephens said. "I just got it a couple weeks ago. Donated, on account of my legs. I thought I was never gonna drive again, and man, that sucked. I've already put a thousand miles on it, and I don't plan to stop until it hits at least five hundred thousand."

What had happened to his legs? Had he been shot? Mangled or burned thanks to the damage an improvised explosive device could do to metal and steel and, of course, the fragile human body? Had he survived a blast with bloody stumps, shredded skin, disintegrated bone?

There were all sorts of ways to lose the use of a perfectly functional pair of legs, and Calvin figured he'd seen them all.

What did it say about him that the carnage of the last blast he'd seen had sickened him as much as the first?

He wondered about the corporal's injuries, but he wouldn't ask. He wouldn't probe someone else's open wounds—emotionally if not physically—just to satisfy his own curiosity. Besides, if he asked, he would be expected to share his own injury. There was something so much more acceptable in being able to say *broken arm, bad leg, amputated foot*, than in Calvin's response: *I went crazy over there.*

But Justin didn't wait for him to ask. "My humvee got taken out by an IED. Broke both legs in more places than the docs wanted to count. Now I've got more screws than Home Depot."

Sorry was the most useless word in the world, but it was the only thing Calvin could think of.

Stephens shrugged it off. "I'm doing good. No brain damage, no more combat, and I learned to dance all over again. My girlfriend dumped me, but that just means she wasn't worth keeping in the first place. I can drive again, I can still please the ladies"—his grin stretched across his face—"and hey, everyone's gotta face a little pain, right?"

Calvin's face grew hot as the guilt flared again. He'd found it too easy to forget that other people suffered, that other people had *real* pain.

"You have family near here?"

He cleared his throat. "Parents and grandmother in Tallgrass. About a hundred and one relatives spread between Oklahoma City and Tulsa."

"Lucky. My dad's an only child, and my mom's family was halfway across the country when I was a kid. I grew up in California, but my grandma and grandpa live in Enid. They've both got some health issues, so Mom and Dad moved back here to take care of them. My mom thought she was going to take care of me, too. Hell, man, I love her, but I'm twenty-two years old. I don't need a nurse...although I'd sure give Val a shot if she was interested. Here we are."

The announcement came so abruptly that Calvin needed a moment to refocus. The brick building in front of them reminded him of a hundred other buildings on a dozen other posts, newer than most, maybe a little more aesthetic than most, but still obviously a government facility.

"The WTU barracks are over there." Stephens gestured to the building next door as he opened his door. He carefully swung his legs out, picked up his crutches, and maneuvered to his feet. "Most of us gimps are on the first floor. The guys with TBIs and PTSD get the second-floor apartments, though there's an elevator if they have to put one of us up there."

At least Calvin could be grateful he didn't have a traumatic brain injury. That was a lifelong sentence without a cure.

Though there was no cure for PTSD, either. It was a lifetime of trying to stay in control, of never letting his guard down, of never letting the darkness defeat him. Decades of fighting, when the last decade had just about done him in. Where was he supposed to find the strength?

Slinging the strap of his bag over his shoulder, Calvin matched his pace to Corporal Stephens's from the parking lot to the door. A figure waited on the opposite side of the glass, posture erect, eyes sharp, imposing and silent.

When Stephens limped through the door Calvin held for him, the figure moved, a low whine in his throat, and nudged his head against Stephens's knee. "Hey, Sarge, did you miss me?"

A man in PT clothes stepped out of a door down the hall, wiping his face with a towel clenched in a prosthetic hand. "Don't flatter yourself, Justin. He's waiting for the schoolkids to come."

"That's okay," Stephens replied. "He can be as friendly as he wants, but he still goes home with me."

The collie barked once in agreement.

Using the crutches as if they were a natural extension of himself, Stephens moved down the broad hall. "Captain Sweet, this is Kyle Danner, and that's the gym. We spend an ungodly amount of our time in there. Staying in shape is big around here. Sound mind and healthy body, and all that crap."

Calvin exchanged nods with Danner and took a quick look around the gym. Physical and occupational therapists worked with a handful of patients; a few more worked out on their own. Everyone—all the patients, at least—was dressed in PT clothes: shorts and T-shirt or sweats, with scars, dressings, and prosthetic limbs on display. It stood to reason, then, the people lacking the scars, dressings, and prostheses were the PTSD guys and some of the TBIs. No hiding his failures here.

An itch started along the back of his neck, like the time he'd gotten poison ivy, spreading down his spine, his arms, and his legs. His parents hadn't told anyone what he'd done, just Gran, and they'd promised him it was his secret to share. This wasn't like going to any post in any town for treatment, where he hardly knew anyone and no one who would be surprised.

He knew people in Tallgrass, had gone to church and to school with them, had been friends with some and not with others. He had worked summer jobs for some fathers and dated some daughters and planned in another eight or ten or twelve years to come back here to live.

Well, he'd come back, though not quite the way he'd planned. Now it was up to him to learn how to live.

* * *

"Bennie, why did we ever decide that we wanted to be nurses?"

Shifting her backpack to her other hand, Bennie wrapped her free arm around Trinity Adams. They'd been friends since seventh grade, when Trinity's father transferred to Fort Murphy, then decided to retire there; they'd finished school together, they worked together as aides at St. Anthony's, and they'd decided to become RNs together. "As I recall, we were tired of making beds, wiping butts, and running ourselves ragged."

"We're still gonna run ourselves ragged."

"Yeah, but we'll get paid a lot more for it."

"Keep reminding me of that, 'cause I think this class is going to kill me."

"Aw, you can't give Dr. Perkins that satisfaction." They reached their cars, parked side by side in the community college parking lot, and Bennie beeped hers. The lights flashed, a welcome glow in the dark night.

"You're right. The old bat probably keeps track of her kills on her office wall." Trinity beeped her own car and tossed her bags inside. "Enjoy a margarita for me, will you? I'm heading home to study. The story of my life."

With a wave, Bennie slid into the driver's seat of her car, closed, and automatically locked the doors. Work, school, and study were mostly the story of her life, too, she thought as she drove out of the parking lot, but not tonight. Dr. Perkins had let them out early enough that she could catch the last part of the Tuesday Night Margarita Club meeting.

Though *meeting* was an awfully formal word for the weekly dinner, drinks, conversation, and much-needed laughs. Fellowship, Mama called it. She got the same, minus the drinks, from the Ladies' Bible Study and Prayer Group that met at the church twice a week. Though mostly elderly, that bunch was lively enough. They didn't need liquor added into *their* equation.

The margarita girls were pretty lively, too, and no matter what was going on, they always made Bennie feel better. In a town the size of Tallgrass—about sixty thousand, including the fort personnel—it was entirely possible that they could have never crossed paths. But they had two things in common: Each of them had loved a soldier, and each of them had lost him. That bonded them in ways nothing else could.

It was seven forty-five when she swept into The Three Amigos, the best Mexican restaurant in town. In warm weather, the margarita club claimed the patio on the east side of the brightly painted building, but the rest of the year, they occupied anywhere from four to eight tables pushed together in the back of the restaurant. She spotted them as soon as she passed the bar, and affection and pure, unadulterated pleasure welled inside her.

"Bennie!"

A half-dozen voices called her name, and there was affection and pleasure there, too. They scooted chairs, making room for her. After shucking her coat, she circled the table, giving and receiving hugs. When she got to Ilena Gomez, she *ooh*ed over baby John, nestled in his mama's arms. His black hair stuck up at angles, and his coffee-dark eyes grew bright when he grinned at her.

"I swear, Ilena, he's the handsomest baby boy in the whole world."

"Yeah, he gets that from me," fair-haired, pale-skinned Ilena replied, her voice as small and thin as she was.

Bennie snorted. "Not that you aren't beautiful, but that boy's the spitting image of his daddy. I've seen pictures." Juan Gomez had died months before his son was born, but Ilena was determined to keep him alive in John's heart.

Pain twinged in the region of Bennie's heart. She had

wanted babies with J'Myel. He'd suggested on their honeymoon that she get pregnant right away, but she'd kept taking those birth control pills. A husband and wife needed time to get to know each other before bringing a child into their lives, she'd insisted. *You've known me since we were nine,* he'd retorted. *How much more do you think there is to learn about me?*

Lord, she regretted that decision. She'd never wanted to be a single mother, but having some tangible part of J'Myel would have been so much better than having nothing but memories. She had way too many of those.

Their usual waitress, Miriam, stopped by the table to deliver a glass of iced tea, a bowl of salsa, and a basket of chips. "It's good to see you, Bennie. What can I get for you?"

"Good to see you, too, Miss Miriam. Um, let me have a cup of queso and a cup of guacamole. And probably more chips, but I'll let you bring those when I've finished these." The Three Amigos made their chips fresh, and they were the best Bennie had ever eaten.

Once Miriam left, Bennie skimmed her gaze over the group. "Now that I've ordered enough food to add a few unneeded pounds, let me look at all of you. Carly, marriage to Dane certainly agrees with you. You're glowing."

Carly Clark glanced toward the bar, where her husband sat, and smiled demurely. "Thank you."

"Jessy, you always glow." The redhead was short, slim, green-eyed, and gorgeous, and those green eyes were clear and sharp. She'd been sober awhile now, and it made her *more* everything than before. Bennie was so proud of her.

"Thank you," Jessy mimicked Carly, and she shot a

look at the bar, too, where her cowboy sweetie, Dalton, sat with Dane.

"And Therese…" Bennie heaved a sigh. "You're lit up like a Christmas tree. I'm guessing that Keegan was here this past weekend."

The kindergarten teacher's smile could have been mistaken for a self-satisfied smirk. "He got to stay an extra day, thanks to the ice. But he's back at Fort Polk now."

Bennie grinned at Lucy, Fia, Marti, Ilena, Patricia, and Leah. "The rest of you ladies…we have *got* to get us some men! Look how they just shine with happiness and satisfaction, and us…Have any of us even had a date in the past year?"

"I've had a date," Lucy protested. Then she shrugged ruefully. "Though he fell in love with someone else and moved away."

"But he only fell in love with Avi *after* you broke up with him," Patricia reminded her. She happened to be the mother of the man in question, a mother who'd been estranged from her children for twenty years. Those relationships had healed only in the five months since her second husband's death. Bennie knew it had been hard for Patricia, but she understood the children's position better. Her mother had abandoned her, too. She had no idea where Lilly Pickering was, if she was even alive, and if fate somehow brought her back to Bennie, she didn't know whether there was forgiveness for her in Bennie's heart.

"And why aren't you dating, Bennie?" Fia asked, then slyly added, "Don't tell me you haven't been asked."

She *had* been asked. Just a month ago, a doctor at the hospital had asked, but she thought workplace romances were a bad idea. She'd been asked by a couple of guys she'd gone to high school with, but she remembered too clearly what hound dogs they'd been then to imagine herself with either of them now. The youth pastor at the church had asked her out when he'd first arrived in town, but...truth be told, she wanted a man she could be a little naughty with. How could she be naughty with a pastor?

"I'm just waiting for the right guy," she said airily. Maybe. She'd had a lot of loss in her life: father, mother, husband, best friend. Obviously, some people were strong enough to take the risk of second chances—Carly, Jessy, and Therese had. But she wasn't sure, no matter how lonely she got, that she was one of them.

"Aren't we all?" Ilena said with a sigh.

"Speak for yourselves." That was Marti, dipping a tortilla chip into salsa, shaking off the excess, then liberally sprinkling it with salt. "I loved Joshua dearly, and I loved being married to him, but I'm not looking to repeat the experience. I'm fine on my own."

"I'm fine on my own, too." Though Bennie wasn't really on her own. At least she had Mama to go home to every night. "But if Mr. Right came waltzing through that door right now," she teased, "you can bet I'd be waltzing out with him five minutes later. And somebody take that salt shaker away from her. She's gonna swell up like a sponge."

"But I'll be a happy sponge," Marti replied as Fia laughingly moved the salt shaker out of reach.

When it came time to go, it was the same as usual: Bennie truly hated to leave them. There were hugs all around, then Jessy and Carly headed to the bar area while the rest of them left the warmth of the restaurant for the cold night.

"It's times like these that make me miss Florida," Fia said with a shiver.

"Nah, honey, it'll pass. That warm sun's gonna come back." Bennie hugged her close as they stepped off the curb. "You got a ride, doll?"

"Therese is taking me home. Her van is easy to get in and out of." Fia smiled thinly. "My doctor's sending me for some special kind of MRI that they can't do here. I don't know when or where, but maybe it'll give us an answer."

"Oh, I hope so!" Bennie said fervently. For the better part of the year, Fia had suffered mysterious symptoms that every doctor had lazily written off as normal strains and overuse for a twenty-something personal trainer. Last month, though, Jessy and Patricia had gotten involved. Neither had any medical knowledge, but they were both experts at standing their ground and intimidating lesser mortals. They'd demanded answers for Fia, and this doctor was doing his best to find those answers.

"You know, Mama and I pray for you every day, and so does her church group. Doctors are good, but sometimes they need the Lord's guidance to see the big picture."

"I appreciate all the prayers I can get." Fia grimaced. "I have a new respect for what Dane and everyone like him has been through. It's tiring."

As she spoke, Dane and Carly came out of the restaurant. Like Fia, he was limping—probably the cold and damp—but normally, no one would guess watching him that his jeans concealed the prosthesis required by an above-the-knee amputation.

Bennie walked with Fia to Therese's van, called her good-byes, then hurried to her own car. As she started the engine and turned the heat to high, she watched her friends scatter to their own vehicles and smiled. She'd had her share of heartache—more than her share, it sometimes seemed—but at the end of the day, she was a lucky woman. A little lonely, a little heartsore, but very definitely lucky.

Chapter 4

Though the week hadn't been as bad as he'd expected, Calvin was grateful when the weekend arrived. He'd filled out endless paperwork, been examined and interviewed by his care team—doctor, nurses, therapists, a social worker, and a career counselor—and he'd met the rest of the troops in the WTU company. Half of them, like Justin Stephens, had severe injuries, amputations and burns chief among them. More than half had traumatic brain injuries in varying degrees. Some seemed relatively normal, if forgetful. Others had misshapen heads, where portions of their skulls had been blown away, and had lost their communication and motor skills.

And almost everyone had some degree of PTSD. It should have made him feel better that he wasn't alone, but instead it just made him...weary.

He was weary this Saturday morning as he walked down the stairs from the barracks to the parking lot. His father's pickup truck was waiting at the end of the sidewalk, and Justice sat behind the wheel, grinning as he watched Calvin approach.

"You know, when I think of barracks, I always picture a huge room with double-stacked cots and fifty men to a latrine," he remarked when Calvin got in. "This ain't bad."

"The apartments help the guys adjust to what it'll be like when they go home." Calvin always thought *guys*, but there were a dozen or so women in the company, too. "I could be in regular quarters since I don't have any physical disabilities, but they had space available here, so…" He didn't mention that he also had the option of living at home. He didn't want to try to explain that he just couldn't move home again and sleep in his old room, live with his old memories, and bear the scrutiny and worry of his parents and Gran anytime he didn't behave like the Calvin they knew.

The notion struck him hard, made his breath catch and his chest ache. He was no longer the son Justice and Elizabeth had loved, raised, taught, disciplined, and said good-bye to eleven years ago. Since he'd begged off on seeing them this past week, he didn't know if they'd realized that.

He didn't even know who he was now.

Feeling his father's gaze shift between him and the road as he drove, he forced his fingers to unclench and his jaw to loosen enough to talk. "How's Mom?"

"She's fine. Cooking up a storm for you."

Yep, that was his mother: When in doubt, cook. "And Gran?"

"Oh, you know Emmeline."

People had been saying that about his grandmother

for as long as he could remember. Emmeline Wright was strong-willed—hard-headed, most people said—and independent and didn't give two cents what anyone thought of her. She had more quirks than the entire rest of the family put together, and anything she did, normal or not, could be explained by a sigh and a *You know Emmeline.*

Last weekend's ice had disappeared by noon Tuesday. There had been a few relatively warm days, but today the sky was dreary, clouds hung so low to the ground that he couldn't tell where they stopped and the sky started, and rain fell at a steady rate. The thermometer display on the rearview mirror of the truck read 44 degrees, making the rain plenty uncomfortable but with no chance of ice.

"How's your week been?" his dad asked. "What have they got you doing?"

Everything in Calvin tightened. There were people he didn't have to tell a thing to, one of the medical team had told him, but those people generally didn't include family. Families who cared, who worried—family he intended to stay a part of in the future—deserved to know what was going on.

"Right now it's a lot of getting settled. Paperwork to fill out, people to meet, names to remember." From all the talking he'd done this week, Calvin's voice sounded rusty. Once upon a time he'd been as outgoing and chatty as Justin. That was just one of the things he'd lost over the past three years. He would try to regain it because him being quiet was as unnatural as J'Myel being dead.

He flinched, and his right hand slowly knotted into a fist again. He slid it between him and the door so his dad couldn't see.

Justice glanced at him, then injected a deliberately

careless tone to his voice. "Your mama's been fixing up care packages for your apartment. She's got lasagna, chicken enchiladas, meat loaf, pot roast, and biscuits, bread, and cookies, all ready to pop into the oven. She's also packed up sheets, quilts, afghans, and everything else. I reminded her that your last command is shipping your stuff here so you should have it any day, but she reminded me that 'any day' isn't 'today.'"

"The apartment came with furniture, some dishes, and linens." About the only thing he needed was clothing. Besides the jeans and shirt he wore now, everything else he'd brought was Army-issued. But he forced himself to go on. "It'll be nice to have some stuff to make the place more like home."

"Tell your mama that, and you'll make her day. Remember how she wanted to send your favorite quilt to basic training with you?"

The beginning of a smile curved the corners of Calvin's mouth. "Even though we told her no, she had to hear it from the recruiter."

"We were lucky she didn't try to send herself with you. She was so worried about you boys that she hardly slept for a week. I kept telling her you were having a great time, and when you finally wrote and told her the same thing, she finally got back to normal."

They'd turned off Main Street and now were entering the Flats. There was no official sign, no legal designation, but everyone who lived there or around there knew the borders: Cimarron Street to the south, Maple Avenue to the east, the Burlington Northern tracks to the north, and the pasture where Harley Davis kept his meanest bull to the west.

The neighborhood kids used to stand along that pasture fence and brag about how long they could stay on the bull's back if given the chance, but anytime the 2,000-pound animal showed interest in them, they had set speed records backing away from the fence.

Calvin wanted to close his eyes, tilt his head back, and breathe deeply a few times before they reached his parents' house, but he couldn't. Hyperarousal, they called it: gaze constantly moving, focus constantly shifting, making sure there was no danger here, there, or over there. It was a lifesaver in the desert. Back home, it just made him someone to be wary of.

When they turned onto his street, he deliberately shifted his gaze to the left, not looking at a single house on the right side of the street. Not looking at a white house in particular, one with a porch that filled most of the small yard, with bushes growing all along it. The azaleas and forsythias were a wild mess the better part of the year, Golda Ford used to say, *but, oh, when they're all in bloom, they're so worth it.*

When his own house appeared ahead, he exhaled deeply. It looked exactly the way it had the day he'd left. The lawn was close-cropped, and the mailbox at the end of the driveway stood perfectly straight. The house had had a recent coat of white paint, the porch floor and ceiling pale gray, the shutters dark blue. The wooden rockers' deep red color had been updated, too, and sheer white curtains hung at every window.

Everything else in his life had changed, but home was the same, and that made his throat close up and his vision grow blurry.

Justice turned into the driveway and followed it to his

regular parking spot right next to the house. When Calvin climbed out, he looked over at the cottage, a hundred feet behind the house and a hundred feet to the west. Unlike the house, it hadn't received a coat of paint in probably twenty years. That last one had been pale yellow, and more of it had flaked off than remained. Gran liked it that way, though. *An old house for an old woman. We've both lost most of our shine.*

Before he had a chance to lift his foot to the first step, the screen door was flung open and his mother burst out onto the porch, followed by Gran. "It's so good to see you, sweet baby of mine," Elizabeth said, her smile lighting the whole area.

His grandmother slipped past her—she was pretty agile for seventy-six and arthritic—and came to the top of the steps, where she was on eye level with him. She studied him hard for a moment, her eyes narrowed, her mouth thinned. Shaking one thick-knuckled finger at him, she said, "Don't you never again—"

With a deep breath, she cut off the words, then reached out. He expected her to grab his ear—she'd been famous for tweaking the ears of anyone who displeased her—but instead she wrapped her hand around the back of his neck and pulled him close. Hiding her face against his neck, she whispered, "Lord, it would have broke my heart," then squeezed him tighter than an old lady her age should be capable of.

The lump came back into his throat, and his eyes grew wet with tears. He wasn't ashamed of crying. There'd never been any of that men-don't-cry garbage in his family; they were as emotional as the women were. He'd cried when he'd seen his first buddy die, and the sec-

ond and the third. He'd cried over every one of them...
except J'Myel. Something had broken inside him then.
His throat had swollen shut, and his chest had grown
tight, and he'd literally ached to let the tears flow, but they
wouldn't.

That was when he'd learned some hurts were just too
deep for tears.

"I've missed you, Gran," he murmured against her
wiry gray hair.

"Of course you have. I'm one of a kind. No one could
ever take my place." After an extra-tight squeeze, she let
go and smiled up at him. A few more cares lined her face,
and her eyes were cloudier than he remembered, her glass
lenses even thicker, but her smile was still as broad, her
voice was still as strong, and—he gave her a quick scan—
her sense of fashion was still just as skewed. She wore
an orange Halloween-decorated sweatshirt under denim
overalls, with a pair of high-topped hot pink tennis shoes.

He climbed the steps, gave his mother a hug, then let
Gran twine her arm through his and lead him inside. "Just
wait until you see all the goodies in the freezer for your
new place. We've been cooking all week."

Behind her back, Elizabeth quirked one eyebrow.
"We?" she mouthed.

Calvin acknowledged her with a nod. Everyone knew
Gran didn't cook so much as take credit for it. *Taught
Elizabeth everything she knows in the kitchen,* she'd always bragged, while her kids insisted that if one of them
hadn't learned to cook, they would have starved, because Gran's talents ran to opening cereal boxes and
burning toast.

"Lunch is almost ready, son," his mom said, bumping

shoulders with him. "You just relax here with your daddy for a bit while Mama and I get it on the table."

He nodded, then turned to look around the living room. They'd gotten new furniture since the last time he'd been home, though Justice's beat-up old easy chair still sat with good views out both the front and the side windows. The TV wasn't new. He hadn't seen one that boxy and heavy in years.

Justice followed his gaze and patted the television on his way to his chair. "It's not as bad as those giant old console TVs from my younger days."

"But it's close."

"Your mom and me, we don't need the newest, trendiest digital stuff. This TV works, and that's what matters."

His parents had always been tight with a dollar. Fiscally prudent, his mom called it. Use it till it broke, was their motto, and when it broke, fix it. If it couldn't be fixed, then and only then did they buy a new one. The upside was that they were well prepared for retirement, and for them, there was no downside.

Calvin's gaze continued around the room, so familiar and full of memories, then finally stopped on the pictures that covered most of one wall. Some were black and white, and on some, the years had washed out the colors. A few were posed, like the thirteen portraits covering Calvin's school years, but most were candid shots. There was at least one picture including every member of the extended family—and that was saying a lot, given that Gran had had seven children, and there'd been four on his father's side—but most of them were of Calvin, J'Myel, and Bennie.

Grief spreading through him, he walked to stand directly in front of one picture in particular. It had been high school graduation, and he and J'Myel stood on the football field out behind the high school, their arms around Bennie, the three of them in blue gowns with blue and gold tassels on their caps. Bennie wore a gold shawl with her gown, the reward for her perfect grade point average and being valedictorian, and they'd all been so... relieved. Excited. Happy.

Yet he remembered being sad, too. Thinking that after that night, things would never be the same again. That it really was a turning point, the end of being a kid, the accepting of responsibilities, the beginning of becoming an adult.

"She still lives down the street with Mama Maudene."

Calvin stared at the picture a moment longer before glancing at his dad. Justice was folding the Tulsa *World* into quarters so he could do the crossword puzzle. Then Calvin looked back at the photo, this time focusing on Bennie. The days of going natural with her hair had long since passed by senior year; she'd straightened the hell out of it then. Her eyes, like his own, were dark-chocolate brown, her skin a creamier version of his and J'Myel's. He remembered the day he'd looked at her and realized for the first time that she was more than a great fisherman, a fast runner, a daredevil on a bicycle, and an outstanding first baseman: She was a *girl*, and a pretty one. They'd been in tenth grade, and Calvin really hadn't known how to handle that realization. When he'd said something about it to J'Myel, J'Myel had snorted. *Bennie? Get outta here. She's our buddy. You know, like, a guy.*

And then ten years later, J'Myel had married her.

There were no more pictures of Calvin with Bennie, but there were plenty more shots of him and J'Myel. The two of them in basic training, at infantry school, in Mosul, Bagdad, Kirkuk.

Calvin couldn't walk away from those pictures fast enough. He sat so his back was to them, and he kept his gaze fiercely, narrowly ahead.

"There's a game on if you want to watch it," Justice said.

"Nah, I'm okay." He rested his forearms on his knees. "How's business?"

"We stay busy. Everyone wants tile in their houses— except your mama. Right now we're doing a project for a retired general who wants the Army Seal in the middle of the foyer. So we're cutting little pieces of tile to make cannonballs, a suit of armor, and flags. It's beautiful— we're about half done—and it's labor-intense, which means pricy. So the general's happy, and so are we."

Painstaking, repetitive work. That sounded like just what Calvin needed. When he had to focus hard on what he was doing, time went faster and things went better. It was when his mind wandered that he worried.

But a call from the hallway was going to keep him focused enough. "Dinner's ready!" Gran yelled. "Bring your appetites, your blessings, and your thanks to the cooks."

*   *   *

Lucy had finished her Saturday chores and was considering a trip to Sam's in Tulsa to restock her baking ingredients and wondering what Joe was up to. She could easily make the journey alone, but it was always nicer with someone to talk to on the long drive—and face it, to heft those fifty-pound bags of flour and sugar into her cart and then her car.

After wiping down the kitchen counters, she walked into the living room, rubbing lotion into her hands, her fingers bumping over her wedding rings every time she swiped. There on the sofa lay Norton, back scooted against the cushions, a pillow under his head, and nestled against him, tucked into the curve of his chin, was the pitiful kitten Joe had rescued last week. Lucy had tried to send it home with him, but Joe had tap-danced out of it, leaving her with a kitten she really didn't want.

Both animals lifted their heads to look at her, then resumed their usual task of doing nothing.

When the doorbell rang, Lucy was surprised. No one came over without calling first. Well, Joe did, but civilized grown-ups didn't, and he only rang the bell on the times he was too lazy to dig out his keys. She checked the peep hole—a few years ago he had lowered the old one so she could see—then she pulled the door open. "John! What a pretty boy you are. And so happy." She swung him from his mother's arms, then added, "Hi, Ilena. Come on in. What brings you two out on such a gloomy day?"

"It's not so gloomy. The sun's there. You just can't see it for the rain." Ilena slipped off the quilt that was keeping John dry, then shrugged out of her coat and hung both over the back of a kitchen chair. "Where's Joe?"

"Did you hear your silly mama?" Lucy said in a baby-soft voice before making smoochy sounds at John. "I'm going to put a sign on both doors that says, 'Attention: Joe Cadore does not live here. He just spends way too much time here. His house is the white one'—and I'm gonna paint an arrow pointing that way."

John laughed delightedly, making the lost-her-chance wife and mother inside Lucy embrace her tightly from inside out. A couple minutes with Ilena's cutie patootie, and she was a happier woman. That was a lot of magic for a five-month-old to wield.

"And why does Joe spend so much time here?" Ilena asked slyly.

"Because I feed him."

Ilena blew a raspberry.

"Because he can dump strays on me and I take them."

"Oh, Norton's not a stray—" Looking over at the dog, all comfy on the couch, Ilena broke off. Circling around, she sat on the coffee table for a better look. "What's the name of the little teeny guy lying way too close to Norton's mouth? Dinner?"

"I thought of that, though for Norton, he'd only be an appetizer. I also considered Conair since it took me two hours to thaw him out from last week's ice storm and get him warm and dry again. And I gave some thought to Keurig because I drank a dozen cups of coffee to stay awake that night for fear he would die if I closed my eyes. The last option was Lazy Bum, for Joe, who brought him into my house, wrapped him in a towel, and said, 'Here you go, Luce. Happy Saturday.'"

Ilena cautiously lifted the kitten from the couch, settling him on her lap. Norton's suspicious gaze never left them. "Which one did you settle on?"

"Sebastian."

"Poor Sebastian. Sweetie, your name's bigger than you are."

Lucy and John watched Ilena gently stroke the kitten before Lucy said, "Hmm...you know, John will need a pet before long. A little boy would probably love a little kitten who could snuggle with him and purr when he babbles."

"Oh, no," Ilena said in her sternest voice. "I'm already coping with one nonverbal creature who needs constant care. I'm not adding another."

"Darn," Lucy said, though she wasn't really disappointed. She had never said to herself, *I want a half-frozen kitten,* but since she'd gotten one, she was making the best of it. Besides, Norton curling up to sleep on his bed with Sebastian and his yellow ducky sharing equal places of honor guaranteed her at least one smile a day.

Ilena replaced the kitten next to the dog, then stood up and brushed her skirt down. "I came to talk to you about your business."

Pleasure skittered through Lucy, settling somewhere in her chest.

"Remember my old boss Brody? Actually, I probably talked more about his wife the witch than I did him."

Lucy nodded. The conversations were memorable for two reasons: because it was out of character for Ilena to talk badly about someone else, and because the wife really had been a witch to all the poor unfortunates who crossed paths with her.

"Alicia Anne fancied herself a caterer, so Brody bought a little place for her to set up shop in. Before she actually cooked anything in the new building, she decided the summers here were too hot, so he sold the real estate office and they moved to Florida."

"Because of course it never gets hot there."

Ilena grinned at Lucy's snark. "Anyway, Alicia Anne won't let him sell the building because…well, even Brody doesn't understand why, but he figures he should recoup at least some of his investment, so he's looking for a tenant. He completely redid the kitchen for Alicia Anne, though she decided they had to move as soon as that was done, so the dining room needs work. The rent is really reasonable—"

She stated a number that raised Lucy's brows. She could totally pay that for a year from her savings, which was how much time she'd given herself to prove Prairie Harts could succeed. She wasn't expecting total self-sufficiency, much less a profit, in that time, but at least some evidence that either or both were somewhere on the horizon.

"The downside is that the location isn't the best—one of the reasons Alicia Anne changed her mind, I'm sure. It's on North First Street." Ilena wrinkled her nose and raised her brows. "But you see the potential, don't you? You want to go see it, don't you?"

North First was that section of street leaving town that every town had: empty lots, a motel, a flower shop, a gas station, a garage. It lacked the charm of downtown Tallgrass and the commercial traffic of East Main and the first few blocks of South First. But a kitchen she could afford…a space that met her needs both for catering now and a bakery/restaurant later…

"Of course I want to see it. Can we go now? Just let me clean up."

After handing John to his mother, Lucy went to the bedroom, opened both closet doors, and stared for a moment before pulling out a brand-new pair of miracle-fiber jeans that were like Spanx for her entire lower body. Even her feet looked better in the jeans. She added a snug-fitting sweater that stopped an inch below her waist and boots that barely cleared her ankles—her punishment for having fat ankles and calves that wouldn't fit in a pair of knee boots to save her life. She put on rings, bracelets, a necklace, and perfume, and headed back to the living room.

"Oh, I like your hair down, Lucy," Ilena said happily. "You're so pretty."

A flush warmed her face. She had never had the delicate/pale/blond beauty Ilena took for granted, but she *was* feeling happier with her own self these days. Not pretty yet—still too round for that—but getting there.

"And you went shopping! How many sizes have you lost?"

"Two. Three if I don't breathe."

"Oxygen's overrated." Ilena hefted John to her shoulder while Lucy gathered her coat, purse, and keys, then they piled into Ilena's SUV for the short drive to the restaurant.

It sat alone in the middle of a block that was only half the usual size. The parking lot was gravel and bumpy, and patches of yellow weeds attested to how rarely it saw traffic. The building was sandstone across the front, brick on the sides, and large windows looked in on a largely empty room with construction debris on one side and a dusty display cabinet on the other. It was kind of sad and lonely looking, but Lucy could all too easily envision landscaping, scrumptious pastries in the display case, a homey dining room, and the wonderful, yeasty, buttery aromas of deliciousness in the ovens.

She absolutely loved it.

Chapter 5

Come walk with me to deliver that pie I just made."

Bennie looked up from the middle of her bed. Her laptop was open on one side, her tablet on the other, and a good old-fashioned textbook sat in the middle. Except for a break for lunch, she'd been studying all day, and she was pretty sure her brain had run out of room for new facts a while ago. Taking off the glasses she had to wear after a few hours of digital reading, she pinched the bridge of her nose, then smiled at Mama. "You're giving that coconut cream pie away? And here I thought you'd made it for me, since I'm the biggest fan of your pies in the whole universe."

"I made one for us, too. Come on. Put some shoes on and let's get us some fresh air."

Because she did need fresh air, and because she didn't like Mama wandering off through the neighborhood alone, Bennie swung her feet to the floor and slid them inside her favorite scuffed-up clogs. They had a wedge heel that kept her jeans from dragging on the ground, and nubby wool socks would keep her feet warm.

Brushing curls back from her face, she followed Mama to the living room and slipped her arms into her favorite jean jacket. Already wearing her own jacket, Mama waited at the door, a plastic cake carrier carefully balanced by its handles.

"Which of our neighbors is the lucky one today?" Bennie asked as they made their way down the steps, then along the sidewalk to the street.

"I haven't decided yet. Might be the first one I see. Might be the last house I pass before I decide to come back home."

Mama's method was no more scientific than that. Knowing that, on cool fall days when she baked pies and tarts from the apples that fell in their yard, the whole neighborhood would be out on their porches or in their own yards, hoping her randomness would pick them.

"It's a lovely day to be out, isn't it?" Mama asked with a satisfied sigh.

The temperature was just low enough that Bennie could have used a heavier jacket, and the sun had no intention of coming out to play. The rain had stopped, though. Plus, Mama routinely announced that every day a person woke up was a lovely one—as opposed to the alternative—and no one ever won an argument with Mama.

"Tonight's trick or treat."

"Oh, yay." *Not.* Bennie had been officially over Halloween since high school. All the day meant now was too much candy, too much spending, and too many parents giving their kids an early start on the idea of getting something for nothing.

Mama, on the other hand, had a decidedly different point of view. "What are you dressing up as?"

"A hardworking student who needs to learn microbiology before the test on Tuesday."

Mama gave her a chiding look. "I'm going to be a witch. I have a pointy hat and a wart to put on my nose, and I'm going to wear my ruby slippers. I've been practicing my cackle. How does this sound?"

She unleashed a laugh that made Bennie laugh, then fake a shiver. "Spooky."

"Nobody will dare prank me. They'll be too scared."

She was right about the first part. There wasn't a kid in the neighborhood who would think of toilet-papering her yard or egging her house, but it wasn't because they were scared of her. It was a matter of respect and love, though if they needed a little fear to keep them on the straight and narrow, Bennie would be happy to provide it.

"And we have a winner." Cheerfully, Mama turned into the next driveway, her short legs making long strides while Bennie dragged in dismay. The Sweet house. Had Mama planned to come here all along, or had she just chosen the family because Justice, sitting on the porch, was the first neighbor they'd seen—

Bennie's feet came to an abrupt halt without input from her brain. That wasn't Justice sitting still as a statue in the red rocker. No, it was a younger version, a taller one, a leaner one.

It was Calvin.

"Mama!" she whispered, but by now her grandmother was just a few yards short of the porch steps.

What was she supposed to do now? Of course she knew what Mama expected of her: following along obediently, smiling, and being friendly. But that wasn't Bennie's first choice. Maybe standing at the end of the driveway like a fool while Mama dropped off the pie? Mama *never* just dropped off a pie. She would stay and visit, say hello to Justice and Elizabeth, and give Miss Emmeline an opportunity to take credit for teaching her how to make that special meringue.

Or she could run back home like a coward.

Oh, no. Benita Pickering Ford was not and had never been a coward. She'd been standing up for herself all her life, knowing first her daddy and then Mama had her back, but she hadn't relied on them too often. She fought her own battles and stood up to her own bullies.

And Calvin Sweet wasn't going to change that.

Stiffening her spine, she strode along the driveway, reaching the steps just a few seconds behind Mama. She followed the old lady up, folded her arms across her middle, and waited strong and steady for the confrontation to come.

"I heard you were in town," Mama said with a broad grin. "About a week, isn't it, and you haven't come to see me so I can hug your neck yet."

"I, uh…" That may have been all he meant to say. It was hard to tell since Mama had hold of his neck, and it was even harder to tell from ten feet away if she was hugging him or strangling him.

J'Myel had always accused Mama of using a hug as an excuse to get him into a headlock. *That's because you've always been up to something,* Mama responded. *For every hug you deserve, you've probably earned two headlocks.*

Bennie's chest tightened. After J'Myel died, she'd

become an expert at breathing using just a tiny portion of her lungs. Filling them took too much effort, gave her mind too much time to run through a million precious memories. In the moments it took her to breathe deeply, a tear could fall, and the first one was always followed by a flood of tiny, salty, anguished ones that didn't end until she was a limp, exhausted, soggy mess. And she would not let Calvin turn her into a soggy mess.

With her hands tightened into fists, she took another breath, then slowly directed her gaze past Mama to finally settle on Calvin for the first time in years. At the moment, she couldn't remember exactly when things had started going wrong between them, when J'Myel had stopped starting every sentence with *Me and Calvin...* It had been years. A lifetime. Too much time had passed, too many hurts, to ever forgive.

He was six feet tall, but even after all the years of working out and literally running for his life, he was as lean as ever. J'Myel had bulked up tremendously. When he'd come home for their wedding, he'd had to borrow a dress uniform from one of his friends because his muscles didn't fit into his old one anymore.

Calvin was still sleek, muscular but not-in-your-face so. There were a few hard lines etched into his face, and his eyes were flat—not emotionless, but wary. Unwelcoming. There was none of the mischief or the gleam she'd always associated with him, none of the pleasure at seeing her.

Well, that was only fair, because she wasn't feeling any pleasure at seeing him, either. Her chest hurt, and the air simmered around her, and she wanted nothing more than to vent her anger, to stomp her feet, to stare right through him, to freeze him to the core.

All he'd said so far was *I, uh*..., but Mama didn't need silly things like responses; she could keep a conversation going all by herself with minimal effort. After a good long hug, she stepped back and gestured Bennie's way with one elbow. "Well, Calvin, say hello to Bennie, or did you not recognize her there? All growed up, dressing like a woman instead of a tomboy, and she finally quit torturing her hair."

"Mama." Heat rushed though Bennie, but she steeled herself for his gaze, sliding head to toe as if he were confirming that she had indeed grown up, morphed from buddy into woman, and gone natural. She hoped he didn't think she'd dressed up for him because obviously she hadn't. Obviously she wouldn't even be there if she hadn't been tricked. Her jeans were almost as comfortable for studying in bed as sweats, and the dappled gray sweater was flattering. Nothing special.

"Say hello, Calvin," Mama prompted.

Lines appeared at the corners of his mouth. "Hello, Bennie."

Mama beamed. "Now you say it back, Bennie."

Bennie would bet matching lines had formed around her mouth. She knew her teeth were clenched so tightly that it was a miracle sound could escape. "Hello, Calvin."

Mama appeared oblivious to the tension, but Bennie knew better. The old woman wasn't oblivious to anything, no matter how she might pretend.

"I brought you one of my famous coconut cream pies," Mama said, lifting the carrier to bring his attention to it. "I remember how much you loved them. I'll just take it inside and say hello to your folks and to Emmeline. Here, Bennie, you have a seat and make yourself comfortable for a few minutes."

Why? Why was Mama putting her through this? She knew everything that had happened between Bennie, J'Myel, and Calvin. She *knew* how he had let Bennie down, how he'd broken her heart even when it was already breaking.

But Mama was a woman of grace and forgiveness. She thought some of that had rubbed off on her granddaughter.

Bennie scowled at her grandmother's back all the way to the door. Wishing she had her big coat with pockets to hide her fists and a hood to hide her face, she turned to stare out at the street. One minute ticked by after another, nothing but silence in the air. She didn't mind silence. She wasn't intimidated by it. She could stand right there, chilled to the bone, and say nothing until Mama finished visiting with the family inside. Wouldn't bother her in the least.

So she couldn't begin to explain why the next sound she heard was her own voice, hostile and thick and as cold as the air. "Why are you here?"

More quiet, then finally came the creak of the rocker. "I go where the Army tells me."

She closed her eyes. He had a man's voice now, deep and steady, though she would bet he still had the ability to hit some notes that were high for even her when he was excited. *Squeaky,* J'Myel used to call him. *Squinty,* Calvin responded, a reference to the glasses J'Myel had hated.

"How long will you be here?"

"As long as they say."

Oh, God, had he been assigned to Fort Murphy? Was he going to be living in her town for the next however many years, where she could run into him every time she left the house? Could she bear seeing him at odd times, caught off guard and overwhelmed with memories?

Tallgrass was a decent-sized town, she reminded herself while struggling to steady her breaths, and the fort was even bigger. Since he would work on post and she was at the civilian hospital, and he would hang out with his Army friends and she would stay with her friends, it wasn't likely they *would* run into each other. Maybe in the neighborhood here, but she would be on alert. She could avoid him as thoroughly as he'd avoided her the past five years.

That was what she would do: avoid him when she could, ignore him when she couldn't. The way he'd avoided her. The way he'd ignored her. It was a plan she could live with.

So she was doubly surprised when her body turned to face him of its own volition and the next sound she heard, once more, was her own voice. "Why didn't you ever say *I'm sorry*?"

*   *   *

As Calvin's hands tightened on the arms of the rocker, Bennie's hand flew to her mouth as if she wanted to capture the words and force them back inside. A sharp wind from the west made his eyes water. Not sorrow. Not guilt. Not the anger of her and J'Myel's betrayal.

He was sorry, all right. He was sorry J'Myel had let him down. Sorry Bennie had thrown away more than fifteen years of friendship with *him* in favor of staying on J'Myel's good side. Sorry that J'Myel had died and sorry that *he* had lived when so many good people hadn't.

"What do you think I owe you an apology for?"

She blinked, her brown eyes going even darker with emotions flitting through them. She really was *all growed up*. She'd been pretty when he and J'Myel had left for the Army, but in the years since, she'd matured, gotten all soft and womanly. Curls framed her face, and her curves had filled out, rounding her breasts and hips. Any man would give her a second glance, would go out of his way to speak to her, learn her name, earn a smile from her...if he didn't already have a history with her.

Annoyance settled in her eyes as she freed one hand long enough to make a dismissive gesture, one he'd seen from her a thousand times. "Not an apology. Sympathy. When J'Myel died. My husband. Your best friend."

Too restless to sit any longer, Calvin surged to his feet and walked to the end of the porch. From the corner of his eye, he could see his father through the window, sitting in the old easy chair with the newspaper, and he knew from experience that the women were in the kitchen, gathered around the table there to gossip.

Probably about him.

Shoving his hands into the pockets of his jeans, he faced Bennie, though he had to focus every second on keeping his gaze from darting away. "He wasn't much of a friend the last few years," he said flatly, refusing to acknowledge even to himself how deeply those words hurt. "And neither were you."

She didn't have anything to say to that. She tried. Her

lips parted, then closed, parted again, then closed again. There just wasn't any defense to the truth.

Even though it was the truth, he still could have sent a card. People who hadn't known J'Myel and Bennie even a fraction of the way he had, had sent cards, maybe even flowers. Calvin could have, probably should have, but the time for that was long past. The fact that he hadn't was just one more in a very long list of regrets.

Bennie at a loss for words was a rare thing, and he couldn't remember it ever lasting more than a moment. This time it dragged on, the tension obvious in the way she stood, the way her jaw clenched. He could imagine words building up inside her with such pressure that they would eventually explode, erupting in bursts that made no sense until anger finally forced them into some kind of order. Volcano Bennie, J'Myel had once called her, though after she'd chased him down and tackled him to the ground, he'd never done it again.

After a moment, she breathed in deeply, then blew the air out through her mouth. "Tell Mama I had to get back to studying. Tell her to call me when she's ready to come home."

Without waiting for a response, she turned on her heel and headed off. He watched as she reached the sidewalk, then the driveway, then turned left onto the street. He watched until she was little more than a hazy figure, striding across her own yard, up her own steps, into her own house.

And finally he released his breath. He shifted so the wall of the living room was at his back, and finally, oh, God, finally, he looked down the street to the right, his gaze zeroing in on a white house on the other side with a front porch that filled most of the front yard. A house where he'd spent probably half of his life, where he'd built forts and played basketball and slept in a tent out back on hot summer nights.

It had been just J'Myel and his mom in the house. His parents had divorced, and his dad had taken a new job in Seattle. They'd stayed close, though, the three of them, and J'Myel hadn't given up hope that his parents would get back together until the summer he'd turned sixteen, when his mother began dating for the first time since the divorce.

As far as Calvin knew, Golda Ford had never remarried. She'd stayed in that house, working as a paralegal for a local law firm, tending her overgrown bushes, and fretting over her son. What mother didn't fret about a son at war?

Then, after J'Myel had died and was buried with honors at the Fort Murphy National Cemetery, Golda quit her job, put the house for sale, packed up, and moved to Edmond to be closer to her family. His death had broken her heart and maybe her spirit. But what mother wasn't heartbroken at the death of her son?

The bleakness he'd lived with so long was starting to settle, like clouds so heavy with gloom that they had no choice but to sink low to the ground. He squeezed his eyes shut, pressed the heels of his hands to them, and breathed deeply, evenly, pushing it away with every fiber of his body.

"Calvin?"

A hand, soft and capable despite its age, clasped his forearm, and he jumped, jerking away, putting a half-dozen feet between himself and—

Mama Maudene. She was giving him a look, part knowing, part curious, all sympathetic. She reached out, hesitated as if to give him time to adjust, then gave his head a soothing pat. "If you had any hair to speak of, I'd brush it back," she said quietly. "All you boys who practically shave your heads bald . . . You know, the Army lets you have hair. I see it every time I go to town."

Calvin focused on calming his breathing, on controlling the fear that had, for an instant, ricocheted through him.

"Did my granddaughter go home without me?"

He swiped a hand across his face, drying the sweat that had popped out on his forehead. "Uh, yeah, she did. She said for you to call when you were ready to leave."

Mama snorted. "That girl. She acts like I never walked the streets alone. I moved here, just me and my kids, long before her daddy had even noticed girls, and we not only got along, we prospered."

He'd heard the story before: how she'd divorced her husband back when it wasn't common, how she'd moved west and raised her kids without any help from their father. *You took them away, now you take care of them.*

"She also said to tell you she had to study." He had no intention of saying anything more, none whatsoever of showing any curiosity, but there it was before he could think better of it. "What is she studying?"

"Nursing. My girl's going to be a registered nurse." Mama's smile was filled with pride. "She says she's going to specialize in geriatrics or pediatrics. I tell her, she spends enough time with old people as it is. Besides, if she works in pediatrics, maybe she can borrow me a great-grandbaby, because I don't think I'm going to get one any other way."

Calvin could imagine Bennie with a baby, but not J'Myel's. Back when he'd heard they were dating, when the best, deepest friendship he'd ever known had turned ugly and mean, he hadn't been able to wrap his mind around it. He'd realized Bennie was a woman, not their childhood pal, their bud, but he hadn't known J'Myel had come to see her as more, too. Them being more than friends? Kissing, having sex? Making plans for a wedding, a family, a future? There'd been something disconcerting about it. It had taken Calvin a while to get used to the idea, to try to be happy for them when deep inside he felt lost and left out and jealous. For more than half their lives, they'd existed as parts of one whole, and suddenly he was the outsider looking in.

"Come walk me home, Calvin," Mama said, taking his arm without waiting for an agreement. She knew he wouldn't refuse any reasonable request she made—and more than a few unreasonable ones as well.

He let her draw him to the steps, following the invisible trail Bennie had blazed a little while before. The air chilled him through his shirt and felt good on his skin, the dampness a reminder of his time stationed in Washington. When he breathed deeply, he smelled autumn: browning leaves, wet ground, a wisp of smoke drifting up from someone's fireplace. It smelled good and sweet and fresh.

"Your folks are awfully happy to have you home again," Mama commented before giving him a sidelong look. "You're not quite as pleased to be here, are you?"

A faint smile tugged at his mouth. "No, ma'am."

"I understand. All three of my children chose to leave home."

"So did you."

Her laughter touched old memories inside him. "That I did."

"Is Brenda still in Stillwater?"

"Yep, teaching economics at OSU, and Roland is still lawyering in Ada. They're my pride and joy—my kids and my grandkids. Just like you're your mama's and daddy's and Emmeline's pride and joy, and J'Myel was Golda's and Steve's."

Calvin's chest tightened. There was joy for his family, that he was alive, but what kind of pride could they find in him now?

Every day you survive is another day that counts, Chaplain Reed back at Lewis-McChord had told him. *Every day you don't die is another chance to make things right.* And Calvin was determined to make things right. Some days it seemed like a losing battle, but he was trying. He wouldn't stop trying.

When they reached the Pickering driveway, Mama looked at him earnestly. "I hate to poke in your business, Calvin, but can I tell you something?"

The smile that had almost formed earlier was back, stretching broad enough to make long unused muscles feel odd. "Mama Maudene, you've been in my business since I was a baby, and you never hated it even once."

"You're right on both counts," she admitted before gazing off into the distance. "That girl of mine... you've helped her through some really hard times when she came here with no daddy or mama. All those years you were the friend she needed when she needed it. My heart tells me you've reached some really hard times. Give her a chance to give back. Let her be the friend you need."

He loved Mama the way he loved Gran, but he couldn't give her the answer she wanted. *Let* Bennie be his friend? Hell, she didn't want to share the same air he breathed. Those few minutes back on his parents' porch had made it clear that she would have been happier if she'd never seen him again.

But he didn't have to give Mama any answer at all because suddenly she was in a rush to get inside. "Thank you for walking me home, Calvin. I've got to get in and put on my costume and do my makeup and make sure we've got enough candy for the trick-or-treaters tonight." She released his arm and started down the sidewalk, doing a crablike sidestep so she could continue to talk to him. "Why don't you borrow some of your cousins' kids and walk them around the neighborhood? I'll be sure and save you some special treats."

"I think I'll skip it, but thanks."

Mama was on the porch by then. "You and Bennie are old fuddies. Enjoy your TV watching while I'm having fun scaring and treating the kiddies."

He watched until she was inside—old habit—then raised his face to the sky. Rain was starting to fall again, cold and uncomfortable. It wouldn't stop the trick-or-treating, though. Mama's treats were too well known in the neighborhood. Even if the little buggers had to crawl on ice to go to only one house, it would be Mama's.

He would be back in his bland apartment—yes, probably watching TV—before the goblins and ghosts and zombies came out. If that made him an old fuddie, so be it. The description was the only thing he had in common with Bennie anymore, and hopeful though he was trying to be, he couldn't see that changing.

Chapter 6

Tell me again why we're not staying home to answer the door for trick-or-treaters."

Joe looked down the hallway toward Lucy's bedroom, where she was just out of sight but making plenty of noise. "Because we decided last time that this year we'd rather be anywhere but here."

"Oh, yeah. I think it was the mothers who did it for me. Witches' hats with everyday clothes, vapor cigs in one hand, and their very own candy bag in the other." Lucy lowered her voice to a rasp, punctuating words with a hacking cough. "'Hey, Taylor Leigh, be sure to get your mama something that goes good with Bud Light.'" She coughed again to get her own voice back to normal. "You're sure that wasn't a big kid in costume as a bad mother?"

"I'm sure. Her son is on the junior varsity football team. She asked me once if there was anything she could do to help him get moved up to varsity." He winced at one of the worst moments of his football career. Thank God the athletic director had walked in at just that moment.

At last Lucy began making the sort of noises that meant she would be coming out soon: spraying perfume, which made Norton sneeze, then throwing his yellow ducky onto his bed with a squeak, which made Sebastian meow and pounce on it. Joe had suggested they dress up, since he pretty much lived in gym clothes and she wasn't much better. Her loose, unstructured clothes that had been bought for comfort were practically falling-off too big now. Just once he would like to see her in something snug and clingy, to celebrate the achievement of her forty-pound weight loss.

At the sound of footsteps, he quit pulling at a loose string on his jacket and looked up. His tongue stuck to the roof of his mouth, his gut tightened as if he'd just been sucker punched, and the little voice that lived in his head couldn't stop chanting *Lu-cy, Lu-cy, Lu-cy.* Then it added a made-up-on-the-spot cheer: *Who's the luckiest guy in town? Lucy's guy.*

She wore a dark red dress that had long sleeves and a short hem that showed a lot of the muscles she'd built pounding the pavement since last May. The fabric plunged between her breasts and wrapped around her, classy but sexy. Her hair was down, its subdued brown picking up red tones from the dress, and her jewelry was minimal. Gone were the chunky rings and office-sturdy watch; small diamond studs nestled in her ears, a delicate watch circled her wrist, and a diamond pendant in the shape of a star hung on a thin gold chain around her neck.

And she wore her wedding rings, of course. He'd never

seen her without them and really never expected to, though he couldn't deny a faint hope...a hopeless wish...

Stopping a few feet in front of him, she raised both brows in a *well?!* sort of way.

He didn't have anything smart or funny or brash to say. When was the last time that had happened? So instead he swallowed hard and simply, honestly said, "You're beautiful, Luce."

Her cheeks turned pink, and she raised one hand like she was going to pat, fix, or adjust something. He caught her fingers instead and tugged her toward the door. Her coat was already lying with his on the back of the love seat. He held it for her, catching the gold and black silk scarf lying with it before it could slither to the floor.

In all the years they'd known each other, this was the first time he'd helped her with her coat. Not because his mother hadn't done her best to imbue him with a touch of chivalry, but he hadn't wanted to let touching Lucy become too easy. At first, she hadn't been ready to consider any man other than Mike in her life, and in case she never was ready, or found some other guy when she was—like Dr. Jerk Ben—he hadn't wanted her to break his heart.

"Where are we going?" she asked, lifting her hair from under the coat collar, then snagging the scarf from his fingers. She pulled it this way and that, then looped it around her neck. It looked more put together than the scarves he threw around his neck.

"We have reservations at Sage."

Lucy's eyes widened. "We can't afford Sage."

He gave her a level look. The place was Tallgrass's fanciest restaurant. Given a choice, he would be a lot more comfortable at Holy Cow for steaks, or Luca's for Italian, or Serena's for fried chicken and mashed potatoes, but tonight was special. "Don't worry about what 'we' can afford, because I made the reservations, and I'm picking up the check. Besides, high school head football coaches make more money than you think."

"I know. Better to put all the school's extra money into coaches than English, calculus, or science teachers."

He made a face at her before opening the front door. The streetlights appeared like haloes in the light rain, but that wasn't keeping the kids in their houses. They trailed along the sidewalks in groups, some accompanied by parents, some with big brothers and sisters. A half-dozen voices called, "Hey, Coach!" before they made it to Lucy's car.

She dangled the keys. "You want to drive?"

"For the safety of everyone on the streets tonight, yes." He snatched the keys from her, then steered her to the passenger side of the car.

"I'm not a bad driver," she retorted as she slid into the passenger seat.

"You won't win any prizes. Besides, guys drive on dates." The words echoed in his head, too late to retrieve. Sure, he'd asked her to go to dinner tonight, like a million times before, but he didn't want this to be like all those other times. He wanted to be a man taking a special woman to dinner at the nicest place in town, talking about... well, man-woman things. Seeing if she might be interested in other man-woman things.

He probably should have mentioned that to her. She probably thought this was just another of their Saturday evenings: two friends sharing a meal, picking up their own tabs, then going home to watch football or old comedy reruns on TV.

"Is this a date?" Lucy asked as soon as he slid into the driver's seat.

He was glad the night hid his face because his cheeks were getting hot. But he couldn't hide the hoarseness in his voice as he started the engine. "A beautiful woman and a gorgeous man, all dressed up, going out to the best restaurant in town to celebrate...if it looks like a duck and it sounds like a duck..."

"Did I say you were gorgeous?"

"Not tonight." He looked at her, and automatically his grin formed. Looking at her made him happy. Talking to her. Arguing with her. Just plain being with her. "But you have plenty of times before."

She *pfft*ed. "Everyone tells you that." Then, "Celebration?"

"You've got kitchen space. Prairie Harts is one step closer to opening its doors."

"I may be one step closer to losing my shirt," she mumbled. "Joe, what do I know about running a business?"

"You've been learning. You'll keep learning. You know what I tell my boys. Whether you think you can or you think you can't, you're right."

"Yeah, I believe Henry Ford said that." Her tone was dry, but it didn't hide her nerves. "You know how many small businesses fail in the first year?"

"You're not going to be one of them." As he stopped at a red light, Joe reached across the console to claim her hand. "Luce, what happens if you do fail?"

Her blue eyes jerked his way. "Do you think I'm going to? Was that other stuff just talk?"

"No. I'm just asking you a question. What happens if the business doesn't make it? What do you do?"

"Well...I don't plan on giving up my regular job right away. Even if I did, I've got Mike's life insurance and some savings of my own. So I guess I'd eat my inventory, then go back to life as usual."

"Will you be heartbroken?" He'd seen her heartbroken on a few occasions, and God help him, it had just about broken him. "Will you crawl into bed and never come out? Will the earth stop spinning and the stars burn out and the sun turn to ice?"

"Of course not," she said grudgingly. "All that happened when Mike died."

Not for the first time, Joe envied Mike Hart. He'd never met the man, but Mike had had everything. He'd loved his job, his family, his country, and God, how he'd loved his wife. And on top of that, Joe was pretty sure that if they had ever met, they would have been best buds.

But Mike was gone, and Lucy needed someone who was here, and Joe needed her.

The light changed, and he released her hand to return his to the steering wheel. "If the business fails, you're not going to be broke or homeless or destitute. You'll just be disappointed. But life will go on, and at least you'll know you tried. You won't look back in twenty or forty years and wonder what could have happened."

Just like he didn't want to look back and wonder what could have happened between them if only he'd tried. Asked her out. Kissed her. Let her know that he wanted to upgrade their relationship from friends to more.

So damn much more.

* * *

It seemed Bennie wished away half of her week. Thursday had become Friday's Almost Here. Friday, of course, was Thank God It's Friday. Then Sunday was Dear God, It's Almost Monday.

This week's Friday's Almost Here was almost over. She'd worked her regular shift at St. Anthony's, put in nearly three hours for another employee, then sat through Dr. Perkins's class, physically present but her mind wandering. She'd thought too much about everything except microbiology, so now that class was over, she was sitting at a tiny table for two in the back of Java Dave's, a rich, creamy, full-fat coffee drink in front of her, hoping the caffeine would give her enough of a jolt to keep her thoughts under control.

Java Dave's, like the Starbucks on the east end of town, was popular with high schoolers who should be home studying or getting ready for bed, in Bennie's opinion. A coffee shop should be a nice place to relax and enjoy good coffee, not listen while a roomful of hyperactive teenagers drank too much caffeine and made too much noise.

Feeling your age tonight, Bennie?

She grimaced, then lifted her cup and took a steamy long, sweet breath, followed by a longer, sweeter drink.

As a particularly loud burst of laughter echoed through the room, a voice cut into her thoughts. "You remember being that young?"

Despite the warm air and the hot drink, a chill ran through Bennie. Her fingers tightened enough around the cup to raise the level of the liquid inside, and for just an instant, an ache zigzagged through her body like a way-ward lightning strike, burning, searing, and catching her breath.

She forced her fingers to loosen on the cup, and slowly she raised her gaze to the man standing beside the table. So much for her theories that (a) they weren't likely to run into each other around town, and (b) she would be prepared if they did.

"I'm still young," she said, wincing at how prim she sounded, then followed it with a shrug that did little to ease the tension in her shoulders. "But even when I was that young, I wasn't loud and raucous."

He snorted, and something inside her clenched. Lord, how she'd missed that sound, that attitude, that—that Calvin-ness. "I believe I recall you being thrown out of the movie theater one night, and Pastor Howell had to give you the evil eye more than once during the Sunday morning service."

"You and J'Myel were thrown out of the theater, too, and you both got the evil eye in church far more often than I did." She breathed and found the tightness in her chest had eased. Her heart was thudding, and the lightning-strike burn was still sizzling, but breathing was good. She was happy with breathing.

He stood there, a sense of restlessness about him, as if he might bolt at any moment. His expression was stony, defensive and protective, a little angry and a little bit lonely, with more emotions she couldn't read. This was hard for him, coming back to his and J'Myel's stomping grounds, seeing the Ford house, seeing Bennie and Mama and old acquaintances, and not seeing J'Myel. She knew because it had been hard for her the first year after J'Myel died. She hadn't known whether to run away to get a new start or stay where she could wallow in the memories. Calvin looked like he was wondering the same thing.

He stood still enough to blend into the wallpaper...if he weren't handsome enough to draw interested looks from the women at the nearest table. His jeans fit snugly, like his gray T-shirt, and his black hoodie made him look ten years younger. He'd had a passion for dark hoodies that drove Gran crazy—and a passion now for giant-sized cups of coffee, cradled in his long fingers with the care he once might have used for a football or a basketball. Black, it looked like. No cream, no sugar, no whipped cream, cinnamon, or caramel. He needed to learn how to properly indulge when it came to caffeine.

She glanced past him, at the tables packed with kids, then made a gesture toward the chair opposite her. He hesitated—that wasn't the Calvin she'd known—then slowly slid into the seat. Immediately he turned it so that his back was to the wall, so that he looked at her peripherally. Like seeing her face-on was unappealing.

She didn't know what to say. He didn't appear to, either. Lord, had they ever found themselves in this situation before? Even the very first time they'd met, when she'd still been red-eyed and teary over her father's death, it was like they'd known each other forever. J'Myel had been a smart-ass, but Calvin's friendship had been the first hope she'd found since the funeral. He'd let her feel like a normal kid, talking when she needed to be distracted, listening when she needed to talk, and doing nothing at all when that was what she needed.

The silence continued, tension mounting, crawling along her skin until she blurted out the safest thing to come to mind. "Where were you stationed before you came here?"

Some emotion flashed across his face. Relief that she hadn't jumped right into the issue of him and J'Myel with both feet?

"Joint Base Lewis-McChord. In Washington State."

A long way off. Practically as far as he could get while staying in the contiguous States. "I hear it's beautiful up there."

"If you don't mind the rain."

"Which you don't." *He must be part fish, as much as he likes being wet,* Elizabeth Sweet had once remarked. *More likely part fungus,* J'Myel had snickered.

How could a memory be so sweet at the same time it hurt her heart? All the good times they had shared... The three of them had been inseparable, but they'd each had their roles. J'Myel was the joker, the clown who never took anything seriously. Bennie was the bossy one who tried to keep them in line but failed—exasperatedly and happily—as often as she succeeded, and Calvin... He'd been the rock, the one she'd shared laughs with while J'Myel was being goofy, the one she'd discussed serious subjects with, the one she'd turned to in times of need: her first birthday without her daddy, her first boyfriend breaking up with her for another girl, her worries about Mama and school and life. He'd gotten her through all of them.

And now she couldn't think of anything to say to him.

"Mama says you're going to nursing school."

She grasped on to the question quickly. "Getting my associate's degree. OSU has a program through the community college here. After this semester, I have one more year, and then I figure I'll work for a while before I finish my bachelor's."

"She says you want to work with babies."

"Or the elderly. They both like me." She shrugged, hoping the immodesty she was aiming for came across. "Believe it or not, everyone likes me."

"I believe it." He wasn't looking at her when he said it. Instead, his gaze shifted over the dining room, landing briefly at each table. When he'd finished the visual survey, he started again.

Was it so hard for him to look at her? Was it guilt? Discomfort? Sadness? Regret? Lord knows, she felt all those things with regard to him. And anger and betrayal and…something small, isolated: something better, happier. Gratitude? Was she grateful he'd returned home? To see him again, to hear his voice, and to remember happier times? No. Maybe someday, but she wasn't ready for it yet.

But she was grateful for his parents that he was back. They had missed their only child. They needed some time where they could look at him and touch him, reassure themselves that he was okay. She imagined Elizabeth Sweet had awakened every morning for the past two weeks, thanking God, "My son is *home*."

"You keep in touch with many people from school?" he asked, his voice steady, cautious.

A slow breath lessened the tightness in her chest. Everyday conversation—she could handle this. "Trinity Adams is in my class at school and works my floor at the hospital. She's been married and divorced twice but not to the fathers of either of her kids." Bennie loved Trinity, but she didn't envy her friend's situation. She'd been raised that there was an order to things—love and marriage came before babies, and commitment came before any of it—and no matter how old-fashioned it seemed to some, Bennie still believed it.

"Hence, the divorces."

"Ooh, a man who uses *hence* correctly." The teasing came automatically, Bennie's brain forgetting that her heart wasn't anywhere near forgiving him yet.

His automatic response to her teasing in years past—a smile that spread ear to ear and scrunched up his eyes—didn't put in an appearance. Instead, his mouth thinned, and his eyes went flat as a muscle in his jaw twitched a few times.

And a man who's lost his sense of humor. What else? she wondered. What other parts of himself had he sacrificed in his years of service? "Rickey Duncan is senior pastor at the big Baptist church in town. Whoever would have guessed that drugs, alcohol, and sex would lead him straight to God?"

Calvin's stiffness slowly faded. "Wasn't he the one we thought most likely to spend the rest of his life in prison?"

"Yup. He reminds people of that in his sermons sometimes." She thought for a moment. "Bethany Green is our U.S. senator. Shay Barefoot is a doctor. Marc Harjo *is* spending the rest of his life in prison. The Holloway twins were killed five or six years ago when they tried to beat the train across the railroad tracks."

"Kind of hard to feel sorry for someone who messes with a train."

She nodded. "Most of our class are living normal, everyday lives: going to work, getting married, having kids. Some of them drink too much or smoke too much weed.

Some run around on their spouses or mooch off their parents. Some ran far away, and some are trying real hard to get back."

A muscle twitched at the corner of his left eye. "You didn't run away."

She could have. College would have been an easy out for her. Get a degree, get a job outside the state, settle someplace where she'd be no one's friend, no one's family, where she could find out what she was made of.

"Why would I want to leave?" she asked. "I love Tallgrass. The happiest years of my life have been here."

He took a long drink, and when he lowered the cup, bold, dark wisps of steam perfumed the air. "J'Myel wanted to leave."

She caught her breath that he'd brought up J'Myel, and without anger or resentment in his voice. Granted, there'd been no other emotion in it, either. "He intended to come back here when his Army time was done."

Calvin shook his head. "That wasn't his plan in the desert. He talked about settling in Chicago, New Orleans, Los Angeles, Seattle."

If the two of them had been on speaking terms then, those conversations must have taken place well before she and J'Myel got married. Maybe being with her had changed his mind, because there had been no way on earth she would have moved to Chicago, New Orleans, Los Angeles, or Seattle, and he'd known it.

Insecurity sparked inside her. He *had* known that, hadn't he? Had understood that much about her? Naturally, his years in combat had changed him. He'd had to grow up, grow tough. Instead of planning their future ten years down the road, he'd had to concentrate on surviving each day. But with all the changes, he was still the boy she'd grown up with, the man she'd fallen in love with. And he'd loved her.

But she hadn't known his plans, beyond coming back to her; he'd never wanted to discuss them. She hadn't known any of the new friends who had replaced Calvin; he hadn't wanted to talk about them, either, not when time was precious. She hadn't known anything about his life but what he chose to share in e-mails and phone chats.

Unsettled, she fingered the necklace she always wore, a gold heart on a chain, a gift from J'Myel. With a shrug, she pushed on with the conversation. "His mom moved to Edmond. Too much sadness here for her."

Calvin didn't say anything like *I heard that.* She was sure he had. Once the falling-out had occurred, Mama and Miss Emmeline had kept each other filled in on the grandkids' lives. Bennie was sure at least some of it had been passed on.

The young kid behind the counter flashed the lights once, and a chorus of groans came from around the room. Bennie glanced at her watch, surprised by the lateness of the hour. "It's closing time."

She threw her cup and napkins in the trash, then, with Calvin behind her, wended her way to the door. The temperature was in the fifties, and the weather folks were predicting typical November weather for the weekend with highs in the seventies. "I'm parked over here." She gestured toward her vehicle. "Where's your car?"

"Your guess is as good as mine."

His cryptic answer earned him an unwavering look. He lifted one shoulder. "It got stolen before I left Washington."

"Then how did you get here?" She gestured to Java Dave's. She knew the Army had provided transportation to Fort Murphy.

"A friend with a car was going out to Bronco's and invited me, but cowboy bars aren't my thing, and I've had only one decent cup of coffee since I got here, so I asked him to drop me off. I'm going to meet him there."

"You want a ride?"

"No, thanks." He walked with her to her car and stood there on the sidewalk, hands stuffed inside the hoodie's pockets. She unlocked the driver's door, swung her purse to the opposite seat, then straightened, her hands gripping the door frame. She felt the need to say something at least halfway conciliatory, but since she couldn't think what, she smiled stiffly, got inside her car, and slowly backed out of the parking space. He didn't wait for her to drive away before he began walking again.

She watched, gaze flitting between her driving and him, as he took the shortcut behind the courthouse, his lanky legs climbing the gazebo steps, crossing the warped boards, climbing down again on the other side. A few more strides, and he was in the shadows of a giant oak, and she was ticking off the teenagers kicked out of Java Dave's. She accelerated to a normal speed, traveled the block to the red light at the intersection of Main and First, and glanced to her right.

The bar Calvin was headed for was three blocks away on the right side of the street. If she hadn't been looking for him, she wouldn't have spotted him, already halfway there, sticking close to the buildings, walking in the dim light under the awnings of the shops.

As a kid honked a horn behind her, she noticed the

light had changed and she pulled away from the intersection. Within a few minutes, she was home, letting herself into Mama's, warm and sweet-smelling and safe. After chatting with Mama a few minutes, she carried a glass of warm milk and her backpack into her bedroom. She intended to complete the studying Calvin had interrupted at Java Dave's, but concentrating on microbiology was hard when her heart was all fluttery and unsettled.

Calvin had seen some awful things in Iraq and Afghanistan, things no naïve kid from Oklahoma should have to see. That had to be the reason he'd changed so much, the reason he and J'Myel had fallen apart, why he hadn't been able to send even a damn note of sympathy for the funeral. Maybe she shouldn't be angry with him. Maybe he was the one deserving of sympathy.

Probably he was. But it wasn't about just them. It was about J'Myel, too, and the disrespect Calvin had shown him. And it was about, heavens, every emotion that simmered through her at the thought of him, that could so easily boil over at the sight of him. It was about who they'd once been and what they'd since lost.

Bennie had experience with loss—her mother, her father, J'Myel, Calvin—but the others were gone: Lilly disappeared God knows where, Daddy and J'Myel in the grave. Calvin was the only one still here. The only one she could at least find out why.

*   *   *

"Do you like dogs, Captain?"

Calvin dried sweat from his forehead, then tossed the towel over the treadmill controls before focusing his attention on Captain Kim, one of the psychologists with the unit. "My grandmother used to send her Labrador retriever swimming at the lake with us. He never let me get in water deeper than my waist. Other than that, I guess I liked him fine."

"Did you have a pet of your own?"

"It was hard enough with my mother expecting me to be clean and shiny and well behaved all the time. Would've been impossible for me and a dog." The treadmill beeped and slowed to a stop, signaling that he'd reached his five-mile goal. "Why the questions? You have a dog you're trying to get rid of?"

She smiled. "Nope. My pilot program is starting today, and you're one of the lucky guys taking part."

He'd heard of programs involving patients with various animals, especially horses. If they could help troubled kids and physically disabled patients, he wasn't surprised they'd be doing some version of it with soldiers.

Both the physically disabled and the troubled.

"What does this program involve?"

The captain, with black hair, dark eyes that sparkled, and an impossibly white smile, made a note on her tablet, then shook her head. "You'll find out as soon as I gather the others. Meet us at the front door in fifteen minutes."

"Can I shower first?" His skin was sticky, and his PT clothes were soaked, smelling more than a little ripe.

"If you can do it in fifteen minutes. But it's really not necessary. You'll probably need a shower when we come back anyway."

Giving her a cynical look as he stepped off the treadmill, he dryly said, "I'll make it quick."

He kept his word. With one minute to spare, he arrived

back at the entrance, where the captain was waiting with six other patients. All of them, Calvin had learned by now, diagnosed with PTSD.

A van drove them to the middle of town before turning north. Just before the railroad tracks, the driver turned back east again, and a moment later deposited them in the gravel parking lot of the Tallgrass Animal Shelter.

Three women were waiting outside for them: two tall, cool blondes and one short little redhead. Calvin's gaze skimmed across them before going to the dogs lined up along the fence, some barking, some watching in suspicious silence. A few were so greedy for attention that it seemed they might piss themselves if they didn't get it right away, while a few others looked as if they'd rather starve than take food from a friendly hand.

He understood the theory behind animal therapy. Caring for someone or something more helpless, more dependent on others, was supposed to help rebuild trust— both theirs and the dogs'. It was supposed to get them out of the dark places in their minds, to remind them that there was innocence and good in the world, that they could make a difference in someone else's life, that they had value.

It was a hell of a burden to put on a bunch of unwanted, malnourished, mistreated, and rehabilitating animals.

One of the blondes started the conversation. "Hi, guys, I'm Meredith. I'm the part-time vet here and full-time owner with my partner, Angela, and this is Jessy, who helps us keep things relatively under control. Rae"—she gestured toward Captain Kim—"offered us some warm bodies to help out here, and believe me, we're *always* grateful for warm bodies. There's never any shortage of unwanted dogs, and we're perpetually understaffed, underfunded, and overworked, so we're incredibly grateful for you."

The other blonde took over. "We work on a first-name basis around here. The three of us are easy enough to remember—Meredith, Jessy, Angela—and fortunately, the rest of you, dogs included, all wear name tags. We do have some cats who are also tagged, but you'll probably never get close enough to have any interaction with them. They prefer to be worshipped from afar."

Along with the Lab, Gran had had a cat. It had had three legs and was blind in one eye, and it gave the Lab so many vicious swipes with its paw that he'd whimpered and hidden when he saw it coming. Calvin had had to hide from it a few times, too. He hadn't worshipped it— hadn't even liked it—but he'd had a very healthy respect for it.

They divided into groups, Calvin finding himself alone with the redhead. She was close to a foot shorter than him, but she moved fast and talked slow, the sharp edges of her words softened by a lazy Southern accent that reminded him of basic training at Fort Benning, Georgia. She wore shorts and a top that exposed her legs and arms, thick-soled sandals, and a platinum-set diamond on her left hand.

He followed her inside the shelter and through to the backyard, where she took two pairs of gloves and two rakes from a storage shed built against the outside wall. "It's your lucky day, Calvin—lucky that it's not cold, raining, or snowing, that is, because we're cleaning the yard."

"Cleaning?" He accepted a rake, then looked past her.

"Oh. 'Cleaning.'" There were a lot of dogs at the shelter, some inside at the moment, the rest outside, yapping at them or keeping their distance. A lot of dogs equaled a lot of dog sh—

"We call it poo, but feel free to use whatever word fits best for you. I'll tell you, if they could clean up after themselves, they'd be the perfect creature."

"More perfect than the guy who gave you that ring?"

She eyed it a moment, then shrugged. "Well, he does clean up after himself. Mostly. How long have you been in Tallgrass?"

"A couple weeks. How long have you been working here?"

"About six months. These guys saved my life, so I try to return the favor."

He didn't ask, didn't want to know, didn't care, except somewhere inside, maybe where his mom and dad had ingrained in him to care. As they began raking dog shit, er, poo into piles to shovel into the nearby wheelbarrow, he asked, "How?"

Jessy looked at him, her eyes the clearest, cleanest green he'd ever seen. "I'm an alcoholic," she said evenly, without self-consciousness or embarrassment. "Getting a job here helped me stop drinking."

Would he ever be able to state his problem as easily as she did? To set aside the shame at how weak he'd become, to admit that life had overwhelmed him so deeply that he hadn't wanted to live? He wanted to get to that point. If he was going to be in this world, then he wanted to *be* in it. To accomplish things. Love people. Laugh. Be happy.

Right now he'd settle for not hurting.

"Congratulations," he said shortly.

"It's an ongoing battle, but I've got support. From my fiancé"—she waggled her fingers, drawing attention to the ring—"his family, my friends, and my babies." At that, she bent to scratch a young beagle under its chin. "You guys are sweet babies, aren't you?"

A half-dozen more dogs crowded in for their scratches, and she accommodated them all before returning to the raking.

Calvin had family and friends. Not close friends, like he, J'Myel, and Bennie had been, but friends who'd been where he'd been and seen what he'd seen. Friends who'd found some weakness in themselves and dealt with it better than he had.

Friends who were scattered everywhere around the world but here. And the guys with PTSD in the WTU company—they'd been there, done that, gotten damaged in the process—but they weren't friends. Maybe someday they would be, maybe not. But they hadn't coped any better than he had to wind up in the WTU.

He and Jessy started raking in the back corner of the fenced yard. By the time they'd cleaned a nice-sized section, one of the standoffish dogs, a tall muscular mix of breeds, circled in the middle of it and added a new pile.

Jessy grinned as she pushed her hair from her face. "It's like every kind of cleaning I've ever done. You get about ten seconds to enjoy it, then the crap starts piling up again."

Calvin had heard similar comments from his mom. *I just finished the laundry, and there you are in dirty clothes. I just washed the last dish, and now I have to dirty new ones to fix dinner.*

"The solution would be to not waste time in futile tasks that you'll just have to do again."

"Oh, this is not futile. Setting aside the obvious downside of a yard full of poo, there's the secondary and more offensive scourge: flies. You know in Oklahoma, they're classified as instruments of torture. If we don't keep the yard clean, they'll carry off animals and small workers, and since I'm the smallest one here..."

Calvin's laugh was rusty. The poo did smell something awful, but there weren't any flies to do battle with today, and it was a nice, cool, sunny day to be out. It was a good change from his last job of dealing with troops to his most recent assignment as a professional patient. Things could be worse.

By the time they'd cleared the back third of the yard, other teams were finishing the job in the side yards. While explaining that a kind rancher who had more land than he used would haul the poo away for them, Jessy returned their tools to the shed, then led him inside. As they passed through the storage room, he caught a glimpse of a cat black as midnight except for a white spot on his forehead. The animal moved silently, elegantly stalking along an upper shelf, tail lazily above him. He reminded him of Gran's old cat, not in looks but in the stealthy way he moved that suggested confidence, brashness, pride, and trouble.

About half the space of the shelter was filled with kennels. Just the number of dogs outside was disheartening, but adding in those who remained in their kennels was depressing. "Where do they all come from?"

"Some are pets who've been surrendered by people who were moving or because their owners have died.

We're a no-kill shelter, so we take some in from shelters where they're scheduled to be euthanized. Some are strays who aren't tagged or chipped, but most of them are dumped. Your dog has puppies you don't want, so you take them for a drive, toss them out somewhere far from home, and problem solved."

She pointed out the kennel dogs recovering from spaying, neutering, or injuries they'd had upon arriving. A few were large animals, a couple of German shepherds and mixes, who reminded him of the working military dogs in Iraq and Afghanistan. Beautiful animals, smarter than the average soldier. And sad. These guys were sad, too.

"You don't put any of them down," he repeated, wanting confirmation as he looked at them.

"Only when their condition is so far gone that Meredith can't help. We don't let them suffer."

Physically maybe, but what about mentally?

One of the shepherds became aware of his attention, stood, and moved to the front of its cage. Almost silently, it drew back its lips to show a deadly set of teeth, then exploded into cringe-inducing barks.

"Heidi," Jessy chastened. "She considers it her job to shake things up around here every few hours. She's not ready yet to put up for adoption. We're still working on her manners."

"Too vicious?"

"Oh, no. If she didn't know she was safe in her kennel, she'd be huddling in the back corner, whimpering and shaking like a leaf. She's so afraid of people that Meredith had to sedate her to bring her here. Meredith's been working with her, but progress is slow. I told her, first thing, she needs to give that baby a name to be proud of. Heidi's fine for a little girl with blond braids, but not for a hundred-ten-pound authority figure of a shepherd."

"Yeah, maybe something like Bear, Killer, or Fang would fit better," he agreed. "Or maybe Jessy."

She flashed a grin at him. "I like you, Calvin Sweet. We're gonna have fun here."

Chapter 7

Do you suppose I could learn to knit and make a gift in time for Christmas?" Bennie wondered aloud as she picked up a booklet of patterns for knitting scarves with various embellishments. Though she'd been speaking to Marti, on the next aisle looking at jewelry-making material, it was a shop clerk who answered.

"One of those scarves would be pretty simple. Once you get started, it's really just a matter of keeping it going until you've got it long enough. Is that what you were thinking of?"

"Actually, I was thinking about a blanket for our friend's baby."

Marti glanced over the top shelf that separated them. "Then why were you looking at patterns for scarves?"

"Marti, please don't expect me to be rational and logical on my day off. It's been a long week. Work, class, and—" Bennie practically bit her tongue before Calvin's name could get out. She'd never told anyone in the margarita club about Calvin and had never thought she would. Had *never* thought the Army would send him back here. What were the odds of that?

Hard to calculate, especially since she didn't even know what Calvin's field was. He and J'Myel had gone into Infantry together, but after Calvin had earned his bachelor's degree, she assumed the Army had put him someplace where they could take advantage of his specific education. By then, the great divide had appeared, and none of them had tried to cross it.

"You're off Sunday, too," Marti reminded her, shaking Bennie's thoughts back to now.

"Breakfast, Sunday school, church, after-church dinner, studying, evening church, bed. Show me a spare minute."

"Hmm. Well, Sunday's a day of rest for me," Marti said, "which means my Saturdays are pretty calm, too."

Calm probably came pretty easily when Marti didn't go to church or school, wasn't living with anyone, and didn't have to worry about meals. Everything she put down was exactly where she left it when she wanted it again, and if she wanted ice cream for breakfast, popcorn for lunch, and cotton candy for dinner, she got exactly that, without any lectures on balanced diets.

Bennie wouldn't trade places with her for the world.

The shop clerk was still waiting to explain the intricacies of knitting, but Bennie made a face. "You know, I think I'd rather try a quilt. Cut out pieces of material, sew them together, quilt them... I'm pretty sure I can do that while 'knit one, purl two' is a foreign language. Besides, Mama used to quilt. She'll help me." Mama would help make little John Gomez's first Christmas quilt something really special.

"We have some beautiful quilting fabric over here, along with pattern books," the sales girl said. "If you're a beginner, you might want to try a simple nine patch, but if your mother's experienced and working with you, you can do an appliqué piece so beautiful you'll cringe to see the baby touch it."

"When Joshua and I moved here, my mother gave me a chest filled with baby blankets and quilts and garments," Marti remarked, holding a large dangly string of beads to one ear and studying herself in the mirror. "They'd all been gifts to me when I was a baby, but she was sure I would get them dirty. Overflowing diapers, spit-up, drool—you know, all those nasty things newborns do. So she never dressed me in the clothes or wrapped me in the blankets."

"At least she gave them to you in pristine condition so you could use them with your own baby if you have one."

"You'd think, but you see, now they're thirty-plus years old. They're *vintage* baby clothes. Heirlooms. And I couldn't possibly dress my infant in family heirlooms except for special occasions."

Bennie laughed at Marti's wry head shake. She'd heard a lot of stories about Marti's mother, Eugenie. She was currently in her fourth widowhood—or was it fifth?—and each husband who'd passed had left her with even more money than before. She lived in Florida, where the world rotated around her, dated endlessly, and sent frequent dispatches to Marti and her brothers. As far as Bennie knew, Eugenie had never visited Tallgrass and, with luck, Marti liked to believe, never would.

The margarita sisters liked to remind her that luck could and often did change.

Following the clerk, Bennie found herself in the fabric section, surrounded by bolts of material in more colors and patterns and fabrics than she'd ever imagined. Immediately, Mama's opinion on dinner buffets came to Bennie's mind: *Too many choices is just too many choices.* How was she supposed to pick only six or eight fabrics for John's quilt when they were all beautiful and colorful?

The clerk's smile was a tad smug. "I'll let you look and check back in a few minutes."

Bennie browsed baby-patterned material, little boy themes, Christmas themes, jewel-toned solids, high school and state university logos, and specialty fabrics. There was a hand-painted fabric that she absolutely loved, but it cost more per yard than her college classes per credit hour.

She was exaggerating a little. Okay, maybe a lot, but still...The idea of working with the gorgeous material made her smile, as well as the idea of John teething and slobbering all over it.

Her meandering had taken her to the front windows of the craft store. She was glancing outside, acknowledging that she would have to come back with Mama to help her make choices, when a familiar figure on the sidewalk caught her attention. Rickey Duncan, tall and broad-shouldered, was deep in conversation with a man whose back was to her, but when she waved, Rickey's face brightened, and he waved back, gesturing her to join them.

Then his companion turned, and Bennie's breath caught. There were a boatload of tall, slender, muscular black men in town. She had to start reminding herself that any one of them, seen from a disadvantageous position, could be Calvin.

Leaving the few items she'd selected to buy on the measuring table, she slipped out the nearby door, a ready smile on her face. "Rickey!" she said with real pleasure as she stepped into his embrace. Their old friend who'd taken the drugs, sex, and rock-'n'-roll path to the ministry was easily one of the most cheerful people she knew. He was so grateful for the life he lived—wife, kids, friends, calling—that when he said he couldn't complain, he truly meant he couldn't complain.

Bennie wished she had that kind of utter and complete gratitude.

"I'm trying to persuade Calvin to drop in on our service tomorrow morning," Rickey said as she stepped back to include the other man in their small circle.

"If I visited your church, Emmeline would track us both down for a come-to-Jesus meeting, and it wouldn't be pretty," Calvin said. His gaze flickered across Bennie's face, away, back again, then away. She didn't know if he was aware of it, but his feet were shifting, too, like he was looking to get away before he'd fully arrived. Was it just her that made him want to run? Though her skin should be plenty thick enough with all her heartaches, the idea stung. But it beat the alternative, that everyone made him so antsy he wanted to escape. That was entirely too sad a possibility.

"Everyone in town knows the Sweets and the Pickerings and Miss Emmeline's people founded that church over in the Flats," Rickey said, "and not one of them's ever gone anywhere else since."

"We make allowances for weddings, baptisms, and funerals," Bennie teased.

Across the street, a horn honked, and Rickey waved in that direction. Bennie glanced across at a silver minivan with Rickey's wife in the passenger seat and their four kids crowded into the driver's and left rear seats, heads stuck out the windows, taking turns calling their daddy. "I'd better go before they make a real disturbance. Calvin, it's really good to see you." Rickey enveloped Calvin in a hug. Bennie had expected it—most pastors she knew were huggers—but Calvin hadn't, and she watched how stiffly he held himself. Was hugging something else he'd given up along with J'Myel, visits home, and her?

That little sting inside sharpened its bite.

After another blast of the horn, Rickey called, "I'm coming," then trotted across the street at the first break in traffic.

"Are all those kids his?" Calvin asked quietly.

"Yep. And one more on the way. They'll have five under the age of six."

"Wow."

She felt the same in a stupefied kind of *Don't they know what birth control is?* way.

As the Duncans drove away with one last wave, Calvin faced the building, his gaze sliding across the bright sign overhead. " 'Crafty Minds,' " he read before glancing at her. "Even in vacation Bible school, the stuff you made with ice cream sticks was crooked and fell apart before we got home. Don't tell me you finally learned to use glue or knit or thread a needle."

Huh. That look in his eyes showed a tiny bit of the humor she'd always loved about him, and with a little effort, the set of his mouth could almost become a smile. Lord, how she'd missed his smiles.

"I'll have you know I've watched Mama do all those things a million times. She's even let me help cut out quilt pieces before." She glanced inside and saw Marti, still lingering on the jewelry aisle, trying to pretend she wasn't paying more attention to Bennie and Calvin than she was to the merchandise. *Nobody special,* Bennie would say when she asked. *Just some guy I went to high school with. He and J'Myel and I were friends.* With the right degree of carelessness and no guilty look in her eyes, Marti might even believe her.

Why shouldn't she? It was true. Mostly.

"My friend Ilena had a baby this summer. Kid's got a wonderful mom and a dad who—" Breaking off, she swallowed hard. Combat deaths could be hard to talk about, especially with someone with firsthand experience. She knew Calvin had lost friends, and those losses had hit him hard. How accustomed was he to a discussion of death that, on the surface, seemed casual? Less than she and the margarita girls, that was sure.

She moistened her lips before continuing in the most normal voice she could force. "A dad who died in Afghanistan before he was born, plus eight or ten godmothers. I want to do something special for John's first Christmas, so I was checking the possibilities."

She'd been right that it wasn't an easy topic for him. A hard look swept across his face, and he took a few steps back, scuffing his feet on the pavement. She thought again that he was emotionally preparing to flee but not necessarily from her this time. He was just itching to run in general.

The bell dinged behind her, and Marti came to stand next to Bennie. Maybe it was the appearance of a gorgeous woman that eased the lines of his face, or maybe it was just the interruption itself, the third person to change the direction of the conversation. Whatever, Bennie actually felt the air around Calvin soften.

"There I am looking at beads and loops and lobster claws, and you're standing out here talking to a man." Marti stuck her hand out, but just as surely as Rickey hadn't given Calvin a chance regarding the hug, she wasn't going to give him a chance to refuse the handshake. He seemed to realize that and offered his hand, his long brown fingers easily, perfunctorily gripping hers.

For a moment, Bennie envied Marti the touch. She and Calvin had always been generous with physical contact—a punch here, a hug there, shoulder bumps everywhere. They had been so comfortable together that the awkwardness now just about broke her heart.

"I'm Marti Levine."

"Calvin Sweet."

"Oh, the plays on words I could make with that name."

Something of a smile flitted across his face. It wasn't the first time he'd heard that remark, Bennie knew. His last name had been a source of teasing since he started kindergarten.

"But I won't." Marti directed her gaze at Bennie. "You've been holding out on us."

"Calvin's parents live down the street from Mama and me. He just came to town a few weeks ago."

Marti nodded, her sleek ponytail bobbing. "Are you married, Calvin?"

His face darkened a shade. "No."

"Looking?"

Another shade of embarrassment as curiosity deep inside Bennie perked its little ears. "Not at the moment."

"Like to have fun?"

"Marti," Bennie chastened, telling herself it was just curiosity. The old friendship, the nosiness she'd inherited from Mama. Nothing more. "We're going back inside now to finish our shopping."

As Bennie shoved Marti back into the store, her friend caught hold of the door. "If you decide your answer is yes, Calvin, I know a lot of wonderful, fun, beautiful, available women who would love to meet you."

To Bennie's surprise when she turned around again, Calvin was still there. She'd thought he would take advantage of the distraction to get the heck out of Dodge. He stood there, though, balancing lightly on the balls of his feet, hands shoved into his jacket pockets, and that almost-a-smile was back in place. "Matchmaker, weird, or just desperately seeking?"

"Matchmaker. I'm sure the only thing Marti has ever been desperate about was her husband's death. That was tough for her, but of course, that's true of all of us."

"All?" he echoed.

"My best friends here in town." Again, she hesitated a moment before plunging in. "You've heard of wives' clubs. Well, we've got a widows' club. The Tuesday Night Margarita Club. All our husbands died in the war."

Bennie was used to various reactions when she told people about the margarita club. Some people instinctually understood the club for what it was: a group of women helping each other through the worst times of their lives. There were some, though, who heard "widow" and imagined a bunch of heartbroken women, complete with black scarves and veils, who sat in gloomy rooms talking endlessly about their dead husbands, God rest their souls. To ensure Calvin wasn't in that last group, she added, "Forget the widow part. Just hear the best friends part."

"Is it a support group?"

"Yeah, it's a lot of that. It's a sisterhood. An adventure club. A steady supply of work and relationship advisors, babysitters, shoulders to cry on, caretakers, caregivers, prayer warriors. Our youngest is twenty-three, and the oldest is in her fifties. We've got Christians and agnostics, with kids and without, and we cover the spectrum in pretty much every other way."

"Sounds...depressing."

She shrugged. "When a person's gone through an experience that's out of the norm, it always helps to find someone else who's been through it and not just survived, but flourished. Why should every one of us have to struggle to learn things that those ahead of us have already learned?"

"Makes sense." Delivered with a shrug that said he wasn't convinced but wouldn't argue. "Look, I, uh, have to go. I'll...see you later." With a nod, he turned on his heel and strode off down the street before she might argue. Surely he found death to be depressing, too. He'd damn well better have been depressed by J'Myel's death, if for no other reason than it meant their last chance to salvage their friendship had been forever lost.

She watched him for a moment, then returned to the

craft store, pushing his words out of her mind. Her days of having to convince anyone of anything were long gone. When it came to the margarita girls, all that mattered was that she loved them, and they loved her right back. Anyone else's opinion or discomfort belonged entirely to that person, and it was their loss, not hers.

But, Lord, did her losses have to be so impressive?

* * *

Balancing a twenty-five-pound bag of sugar on one hip, Lucy slid her key into the back door of her new shop, shoved the door open with her foot, and made it to the nearest stainless table before the bag slipped free. It landed on the metal with a thump, then she slung her purse over her shoulder and went into the kitchen, turning on lights on the way. The room was filled with the kinds of equipment and space she had only dreamed of. There would be no more locking Norton in the bedroom while she baked, no more storing goodies in the guest room for safety. When her parents came for their next visit, she would once again have a bed for them to sleep on . . . and something wonderful to show off to them.

A couple of thuds sounded from the store room, then footsteps came to the kitchen door. She was standing at what would be her primary workspace, rubbing her hand lightly over a mixer that made hers at home look like a shrinky-dink model. There were ovens, burners, prep tables, sinks, fridges, freezers—plural. More than one of each.

She knew she was grinning ear to ear. She had been for the past week.

Hands propped on his hips, Joe watched her with his own grin. "As soon as we finish unloading the car, it's time to baptize this place by fire."

"Ouch, fire and bakery don't belong in the same sentence." She imagined the scene covered with soot, debris, water running everywhere, and firemen zapping down hotspots. "I prefer to think of this room as my pool, and I'm about to dip my toes into it for the first time."

"Well, whatever you're doing, you've got a lot of stuff to fix for tomorrow, and I'm your only help."

A few dozen miniature cupcakes, three dozen blueberry muffins, two large pans of cinnamon rolls, an assortment of fruit turnovers, and enough cheese Danishes to tempt her to sample. A small portion was going to her own church; the rest had been ordered—her second bona fide sale—by the church one of Joe's assistant coaches attended.

"You know, I can call the girls to help." All of them had volunteered at dinner Tuesday night, albeit in a wonderful rushed, *Me, too!* sort of way. Because they were the kind of people who always helped whenever they could, she had no doubt they'd show with one phone call.

"Or I could call the boys," Joe said with a broad grin. He was as confident of his team jumping when he called as she was of her margarita sisters. The only thing the Tallgrass Eagles loved more than football was their coach. If learning to bake, decorate cupcakes, and do dishes would make their coach happy, they would bake, decorate, and do dishes.

"Let's see how far we get on our own," Lucy said, thinking how those boys could inhale two dozen cupcakes in two bites. She headed outside, lifting her face to the blue sky and warm November air, breathing deeply as she slung a large canvas bag over one shoulder, then hefted a box of supplies. For two days, she'd planned what she needed at the shop—that was what she'd decided to call it instead of bakery or kitchen; it was quainter. She'd gone over her recipes, listing every tool, spice, bowl, toothpick, ingredient, whatever. She'd added every baking pan she owned, every tray, bought new brooms and mops and buckets, dish detergent and soap, washcloths, towels, paper towels, toilet paper, everything she could possibly use. She was convinced she'd forgotten something vital, but with her gaze skimming over the box filled with every natural and artificial flavoring known to woman, she couldn't think what it was.

Once her car was emptied, Joe asked, "Where do we start?"

"Unpacking and organizing, I guess." She had spent every night but Tuesday—margarita club—and Friday— Joe's football game—at the shop cleaning and envisioning what would go where. All that envisioning hadn't gelled into a plan yet. "Every time Mike and I moved, we rented a two-bedroom house with a decent yard and a patio or deck, but each house was just different enough that our stuff didn't quite fit. The kitchen cabinets would be configured differently. The new living room would be ten feet longer and four feet narrower than the old one. And curtains…In my attic, I have enough window treatments for four or five houses, tall windows, short ones, formal, casual, sheer, blackout. This is like unpacking into a new kitchen on a giant scale."

"You're making too big a deal of it." Joe plopped a

stack of baking trays on the top shelf, turned, and picked up a stack of dish towels.

Lucy went to stand beside him. "Too big a deal?"

"What's the problem?"

She looked up to meet his gaze, then kept tilting her head until she could see the trays. For extra emphasis, she rose onto her tiptoes and stretched her right arm as far over her head as she could. Her fingertips were still a foot short of the trays.

She was lowering back to her soles when she caught a whiff of his cologne. She wasn't one of those people who could identify every spice or flavoring by smell, but whatever fragrance he wore was perfectly suited for a kitchen. If she closed her eyes and breathed deeply, it brought to mind a toasty fire, spiced coffee, chocolate, something sweet and buttery. It was homey and sexy and warm and shivery, and if one of them didn't move soon, she was going to swoon—or worse—right there. She was actually leaning toward him, drawn as if she had no will to resist, her nose seeking the source of the fragrances, sniffing up the length of his arm to—

"Okay, I see your point." Joe stepped away so quickly that it was a wonder she didn't lose her balance. Had he realized she was getting too close? Had he wondered what she was about to do? Or had he been totally unaware of her savoring his scent right next to him?

Joe could be totally clueless at times, no doubt about that. And her tender ego preferred to believe that than to think he'd moved away deliberately.

He went into the store room, returning with a step-ladder. Collapsed, it fit neatly between the wire rack and the wall; unfolded, she could reach any shelf in the room.

Then he moved the trays down three shelves, where she could retrieve them without risking her dignity or her life. "Better?" he asked.

Four feet and a stepladder between them? Enough space that she couldn't be sure she still smelled a hint of his scent or whether it was memory tempting her? So far apart that if she swooned, she would face plant right onto the cushy rubber mat that fronted the worktable instead of his arms?

She smiled weakly. "Yeah." *So much better.*

* * *

Normally, Calvin didn't sleep worth a damn, but Saturday night was an exception to the rule. He'd conked out on the couch while watching TV, staggered into the bedroom somewhere around midnight, and would still be snoring if the ring of his cell phone hadn't woken him shortly before one in the afternoon. As far as he could guess, he'd slept about fifteen hours. Who knew that could make a man feel as crappy as only two or three hours?

He'd showered and just finished dressing when the bell sounded at the door. Trying to rub away the thickheadedness that plagued him, he opened it without checking the peephole. His mom, dad, and Gran, all dressed up from church, stood together, broad happy smiles on all their faces.

Something surged deep inside him. Not happiness exactly. Maybe it was pleasure. He'd gotten so far from good emotions that when they occasionally reappeared, it was hard to identify them precisely. But seeing his family smiling like that, so obviously glad to see him, made him want to smile in return.

Elizabeth stepped forward first, hugging him, running her fingers through his hair as if there was enough of it to need straightening. "You look like you just got out of bed, son, and here it is dinnertime. You're getting lazy in your old age."

"Huh. Don't malign all us old folks. I'm seventy-six, and I don't sleep till afternoon." Gran moved his mom aside, and he bent low to accept her hug, the brim of her hat flopping against his face. She kissed his cheek, then pulled a white handkerchief from somewhere and wiped away the lipstick. "You're a handsome boy, but harlot red just isn't your color."

"Mama!" Elizabeth exclaimed, but Justice just shook his head as he extended his hand. "You missed a good service today."

"I bet you say every service is a good one."

"I wish I could, but this pastor doesn't often hit the target, and on the rare occasions he does, he still bores the congregation to sleep before he does it. Today was one of his better days."

"Justice!" Mom exclaimed, then shook her head before linking her arm with Calvin. "Give us a tour of your new place, son."

It was a one-bedroom apartment, nothing much to see: living and dining room, small kitchen, bedroom, and bathroom. It was a world away from his last apartment, though, back in Washington. Chaplain Reed, the only person to ever visit him there, had taken one look around and known that something had gone seriously wrong in Calvin's life. That was how low he'd sunk.

Pushing that thought away, Calvin extended his free hand toward the living room. "That's where I watch TV. Over here is where I microwave the food you sent home with me last week." He gestured toward the kitchen, then led them the few feet to the bathroom door. "Here's where I shower. Notice—no wet towels on the floor. And here's the bedroom."

"Not nearly inviting enough to sleep away the whole day," Gran muttered after poking her head through the door.

"Hey, I'm up in time for dinner. That's what matters, isn't it?" he retorted.

"I'm sure your mama would say it's church that matters, but you can't nourish the spirit if you don't nourish the body." Gran gave him a poke. "And my body's in need of nourishment. Come on. If we don't get to the restaurant before the Mount Zion congregation, they'll polish off the buffet like a flock of vultures."

Calvin blinked. "Restaurant? We're going out to eat?"

"Don't act so surprised," his mom said. "We do that from time to time."

"Not on Sunday. Never on Sunday." The first time in his entire life that he'd ever sat down to a Sunday dinner at anyplace besides his mom's table or a church basement table was at basic training. It hadn't seemed right at all.

"The benefit of eating out on Sunday is the same as every other day," Gran put in. "No planning, no cooking, and no dishes to wash." She grinned. "And the buffet at Zeke's is a thing of beauty. Now let's go before the Mount Zioners beat us to it."

Calvin followed them out, locked up, then offered to show Gran to the elevator. She flashed him a chastising look, grabbed hold of his arm, and made her way regally down the stairs. It was a nice day, the sun shining, a little chill in the air. Brown leaves clung to the trees, and acorns crunched under their feet as they walked to the car.

On the drive off post and across town to Zeke's, Elizabeth and Gran chatted about who'd been at church and who'd missed, who had worn what, said what, and acted how. Idly he wondered if Bennie had been there, if she was still a regular or if time and circumstances had made it easier to occupy herself elsewhere on Sunday mornings.

Running into Rickey Duncan yesterday had been a surprise. Turning at the sound of the store bell and seeing Bennie had seemed…right. He'd never known her to have a creative bone in her body, though she threw one hell of a fastball and could outfish everyone he knew. Though she'd been dismissive of any potential crafting talent, he tried anyway to imagine her knitting or sewing, but nope, the image wouldn't form. The Bennie he'd known had liked to be on the move, not stuck inside doing girly things.

If she had a more girly nature now that she was grown, it was only fair, because she'd certainly grown into a girly sort. Her curls, her flawless skin, her laughing eyes, her curves…he would never be able to think of her as just one of the guys again. He wasn't sure how he'd managed to remain oblivious to her charms back when they saw each other every day.

The parking lot at Zeke's was mostly full, though Gran noted with satisfaction that she didn't recognize any cars from the Mount Zion congregation. "That pastor of theirs tends to be long-winded. It takes a lot to get him to shut up."

"Speaking of people who don't shut up," Justice murmured to Calvin as they followed the two women across the lot.

Calvin grinned. Elizabeth and Emmeline were both talkers. An awful lot of his childhood memories included one or both of them going on about something, while Justice read his newspaper, worked his crossword puzzles, or watched his football games.

"Miss Sunday dinners at home?" Justice asked.

"I go away for eleven years, and they get rid of the tradition."

"Nah, it's not gone. Just sometimes your mama doesn't feel like cooking, and Emmeline's on a no-fried-foods kick, and no one can agree on what they want. So once a month or so, we come here. But trust me, Cal, nothing's changed, nothing important, at least. We still host the Fourth of July cookout, we still volunteer at children's church, we still get together and complain about having to go to your auntie Mae's for Thanksgiving, and we still fill every spare space in the freezer and the house with pecans when the picking starts out at Mayville's Nut Farm."

"Just like squirrels storing acorns for winter."

Justice grinned as he held the door open and gestured for Calvin to enter first. "That we are. And it pays off, too, in the dead of winter when the trees are shaken bare and we've got a fresh pecan pie sizzling in the oven."

When they got inside, two lines formed. Zeke's was a pay-before-you-stuffed-yourself buffet. The food tables were so long, so many, and heaped so high that it was almost shameful. After Gran found a suitable table where she could see all the comings and goings while they ate, Calvin picked up his plate and approached one end of the line, just strolling along, looking at all the choices. There were breakfast foods, fresh fruits, salads, and rolls. Next up came the hot meats: Beef roast, steak, meat loaf. Chicken fried, grilled, baked, or cooked with dumplings. Grilled fish and fried shrimp and ham and pork chops, and a half-dozen sides for every entrée. There were bars for hamburgers, hot dogs, tacos, and baked potatoes, and another six long tables filled with desserts.

He kept moving slowly, staying out of everyone's path, remembering the days at Lewis-McChord when, if he went home from work without grabbing fast food, he just didn't eat until the next day. There hadn't been a meal worthy enough of getting dressed and going out for the sole reason of buying it.

He'd been *really* depressed then. As opposed to mildly overwhelmed right now. The lines were long, people taking their sweet time while overfilling their plates, and the noise level was somewhere between jet engines and too-close-for-comfort artillery fire. Crowds and noise were just two of the things that made him edgy.

Suddenly Justice appeared at his elbow. "Come on down here. I'll show you the best stuff they have. Their roast beef is almost as good as your mom's, though I'll deny saying that till I go to my grave. The mashed potatoes have just the right amount of garlic and butter, and the collards are—well, collardy. The fried okra is as good as your mama's, too, and when you're done with all that, they have a blackberry cobbler that, I swear, they lifted from her recipe."

Calvin was relieved to follow along. Food was supposed to be simple: You're hungry for this, you eat this. You're hungry for that, you eat that. The problem was, he was hardly ever hungry for anything. He knew he had to eat, so he settled for protein bars or whichever of his mom's dishes was up next in the freezer.

"Looks like we're sharing a table," Justice said as they began weaving their way back to their seats. "I'd never admit Emmeline's right, but if you want a decent meal on Sunday, you do have to get here before the pastor finishes up the sermon at Mount Zion. They overrun the place, and everyone else just has to try to work around them."

The table for four the family had originally chosen was now pushed together with another one. His parents had the seats at the nearest end; two hats with ribbons and flowers were bent over the middle of the table until their brims bumped while the two old ladies talked; and one occupied seat waited at the end with an empty chair for him.

Occupied by Bennie.

"What a coincidence," he said as he placed his plate on the table, then squeezed into the seat, bumping Mama in the process. She turned, squeezed his cheek with her fingers, then pulled his face to her neck for a quick hug without missing a beat in her conversation with Gran.

"The ladies get tired of cooking and planning and cleaning," Bennie said as she slipped a paper wrapper from her straw.

"So I've heard. But what happened to Mama and her *too many choices is too many choices*?"

Eyes open wide, Bennie shrugged. "Things change, you know."

Oh, hell, yeah, he knew.

Bennie was meticulously buttering a sweet yeast roll. Watching her calories and cholesterol? Or just trying not to slather butter over her pretty church dress? It was purple, not a pale, puny shade but dark, vibrant, the color that used to be reserved for royalty. The rounded neck showed a hint of cleavage, and the sleeves hugged her slender arms. That was all he could see with her sitting. Did it end above her knee or closer to her ankle? Was the skirt full and swishy, or did it cling to the curves it covered? Were her shoes sensible, utilitarian, or did they have heels that did her legs justice?

Dampness warming his forehead, he swiped a napkin across it, then crumpled it to one side without looking at her. There should be a warning going off in his head: inappropriate thoughts about an inappropriate woman. She was his childhood friend—J'Myel's widow, for God's sake.

He was out of the diving-into-danger business for good, he reminded himself grimly. And if he got back into it for any reason, it damn well wouldn't be with J'Myel's girl.

Chapter 8

It was a strange thing to sit in a room filled with happy, talking people and be half afraid to lift her gaze from the plate of food in front of her. It wasn't even as if Bennie hadn't been prepared for this. When Miss Emmeline decided she wanted to eat out after Sunday morning services, she always insisted Mama and Bennie come along, and it was fair odds from now on that Calvin would come, too, even though he'd skipped church. Eating dinner together on Sundays was a family thing; it was what the Sweets and the Fords and the Pickerings did.

As she reached for the pepper, she risked a quick peek at Calvin. He hadn't shaved this morning, not that it made much of a difference. J'Myel had grown a mustache at fifteen, a beard at sixteen, while Calvin was still lamenting his baby face when they left for basic training.

It wasn't a baby face any longer. The softness was gone; lines etched into the skin at the corners of his eyes and mouth, and his eyes were shadowed, as if he'd seen things he would never forget. The last eleven years had been tough. The war had changed him. Changed everyone. How much was the only question.

How much had it changed J'Myel? She honestly couldn't say. Sure, he'd grown up, lost some of that boyish charm, gotten a bit more serious. He hadn't been the kind, though, who talked about bad things. In his e-mails and calls, he'd always been upbeat, telling jokes, relating funny stories. He hadn't wanted to worry her, had wanted to keep things as normal between them as they could be when they were thousands of miles apart.

But if he'd come home, would he have had memories he couldn't share, feelings he couldn't express? Would the rest of his life have paled in comparison to the adrenaline-fueled years in combat?

Would he still have loved her?

Would she still have loved him?

Always. Maybe with a few changes, but always.

Sad, grim thoughts, and drat it, Bennie was *not* a sad, grim person.

"How are you settling in at Fort Murphy?" she asked, forcing normalcy into her voice.

Calvin's fingers tightened on his fork, and the little shrug he gave barely caused a ripple. "It's okay."

"Did you ever think the Army would send you right back where you started?"

"It was pretty much inevitable."

She wondered what he meant by that. The Army had plenty of forts all around the world. Every soldier got to see his share of them, though when she'd asked J'Myel once what the odds were of him getting assigned there when he returned from Afghanistan, he'd replied slim to none. Of course, according to Calvin, J'Myel hadn't wanted to come back here. She still wasn't sure how she felt about that. Mama would say J'Myel's death made it a moot point.

"So what keeps you busy besides work?"

"Not much."

That was one subject shut down. On to the next. "Have you replaced your car yet?"

"I've looked. Haven't found anything I liked."

"Why? Because they all have four doors, hoods and trunks, and windows that actually work?" she asked with a snicker. J'Myel's first-ever car had been a brand-new Mustang with the biggest engine available, even though the payments and insurance had eaten him alive. Calvin's had been a beater that even Gran had looked at with disdain.

The question earned her a smile, sending something coursing through her—satisfaction or maybe even pride that for just an instant, she'd lightened the somberness in his eyes. "It's transportation," he said. "My old cars get me where I'm going just like the new, expensive models."

"Being frugal is one thing, but you could compromise. Get something that hasn't flipped the odometer three or four times and doesn't need industrial adhesive to hold the mirrors on."

"I've had a car or two with all their mirrors intact."

"The one that was stolen?"

"Yeah, as a matter of fact. Though two of the windows were broken out. Hey, plastic, Velcro, duct tape, and superglue can fix anything."

She laughed, and for a moment, the sensation was so familiar, so dear. Laughing was how they'd spent most of their time together. It felt sweet and innocent, lifted her mood, and brightened her day.

"Your own car didn't look brand new the other night."

"It's not. It's five years old, and it's been a good and faithful servant. Besides, I'm a poor college student." She didn't add that she loved her little red Volkswagen as much as he'd loved his beaters.

"You know, the Army will pay for your schooling if you agree to be *their* good and faithful servant for a few years."

"*Pfft.* Me wearing combat boots and saluting and PTing? Yeah, that's not gonna happen." She caught Mama glancing her way and winked at her. "I'm staying right here where the good Lord planted me. Besides, St. Tony's is picking up some of the costs, and they can't stand me at attention or send me anywhere in the world on a whim."

"Yeah, there is that," he murmured in agreement.

The older folks began gathering their things, preparing to leave. She and Calvin obediently followed suit, rising, pushing their chairs back under the table, trailing them out the door.

In the parking lot, Gran linked arms with Mama before smiling blithely at them. "Calvin, why don't you ride home with Bennie so Maudene and I can talk awhile longer?"

Mama's smile was just as innocent. Bennie, Calvin, even Elizabeth and Justice, gave the two old ladies chastising looks, but they wandered on, pretending to be oblivious, though everyone knew they were *never* oblivious.

"Or I could ride with Bennie," Elizabeth said, sliding

her arm through Bennie's and giving her a wink, "and we can catch up. We don't get many chances to visit with just each other."

All of them knew their kids' friendship had ended badly. Mama, for sure, had heard Bennie's every rant and sob on the subject, though how much Calvin had confided in his family, she could only guess. Either way, Mama and Gran had apparently decided it was time to set old grudges aside, maybe not to forget but to do their best to forgive. Mama and Gran were big on forgiving. Elizabeth was big on forgiving, too, but she wasn't nearly as pushy as the older ladies.

She looked from the women to Calvin. His face was expressionless, his shoulders tense, gazing off into the distance as if the conversation didn't involve him at all. A week ago, Bennie had gone all stiff, too, at the idea of being alone with him on the porch, but today . . . she'd already spent time at Java Dave's alone with him. It hadn't killed her—truthfully, it had filled some need in her that she hadn't even been aware of—and if she kept doing it, maybe someday she could ask him her questions.

Like what had ended his and J'Myel's friendship.

Like why he hadn't contacted her when J'Myel died.

Like what the last few years had been like for him, because she did care. Not in conjunction with J'Myel, with her own grief and sorrow, but just because she did. Because he'd been one of the two best friends in her whole life, and it hadn't been her choice to end their friendship, and he mattered.

It was kind of a surprise to her, to think it that bluntly: Calvin really still mattered. In spite of everything.

"It's okay," she said, stepping so that her shoulder

bumped against his. "I'm parked right over there." To the others, she announced, "We'll see you at the house."

"Someone should tell the old ladies no once in a while," Calvin murmured as they walked to the car, where he had to adjust the passenger seat a foot or two before he could even slide in. Once he got in, he looked around exaggeratedly as if trying to find a place to put his elbows and knees. She loved her little Bug, but no doubt, it was intended for passengers of slightly smaller stature.

"Yeah, why don't you volunteer for that? You can run faster than me."

He snickered. "It doesn't matter how fast we run. We have to go home eventually, and they'll be waiting. Like the time we got put off the school bus for talking smart to the driver and had to walk home so we went to the pond and skipped rocks for a couple hours instead."

"And when we stepped out of the woods into the street, there was Gran waiting on your porch and Mama on hers. They were a fearsome sight." She shuddered, and they shared a small chuckle at the memory.

The silence returned, a few moments passing, before he spoke again. "I can't believe someone who drives a toy car makes fun of my beaters. You're gonna have to pry me out of here with a shoehorn."

"Do they even still make shoehorns?"

"I don't know, but I can guarantee you Gran and Mama both have a few tucked away somewhere."

She *hm*ed in agreement. Both women had a room in their houses for old tools, doodads, and whatnots. It was like visiting a vintage prairie museum, a lesson in history and the value of never throwing away anything.

As they followed Justice onto Cherokee Street, Bennie

glanced ahead. "Looks like you guys have company. You expecting anyone?"

Calvin had turned his head to study the Ford house as they drove past. He snapped back around so quickly that she was surprised she hadn't heard the sharp crackle of whiplash. Justice turned into the driveway, slowly drove past to his usual parking space, and Calvin had a minor eruption right there in her car. "Son of a bitch, son of a—Stop the car, stop, damn it, let me out!"

Shocked into speechlessness, she hit the brakes so hard that the entire vehicle body rocked forward, then back again. Before the motion stopped, Calvin was out of the car, his long legs eating up the ground between him and the man standing beside the strange car. "Oh, this doesn't look like the start of a happy reunion," she whispered, shoving the gear shift into park, then scrambling out.

Closer, she could see it wasn't a man at all but a boy, maybe sixteen, shorter than Calvin, long and thin and boneless, the way some teenagers were built. His black hair was shaggy, his T-shirt was stained, and his gray hoodie was cheap and worn. "Hey, dude," he greeted when Calvin got closer. "How's your arm, man? You already got the cast off? That was quick, or has that much time really passed?"

Calvin didn't slow until he'd grabbed the kid's shoulder, crumpling shirt and jacket in his hand, and pushed him back against the vehicle. "What the hell are you doing here?"

The boy relaxed, as if leaning against a dirty car on a chilly day was no big thing to him. "Don't be so ugly, dude. I came a long way to bring the stuff that you forgot in my *neighborhood*. You remember? Crappy place?

Run-down, no lights? *Undesirables* hanging out in our park?"

Bennie's gaze flickered from the boy to Calvin, and her breath caught. She could count the number of times she'd seen him angry on one hand. The word didn't even come close now. His breathing was ragged, the muscles in his neck and shoulders knotted. Sweat dotted his forehead, and his skin stretched across his skull, as if all the dark emotion in him had bubbled up until his skin didn't fit anymore. His eyes were open wide, barely blinking, and there was nothing in them but cold.

A shudder racing through her, she took a few steps closer even though what she really wanted to do was jump in her car and drive home. Justice took the same few steps from the other side. The women remained inside the car, their heads swiveled around to see.

"The stuff I forgot?" Calvin repeated, for half a moment sounding reasonable and conversational. Then he leaned even closer, looming over the boy until their foreheads and noses almost touched. "The stuff I *forgot*? Oh, you mean, like this car. No, wait, you *stole* it. My wallet, my keys, my cash, my debit card. You ripped me off, and now you're *returning* it?"

"Most of it," the boy answered cockily. "Well, there was a protein bar in the glove compartment. I ate it. And I borrowed the workout clothes in the back. Guy's gotta wear something. And of course I needed some of the money to get this piece of junk here. Gas ain't free, you know."

Justice's feet crunched on gravel as he abruptly came closer. If Calvin's outrage worried the older man, he gave no sign of it. Instead, a big grin spread across his face. "So this is the boy you told us about, Cal? The one that helped you out?" Justice charged in, right hand extended, clapping the boy on the shoulder with his left hand. "Justice Sweet. Come on over and meet Calvin's mama and his gran." He steered the boy away from Calvin before asking, "What's your name?"

"Diez." The kid gave Calvin a smug look over his shoulder.

Justice's forehead wrinkled. "Diez? Isn't that Spanish for ten? What was your mama thinking?"

Diez imitated the frown. "Justice? Isn't that English for 'only if you're white and have money'? And you ain't even white. What was *your* mama thinking?"

"Fair enough," Justice said with a chuckle. He guided Diez toward the house, where the women were now out of the car, anxious to greet him. What kind of help had he given Calvin? Bennie wondered. It must have been substantial, considering Justice's welcome—and pretty touchy, considering Calvin's.

For the first time in a long time, she regretted making clear to Mama and everybody else that she didn't want to hear one single thing about Calvin's life without her. She was curious by nature and becoming downright nosy with every minute she spent around him.

As the space between Calvin and Diez grew, the tension shrank, though it still hovered tight around Calvin. His hands were shaking, faint tremors that slowed with each breath he took. Grimly, he dragged one sleeve across his face, then turned his head from the sight of his family gathering around the boy. He shifted his weight a time or two, dried his palms on his jeans, then breathed deeply. Like a rabbit getting ready to bolt.

All those endorphins released by running were supposed to make a person feel better, but Bennie wondered…If Calvin took off, would he ever stop?

"Come on, kids," Justice called back. "Elizabeth made her special strawberry cake this morning. I've held out as long as I can."

When Calvin didn't automatically move, Bennie walked to him, then did a slow circle around the car, noticing dings and dents and rust, two missing windows, and cracks in every other one. The front passenger seat was nothing but foam, the cover long since worn away, and the headliner hung like a drape in some belly dancer movie. "Yep, this is your car."

He glared at her across the roof. "It was, until that punk stole it."

"The punk returned it, so unless you collected from the insurance, it's yours again." She touched the antenna, broken in half and dangling. "Could you actually get an insurance company to cover it?"

He scowled again. "You're not funny, Benita."

"What kind of help did he give you?"

Calvin rested both hands on the roof. "He didn't give me any damn help at all."

"He seems to think he did."

"Yeah, well, he stole my stuff. Does it really matter what he thinks?"

She studied Calvin a moment, curious about his anger—to be honest, still shaken a little by it. Outbursts were more her style. Her temper flared, she pitched a fit, and then everything was fine again. But even she had never been that angry before. Except once, when J'Myel had died, when she'd screamed with fury at God.

"He returned the car," she pointed out again, her tone

mild. "Though he doesn't look old enough to have a license."

"He had *my* license."

The image of the tall, skinny Latino kid passing for a tall, skinny black man made her want to smile, but she restrained it. "I'm heading inside to meet Diez. I'll try to leave some cake for you, but you know how I love your mama's made-from-scratch strawberry cake. Don't wait too long, or you'll get nothing but crumbs."

* * *

As Bennie had done, Calvin circled the car slowly, his breathing shallow. Of all the outcomes he'd considered to his run-in with Diez, this had never occurred to him. What kind of thief drove two thousand miles to return the car he stole? How did he plan to get back home to Tacoma? Steal someone else's car? More likely, he wouldn't go back. Didn't seem anyone there had given a damn about him.

Calvin didn't care about the car, or the money, or the wallet, though it had sentimental value. He'd accepted two months ago that everything was gone. Given that he'd just tried to kill himself and brought a premature end to his Army career, the possessions hadn't mattered.

But now he was home. He was getting treatment. He was starting over. He was running into family and friends. None of whom, outside of his parents' house right that very moment, knew what he'd done. Who knew if Diez would keep his mouth shut? Who knew what he was telling Bennie and Mama right now? The kid was a thief. He couldn't be trusted.

He returned the car. Bennie's voice echoed in Calvin's head. Calvin had figured Diez had long since sold it for food, a place to sleep, drugs. He'd known the night they met that the kid was homeless and hungry. Runaway or abandoned, it didn't really much matter. A kid too young to take care of himself was doing his damnedest to do just that.

And he'd saved Calvin's life.

Wearily, Calvin rubbed at the ache between his eyes, then slowly walked once more around the vehicle. It didn't look any worse for wear after its time in the kid's possession, if that was even possible. So it had a few thousand more miles on it. Calvin had always thought it would be cool to watch the odometer flip over to 500,000 miles. He was that much closer to it now.

Shading his eyes, he looked through the window. The front floorboard held piles of wrappers from McDonald's cheapest hamburger, while a ball cap and his old PT clothes occupied the front seat. The backseat held a pillow and two thin blankets, a flashlight, a pack of batteries, and a pile of community magazines, the kind they offered free inside the entrances of restaurants and stores. There was also an extra pair of shoes, some socks, and a container of baby wipes. Clearly Diez had been living in the car.

In terms of material comforts, Calvin had lived a few tougher places, but not by much. But damn if he was going to let himself feel sorry for the kid.

Frustration bubbled inside him, tempting him to turn onto the street and walk until there was no place left to put his feet. He wanted to run away, but if the past couple years had taught him anything, it was that there really wasn't any such thing. Wherever you went, there you were: never away, just someplace else.

The key was learning to cope in the place where you had to be.

Sometimes he had great hope for his learning. Others, it was overwhelming in its neverendingness.

Going into the house took narrow focus and a stubborn need to be in the same room with Diez to monitor what the kid might say. Calvin forced one foot in front of the other, climbing steps, crossing the porch, walking through the door. They were scattered around the room with Diez on the couch between Elizabeth and Gran, and everyone held a dessert plate with a heaping slice of strawberry cake. There was an instant of silence, all eyes turning his way, which ended when he closed the door.

"Have a seat, Calvin," Mama said, "and I'll fetch you some dessert."

"Thank you, Mama, but I can help myself." He glanced once at the look on Diez's face, part smug, part something else, before heading to the kitchen.

Not everyone was scattered around the room, he realized belatedly. Bennie stood at the kitchen counter, using Elizabeth's engraved silver cake server to transfer a slice of three-layer cake to a dish. He'd wondered earlier whether her skirt was long and full, whether her shoes were sensible. Every man who'd seen her today had been rewarded, because the skirt clung to her hips before ending above her knees, and her shoes had little substance with wicked heels that made her legs long and lovely.

Tomboy Bennie, whose wardrobe had consisted of jeans, T-shirts, shorts, and ball caps with only the occasional church dress, had found the woman within her, and she was breathtaking.

His old buddy Bennie. Breathtaking. Wow.

"That boy out there sure knows how to talk," she said, apparently knowing without looking who had joined her. "And eat. This is his second piece of cake." She pivoted then, holding the plate, licking a bit of pink frosting from her fingertip. Aw, man, it'd been a long time since he'd tasted frosting from a slender finger. "It'd be my guess he doesn't eat regularly."

"Yeah, me, too." When he approached the counter, she moved to one side, giving him room to claim his own piece of cake. Her fragrance remained in the air, sweet and tantalizing.

"Does he have family in Tacoma?"

"Don't know."

"How did you meet him?"

He gave her a sidelong look. "What'd he say?"

"That it was a long story. One you're not planning to share, either, are you?"

"Nope." Maybe someday, after more treatment, more healing, more living, maybe then it wouldn't be such a secret, but today was a long way from someday.

After setting his plate and fork on the kitchen table, he took the milk from the refrigerator, filled a glass, then wordlessly offered the carton to her.

She scoffed. "Yeah, you go tell the kid who just drove cross-country by himself that he should drink his milk. I think he's real happy with the Pepsi your mom gave him."

Calvin would have liked to believe he could have done the same at that age. Truth was, he would have hated it after the first day or two. He'd been taught independence, but he'd also loved the comfort of his own bed at night and the security of his parents down the hall. Didn't seem Diez knew much about either.

With a faint smile, Bennie left the kitchen, her heels clicking on the wood floor. Calvin sucked down a big swallow of milk, topped off the glass, then turned and stopped. The man of the hour—the thief, the boy—was standing just inside the doorway, holding an empty glass. "What?" Calvin prompted irritably. "You couldn't get one of the ladies to get you a refill?"

"They offered. I told them my hands ain't painted on." Diez circled wide toward the kitchen table. Calvin made a similar move in the opposite direction, giving him access to the refrigerator.

"You're welcome," Diez said after removing a can of pop from inside.

"I didn't say thank you."

"I know. Just 'cause you forgot your manners doesn't mean I don't know mine." He opened the pop and poured it into his glass. "I brought your car back without a scratch on it. Not that you would've noticed a new one."

"It took you long enough."

Diez shrugged, lifting only one shoulder with a touch of arrogance. "I didn't plan to keep the car. I tried to find you at the post, then finally heard you'd been transferred out. There wasn't enough money in here"—he pulled Calvin's wallet from his hip pocket—"to pay for the trip, so I had to stop when the cash ran out until I made some more."

Made some? Or stole it? But Calvin didn't ask. The kid said *made*; he probably did earn it. There were ways—unscrupulous bosses looking to hire on the cheap, day laborer jobs, panhandling, hell, even picking up plastic bottles and cans.

Looking as if he knew exactly what Calvin was thinking, Diez scowled and tossed the wallet to him. "It's all there but the money. Your driver's license and your military ID and the pictures. That Bennie...she sure grew up, huh?"

Calvin didn't check the contents of the wallet. He just slid it into his own hip pocket and immediately got that old comfortable feeling that came from carrying it there for eleven years. "When are you leaving?"

Diez rubbed the toe of one shoe on the floor and avoided Calvin's gaze. "Soon. Your mom asked me to stay for supper."

Not his problem, Calvin reminded himself. He hadn't brought this kid into the world, hadn't invited him into his life. If he was homeless, that was *his* problem, his parents', society's, but most definitely not Calvin's. "Where are you going?"

Damn. Where had that come from?

"I dunno. South, I think. I miss the warm weather."

"How're you going to get there?"

The kid's discomfort disappeared behind a big grin. "I know how to hitch a ride. I used to do it with my dad. Well, sort of my dad. He was my brothers' dad, but not me or my sisters'. Anyway, he'd take me with him sometimes when he was too broke for the buses."

"So you intend to hitchhike from here to someplace south to do what?"

"You ask a lot of questions."

"You don't have many answers."

Diez lifted his chin. "I got plans. They're just none of

your business." Turning on his heel, he returned to the living room with his pop.

Calvin waited a minute, picked up his cake and milk, and tried to will himself to go to the kitchen table to eat, but it didn't work. When he moved, he walked down the hall and turned into the living room. He sat on a wooden chair Justice had dragged in from the dining room, nearest the door and a quick escape if needed.

It was Mama that interrupted the light chatter that felt like it would go on forever. "Where's your mama, Diez?"

Everyone's gaze swiveled to him, including Calvin's. The kid's skin darkened, and his eyes shifted from item to object before finally meeting Mama's. "She's in Tacoma."

"Where?" Mama's voice was low and doubting. Calvin knew from experience that it was damn near impossible to get anything past her. She had a sixth sense about people, when they could be trusted or they couldn't, when they were being truthful or when she needed to just send them on down the road. No teenage boy was going to outwit her.

"With my brothers and sisters."

"And she just let you up and take off to Oklahoma all by yourself? You don't look like you're anywhere near sixteen."

Diez's fingers clenched around the fork as he took a huge bitc of cake. When he was able to speak again, he said, "She don't mind. I look young for my age, on account of being so skinny."

Calvin scraped the last bit of strawberry frosting from his plate, sucked it off the fork, then said flatly, "You look young for your age, on account of being only fourteen."

Elizabeth's and Gran's eyes widened, and a scowl

came across Justice's face. His gravelly voice went into lecture mode. "You can't just take off and drive a car that doesn't belong to you cross country at fourteen. It's too dangerous. Son, you can't even legally *drive* at fourteen."

Mama rolled her eyes at the comment. "And yet he did it, Justice, and here he is, safe and sound." She sat in Elizabeth's favorite glider, ankles crossed, hands folded in her lap. "Did your mother run out on you or you on her?"

If Calvin could expend the energy to feel sympathy, now would be a good time. Diez's face was flushed and hot, and he was struggling to maintain the smug, smirky behavior that was all Calvin had seen from him. He leaned forward, set his dish on the coffee table, then held his pop in both hands and tried for a casual shrug. "A little of both, I guess. She went to rehab, my brothers went to their dad, and my sisters went into foster care. The group home they put me in, because of my age"—he shot a scowl at Calvin—"wasn't really my kind of place, so I checked myself out."

Calvin glanced around the room, checking out the sympathetic/aghast/heart-hurting looks on everyone's faces. He was in a roomful of parents and one would-be parent, good people who couldn't help sympathizing with every child less fortunate than their own. They were already wondering how they could help Diez, and Calvin would bet for sure the first step would be letting him spend a night or two here in the Sweet house. He didn't like the idea—*hide your valuables, keys, and money*—but he knew how much sway his opinion would have in the face of Elizabeth's fearsome mother instincts.

"We should call the police," he said before the magic invitation could come out of someone's mouth. They all

turned to face him, Diez's expression dark and belliger-
ent. The only one Calvin expected any sort of support
from was Bennie; after all, she worked in the real world;
she knew a person couldn't just take kids in off the street
and into his home, couldn't take them at their word.

But she wasn't leaning his way at all. She sat, legs
crossed, her attention shifting from one adult to the other,
finally resting on Mama. The old lady smiled and nodded.
For whatever reason, that famous instinct of hers had
deemed the kid worthy—and trustworthy—and Bennie
and the others would follow her lead.

Are you crazy? he wanted to ask, but he knew better.
Nine or twenty-nine—even when he was forty-nine, for
that matter—that was just something he couldn't get
away with saying to his parents.

Damn it, he'd chosen to stay in quarters rather than
move back into his parents' house for a lot of reasons,
but none of them mattered now. As long as his parents'
misguided gratitude welcomed a punk stranger into their
home, Calvin would be staying there, too.

Chapter 9

Benita was saying her good-byes so she could go home and study when Calvin came in from the kitchen, stalked to the sofa, and stuck out his hand. "Keys," he said flatly.

"Oh, son, you're not leaving, are you?" Elizabeth asked as Diez dug in his jeans pocket. Concern softened her voice and her eyes.

"I'm just going to pick up some stuff from home. I'll be back."

He wasn't happy about the situation, and Bennie couldn't totally blame him. But Mama could learn more about a person in less time than anyone else Bennie knew, and that little nod of hers had meant she trusted Diez. If Mama had invited him into *their* house, Bennie would have trusted him, too...but she still would have kept an eye on him.

Calvin followed her out the door, and together they

descended the stairs. "Interesting kid," she remarked. "How'd you meet him again?"

His answer was a scowl. Okay, still not talking about that. "That stuff you're picking up from home wouldn't happen to be a uniform, boots, whatever you need to spend the night?"

"You think I'd leave them alone with him?"

"No." She grinned. "Wow, it'll be like having the kid brother you never wanted."

His grunt wasn't amused.

As they approached the two cars at the end of the driveway, she said, "I can drive you over to the fort if you want. You know, if maybe you didn't want anyone to see you in that heap. I'm surprised that when you park it, someone doesn't come along and haul it off for junk. It's so rusted, though, it probably doesn't even have any scrap metal value."

He dragged his fingers over his head. "I think you have car envy. You're driving a nothing-special little kid car like a million other people in this country, while my vehicle is unique."

"That's one way of putting it," she said with a choking laugh. "The others that come to mind are junk heap, POS Ford, hoopty-mobile, rattletrap, and my favorite, possible health hazard. You up on your tetanus shots?"

They stopped between the cars, and Bennic hesitantly reached out. The tips of her fingers brushed his forearm just for an instant before he turned toward his car. "Give the kid the benefit of the doubt, Calvin," she said, the brush-off so sudden that her hand just hung there in midair before she had the sense to lower it again, skin tingling. "He did return your belongings. Maybe he just wanted to do the right thing. Maybe you made that big of an impression on him. But the boy can obviously use some friends."

He gave her a dry look, as if the last thing in the world he wanted was a new friend. But the look reminded her that Diez wasn't the only one who could use friends.

"I guess I'll see you later," she said, climbing into her car. Elizabeth had invited her and Mama for supper, too, so by six o'clock she would be back over here.

He substituted a scowl for a good-bye and didn't seem to notice her wave as she drove off. It seemed silly, on a nice day like this, to drive the short distance between their houses, but she was in her prettiest heels, and no matter how many women lived their lives in killer heels, she accepted that, for her, at least, heels were *not* made for walking.

After changing into jeans and a sweater, she spread out on the couch with her tablet, her laptop, her textbook, and a bottle of water. She actually made a stab at studying, too, but the house was so quiet, and she had questions. Never a good combination.

She had been living here with Mama about a week when she began questioning Mama about the school she would go to, the kids in the neighborhood, why her mother had left, why her father had to die, and about a dozen other subjects. Mama had laughed and said, *Girl, you are curious.*

Mom said nosy, Bennie had responded, *and she said I get it from you.*

Better than anything you got from her, Mama had murmured under her breath. It was the only time she'd ever said anything against Bennie's mother.

What Bennie had gotten from Lilly Pickering was flecks of gold in her brown eyes, curls that had driven her to spend countless hours with flatirons, a great laugh, and a small empty place in her heart that could stay silent and ignored for months and then suddenly throb. *Why why why? She had a right to leave Daddy if she didn't love him anymore, but why did she leave me? I wasn't part of their arguments; I wasn't the one who made her scream and throw things and stomp out in anger. She was my mother. She was supposed to love me more than life itself, and instead she walked away and never looked back.*

Bennie rubbed her fingertips lightly over her chest as if it might soothe her heart. The inescapable conclusion was that Lilly had never loved Bennie the way a mother should have. Thank God Bennie had had Daddy and, when he was gone, Mama.

Who did Diez Cooper have?

Unable to focus even a few minutes on microbiology, finally she laid the material aside, snagged a photo album from the bottom shelf of the coffee table in front of her, and lifted it onto her lap. The book was one of two dozen Mama had filled with snapshots meticulously dated and identified in her spidery writing before filing in chronological order. She was in the process of scanning them into the computer, typing the information, and uploading it all to the cloud, so the whole family could view them. Bennie couldn't imagine looking at them any other way than in the musty albums.

This album covered the year Bennie was nine. The year her father died, when she'd come to live in Tallgrass. She had cried a lot that first year, but truthfully most of her memories were good ones, thanks to the boys who'd taken her into their tight-knit friendship and given her a place to belong. To be happy.

She turned the pages slowly, admiring pictures of Montie Pickering, tall and always grinning. It had broken his heart when Lilly left—as much for Bennie's sake as his own—but he'd met a new woman just months before the accident that killed him. He'd been serious about her, because for the first time with all his dates, he'd made plans for Bennie to meet her. Her name was Shel, and Bennie's first meeting with her had taken place in the ER, where they'd cried over his body in each other's arms. Shel had stayed with her until Uncle Roland made the drive to Norman, until Mama and Aunt Cheryl had come.

Roland and Cheryl had emptied out the apartment, arranged the transfer of Montie's body to Tallgrass for burial, had taken care of all the details involved in leaving a place for good. Mama had taken care of Bennie. Both her aunt and her uncle had offered to take Bennie into their homes, but Mama had refused them. Her heart was breaking; her grandbaby's heart was breaking; and by the grace of God, they would break and then heal together.

Bennie swiped a tear from her eye and smiled at the photo of her and Mama, Cheryl and Roland and his wife, Zena, then at the one opposite: J'Myel and Calvin. If she hadn't come to Tallgrass, she may have never met the boys, and she certainly wouldn't have become best friends with them. She wouldn't have fallen in love with J'Myel, and she wouldn't be seeing Calvin again after so long.

Things worked out the way they were supposed to, according to Mama. Sometimes it was a happy thought that comforted Bennie—that she'd been destined to be

Mama's granddaughter, Daddy's daughter. That fate had meant her to live in Tallgrass, to meet the two boys, to have a childhood as nearly idyllic as possible.

Sometimes the thought left her feeling blue: that her father had died so young, that J'Myel had died even younger, that Bennie's heart had taken such a beating.

She didn't know how long she sat there, lost in memories. She returned the photo album to its shelf and her attention to her studies. At five, Mama gave her a reprieve by dutifully calling to remind her about dinner. Assuring her that she wouldn't be one second late, Bennie set aside her books. After careful consideration, she dressed in a white open-necked shirt, khaki trousers, and magic black shoes that were comfortable *and* sexy. She made sure her curls weren't flat or lopsided or tangled, freshly applied her cologne, touched up her makeup, and changed earrings twice before realizing she was primping. Decisively she walked away from the mirror.

She couldn't resist glancing over her shoulder to see if her butt looked as good in these pants as she'd remembered. Indeed, it did.

Her knock at the Sweet door was opened by Justice. Though he smiled at her as heartily as he always did, there were a few stress lines on his face. Bennie hugged him, as she always did, and said, "I see by the presence of the junker that Calvin is back."

"Yes. He came in, threw a bag down at the foot of the steps, and has been sitting in the corner growling from time to time at the boy. Not much of a gratitude attitude, but maybe he needs some time to get to that point."

Having a gratitude attitude was one of their pastor's favorite teachings: If you're grateful for what you get, then you'll get more of it. One good deed begets another, and so forth. Bennie could see where Calvin definitely needed an attitude adjustment, but she would love to know how gratitude and Diez fit together.

Hearing Mama's and Elizabeth's voices in the kitchen, Bennie hung her jacket in the closet, then walked to the double-wide living room doorway to see which corner Calvin had banished himself to. He was in the one most distant from the door, sitting loosely in a dining chair, wall to his back, giving off restlessness and edginess in waves. His attention was primarily on the sofa, where Emmeline and Diez sat facing each other from opposite ends, cards in their hands.

"Ah, Miss Emmeline, you roped someone into playing hearts with you," Bennie said, moving farther into the room. The old lady didn't spare her a glance, but Diez looked up and grinned with an approving look.

"This isn't hearts," Emmeline said, studying her cards. "It's Texas Hold 'Em. You know, poker."

Bennie feigned scandal. "Diez, you're teaching Calvin's seventy-six-year-old gran to play poker?"

He grinned again. "No, dude. She's teaching me."

A growl came from Calvin's corner.

"Miss Emmeline, where did you learn to play poker?" Bennie half expected to hear *from Elizabeth's daddy, God rest his soul.*

Instead she got a wicked smile. "Maudene taught me. She learned on the Internet. It's full of wondrous things. I'd get my own computer to check it all out, but she says she's still got about two million things to show me, and that's not even counting Pinterest."

"Remind me to have a talk with Mama about online

gambling." Bennie wandered over to the corner where Calvin sat. This close to him, she could feel the tension in the air and wondered how he kept from giving himself high blood pressure, migraines, and a stroke. He'd been so laid back when they were kids that teachers had joked about having to wake him up during lectures, but he'd always known exactly what they'd been saying.

Now he reminded her of a rock tossed into a pond: landing with a splash, sending out tiny disturbances into infinity, except *he* was the rock and the ever-widening disquiet was his life. What had thrown him in? she wondered sadly. And what could help him find peace?

* * *

Two-a-days for Joe's team meant he mostly stood on the sidelines, gave advice, and reviewed each player's performance. Two-a-days in his personal life meant he was pretty much guaranteed to see Lucy twice a day, for their morning and evening walks. It was a hell of a good way to start and end the day. Kind of like waking up beside her, then going to bed next to her eighteen hours later.

Well, not really, not when the beds they were sleeping in were in different houses, and if they were sharing a bed, they would be doing so much more than sleeping. Maybe someday...

As he let himself into her house Sunday evening, he imagined the names his brothers would call him if they knew what a geek this thing with Lucy had turned him into. He had three of them, and two sisters, all older and stronger than him. Joey and Bella Cadore were tall, blond, and a force of nature, and they'd produced six versions of themselves, with Joe being the runt, Lucy liked to say. His brothers liked to say the exceptional Cadore genes were running low by pregnancy number six, explaining why Joe was mostly just average.

Norton met him at the door, then immediately led him to the couch, where Sebastian was stretching his tiny little claws. Joe was Norton's staunchest defender, but even he had to admit the dog had gone a little daft over the kitten. "You'll never have pups of your own," Joe remarked, scratching behind the dog's ears, "but your paternal instincts are as good as anyone's."

"Or maternal instincts." Lucy came down the hall from the bedroom, moving as if she'd undertaken the teenage-boy helmets-and-pads two-a-days this weekend. He wouldn't make fun of her. He was a lot more active, and all those hours in the kitchen Saturday had brought out a few pains in him.

"You wanna skip the walk?" He was tough when needed, but missing one workout wasn't going to hurt her. Besides, he was sure they'd burned plenty of extra calories on Saturday, even given that he'd tasted one of everything she'd made.

Using a band wrapped around her wrist, Lucy pulled her hair back into a ponytail and secured it. "No, I think moving will actually make me feel better."

"Who knew cooking was so hard on the body?" he teased, earning himself one of her chastising looks.

"Every mother and wife who has to do it every evening after a full day at the job while taking care of the house and the kids," she said dryly.

She sat down at the kitchen table to put her shoes on, and he leaned against the back of the couch to watch.

She was wearing a T-shirt for a 5K sponsored by the post hospital; her margarita girls had walked with her, and he'd run with his team. The shirt was a little too big, but not in the swallow-her-whole way she used to hide her body. As for her bottom half, there was nothing too big there. She wore yoga pants that clung to her curves and ended mid-calf, which emphasized the remarkable change in her calf muscles since taking up walking with him last May. The first day she'd put them on, a week or so ago, she'd caught his wide-eyed look and asked, "Too much?"

He'd thought about Goldilocks and the littlest bear and replied in a voice far too awestruck for his pride, "No, they're just right." Never let it be said that Joe Cadore wasn't a witty conversationalist.

After grabbing a water bottle and her keys, she waited while Joe hooked on Norton's leash, then the three of them left, followed by a pitiful wail from the kitten. "When Sebastian is bigger, you should get him a leash and a harness so he can come with us," Joe said.

Lucy gave him one of her looks. "He's Norton's pet. Let him walk him."

"Like you walk Norton?"

She dished out another look. "I had Norton for a year before you moved in. I fed him, let him out, walked him, cleaned up after him...boy, did I clean up after him. Then you moved in. You came over that first day to introduce yourself, your face lit up, and you said, 'Gosh, Mrs. Hart, you've got a puppy! Can I play with him? Would he like to go for a walk?'" She shook her head with no sympathy. "You made him fall in love with you, and after all this time, there are no take-backs. You cannot move from that house or have another dog as long as Norton lives, or you'll break his heart."

There was always a lot Joe could defend about his behavior on any given day, but of that particular memory, he had only small corrections to offer. "I didn't call you Mrs. Hart. And I didn't say 'gosh.'"

She shrugged but didn't change her words. At the sidewalk, where they normally turned left, she chose right instead. They passed only a couple of neighbors as they walked to First Street, where, not surprisingly, they turned left again. Three blocks down on the opposite side of the street was the bakery. Lucy gazed at it with such pride, while Joe looked at her the same. Opening up this shop was a big deal for her. When she'd lost Mike and the future they'd planned, she also lost a big part of her self-confidence. Joe was proud she was doing this—and prayed every day that it paid off for her—because somewhere along the way, she'd stopped taking chances. The only thing worse than failing, his dad used to say, was not trying at all.

The only thing worse than that was giving up, and damned if he would ever let Lucy give up.

"It needs a sign," she remarked, her face flushed with a smile.

"Yep. And some gravel to fill in the parking lot ruts."

"Yeah. I think I'm going to do the dining room with a beachy vibe."

"I thought you didn't like the beach." He'd done his best to talk her into a tropical vacation last summer, but she'd turned him down. He'd gone anyway, and he'd had fun, but he would have had more fun with her.

"I'm a California girl," she reminded him. "I learned to

swim practically before I could walk. I love the ocean and the sand and the seagulls and the dolphins and the shells and the sky and the relaxation and the vibe." She paused a beat. "I just don't love swimsuits in a size—"

She mangled the next word badly, but he didn't ask her to repeat it. When she'd lost Mike and her future, she'd gained weight and lost her self-confidence. It was too bad, too, because she wasn't one of those *if* girls. People didn't look at her and say, *She'd be so pretty if she would just lose weight,* or *She's got such a pretty face if only she wasn't so heavy.*

She was beautiful. She'd been beautiful pre-widowhood when she was thin. She'd been beautiful before she started dieting and exercising and lost forty or so pounds. She was beautiful now, and whether she lost weight or gained it, she would still be beautiful. And funny. And smart.

And damn, he was pathetic.

After a moment more, with a soft sigh, she pivoted and headed south. They walked fast enough to make easy conversation a struggle for Lucy. It wasn't as much of a workout for him, but he got paid to work out five days a week. For him the walks fell outside the range of fitness and into his fun time. Spending time with Lucy, even Saturday working his butt off in the bakery, was always fun.

They reached the west side fire station before he realized how far they'd gone. The sun was sliding down, stealing what warmth the day had had, and Lucy had zipped her jacket halfway and shoved her hands in the pockets. The firehouse doors were open, though, and the firefighters were in lawn chairs around a propane grill that was putting out some pretty amazing aromas.

"Hey, Lucy, hey, Coach," a half-dozen voices called. Through Joe and Lucy's summer walks, the firefighters had been unfailing in their supply of encouragement, dog cookies, and cold bottled water.

Lucy chatted with them while Norton dragged Joe to the cabinet where the cookies were stored. One of the men hefted out the big plastic jar and unscrewed the top before fixing his gaze on Joe. "Hey, Coach, exactly what's up between you and Lucy?"

"We're neighbors."

The guy stole a look at her. "Is that all?"

"And friends."

The guy looked at her again, and suspicion reared in Joe's mind, tightening the same jaw muscles that had always twitched around Ben Noble. That was the same expression Dr. Jerk had worn every time he'd looked at Lucy. Hell, it was the same expression Joe wore all too often around her. "Very good friends," he emphasized.

"Like, with benefits?"

Joe's teeth clenched, though he covered it with a smile. If he could leave it at that, the firefighter—Tompkins, according to his name tag—would get the wrong idea and back off, and it wouldn't even require a lie. But damn it, he couldn't leave it at that. What if this guy was Lucy's Mr. Right? What if Joe let him believe they were more involved than they really were and Tompkins never asked her out and she lived the rest of her life alone?

"None of your business," Joe said evenly, silently wishing Norton would chomp on Tompkins's fingers as he took the first cookie.

Tompkins grinned. "So that's a no to the benefits. Good. So you have no reason to mind if I ask her out.

Huh." He tossed a second cookie to Norton, then strolled off to join the other firefighters and Lucy.

Joe scowled as he scratched Norton's head. Last summer he'd thought he had plenty of time to work up the courage to let Lucy know he was interested in more than friendship, then Dr. Jerk came along. In the months since they'd broken up, Joe had thought he still had time, no rush; after all, she hadn't looked at another guy twice. But now this guy . . .

Joe didn't want to stand in the way of Lucy's possible Mr. Right, but damned if he could step back without putting himself up for consideration first. Letting her know how he felt. Showing her how he felt.

Because the only thing worse than failing was not trying at all, and the only thing worse than that was losing Lucy.

* * *

When Calvin was a kid, the women in his family occasionally claimed to suffer from what they called a sick headache—the kind where it hurt to open your eyes, where the muscles in your neck were on the verge of spasming and your stomach was heaving like a bobber in a creek after a heavy rain. His started during dinner, with his parents, Mama and Bennie, and Diez crowded around the dining table. The conversation was too loud, the food smells too rich, Calvin's mind too frazzled.

When the food was mostly gone and everyone was overstuffed, Bennie shooed the parents and grandparents into the living room, filled her hands with dishes, and bumped Diez's shoulder as she passed. "Why don't you guys help me in the kitchen?"

Diez stood immediately, gathered dishes, and followed her. His words drifted back into the dining room. "I can do this. You go sit."

Bennie's laugh was amused and sweet. "I don't believe I've ever sat after a meal while someone else cleaned up. In my family, cleanup is the young people's thank-you for the older folks' cooking."

"In my family, cleanup means throwing away the fast-food wrappers."

As the water came on in the sink, Calvin pressed his fingers to his temples, wishing he could squeeze away the pain, wincing at the brightness of the overhead lights, the clanking of silverware, the lingering aromas of dinner turning sour. He needed a bed, a dark room, and endless silence. Except voices intruded on the silence eventually, most of them belonging to people who were dead. Old jokes, old arguments, odd moments out of time.

At times like these, he wanted to forget all those people, all those emotions, including—especially—J'Myel. He wanted to wake up one morning with everything gone: who he was, who he'd loved, what he'd done. Amnesia sounded like the greatest gift he could have.

Then, in the kitchen, Bennie laughed. Farther down the hall, in the living room, Elizabeth's and Gran's sopranos blended in an a capella version of "Amazing Grace." Their voices were sweet, the hymn so familiar, one of the first he'd ever learned. He sat back, closed his eyes, and let the words wash over him, and the peace he'd always associated with the song seeped, just a little bit, over him. He'd been lost, God, for so long, wanting desperately for the pain to stop. He'd given up hope, so much that death seemed the only option, but he'd failed at that for a reason. More punishment, he'd thought, but as another of Bennie's sweet laughs drifted in from the kitchen, he knew he'd been wrong.

Through many dangers, toils, and snares, I have already come. 'Tis grace hath brought me safe thus far, and grace will lead me home.

He was home. If anyplace could save him, it was home.

Fingers trembling, he pressed the heels of his hands to his eyes. In that instant, he believed he had a chance. He could learn to treasure those memories and voices from the past. He could reach the point where he could think of J'Myel without his heart breaking in two. Next week, tomorrow, ten minutes from now, the doubts and darkness might start burrowing their way back, but at that very moment, he thought he just might survive this.

The rich aroma of coffee drifted on the air as steady footsteps approached from the kitchen. Bennie, not the heavy clunk of Diez's size twelve sneakers. Elizabeth and Gran were singing again, and Bennie hummed along to "I'll Fly Away." He'd forgotten that she had the sweetest voice in their church choir.

He dropped his hands from his face but not before she caught at least a glimpse. "You have a headache?"

"Yeah." Not as bad as before, though. The queasiness, the sweaty palms, and the spasming muscles were mostly gone, leaving behind a dull—and manageable—ache.

"A couple of aspirin and a cup of Benita's best brew should take care of that. If it doesn't, apple cobbler and vanilla ice cream will."

"And if that doesn't?"

She picked up the rest of the dishes and gave him a broad mischievous smile. "Oh, honey, if cobbler and ice cream don't cure what ails you, it's time to call the undertaker 'cause you're past saving."

Once again she left the room, and once again her conversation filtered from the kitchen. "The storage bowls for the leftovers are in the cabinet right there. Don't bother keeping the gravy. Miss Elizabeth would rather make it fresh than reheat what's left."

Cabinet doors opened, then closed. "Why do you call her Miss?" Diez asked.

"Because I was raised right," she replied swiftly, then relented. "It's a way for kids and young people to show respect to older people."

"So should I call you Miss Benita?"

A scuffling sound followed. Calvin knew from too many personal experiences that Diez was trying to avoid the kitchen towel she was snapping at him. "You are not that young, and I am not that old," she said primly.

Bennie and Calvin were four months apart in age, but he felt that old. Sometimes it wasn't the age; it was the mileage.

He sat a few minutes longer, listening to the music—his father's bass had joined in on "Down to the River"—and the kitchen talk before shoving to his feet. He pushed all the chairs under the table, straightened the embroidered tablecloth, and swept the crumbs into his hand, then went to the kitchen door. Diez was at the sink, hands in soapy water, and Bennie was loading the dishwasher and in the middle of a story.

"—had just gone to live with Mama, and she sent me

in to do the dishes after dinner. We'd had fried chicken, mashed potatoes, and gravy, and of course she used her cast-iron skillet for the chicken and gravy because Mama would never fry it in anything else. Anyway, doing dishes by hand was a new experience for me, and I was actually kind of enjoying it. I left the skillet for last, and when Mama came in to check on me, I was standing at the sink, singing and just scrubbing away at that skillet with cleanser and one of those stiff scrubber pads."

Calvin leaned against the doorjamb. He'd heard this story a few days after it took place, and he and J'Myel had practically rolled with laughter that she hadn't known any better. They were *boys*, and they knew just how particular women could be about their cast iron.

"All of a sudden, I heard this shriek from behind me. I jumped about six feet and dropped the skillet on the floor—left a big dent in the wood—and Mama came rushing over, practically in tears. 'Oh, dear Lord, girl, what are you doing?' she wailed, and she grabbed that skillet and the cleanser and the scrubber and sent me from the room until she got herself under control."

Diez watched her laugh, his grin tinged with confusion. Bennie was like that—she could make you smile even when you didn't understand what she was talking about.

Shoving off from the door frame, Calvin walked into the room and began gathering coffee cups from the cabinet. "All the cooking in a cast-iron pan helps season it—makes it nonstick and easy to clean. You clean it with an abrasive, it takes off that seasoning and all you're left with is just another pan."

Bennie nodded. "That skillet had been passed down to Mama from her own grandma, and not once in all those years had it ever been scrubbed. She swore it took more than ten years of constant use to get it back to the condition it was in before I cleaned it." She reached into the cabinet above the dishwasher, pulled out a bottle of aspirin, and handed it to Calvin, her fingers brushing his.

Soft. He'd missed that.

"I bet it was a long time before she made you wash dishes again," Diez remarked as he rinsed a baking pan, then set it in the drainer.

Calvin and Bennie exchanged a look, then she burst out laughing. "Oh, child, I washed dishes every day after that, only for the next year she stood there supervising me. Doing things wrong is *not* a way to get out of work in Mama's house."

A yearning to join in her laughter started somewhere deep inside Calvin. He wanted to laugh the way he used to, with his whole body, until he felt weak from it, until tears streamed down his face. Even in combat, he'd found reasons to laugh. But the best he could manage now was a smile, and it slipped away too soon.

After washing down a couple of aspirin tablets, he filled four cups with coffee and carried them, two at a time, into the living room. He was returning from delivering the cream and sugar when Diez asked, "Why'd you live with your grandma?"

Bennie closed the dishwasher, started it, then leaned against the counter. "My father died."

"Where was your mother?"

"Didn't know. Still don't. She left a few years earlier."

"Why?"

That had been the million-dollar question for Calvin back then. Why had her mother left her behind? Leaving her husband was one thing—J'Myel's parents were divorced—but leaving her kid? He'd known, even at nine, that if he ever had kids, he would never do that to them, no matter what.

"I asked that question a dozen times, honey," Bennie said. "Daddy said she was a free spirit. Mama said she had a hard time accepting responsibility. Aunt Cheryl said she was just selfish. Truth is, *why* is the most useless question out there. Even if there's a reason, it's never a good enough one."

Calvin knew all the way through his soul that was true. He'd asked *why* a million times: Why had J'Myel changed so much that he'd wanted nothing to do with Calvin? Why had he died? Why had Calvin lived? Why hadn't Diez left him alone? But he also knew it was damn near impossible to stop wondering.

He imagined Diez had a few *why*s, too. Why wasn't his father in his life? Why had his mother chosen drugs over her kids? Why did his brothers have a family who wanted them and he and his sisters didn't? Why had he ended up homeless and hungry in a crappy abandoned house in a crappy abandoned neighborhood when his biggest worry should have been making the basketball team or impressing the girl down the street?

Why did so many people have life so easy while others had it so damn hard?

None of it was Diez's fault, though Calvin suspected Diez might not find comfort in that, knowing he'd wound up where he was because of other people's bad decisions.

Life was damned unfair...but Calvin didn't have to be. As long as the kid kept his mouth shut about how they'd met, the least Calvin could do was not make things any harder for him.

That wasn't so much to ask, was it?

Chapter 10

The stiffness was gone at least temporarily from Lucy's joints by the time they got home. Automatically they headed around the house to the back door. It was fully dark now, and the porch light shone its yellowish-white light on them as she dug her keys from her pocket. "You want to come in and have a sandwich?" she asked as she slid the key into the lock. The question was only a formality; unless one of them had other plans, they always had dinner together after Sunday evening walks.

She had opened the door an inch or two, allowing pitiful meows to escape, when Joe said, "No. Thanks. I have...stuff to do."

She looked at him, surprised. He always had *stuff* to do, but eating ranked high on the list. Maybe he had to review video of Friday night's game, or study video of their opponents for next Friday's game. Maybe he had to do laundry...though he could sprawl on her couch, watching TV, and somehow sense the exact moment he needed to run back home and add fabric softener or take clothes from the dryer.

Maybe he had a date.

He'd been awfully quiet since they'd left the fire station. The few words he'd said had been directed at Norton, maybe because he'd been thinking about showering, getting dressed, sitting down to a meal, having a drink, with someone else. Lucy had heard the new advanced math teacher was gorgeous and single, and several of his players had sisters who were college-age or older and would appeal to any guy with functioning eyes in his head.

"Oh," she said. "Okay. I'll take Norton—" She reached for the dog's leash and bumped hands with Joe when he held it out. Her fingers fumbled and dropped it, and Sebastian chose that moment to slip his skinny body through the opening between door and jamb. He shot off across the patio, and with a commanding bark, Norton spun around, knocking first into Lucy, then into Joe, and raced after him.

Lucy's knees buckled, and she fell against the door frame. Joe lost his balance, too, and fell against her, his body barely making contact with hers before he thrust out his hand to brace himself. Still, it was a lovely place to be in, sending warm tingles through her, tightening her lungs until only tiny breaths could get through.

His hand still resting on the wood frame above her head, Joe huffed. "Odd how a dog can knock down people two and three times his size." His voice was soft and sounded kind of funny, like he couldn't quite catch his breath.

"Yeah." She sounded even funnier, maybe because her

internal temperature was steadily climbing, using all the oxygen inside her body to feed the flames. Her position was awkward, but she was afraid to straighten, afraid any movement on her part would startle him back into his usual pesky-brother mode. She didn't know exactly what she was hoping for—*Lucy liar, pants on fire*—but pesky brother wasn't it.

You're hoping he'll kiss you, a voice whispered in her head. It sounded like Jessy. And Marti. There were some definite high pitches belonging to Ilena and a bit of Patricia's husky maternal tones.

And finally her own wistful little voice spoke up. *Yep, you definitely want a kiss. A curl-your-hair-and-straighten-your-toes kiss. A take-your-breath-away-and-make-you-soar kiss.*

It's been a long time since we've had a curl-our-hair kiss, Marti and Fia and Leah sighed together.

His face shadowed from the way the light shone down on him, Joe gazed at her a moment, and then he sort of, maybe, oh, yes, definitely leaned toward her. Her breath froze, her cells went on alert, her fingers curled into tight fists to keep from grabbing him and yanking him to her, and just as his lips touched hers, a little ball of fur ran between her legs and a bigger bundle hit the door with a splat, knocking it open so hard that it bounced off the wall. She looked to make sure Norton was all right . . .

And Joe's kiss landed on her ear.

Her *ear*.

Heat flooded her face, and her first impulse was to babble: *My fault, sorry, I shouldn't have looked away, can we try that again, because even for a kiss on my ear, it felt pretty damn good.* But Joe didn't give her the chance.

His mouth pursed like he didn't know whether to laugh or scowl, and he put breathing distance between them. "Six o'clock in the morning, Luce. Be ready."

Shoving his hands into his jacket pockets, he stepped out of the light and headed to his own back door. She watched until he'd gone inside, then slowly went into the kitchen. After shutting the door, she flipped on the lights and found Norton and Sebastian sitting in identical positions in the middle of the floor, the mutt too close to a hundred pounds and the cat who would probably never see ten pounds, both looking as innocent as the day they were born.

"Thanks, guys," she said dryly. "Heaven forbid you give me two minutes...well, maybe five...for a curl-my-hair kiss. I should interrupt your dinner every couple seconds as payback."

Their only response was to continue staring at her, Sebastian adding a slow blink.

She gave them clean water and dished their food, then pulled her cell from her pocket, dialed Marti's number, and prepared for the biggest, shrillest shriek ever. When her bestie said hello, she responded with four breathless words. "Joe just kissed me."

Marti didn't disappoint. Her scream could have curdled milk, forcing Lucy to hold the phone away from her ear until it faded. "Lucy Lu! Oh, my God! Was it wonderful? Was it everything you'd hoped for?" Her voice turned sly. "Did it curl your hair?"

Pulling out the band that held her hair, Lucy examined a strand of it. "Nope. It's still straight, plain, and mousy brown."

Despite her earlier excitement, Marti said primly,

"This does not surprise me in the least. Him kissing you, I mean. Avi nailed it when she was here. She said he was sweet on you."

Lucy's brows rose. "Avi said that?"

"To Patricia and her parents. She warned Ben that he was going to have to make nice with Joe when the two of you got together."

"This is the first I'm hearing about it." But the information pleased Lucy. All the margarita girls asked her, both teasingly and not so teasingly, how she could live next door to Joe without falling for him. No one had wondered aloud about how he could live next door to her without falling for her. Not even Lucy.

But Avi thought he had. *Bless you, Avi.*

"Give me details," Marti demanded, and Lucy complied. After her friend finished laughing, she asked, "What happened afterward?"

Sliding into a chair at the kitchen table, Lucy unlaced one shoe, toed it off, then removed the other. "He reminded me to be ready at six a.m. for our walk, and then he went home."

"Hmm."

"What does that mean? You think he regretted it? He was disappointed?"

"Regret, no. Disappointment, hell, yeah. He's kissing a beautiful woman for the first time ever, and instead of the luscious, kissable lips he's dreamed about, he gets a mouthful of ear?" Marti snorted. "Maybe he was embarrassed."

There was so much to respond to in that comment that Lucy didn't know where to start. A beautiful woman? *Her? Beautiful* wasn't the first word that came to any-

one's mind when they thought of Lucy. Well, except for
her parents. And her margarita sisters. And Mike. He'd
thought she was beautiful, and she'd believed it when he
told her so.

And luscious, kissable lips? Joe dreaming about her?
She settled for the one least sensitive to her. "Joe doesn't
get embarrassed. He's cocky and confident and smug, and
he knows everyone adores him, and it doesn't matter how
he behaves or what he does, they still adore him, and he
knows that, too. He's just a big, charming, lovable, overgrown kid."

Marti's sigh was long-suffering. Lucy could so easily
picture her, her size four body curled up on the couch, her
grungy hanging-at-home clothes classier and prettier than
Lucy's dress-up. Scented candles perfumed the air, the
soft lighting flattered her, and her makeup was as perfect
as when she'd put it on that morning. She'd had dinner delivered and picked at it like a bird, and she'd been
serenely reading something literary or watching a classic
movie before Lucy called.

They were so different for best friends.

"Joe *is* big and charming and lovable," Marti said pa-
tiently, "but he's not a kid, Lucy. He's a grown man who's
passionate about a lot of things, and one of them is you.
But he's flying blind here, Luce. You haven't sent him
any signals that you're interested in anything other than
friendship. So he got up the nerve to take the risk and finally kiss you, and—"

"He got a mouthful of ear." Lucy's cheeks heated
again, but she couldn't deny the grin that was tugging at
the corners of her mouth. If it had happened to any of
their friends, she would have found it worthy of a full-

body laugh. Maybe one day, she and Joe would look back on this night and laugh.

Really? Maybe? Or would they both try their best to forget it?

"He's a good guy, Lucy. And you gotta admit, he cleans up better than Prince Charming."

He did. The rest of the time, he was an adorable blend of gorgeousness and scruffiness: the predictable ratty clothes, the beard stubble, the hair that always looked one day past time for a trim. The blond of that hair juxtaposed against the golden bronze of his skin, the blue eyes that saw even things he wasn't supposed to see, the grin and the good nature that made everyone around him happy.

He made Lucy happy, and the idea made her tremble inside. Great friends could grow into great lovers, the way she and Mike had. Or their love could end and destroy the friendship with it. Did she have so many friends that she could risk losing one of the very best?

When she plaintively asked that question, Marti was quiet a long time before she asked her own plaintive question. "Do you have so many chances at love that you can risk turning your back on the very best one?"

Lucy picked up her shoes and padded down the hall to the bedroom. She'd thought Ben Noble might be that very best chance. Even though the odds against them were astronomical, she'd found the courage to go for it. Turned out, he hadn't been, but the important thing was she'd tried. And they were still friends.

Could she find that courage again? Let Joe know that she wanted more? Face the fact that they could lose big, but they could also win big?

Tossing her shoes into her closet, she heaved a sigh.

"Whoever said that things are easier the second time around was full of crap, you know?"

"I know, sweetie. I have it on the good authority of my mother that it doesn't really get easy until the fourth or fifth time." Marti's voice turned very droll. "Doesn't that sound like fun?"

* * *

"You know," Calvin said as he climbed out of Justin's car, "I could have driven tonight. I've got my car back."

The younger soldier heaved himself out of the driver's seat, holding on to the door until he got his crutches in place, then they started across the parking lot. "I've seen your car, Captain, and pardon me for saying so, but calling it a car is an insult to marvels of mechanical engineering everywhere. The only marvel about that thing is that it still runs."

"Quit dissing my car. Everyone does that, but it gets me where I'm going."

Justin gave him a sidelong look. "Come on, Captain. The *thief* who stole it brought it *back*. That's a car worthy of being dissed."

Calvin shook his head in mock dismay. "And don't call me Captain. It's just Calvin." His time in the Army was limited. One day soon, he would be separated, no longer a captain or a *sir*, just a soldier whose Army had no place for him. A soldier who'd never intended to be a civilian again adapting to just that.

After spending two nights at his parents' house, he'd taken his stuff back to his apartment today. Gran had taken him aside Monday night to tell him they would be all right without his sleeping over, that her instincts said Diez was a good kid, and even if her instincts were sometimes wrong, Maudene's never were.

And the kid didn't seem to be taking advantage of them. He'd kept Gran company while Elizabeth and Justice were at work yesterday, had walked the neighborhood with her and listened to her stories and lost a dozen hands of poker to her. He'd helped around the house, was polite and said *yes, ma'am* and *no, sir*, and washed Elizabeth's cast-iron pans exactly the right way without being told.

And the kid was still fourteen. Still skinny and hungry. Still on his own in the world. Though Calvin had never wanted to lay eyes on him again, he couldn't forget those facts.

They reached the restaurant door and a young woman coming out with her friends held the door for them. Her gaze slid over Justin's crutches, his awkward movements, then reached his face, and a smile of definite woman-man interest spread slowly across hers.

God bless the women who could overlook a guy's handicaps and still give him that I'd-like-to-get-to-know-you smile.

Justin gave her a similar smile, glancing at her over his shoulder as they crossed the vestibule and entered the restaurant proper. There he shook his head and murmured, "Damn," with great feeling.

The Three Amigos was Tallgrass's most popular Mexican restaurant. When Justin had knocked at Calvin's door, suggesting dinner there, Calvin's first impulse had been to turn him down. And do what instead? he'd wondered. Eat more of his mom's food from the freezer in front of the television with a thousand channels and nothing on?

He could meet some of Justin's friends, Justin had added. If he was staying in Tallgrass, he needed to meet some people.

And because he was right, because meeting people and making friends was something his counseling team recommended, here Calvin was, following Justin to a large round table at the back of the bar. Three men were already seated there, one with that familiar Army look about him and two who made Calvin do a double-take. He'd never really known many twins, especially big cowboy types who were damn near identical. One was heavier, the other wore the marks of a tough life, but no doubt, these two were halves of a whole.

Justin handled the introductions as he got settled on a tall stool and stowed his crutches in the corner behind him: Dane Clark, recently separated staff sergeant; Dalton Smith, the more muscular of the twins; and Dillon Smith, the weary-looking one. Justin gave them Calvin's name, no mention of rank or the Warrior Transition Unit. Justin was forthright with everyone about his own injuries—*they're damn hard to hide with these crutches*—but he'd mentioned as part of his invitation tonight that it wasn't his place to share anyone else's issues.

Calvin took the last stool, ordered a beer, and scanned the menu. It didn't appear to have changed much, if at all, in the years he'd been gone. In fact, judging by the tears and the cracks in the laminate, this could actually be a menu he'd handled before, back when he and J'Myel—

Not tonight.

He ordered steak tacos, sipped the beer, and let his gaze slide around the place. Like the menu, it hadn't changed: tiled fountain in the lobby, small rectangular tables in snug quarters, a fake adobe wall topped with an arch enclosing the bar. Mexican folk music played on the sound system, and the smells of onions, beef, and corn tortillas drifted on the air.

"Uncle Sam bring you here, Calvin?" Dane asked.

With his fingernail, Calvin scraped at the label on the beer bottle. It was a simple question with a simple answer, but simple questions could lead to not-so-simple ones. The next logical one would be, *What unit are you with?* Dane being former Army himself and the brothers, living in an Army town, would know that *Warrior Transition Unit* meant something was wrong with him. Having no obvious injuries, that left the assumption of PTSD.

It was nothing to be ashamed of, the shrinks kept telling him.

They didn't have it. *They* hadn't tried to kill themselves. *They* didn't have to live in his head.

Realizing the silence had gone on too long, Calvin gave himself a mental shake. "Uh, yeah, they did. From Lewis-McChord. What about you?"

"From Walter Reed, to the WTU. I left my left leg behind in Afghanistan."

"You from around here?" The Army tried to send troops to the WTU nearest their home of record or their family, though if Calvin had requested it, he probably could have gotten assigned elsewhere. He was glad he hadn't, though the realization took some getting used to. It had been hard coming back here—was still hard—but it would have been impossible anywhere else.

"I'm from Dallas," Dane replied, "but this was as close as I wanted to get. Then I met Carly and..." He finished with a shrug.

Again, Calvin thought of the woman flirting with Justin on the way in. Lucky men.

And then he thought of Bennie and how there was still stuff between them—J'Myel—but being around her still made him feel...better. More like the man he used to be. Made him think of the man he could become, of the future he could have and the woman who could, maybe, possibly share it with him.

She made him feel like he had another chance.

The waitress brought their food, and the conversation turned to sports. Calvin ate, listened, and even contributed a bit from time to time, although he'd found it hard to find much interest in people paid millions of dollars for throwing a ball while he was in the desert hoping to either go home whole and healthy or to die quickly, without any of the suffering he'd seen too much of.

He had his third taco in his mouth, biting into the crunchy shell, when the football talk came to a sudden halt, interrupted by a very Southern voice. "Hey, guys," Jessy Lawrence said, resting one hand on Justin's shoulder, one on Dalton's. Her gaze slid around the group, then stopped on Calvin. "Why, Calvin, I didn't know you know these guys."

Bennie stepped up beside Jessy, her gaze shifting from her to him. "I didn't know you know Calvin."

His hand was unsteady, causing filling to fall from the taco before he slowly lowered it to the plate. Aw, man, what were the odds that Bennie would be friends with the one civilian he'd gotten to know since coming here?

Fairly good, reason forced him to admit. She'd lived here most of her life, and she was an outgoing woman. *That girl of mine,* Mama used to say with pride, *she never met a stranger.*

You mean she'll talk to a post, Gran had always added before they both burst out laughing.

But how was he supposed to justify knowing Jessy? Admit that he and the shelter were both taking part in the animal therapy program?

Not if he could avoid it. Not yet.

Jessy flashed a brilliant smile as she slid her arm around Bennie's waist and hugged her close. "He came by the shelter to look at the dogs the other day. I tried to convince him to take eight or ten of them home with him, but no luck. How do you know him?"

"His parents live down the street from us." Bennie focused her gaze on him. "I thought you didn't like little furry things."

Calvin was grateful for Jessy's quick answer at the same time he wondered if he should take offense at Bennie's own response. That was twice she'd minimized their knowing each other, first with Marti and now Jessy. His parents living down the street sounded a whole lot more superficial than the truth that they had been best friends forever.

Aiming for careless with his shrug, he said, "I like dogs just fine. It was Gran's cat that tried to kill me."

The smile that lit Bennie's face was a wondrous thing, like the sun breaking through dreary winter clouds to light the day. "You should have seen how he tried to hide from that cat. Poor thing had only three legs and was blind in one eye and deaf in one ear and was the sweetest animal you ever saw." She sighed dramatically. "I do miss little Buttercup."

Teasing sounds of derision came from around the table. "You were terrorized by a crippled cat named Buttercup?" Justin asked before joining the others in a laugh.

"Hey, cats are never innocent," Calvin protested before a faint chuckle of his own slipped out. God, it brought back feelings he hadn't experienced in way too long. Sitting at a table with friends, joking, laughing…it was so damn near normal that it made him ache inside. And even though it did stir that ache, it felt so good that he did it again, a serious laugh that released tension he hadn't known he held, that set his muscles free and practically brought tears to his eyes.

The shrinks were right. Life could be better. Not the way it used to be. Everything had changed too much for that. But better than it had been.

Then he caught Bennie's gaze as she smiled at something Dane was saying, and heat, affection, and yearning curled inside him, amending that thought.

Life could even be good.

He'd damn well missed good.

*   *   *

Parades were a big thing in Tallgrass. The first one of the year was for Memorial Day, then there was the Fourth of July, Homecoming for the high school, Veterans Day, and Christmas, and Bennie and Mama hadn't missed one in the entire time Bennie lived there.

Monday was a perfect day for a few hours outside. The sun was shining, the temperature in the seventies, and flags whipped in the steady breeze down Main Street. Bennie and Mama, the margarita girls, and their families gathered on the sidewalk outside the second-floor apartment Jessy used for a photography studio even though, for all practical purposes, she was living at Dalton's ranch.

Bennie had dressed in red shorts and a navy and white striped shirt, her curls held back from her face with a headband in the same colors. Her lawn chair was set up between Mama's and Ilena's, and she held little John on her lap, bouncing him on her knees and making cooing sounds to draw a laugh from him.

"You're so good with him," Ilena commented as she reached across to wipe drool from the corner of his mouth. "You should definitely work with kids when you finish nursing school."

"She should definitely work on getting me some babies of our own." Mama emphasized her words with a raised brow. "If she hurries, our baby and John here can grow up together and be best friends."

"Wouldn't that be lovely?" Ilena's cheeriness was infectious. She was the role model all the margarita girls strived to emulate. She'd loved Juan dearly, and still did, but she'd made peace with his passing, and she woke every morning with joy and hope and the unwavering belief that life was to be celebrated, not mourned.

J'Myel had been gone longer than Juan, and Bennie hadn't dealt quite as well as Ilena. Ilena, though, would be the first to point out that time meant nothing, that she'd had the best reason in the world to push on in the baby she'd carried. If Bennie had been pregnant when J'Myel died...

Heart clenching, she shied away from that path. Losing a husband was tough enough. Being cheated of the homecoming they'd deserved, the everyday life they'd never gotten to share, and the future they'd wanted was enough of a wound. If she added in regrets for the babies they'd never had, she might just retreat into her room and wallow in her grief, the way she had the weeks after his death.

Damn it, life shouldn't be this hard. J'Myel should be there to share it with her.

She drew a deep breath, then exhaled slowly. And Juan should be with Ilena, Paul with Therese, Jeff with Carly. Mike and Joshua should be hanging out with Lucy and Marti, and so on. But Carly had found Dane, Therese was snuggling with Keegan, and Jessy was so in love with Dalton that she could hardly stand still.

And Ilena had John, and Bennie had the best bunch of friends in the whole universe, even if she was, at the moment, lonely and blue in a way her friends couldn't fix.

Then a shadow fell across her, and John lunged forward, arms outstretched. She tilted her head back to smile at Calvin and Diez, standing in the street, one holding two to-go cups from Serena's Sweets, the other balancing three.

She held on to John, wriggly as a worm. "Hey, guys, I wasn't expecting to see you here."

"The Sweet family never misses a parade." That came from Calvin. He wore jeans and a black T-shirt with dark shades and a black-and-gold Army ball cap, and he looked about eighteen. How did he manage that when she usually felt every one of her twenty-nine years?

"Neither do we," Mama said. "Where are you sitting?"

He gestured across the street, and his parents and Gran, all settled in their own lawn chairs, waved in greeting.

"I'm gonna go say hello." Mama set her bottle of water on the ground beside her chair, then maneuvered carefully to her feet. "Diez, hon, if I help you carry those soda pops over, will you walk with me?"

"Yes, ma'am."

She took the two extra drinks from Calvin, then she and Diez headed across the street. The police had already blocked off traffic, so there was no rush, thankfully, because Mama was taking her time.

"You want to sit for a minute?" Bennie asked, gesturing to the empty chair.

"Sure." He lowered himself into the chair but didn't sink back, all comfy like her and Ilena. His spine remained erect, his hands loosely gripping his drink, his feet slightly under him as if he might push back up any second.

"Ilena, this is Calvin. Calvin, my friend Ilena and her little sweetie, John."

The petite blonde leaned forward to flash a smile and wave. "I was wondering when I would get to meet you. Marti and Jessy already have, so I was feeling left out."

He didn't seem to know how to respond to that. All he managed was a faint smile and a murmured, "Nice to meet you."

When John had lunged a moment earlier, Bennie hadn't known which of the two guys he was reaching for. Now he stuffed one hand into his mouth and chewed on it while cocking his head and giving Calvin a measuring look. Must have been Diez who excited him.

Ilena scooted to her feet. "Bennie, if you don't mind

holding on to Hector for a few minutes, I'm gonna go get some hot chocolate."

"Are you crazy? This isn't hot chocolate weather."

"It's November."

"And seventy-four degrees."

Ilena dug her debit card from her huge purse–diaper bag before stuffing it back under her chair. "You drink coffee year round: hot, sweet, caffeine. I do the same, except with chocolate. Want anything?"

"No, thanks. Wave bye-bye to *mamacita*, John." Bennie waved his pudgy little hand, and Ilena blew him a kiss before weaving her way through the crowd to Serena's.

After a moment, Calvin touched the baby's hand, stroking his finger over his soft, soft skin. "Hector?"

"It's one of his middle names. She called him that the whole time she was pregnant, even though we tried to stop her. She thinks because he's her son, she has some say in the matter."

"Imagine that. When you have kids, you'll probably want some say in what they're called, won't you?"

Her heart twinged. "If I have any, you can bet I'll have the only say in it."

John took his hand from his mouth and wrapped it, slobber and all, around Calvin's finger. "I saw that wince," Bennie teased. Reaching into Ilena's seat, she took the always-handy pack of baby wipes and passed it to him so he could clean first his finger, then the baby's hand. John responded by sticking it right back in his mouth.

"How's it working out with Diez?"

Calvin shrugged.

"How long is he staying?"

"I think Gran might have taken him to raise," he joked, then went serious and shrugged again. "I haven't really talked to Mom and Dad about it. They can't just let him stay forever, but he apparently doesn't have anyplace to go, and...they're enjoying him too much to put a damper on it."

"He can go to a foster or group home," she quietly pointed out. "He did go to one. He just didn't like it."

"Can you blame him?" For the first time since he'd sat down, Calvin took his sunglasses off and met her gaze. "What if your family hadn't wanted you when your dad died? Would you have wanted to go live with strangers on a temporary basis, knowing they could return you to the state for any reason, and that the day you turned eighteen, you were going to be put out on your own?"

No, she wouldn't have wanted it at all. It had been hard enough coming to live with Mama, who'd loved her more than anything in the world. But Mama had been family, and she *had* wanted Bennie, and she'd gotten custody of her legally. Taking in a stranger's child from halfway across the country...that was a bigger, tougher deal.

"I'm as softhearted as anyone," she said with a laugh. "I want every kid and stray dog and cat to have a happy, loving home. This is just more complicated than that. Speaking of stray dogs..." She glanced over her shoulder at Jessy, her camera hiding most of her face, and grinned. "Are you thinking about adopting one from the shelter?"

"I can't right now."

"Are you living in the barracks?"

A siren whooped off to the right, and he put his glasses back on and directed his gaze down the street as a police car slowly approached from the west. "Yeah. No pets allowed except service dogs."

"And you don't qualify for one of them, thank God."

Abruptly he got to his feet. "No, I don't. Here comes Mama." He gestured to her grandmother, took a few steps, then turned back. For a moment, he seemed to think better of whatever he'd been about to say, then he blurted it out anyway. "You want to have dinner tonight?"

Her eyes widened, and her lips parted automatically though no words found their way out. Whatever she'd expected, it wasn't an invitation to dinner. Sure, they'd spent a lot of time together, but most of it had been because their families were so close, not because he'd been seeking her out. Besides that night at Java Dave's. And the day outside the craft store when he hadn't fled at the first chance. And now, when he could have refused her offer of a seat while Mama went to visit his folks.

But dinner for just the two of them...he was definitely seeking her out.

With Mama close enough that Bennie could hear her humming, she answered, "Um, yeah, sure. I'd like that." Would *really* like that, she admitted with some surprise.

"I'll pick you up at six?"

A laugh bubbled up inside and overflowed. "Anything to get me into that junker of yours, huh? Okay, I'll see you at six."

As he walked away, Fia leaned over from behind, hugging her around the neck. "Did I just hear you accept a date with Mr. Hard-body there?" she whispered teasingly.

"Not a date," Bennie said automatically even as the word echoed in her head. A *date*? Her and Calvin? It was a strange idea, old buddies who'd abandoned each other going out on a date. Strange…but judging from the tingle of anticipation inside her, not unwelcome. "Just old friends having dinner."

"A handsome man whom I'm assuming is single asking a beautiful woman who's definitely single to go out to dinner is pretty much the definition of a date." Fia waggled a finger at her. "Just admit I'm right. Don't make me call all the girls over here to get their opinions."

"Oh, please, no." If the girls did one thing exceedingly well, besides supporting each other, it was give opinions. And tease. And see right into one another's hearts. Bennie wasn't sure what was in her own heart, but she'd like to find out before she shared. "You're right. That's the definition of a date. But it can also describe old friends just sharing a meal."

"What would you like it to be, sister of mine?"

After a moment's thought, Bennie replied, "I'm okay with either." And she was. Whether she and Calvin were renewing their friendship, making a new one, or maybe starting something totally different and new and intimate, she was okay.

But she couldn't help admitting just to herself that she'd had enough of okay. She wanted more. A boyfriend, fun, sex, passion, a commitment. Something special. Some*one* special.

It never hurt to be open to all the possibilities, did it? Just as long as she protected her heart.

Chapter 11

With winter approaching, Calvin knew better than to waste a nice sunny day. Thanks to the end of daylight saving time, it was already dark early every evening, and no one had a clue when the next snow or sleet would come or when the winter cold would settle in to stay awhile. So after the parade and barbecue from Justice's grill, Calvin went home, changed into PT clothes, loaded up with his cell phone, ID, driver's license, and water bottle, and he left the barracks for a run.

He could have run himself into exhaustion without leaving the post. It was a big area, with trails and roads everywhere. But he exited through the main gate and turned west. He noticed the gates for Fort Murphy National Cemetery, saw that some sort of ceremony was taking place near one of the memorials. He'd passed the cemetery plenty of times since coming home, but he'd kept his glances limited and his thoughts closed off. He didn't like cemeteries, had never set foot in one that hadn't left him feeling creeped out and or melancholy by the time he'd escaped. The history of cemeteries and their graves had never appealed to him; showing respect at gravesides had seemed an empty gesture. Even when he was a kid, the idea of spending time with the dead had freaked him out.

As he jogged on, resolutely keeping his vision focused on a sign two blocks ahead, he acknowledged that at some point he would have to go to the cemetery and pass through its gates. He would have to pass grave after grave filled with people just like him, only he'd been lucky enough to make it home, and then he would reach J'Myel's grave.

Calvin believed in ghosts. He'd seen too many to count. J'Myel's ghost had already eased into his mind around his own house, when he looked at the Ford house, when he found himself in places where they used to hang out together. He had no doubt J'Myel's spirit was inside that cemetery, passing time while Calvin gathered the courage to walk through the gates.

If he could talk, what would he say? Would it be the best bud who had promised Calvin their first day incountry that he had his back? Or would it be the J'Myel who'd held a grudge about something and blown it into a full-fledged life-changing incident?

Sweat was forming on Calvin's forehead, trickling down the side of his face, as he passed the last panel of black wrought iron fence that enclosed the cemetery. This was where the town began, with a storage unit, a gym, and a Starbucks. In the next small group of buildings were an insurance agency, an old-style barber shop, a tiny Mexican deli, and a tag agency. All things that helped to push the cemetery to the back of his mind, where it had stayed hidden so long.

His pace was steady, too fast for a jog, slower than a flat-out run, and his lungs were strong as he inhaled deeply. He'd always liked running and the freedom it represented, but he'd learned in the past few years that it could help ease the depression that gripped him too often. As long as his feet were moving, his heart was pounding, his breath pumping in and out, he could usually close his mind to everything else. And the good feeling lasted after the run. Not as long as he wished, but it was a start. Between exercise and the antidepressants he was taking, he was seeing fewer bad days. It was a gradual thing, but he'd take it any way he could get it.

He had no destination in mind this afternoon, just letting his feet guide him. He passed City Park, where the Sweet and Ford families—and later the Pickerings—attended spring and summer concerts and the Christmas lights-on celebration. There was the squat stone building that had housed their family doctor on one side, their dentist on the other. As much as Calvin hated cemeteries, J'Myel had hated the dentist's office. *It's the drills, man, they freak me out.* Calvin had smirked at him every time they went in for checkups, and J'Myel had returned the favor every time they'd had to accompany their parents to a funeral.

Across the street was the bank where they'd had their first savings accounts started with Christmas money they'd really wanted to spend instead, and on the next block was the convenience store where J'Myel convinced an older girl to buy them their first six-pack of beer. It had cost them twenty bucks and been crappy beer, but they'd thought they were cool.

You guys will regret this, Bennie had taunted them, and she'd been right. She'd taken such pleasure the next morning in blasting the television, clattering and yelling, and otherwise making their hangovers intensify. J'Myel had sprawled on Mama Maudene's couch, one eye pried open, and groaned. "It's a good thing we're not taking her to the Army with us."

Bennie in the Army. At the time, right out of high school, it would have horrified J'Myel, and Calvin wouldn't have been too thrilled about it. Now...she would probably thrive in it. She was smart, capable, and impossible to intimidate. She wouldn't take crap from anyone, she would look out for her fellow soldiers, and she was a motherly, healing sort.

There were a hell of a lot of soldiers who needed the motherly, healing sort.

He'd reached the official western edge of town: the city limits sign posted on either side of the street. Hands on his hips, he heaved a few deep breaths as he crossed the street, then started east again. This time he went two blocks north and made the return run on streets lined with trees, houses, signs of life. There was no order to the types of neighborhoods he passed through: A thousand-square-foot house stood next to one four times its size; old ones beside new ones; starter homes and fix-'er-uppers next to large, gracious beauties. There was one house, three stories tall, built by an early oil-man of sandstone blocks, with a detached guest house, that filled an entire city block, fenced in with wrought iron. *One day I'm gonna dance in their ball room,* Bennie used to say.

Calvin made a mental note at dinner to ask her if she ever did.

He walked the last half mile home, working the kinks from muscles that had gotten overtired from the extra distance. As he stepped into the shower, an ice-cold bottle of water in hand, he did a mental evaluation. Tired, sure, but he'd done longer road marches plenty of times, complete with a fifty-pound ruck. Nothing was hurting, his head was clear, and the muscles in his gut weren't knotted. He wasn't grinding his teeth, his fists weren't clenched, or any of the other things he used to keep a tight grip on his stress. His mood was good, stable, even lighter than usual. He felt right.

He felt *all* right.

When he pulled into Mama's driveway, the screen door opened before he could shut off the engine, and Bennie came toward him. He got out of the car and circled to the other side, opening the passenger door, then focusing his gaze on her. She wore jeans that hugged her curves with a red, white, and blue sweater. Her hair was down, a million curls for a man to get his fingers wrapped up in, and she smelled incredible. Looked incredible. Probably tasted incred—

He gave himself a mental smack.

"Do I need to run back in and get something to cover that seat?" she asked, then ducked under his arm as he pushed the door all the way back. He'd folded and wrapped one of Elizabeth's quilts so it hid every bit of exposed foam. Bennie smiled, slid in, and rubbed her palm lightly over the fabric. "Good as new, huh?"

Calvin closed the door, got in his own side, and fastened his seat belt. "When did you get so finicky? You used to wade in mud, sleep on the ground, stick your hands underwater trying to noodle a catfish from its hole and then gut and clean it."

"I grew up," she teased. "I got a job where I didn't have to do any of that."

"No, you have to deal with sick people, changing their beds, their diapers, their gowns."

"There will come a time, Calvin," she said breezily, "when you'll hurt yourself trying to outrun a bullet or you'll break your ankle while running or some idiot will blast through a red light and crash into your, uh"—she rolled her eyes—"vehicle, and you'll need nurses and aides and be so grateful they're there."

"Oh, I'm grateful, all right. I just wouldn't want to do the job myself."

After settling in, she rested her arm on the open window and smiled at him. "Where are we going?"

"Where do you want to go?"

"Doesn't matter to me. Pick whatever you've been missing."

He considered all the hometown foods he hadn't yet sampled as he backed out of the driveway, then headed east. "How about Bad Hank's?"

"That's always a winner. Plus, they're giving free food to active duty and vets today. But didn't you have Bad Justice's barbecue for lunch?"

"There's no such thing as too much barbecue. Hot links, spicy bologna, ribs, and a baked potato, all slathered with Hank's Devil Sauce." He made a smacking-good sound that earned him a chuckle.

About halfway there, she sighed softly. "Remember when our parents used to let us ride our bikes to Bad Hank's and bring home dinner?"

"Yeah, they made us take the back streets so the only busy streets we crossed were Main and First. At the stop-lights, of course."

"Where we got off our bikes and walked them across, of course."

"Liar. The only time we actually did that was when J'Myel's mom tried to sneak after us about a block back in her car, but we saw her right away."

The easy mood from their laughter lasted until they were parked in Bad Hank's lot. The sky was darkening quickly, the western horizon a dozen shades of pink, red, purple, and gold, and a chill tinged the air. Blues music drifted out the door, along with laughter and some amazing smells.

Calvin held the door for Bennie, and together they followed a waitress to a table in one corner. "There are no small tables in Bad Hank's," Bennie remarked, and the waitress finished for her, "because there are no small appetites." With a flash of white teeth, she went on, "What can I get you to drink?"

Bennie asked for tea. After a moment, Calvin ordered beer. Across the table, she remarked, "So you finally got over that bad experience with your first beer."

"I was thinking about that today. Yeah, a good beer is a treat sometimes."

She fiddled with the gold bracelet around her wrist, then reached up to lift a gold pendant from the rounded vee of her sweater and slid it along the chain. "How are you settling in? It's been...what? Three weeks?"

"Or so." He shrugged, turning his chair so his back was to the wall, gazing out across the dining room.

"You want to trade places?"

The question made him blink. He'd thought he'd been smoother than that.

"I don't mind. I know a lot of people like to have their backs to the walls. Don't want anyone sneaking up on them."

Be strong. Tell her, "Nah, no, thanks. I'm fine." But sitting at a right angle to the table made for difficulty eating and for looking at a beautiful woman who had the ability to make him feel hopeful. On top of that, he'd look like an idiot.

"Okay. If you don't mind."

She picked up her purse and gave him a sly smile that completely altered the meaning of her response. "I never mind."

Once they'd resettled, switched their drinks, and given their orders, Bennie rested both arms on the table, then leaned her cheek against her fist. "Can I ask you something?"

Her question could be totally innocuous, or it could be one of the big-deal ones that the shrink team always wanted to talk about. Muscles clenching in his gut, he shrugged, pretending he didn't care, wishing to hell he really didn't. *Just please, God, don't let it ruin the evening. Don't let* me *ruin it.*

"What happened between you and J'Myel?"

* * *

Bennie was so intent watching for the slightest sign of emotion to cross Calvin's face that she forgot to breathe, a shortcoming she realized as soon as she tried to take a drink and choked on her tea. Coughing and sputtering, she accepted the napkin he offered, patted her eyes dry, and muffled one last cough before laying it aside to watch him again.

There was plenty of emotion crossing his face—anger, regret, bitterness, defeat, failure, sorrow. She had never known any details about their falling-out, just that J'Myel slowly stopped mentioning Calvin in his phone calls and e-mails, and when Calvin did come up, J'Myel was abrupt, hostile even. At some point, everything he said became dismissive, scathing, or derisive, and after a while, it was as if Calvin had never existed.

Bennie had pushed for answers from J'Myel—getting married without Calvin there had seemed impossible— but she'd learned nothing. *Leave it alone,* he'd told her repeatedly. *It don't matter.* He *don't matter.*

She had always thought that must have been her mother's attitude toward her and her father. *We didn't matter, either.* And it had never satisfied her need for a reason. Just one logical understandable reason.

Would Calvin tell her to leave it alone? Would he try to convince her that J'Myel didn't matter? She was wondering when suddenly he slipped from his upright, on-alert rabbit's posture, always ready to flee, and slumped back in his chair. "What did he tell you?"

She fiddled with the pendant she wore, a gold heart that J'Myel had given her right after they started dating. It had been surreal, finding herself intimate with her best bud, falling in love with the kid she'd played and run wild with practically her whole life. The necklace had helped make it more real.

"Nothing," she said at last, "except that he didn't want me talking to you. I was engaged to him. I was supposed to support his decisions." One of her few regrets about her relationship with J'Myel. She should have stood up to him, the way she'd always stood up to other people, grabbed him by the ear like Gran would have done, and had a come-to-Jesus meeting with him.

Instead, she'd let him dictate to her, and she'd lost one of her very best friends. It wasn't possible to have so many very best friends that you could throw one away without feeling the loss.

After another long moment, Calvin unclenched his jaw and shook his head. "Truth is . . . I don't know."

His response left an unsettled dissatisfaction seeping through her. "You must know something, Calvin. You were there, you were seeing him every day, talking to him, hanging out with him. Did you argue?"

He shook his head again, slowly side to side, his gaze distant. After a long time, he sighed, then answered in a low, heavy voice, "When we went in the Army, we were gonna have good times. We knew we were gonna go to war, but we were gonna kick ass and save the world. We were all gung-ho through training, but when we got over there, when we got into real combat, when people were trying to kill us and we were trying to kill them and we were seeing people die—our troops, theirs, civilians . . ."

His haunted gaze met hers, sending a shiver through her, one of pain and regret. Lord, how sorry she was he'd gone through that. He'd seen things no one should ever see, done things no one should ever do, and all his naïve youthful ideals had been shot to hell. He'd had to grow up quickly—and hard.

"It wasn't good times then, Bennie. Our buddies were dying, and we were afraid of dying, and we had to get tougher and stronger. After about three months in Iraq, I went up to our lieutenant one day and said, 'I changed my mind, sir. College is looking real good about now. Can I go home for a while and think about it?'

"He just laughed, and so did I, and he sent me on my way."

Despite his relaxed posture, tension flooded through him. She could see it spreading from his eyes and his jaw, tightening the muscles in his arms and chest, knotting his fingers around the beer he hadn't yet tasted, and reaching across the table into her. She wished she hadn't asked the question. She needed to know, but did her need to talk about it take precedence over his desire not to tell?

"The lieutenant died a couple days later."

"Oh, Calvin…I'm sorry." Dropping the gold heart to dangle on its chain, she took his hand, gently, forcibly unfolding his fingers from the bottle, gripping them in hers. "I'm so sorry."

For a time he stared down at their hands, then slowly tightened his as if he needed to hold on to her. She'd teased him in high school that he had elegant hands for a boy. Artistic creative hands, for a pianist, a painter, a surgeon. He'd laughed, extending his long slender fingers as wide as they would spread, and said he had basketball hands.

"J'Myel…" His voice was husky and thick, the way her own voice got sometimes when she talked about her husband. He cleared his throat, swiped his nose with his free hand, and looked at her again. "I started taking college courses as soon as we got out of training. I worked hard, studied hard. I picked one hell of a career for myself, but going through everything we were going through, I was damned if I was going to come out with nothing to show but a few medals. And that was when things started going wrong with J'Myel."

Though Bennie hadn't made the connection back then, she wasn't surprised now. With his perpetual life-will-always-be-fun attitude, J'Myel hadn't thought much of people going to college. He wasn't going to spend another four years or more sitting in classes, not when he'd just finished thirteen years of it. He was going to live a real life doing real stuff, he'd boasted—not reading about it, not learning about it, not sitting in an office working it like some jerk. She assumed he'd outgrown that prejudice since he hadn't made any snide comments when she'd started nursing school, but he'd been seventy-five hundred miles away. Maybe he'd seen acceptance as his only option at that time.

"When I wasn't working or in class, I was studying. I didn't have much time for going to bars or meeting girls, so—" Abruptly he stopped, guilt flushing his face.

She smiled. "I'm going to presume this was before he and I started dating."

"It was," he assured her. Finally, he took a drink from the beer, his head tilted back, the muscles in his throat rippling ever so slightly under his skin. Was it wrong of Bennie to be thinking what a lovely sight that was when they were discussing her dead husband?

She'd loved J'Myel. Always had, always would. But she had plenty of love left over, and she was much too young to spend the rest of her life in mourning. He would understand. And if he didn't, well, that would be another come-to-Jesus meeting.

"He started hanging out with other guys, guys like him, into partying and good times and living the life," Calvin went on. "When I got promoted ahead of him the first time, he was ticked off. The next couple times, he was really pissed. He wouldn't see it was because he was just doing the bare minimum the job required. He called me college boy and suck-up, among other things. When I finished my degree and got commissioned, he finally got down to the point, to what was really bothering him."

Bennie's shoulder muscles started to cramp, and she realized she was hunched forward, wound tight as a spring. At any moment, whatever was coiled inside her might release, shooting her across the table in a quivering mass. She consciously relaxed her shoulders, rolling them, stretching them down from her neck, as B.B. King and Eric Clapton combined their guitar mastery on a soulful tune coming from the speaker mounted above them.

"*Ambition* was kind of a dirty word to J'Myel." She didn't feel disloyal for saying what everyone knew. His mother was a paralegal, his father a bank finance officer. They'd always encouraged him to study hard, work hard, and make the best life possible for himself.

That ain't me, J'Myel used to say. He was a live-for-today worry-about-tomorrow-when-it-comes sort of guy. If he wanted to do something, he did it. If he had money, he spent it. If he saw an opportunity, he took it, and he never worried about the consequences. He'd been care-free, happy, and always up for anything, and she'd loved that about him. She'd known when he proposed that she would have to be the responsible one in the marriage, and she hadn't minded. She'd been good at keeping him in line.

And she'd honestly thought that before long he would grow out of it. That a couple combat tours of hard living would make college and an air-conditioned office look a lot better—for his own sake, for hers, and for the family they were going to have.

Maybe he would have grown out of it…but time hadn't been on his side.

The waitress interrupted to deliver their food: a regular dinner plate for Bennie, a super-sized one that was loaded to overflowing for Calvin. After she left, they sat in silence a bit longer. Bennie was patient. She could wait as long as it took Calvin to finish.

He released his grip on her hand slowly, the callused skin of his fingertips sliding along her fingers, across her palm, brushing her wrist, before he finally let go. After unwrapping his silverware from the napkin, he squirted Bad Hank's Devil Sauce over his entire meal and stabbed a piece of brisket on his fork, but he didn't lift it to his mouth.

"He said he left home with his best bud." Calvin's affect was flat, no emotion in his voice or on his face. "Two black kids out to save the world, but somewhere along the way I forgot that I was black. I was trying too hard to be white, he said. And that was the last thing he ever said to me."

Bennie cringed. *Trying too hard to be white* was the worst insult in J'Myel's arsenal. She'd believed all this time that whatever had come between the men had been of substance, something that *might* be worth ending a life-long friendship, something that they shared responsibility for. She'd been wrong.

It didn't speak well of her husband.

It didn't speak well of her that she'd acceded to his demands that she cut off contact with Calvin, too. She should have insisted on an explanation, but of course he wouldn't have given it, not when the truth would have tarnished his reckless and fun-loving knight's armor.

Heavens, she'd loved such an idiot.

After being mostly quiet for so long, now it was her turn to talk. "I'm sorry, Calvin. I'm sorry he took that attitude, and I'm sorry I took his side. It was just easier to go along with him than to argue, and I really didn't want to argue. We had so little contact, and I wanted to keep things happy."

She expected him to shrug, brush off her apology. That was what people usually did. Instead, he ruefully shook his head. "I missed you, Bennie. With J'Myel out of my life, then you, it felt like part of my soul had been ripped away."

Her breath caught in her chest, and guilt washed over her. When he'd left town to go to basic, she'd promised she would always stay in touch, that she would be his link to home and real life and normalcy, and she'd done it until J'Myel convinced her otherwise. She was ashamed that her *always* had lasted only six years.

"I missed you, too," she admitted. "I'd seen you guys every single day for nine years, and then you were gone. I didn't know what to do with myself. There was no one to hang out with, to sit with in church. No one to cheer up or to cheer me up or to tease mercilessly. It was tough." On second thought, she added, "Not your kind of tough, of course."

He smiled faintly at that. "So is that enough questions for tonight?"

Her own smile was sly and naughty. "Oh, I have dozens more, but they're all much easier. You know, things like how come you aren't married and how long is the trail of broken hearts behind you and what have you been doing with yourself. But they can wait for another time."

After he'd taken a bite, she smiled sadly. "Thank you for telling me, Calvin. I can't tell you how much I appreciate it." Even though knowing sharpened the shame of her own actions and made her heart feel two sizes too small.

* * *

Eight days had passed since what Joe thought of as the failed first-kiss attempt. He had seen Lucy every day, had spent time with her, and hadn't gathered the nerve to try again, especially since she hadn't said anything about it the next day or the day after or the day after...Did she think if she ignored it, she could pretend it never happened? Did she wish it had never happened? Was friendship all she wanted from him?

"Of all the people in the world to sabotage me," he said softly, rubbing Norton's throat, "you were the last one I expected it from."

The dog's big eyes studied him a moment before drooping shut. On the sofa cushion, nestled against Norton's belly, Sebastian was already snoozing, making tiny whistling sounds with each exhale.

Lucy came in from the kitchen with two bottles of water and a bowl of grapes. After setting them on the coffee table, she pulled a stack of flattened items from under her arm. "Look what I got today." There were bakery boxes in different sizes, bags big enough for a couple cookies, and shopping bags to hold the smaller ones. They were white and green and blue, with the bakery name, address, and phone number and decorated with heart-shaped flowers. "I got business cards, too," she added, pulling a handful from her hip pocket. "Aren't they adorable?"

He took about half the stack of cards, glancing at them before sliding them into his wallet. "Almost as adorable as I am." He feigned a hopeful look. "I am, you know. Everyone says so."

"Aw, you need some ego strokes?" she teased.

"My ego is just fine. Not too big, not too small, but just right." He patted the sofa cushion beside him. With Norton stretching out from the tip of his nose to the tip of his toes, there wasn't much room left. *Thanks, buddy.* "Sit."

"Do I get a cookie if I obey?"

"No, but you can have a grape."

She plopped down beside him, her feet barely reaching the coffee table to rest on the scarred wood. They were both still in their walking clothes. Well, she was. He wore ragged shirts and shorts or sweats all the time. Her ponytail was slipping loose from the band that held it, and her cheeks were still tinged with pink from the exertion and the chill as the sun had gone down.

"How was the parade from your perspective?" he asked, twisting enough on the cushion that he could watch her without being obvious.

"It was great. I love parades. We used to go up to Pasadena to see the Rose Parade, until Mom and Dad finally realized that it was almost as good on TV as in person. No driving, no camping out for a good spot, bathroom right down the hall..." She leaned forward to pick up her water and the grapes, popping one into her mouth and talking around it. "How was it from yours?"

The football team had a long history of riding a float in the parade, right behind the Tallgrass High cheer squad and ahead of the marching band. Since Joe had been in charge, that had changed to walking in the parade. If a bunch of older veterans could walk the two-mile route, the team darn well could.

"There were more people than last year. That's cool." He grinned. "I saw you. John was lying on your lap and you were bent over him while Ilena changed his diaper." Seeing Lucy's smile and the silly faces she'd made to entertain the baby had given him a pain around his heart. Being the youngest of six kids hadn't always been conducive to paternal feelings, especially when the five older ones could outrun him, outsmart him, and outwit him until he was in his teens.

But when he'd become his dad's assistant with a youth football team, he'd found he had a knack for teaching younger kids. He'd continued volunteering through high school and college, and even now he oversaw regular clinics for kids to learn the fundamentals and safety of football. Somewhere during those years, he'd decided he wanted kids of his own—wanted them a lot. Wanted them with Lucy.

"Ilena's lucky," he remarked. It hadn't been easy for her, widowed and pregnant, with her family in South Texas. But with Juan's family little more than an hour away in Broken Arrow and the margarita girls here, she and John were doing fine.

"Yes, she is. I was so jealous of her when we met. I mean, Mike and I had talked and waited and talked, and... here I am."

Joe knew the unselfish thing was to wish she'd had at least that much to hold on to of Mike. He also knew that if she'd been pregnant or had had a child when Mike died, she would have moved back to California to be near their families. He never would have met her, and his life would be a whole lot less than it was now.

"You've still got time, Luce."

"Really?" She made a show of cocking her head, one hand cupped behind her ear. "Hear that? It's the sound of my doorbell and my cell phone not ringing. Guys aren't lining up for the chance to be with me. And it's not a quick and easy process. First I have to meet the right guy, then I have to fall in love with him, and he has to fall in love with me, and then we have to get pregnant and hope it doesn't take forever because I *am* getting to that age, you know, and then we have to wait nine months and pray that everything's okay, and then—"

He shifted uncomfortably, remembering his embarrassment about the kiss, and told himself not to interrupt, but his mouth spoke before his brain engaged. "Maybe you've already met the right guy."

For a moment, she was still, not even breathing, then she turned slightly on the cushion, too. The action put more space between them, but it felt like they were closer, maybe because they were face-to-face.

"Really?" she said.

Yeah. He's sitting right here in front of you looking like a fool. But no matter how emphatically his heart told him to say it, his brain refused to send the words. What if she didn't feel the same way and he ruined the best thing in his life?

She tapped one fingernail against her chin. "Let's see, who do I know? Dane Clark—married. Keegan Logan—engaged. Dalton Smith—engaged. Ben—crazy in love with Avi and as good as married. Dillon Smith—though I don't really know him. Hmm..."

Joe's face flushed, and the flustered feeling spreading through him reminded him of high school and asking Niecy Walker out for his very first date. He'd almost thrown up before he got through the line he'd rehearsed in his bedroom the night before. When she'd said yes, he hadn't known which was more responsible for his elation: the fact that she'd said yes or that he'd survived the asking.

Still wearing a thoughtful look, Lucy went on. "I work with a lot of guys, of course, but none that make me look twice. And there are a few single men at church, but they don't—"

He didn't know what possessed him—some urge spurred on by the teasing tone of her voice, some insanity that he'd been previously unaware of—but he leaned forward, cupped her face in his hands to avoid a misplaced connection, and he kissed her. His heart was beating about a thousand times a minute, and his lungs were as constricted as if he'd just finished a twenty-mile run, and his hands would be shaking if he didn't have her to hold on to, but the instant her mouth relaxed beneath his and her hands came up to his shoulders and a soft sigh vibrated through her, all the nervous tension disappeared and was replaced by a hunger he'd never felt before, not like this.

After a moment—recovering from the shock?—her hands, soft and warm, slid to the back of his neck, then into his hair, stroking and kneading. No longer concerned about where the kiss would land, he let his own hands drift down across the silkiness of her neck, over her T-shirt, down the curve of her spine, settling at her waist, drawing her even closer.

That elation over Niecy Walker agreeing to go out with him was nothing compared to this. This was better than running an eighty-yard touchdown or playing a perfect season or winning the state championship three years in a row. She tasted sweet and light and hot, like everything he'd ever wanted, and she felt... God, like a dream.

When his lungs were burning and his erection was rock-solid and he thought he might just die from the wanting—though it would be a happy death—he forced himself to slide his tongue from her mouth, to end the kiss and sit back, putting a little breathing space between them. Her eyes, rounded and smoky with arousal, stared at him, her lips still parted and tempting and a sweet, deeper pink.

"Whoa." The word just sort of sighed out of her, and her whole body softened, stirring the need inside him.

At the same time, the nervousness raced back, making him swallow hard. "Is that—" His voice was so hoarse that he had to stop, swallow again. "Is that a good whoa or a bad one?"

A smile slowly curved her lips as she leaned forward, cupped her own hands to his face, so soft and gentle against his skin, and for an answer, she kissed him back.

Definitely a good *whoa*.

Chapter 12

When Lucy and Mike were sixteen, they'd had their first make-out session in his pickup, parked in the lot that fronted the beach where they'd spent the day with friends. It had become one of their favorite memories, and every time they'd returned home for a visit, they'd found a way to visit that old parking lot to recapture the sheer joy of that day.

Lucy suspected she was going to feel that way about her couch now. *Sure, it's ratty and stinky and broken down and even the critters won't sit on it anymore, but I can't get rid of it. The second time I felt the magic was right there.*

Man, she'd been afraid she would never feel magic again.

"I've been wanting to do that for a while," she remarked, resting her head on her hand, feeling satisfied all the way down to her toes.

"Bet I've waited longer."

"Bet not. How long?"

He tilted his head back, studying the ceiling while he considered it. "How long have I lived here?"

"Six years." But he knew that. Joe had a mental calendar that was more accurate than a computer. He remembered birthdates, anniversaries, dates of death, worry dates. If a friend told him she was having surgery six weeks from Tuesday, without making a note, he'd be calling her six weeks from Wednesday to see how it had gone. It was his superpower.

That, and curling her hair and her toes and everything in between.

"There you go. How long have you waited? Six days? Ding ding ding, I win."

Lucy kicked off her shoes, brought her knees up to her chest, and curled into the small space between the couch arm and Joe. "That doesn't make sense. That's the whole time you've lived here. You can't have been interested in me all that time."

"First person I introduced myself to?" he asked. "You. Only person whose dog I volunteered to walk and play with and spoil rotten? You. Whose house have I always spent more time at than my own? Yours. Who do I get up early to walk with every day? You. Who did I make nice with Noble for? You."

He curled a strand of her hair around his finger, then reached behind her and pulled the band out so her hair tumbled over his hand. "When we met, Luce, I thought you were gorgeous and funny and sweet and genuine and coming to Oklahoma was the best decision I'd ever made. But Mike hadn't been dead a year. You were still grieving. So I waited for you to show that you were ready to start dating again, and I waited and waited, and then you met Dr. Jerk."

The faint tone—Petulance? Envy?—in his voice made a smile tug at her mouth as warmth curled inside her like a ribbon in a storm. "Uh, calling him Dr. Jerk isn't exactly making nice with him."

Joe gestured carelessly. "He's in Georgia. I only have to be nice when he comes home. And Avi has to be with him."

Back early in the summer, Lucy had wondered why Joe and Ben had taken such an immediate dislike to each other. Separately, they were great, intelligent guys, but together it was ugly. She'd excused it on Ben's part as the situation he'd been thrust into with his mother's husband's death, and she'd thought Joe was just being petty and juvenile after Ben made it clear he didn't like football. Didn't she always say Joe was an overgrown kid?

Who kissed like a very experienced, very confident man.

Suddenly the lightbulb went on in her head. "You were jealous!" Delight twirled through her, wild and out of control, like a young ballerina who'd just discovered the joy of pirouetting.

He scowled. "Hell, yes, I was jealous. I'd been waiting all that time, and five minutes after meeting him, you were planning what schools your babies would go to. You went out on dates with him. You let him kiss you."

Warm and cozy in the glow of her discovery, she reminded him, "There wasn't any electricity."

His blue gaze narrowed. "What about now?" he asked.

Grinning, she slid closer until she could wrap her arms around him and brushed her mouth against his before

·

murmuring, "Come here, Sparky, then decide for yourself."

* * *

It was amazing how a few breath-stealing kisses could
change a woman's outlook on the world.

The bedside clock showed one minute until midnight,
the witching hour. Lucy was already bewitched and had
been all evening. She and Joe had talked, joked, and
watched TV just like every other time, as if nothing had
changed, but when he headed home, he'd given her another of his magical kisses that had set her whole body
to vibrating and made her skin ultra-sensitive to touch.
Even shifting against the sheets in her jammies made her
shiver.

Joe liked her. He really, really liked her. And she really, really liked him.

As she snuggled the extra pillow against her, a tear
rolled from the corner of her eye. Norton's ducky
squeaked as the dog moved in his sleep, and Sebastian
gave a tiny meow from the vicinity of the dog's armpit
before they both resettled. Lucy gazed at the nightstand,
where Mike's picture stood. It was too dark to see more
than a faint glimmer on the silver frame, but she'd spent
so many hours staring at it, crying over it, that she didn't
need to see it. The image was imprinted on her brain.

"I never dreamed I'd love someone who wasn't you,"
she whispered. "Even when we fought and I was so
mad at you I could spit, I knew it would pass because
I loved you too much to stay mad. And when you were
deployed on our first anniversary, and our second and

third, and on three of my birthdays, and then you forgot our fourth anniversary...

"I've been so lost since you left, Mike. I've got our families and the best friends I could ask for, but I need someone to love the way I loved you. Someone who will love me back the way you did." Her voice quavered and dropped until it was practically nothing. "I need someone to have babies with, Mike, and I think Joe's the guy. I've loved him for years—he's one of my best friends—but I think I *love* love him now. The magic is back."

In spite of the bittersweet ache that accompanied the brand-new hopefulness in her heart, she smiled. "You were my best friend, too, before I fell in love with you."

A yawn interrupted her thoughts and made her grin. Leave it to her to get sleepy in the middle of such an important conversation. She was just so sad, and so happy and so full of anticipation.

"You'll always have a piece of my heart, Mike. You'll always be my first love."

Please, God, let Joe be the last.

*   *   *

On Friday afternoon, Calvin reported to the animal shelter with Captain Kim and the other PTSD patients for the animal therapy program. They came three times a week, and he was finding it the best, easiest part of his days, except for spending time with Bennie. The dogs didn't ask questions or probe into painful memories. They couldn't care less what had gone in his past, as long as he was ready with the scratches, walks, play, and treats.

Today he was assigned to exercise duty. The dogs preferred to sleep most of the time they were in the yard so they needed the workout, Jessy explained, and they were easier to adopt when they were already leash-trained.

She was waiting when he went back into the kennel area, with two shepherds who were identical down to the black mask around their eyes and two Lab mixes, one black, the other yellow. "Are you ready?" she asked in greeting.

"I am." He'd run five miles on the treadmill in the gym that morning and still had a pretty good endorphin high going, but these days he never turned down a chance to get a little more exercise in. That would be routine for the rest of his life: antidepressant and anti-anxiety medications and activity. Every single day.

He could live with that.

He took the shepherds, Max and Sheila, and they headed out the front door to avoid setting off a mass escape from the play yard. The air was chilly, though Jessy hardly seemed to notice. She wore her usual uniform of cargo shorts, T-shirt, and heavy-duty sandals. He wore jeans and a T-shirt—soon to be *his* regular uniform—and was glad he'd grabbed a hoodie on the way out the door.

"How's Bennie?" Jessy asked as they headed toward First Street.

"I haven't seen her since Monday." He'd wanted to, but she had class on Tuesday and Thursday nights, and Wednesday night hadn't been his best evening. Got to expect that, his shrink team had warned him. Life would get better, but it would always be a two-steps-forward, one-step-back sort of thing. Wednesday night he'd felt like he'd slid back a thousand steps into a deep, dark abyss.

"She didn't make it to dinner Tuesday, but she usually

doesn't because of school," Jessy went on. "Everyone in town knows that the margarita club meets on Tuesdays, so those silly people at the college should rearrange their schedule to accommodate her."

"I bet everyone does know." From what he'd heard and seen, they weren't rude or obnoxious—just a little bit raucous. Whether it was in spite of their losses or because of them, they enjoyed the hell out of each other every chance they got.

He'd been that way once. He was going to be that way again.

"She's not a little girl anymore," Jessy said. When he gave her a puzzled look, she shrugged. "Bennie. I know you guys grew up together and were buddies all through school. But she's not a little girl anymore."

No, she damn sure isn't.

"I mean, she's fabulous and single, and you're hot-damn and single. You know how often something comes from that—old friends who meet again all grown up and realize they belong together?"

Max dragged his feet, trying to catch a glimpse of the dog barking behind the fence on their right. Calvin coaxed him forward again, then gave Jessy a knowing look. "It's something genetic, isn't it? Women and match-making. If you're alone, you're looking for a guy for yourself. If you've got a guy, you're looking for one for someone else."

Despite the two dogs who, between them, exceeded her own weight, she looked as if she were out for a meandering stroll. She held both leashes in one hand and fluttered the other at him carelessly. "I don't match-make. I just state the obvious. You two have a happy shared history. You have interests in common. You live in the same town. She adores your family, and I know you adore hers because I have met Mama Maudene, and anyone who doesn't adore her isn't friend worthy."

Calvin grinned. "Mama's something, isn't she?"

Jessy bobbed her head. "I've been an amateur photographer for years. I loved taking pictures of places, animals, things, but not people. Long story, too boring for now. But the first time I met Mama, I wanted so badly to spend forever taking pictures of her. She was just so self-assured and joyous at a time when I was a pathetic mess."

Translating to *when I was drinking*. And now Jessy was the self-assured one and Calvin was the pathetic mess. Was she passing on some of what she'd gotten from Mama? Would it be his obligation when he was well to pass it on to the next person who needed it?

They crossed First Street and continued at a decent pace to the west. A half-dozen blocks, a turn or two, and they could wind up at his house.

"Does Bennie know you're in the Warrior Transition Unit?" Jessy asked bluntly.

"No."

"Does she know you have post-traumatic stress disorder?"

"No." He didn't ask how she knew. When her bosses at the shelter had agreed to let a group of WTU soldiers work with their animals, surely Captain Kim had told them the diagnoses. It was only fair.

"I haven't told anyone, and I won't." Her expression turned wry. "Trust me, I know how to keep a secret."

"Thank you." He kept his gaze on the street, aware that the conversation wasn't over yet, not unless he said it was.

"One of the things that contributed to my drinking was guilt. My husband was all excited about coming home from Afghanistan, about buying a house and starting a family, and I... I'd discovered during his last deployment that I liked living alone. I still loved him, but not the right way. I intended to let him enjoy his homecoming, and then a few weeks, a few months later, I'd file for divorce."

He wished she'd been the only person in the entire Department of Defense who'd felt that way, but he'd known too many people who'd gone home to find their spouses gone, their possessions cleared out, their money all spent. He knew a bunch more who'd found their spouses and their marriages and themselves changed, and no matter how hard they tried, they just couldn't make things work anymore.

"A couple weeks before Aaron was scheduled to come home, he was killed," Jessy said. "I grieved horribly for him, but I felt like such a fraud because I'd wanted to be free of him. The guilt was as bad as the sorrow."

She stopped to pull a sticker from the yellow Lab's paw, then ran her fingers through the pads and crevices searching for another. From her crouched position, she said, "Anyway, my point is, I thought I was the only person in the world awful and disgusting enough to feel that way. All the margarita girls adored their husbands. They were all ideal wives and widows, and I was...damn. But when I finally told them about my drinking and how I'd felt about Aaron, they all understood, and one of them in particular had been in exactly the situation I was with my marriage. It was such a *freeing* experience to find out I wasn't alone.

"You aren't alone, either, Calvin."

He let that thought rattle around in his brain while they covered the few yards to where the street made a sharp turn to the left. They didn't follow it but instead circled around and headed back east.

He wasn't alone. Logically he knew that. Hundreds of thousands of troops had PTSD. Some degree of it was more common than not.

He wasn't the only one to attempt suicide, either. More than twenty service members succeeded at killing themselves *every day*. He wasn't the only one to find himself in such hopelessness and despair, but he'd been given another chance.

If he could just let go of the shame and the fear and the self-loathing.

One day at a time. Right now the good days were outnumbering the bad days, which ironically made the bad days even worse. When he'd lived in a constant state of misery, he'd become accustomed to it. Hell, he hadn't even been able to remember what good days were supposed to be like. Now, when the bad days came, they hit hard because he not only remembered what life was like before, but was starting to feel that way again. He was seeing improvement, finding reasons to live, climbing his way out of the darkness, and *bam*, there it was again.

"You can tell me to mind my own damn business," Jessy said. "It won't hurt my feelings."

He believed her.

He also believed that if she cared for someone, their business *was* her business. She wasn't the sort to stand back with her mouth shut when a friend needed her.

And she *was* a friend. The thought made him smile. Who would have imagined that his first new friend in

Tallgrass would be a tiny redheaded white girl from the South?

Deliberately he changed the subject. "Why did you stay in Tallgrass after your husband's death?"

She kicked an acorn that skittered along the street before tumbling into the ditch. "I like the Army community, and I didn't have anywhere else to go. I was never the daughter my parents wanted, so I left home as soon as I graduated high school. They didn't acknowledge my wedding. Didn't acknowledge Aaron's death. So I don't acknowledge them."

"I'm sorry."

Her grin was bright and quick. "Don't be. Dalton's parents and brothers love me, and he adores me. Plus, I've got my margarita dolls." She shook one finger at him. "You can never have too many people who love you."

The conversation for the rest of their walk was a whole lot lighter and came a whole lot easier for Calvin. They traded the four dogs for four more and took a different route. After a third walk—this time Jessy gave him the leads to two prissy little dogs who couldn't have weighed more than twelve pounds each while she took two of the biggest dogs he'd ever seen—he helped Angela clean the yard, then finished out his time with a Jack Russell mix who was still in her socializing phase. The dog didn't know whether to snap and snarl or quiver in the corner hunkered down for a beating.

I don't know anything about socialization, he'd told Meredith, and the vet had laughed.

Sure, you do. You're pretty well socialized yourself. Then she'd explained that all she wanted him to do was be with the dog. Sit in the small room with her and talk to her. No loud noises, no physical contact unless she initiated it. Watch his fingers and toes. Oh, and figure out a name for her.

That last part had been easy enough. In her bold, aggressive state, the dog reminded him of Bennie when they were kids. Her world might have been turned upside down, but she'd never let it show, and she'd landed on her feet, spirit intact. Hoping the dog would have the same good luck, he named her Nita.

When he told the staff her new name, Jessy grinned knowingly as she made a note of it for Nita's kennel. He was on his way out the door for the ride back to the post when he stopped beside Jessy. "You, uh, wouldn't happen to have…"

"Bennie's cell phone number?" She flipped through her phone, then scrawled it on a piece of paper, pressed it into his palm, then squeezed his hand. "Think about what we discussed. You should tell her, Calvin. You should trust her." Her grin grew even bigger. "And don't forget to have fun. You *gotta* have fun."

He wouldn't even think about the telling-trusting part right now, but Jessy was right about one thing: He did need some fun, and he couldn't think of anyone he was more likely to have it with than Bennie.

* * *

Bennie didn't often take an entire evening off to do nothing, and she rarely did it twice in one week. Between work and school and now the holidays coming up, it seemed she needed every minute and then some just to get the essentials done. But when she'd got home from her shift at the hospital, she'd brewed herself a cup of amazing Kenyan coffee—Mama's latest online find—and curled up in the porch swing to watch the sunset and debate the best use of a free Friday evening. Did she want to call one of the girls and go out to celebrate? Get a dose of maternal feelings by offering to babysit John and let Ilena go out and have some fun? Stay right here on the porch swing until the chill chased her outside, or maybe go to bed early? She could always use more sleep.

The screen door creaked as Mama stepped outside, a quilt in her arms. "I was cold, so I figured you could use this." She spread the cover over Bennie, her gnarled fingers smoothing and tucking. "Can I get you another cup of coffee?"

"I can get it."

"Of course you can, but you're already cozy there. Stay. I'll be back in a minute."

Snuggling into the quilt, Bennie breathed deeply. It smelled of fabric softener and detergent, age and love. Mama's grandmother had made the blanket as a wedding gift for her oldest daughter, who'd given it to her first daughter. Technically, it belonged to Bennie now, though it resided at the foot of Mama's bed and would until she passed.

Would its history end with Bennie? If she didn't have any daughters of her own, who would claim it when she passed?

Some cousin somewhere would take it and love it. It wasn't the same as passing it to her own little girl, but it was something.

In her pocket, her cell phone began to ring, the closest thing to an old-fashioned *ring-ring* she could find. She fished it out, glancing at the screen, and a wide smile curved across her face as she greeted, "Hey, Squeaky."

"Don't make me dig up some of your old nicknames," Calvin said.

"I didn't have nicknames. I was above that."

"Yeah, but J'Myel and I weren't, Shorty."

Shorty was probably the most flattering of the names they'd given her, but she'd answered to every one of them. Sometimes with a fist to the nose.

"Are you busy?"

"I'm watching the sun set."

"Unless the earth curves sharply between here and there, it's already set."

"Yes, but the colors in the sky are still beautiful." At the creak of the screen door, she said, "Hold on a minute."

Mama came out, balancing a mug of steaming coffee carefully. She set it on the wood table beside the swing, then said, "Tell Calvin hello for me."

"How do you know it's Calvin?" Bennie asked.

"Because those two boys are the only ones ever made you smile like that. Don't stay out here too long. You don't want to catch a chill."

"Thanks for the coffee, Mama." Bennie warmed her fingers on the mug before tucking her hand beneath the quilt again. "Did you hear Mama's hello?"

"Yeah." A teasing note entered his voice. "She's right, you know. We could always make you smile."

"Because you were both such clowns. How was your week?"

He was silent a moment, as if seriously considering the question. "It was okay. Not bad. How was yours?"

"Always busy. One of my regular patients died this week."

Another silence, followed by, "I'm sorry."

"She was ready to go. She'd been terminal a long time. She told me that her affairs were in order, things were right between her and her family and between her and God, and she really wanted to spend this Christmas in heaven with her husband." J'Myel's first holiday in heaven had been Christmas, too, reuniting with his grandparents and all his buddies, his mama had said; cracking up Saint Peter and Saint Gabriel with his jokes; and adding his off-key voice to the carols.

Golda had wept at the thought, and now unbidden tears filled Bennie's eyes. She cleared her throat and hoped she didn't sound sobby. "I've seen a lot of people die, but never anyone as serene and peaceful as Mrs. Wagoner. That's a gift, you know. To be at peace with death."

Swiping her eyes, she abruptly changed the subject. She'd forgotten for a moment that Calvin had seen too much death to discuss it casually. "So what is it you do these days? Job-wise, I mean."

"I save the world."

The memory of him and J'Myel leaving for basic, chests puffed out like superheroes, made her laugh. "Uh-huh."

"Seriously. I keep mankind safe from itself." Then he chuckled. "Well, that, plus I spend a lot of time scratching Sarge's belly."

Bennie choked in the act of sipping her coffee. Once her sputtering was under control, she said, "I hear that keeping the people who work for you happy is important, but isn't that taking it a little too far?"

"He doesn't mind. Throw in a cookie, and he'll be your best bud for life."

"So the Army's accepting some real dogs these days."

"Hey, Sarge has earned every one of his stripes."

The last of the muted purples and blues in the western sky faded into the inky night. Bennie's cheeks were cold, but thanks to the quilt and the coffee—and the pleasure of talking to Calvin—she was snuggly warm. It was a lovely thing, feeling the chill air, smelling the autumn leaves and wood smoke, surrounded by the quiet night, and hearing Calvin's voice. It was like all was right with her world.

Lights glimmered down the street, marking the houses of neighbors she'd known most of her life. When her gaze picked out the Sweet house, she said, "I saw Diez with Gran yesterday. They were walking and picking up pinecones."

"Aw, man, I hope she's not planning some craft project for Thanksgiving."

Gran's crafting skills were as legendary as her cooking. The problem was she'd given up cooking years ago. She kept doing the crafts. "You know Emmeline. She's probably going to build a turkey centerpiece out of pinecones."

"And light it with candles, like that wreath she hung on her front door when we were in middle school."

"It only took about fifteen minutes to put the fire out," Bennie protested. "And while it was burning, it looked pretty spectacular."

He snorted. "I had to paint that door five times to cover all the scorch marks."

"Better you than me. She still gets a wicked smile when she tells that story." Bennie shifted on the swing.

Her front side was still all warm, but the wooden slats of the seat were letting cold air in to her backside. She should dash inside, grab another quilt, and wrap herself up like a pig in a blanket to trap the heat.

Instead, she asked, "Have your parents decided what they're going to do about Diez?"

She swore she heard Calvin's shrug through the phone. "Mom says the kid's never had a traditional Thanksgiving, so they're going to decide after that. Of course, then they'll need to wait a little longer because he's never had much of a Christmas. I think they want to keep him."

The news didn't surprise her. Elizabeth and Justice had always had enough love for a dozen kids, and they couldn't help needing someone who needed them back as desperately as Diez did. They could make a tremendous difference in the boy's life if the courts would allow them... or they could be setting themselves up for heartbreak.

"How do you feel about that?" Bennie still recalled Calvin's outburst the day Diez had shown up. She'd never seen him get so angry so fast. It had surprised her and made her way too curious about how he and Diez had met.

"When did you get all touchy-feely?" he asked, his tone all but shouting *evasive technique* in spite of its lightness.

"I am the *queen* of touchy-feeliness," she retorted, then waited. She was also the queen of wait-him-out. It had been rare that she couldn't get an answer from either of the boys simply by being patient.

She hadn't lost her touch. After a moment, Calvin sighed. "He could use a good home. And Mom and Gran could use a project."

"Ha! You were always more than enough of a project for them."

"Yes, but I'm grown up now. I don't need to be anyone's project."

There was a tone to his voice, Bennie reflected, something...not bitter. Not resentful. Maybe regretful. Of course he had regrets. They all did. But his seemed *more* regretful. More hurtful. More difficult for her to grasp because he'd always been strong and capable and confident. What had happened to him during those four combat tours?

She didn't want to know. Didn't want ugly images and ugly feelings in her head. She knew war was hell, and that was enough for her. With sincere apologies to Calvin, J'Myel, Justin and Dane and Keegan and Avi and every other service member, she didn't want to know details.

What if J'Myel had survived and needed to share details? What if Calvin needed to share details?

She was Maudene Pickering's granddaughter: also strong and capable and confident. She could do whatever needed doing. If Calvin needed to talk, she could listen. If he needed to share, she could shoulder part of his burden. If he needed to cry, it would break her heart, but she would hold him as long as it lasted. That was what women did for the people they loved.

And whatever was between her and Calvin now, friendship or more—*more*, her little voice voted—she had definitely, always, deeply loved him.

Forcing lightness into her voice, she said, "I have a project of my own tonight, Squeaky, that involves getting out of the cold and having something fabulous to eat. You want to join me?"

When he didn't answer immediately, she went on. "Hey, I'm the easiest date ever. You don't even have to invite me. Are you interested?"

For half a minute, she feared he would turn her down. Then the tenor of the silence changed, his smile carrying through his voice. "I'll be there in fifteen minutes, Shorty."

* * *

Tallgrass, like most military towns, had a glut of restaurants, ranging from fast-food to sit-down-with-linens, from national chains to mom-and-pop one-of-a-kinds. There was Korean, Thai, Chinese, and Japanese; German, Italian, Greek, and an authentic British pub; at least one Mexican place every couple blocks; steak places and chicken places and barbecue places and vegan places.

When Calvin asked Bennie to pick, she'd done so without hemming or hawing. "Sweet Baby Greens."

"Is that some kind of salad place?"

"No. It's the kind of restaurant Mama and Gran would open if they didn't fuss each other to death first, and if Gran knew how to cook. Remember the soul food place we used to go to?"

He nodded. The sign had called it soul food. He'd thought of it as comfort food.

"The old lady who ran it died a few years ago, and it closed down because her daughters didn't want to take it over. Her granddaughter Melia lived in Tulsa, and she kept entering dishes in soul food cooking contests, and she kept winning, so she decided to give it a shot."

"Is it in the same location?"

"No, she moved a mile and a half south of town on First. You can't miss the sign. It's a longer drive, but there's plenty of parking."

Calvin smiled. When they were kids, always starving, nothing had seemed worse than having to walk six or eight blocks to the old soul food restaurant downtown... except the same walk back to the cars when their bellies were stuffed to bursting.

Shifting in the seat opposite him, Bennie gave him a measuring look by the dashboard light. "You ever get serious about anyone while you were gone, Calvin?"

"I dated."

"Not what I asked."

"Well, I didn't go off and get married, did I?"

If she noticed the edge to his voice, she didn't let it show. "But there must have been someone special in all that time. Some pretty girl must have caught your eye." She swatted his arm playfully.

"Yeah, there were a couple. Never serious enough to write home about."

"What were they like?"

You. The answer surprised him as much as it would have surprised her if he'd actually said it aloud. But with twenty-twenty hindsight, it was true: in personality, character, mood, the ability to laugh and make him laugh, they'd shared a lot in common with Bennie, including the blond-haired, blue-eyed French lit major who should have fallen on the far opposite side of the spectrum from her.

"They were nice women." Damn, that sounded lame. "We had good times. But they weren't..." *You.* "They weren't, you know, *the one*."

A large neon sign ahead, looking as if the wearing o' the green for St. Patrick's Day had come early, caught his attention. Bennie had told him he couldn't miss it.

"What kind of name is Sweet Baby Greens for a restaurant?" he asked as he turned into the big parking lot.

"A cute one. They do serve greens—it's not soul food without them—and Melia's last name is Green, and her baby girl has the prettiest green eyes you ever saw."

He chose a parking space on the last row where the nearest car was thirty feet away. "Don't want anyone to ding my ride," he said as he opened the door for Bennie. She slid to her feet, tucked the seat belt with its broken retractor back inside, smoothed a piece of duct tape on the passenger window, then cringed as she carefully closed the door.

"Point made," he acceded. "Silently, but made."

She beamed at him. "One day you're going to meet a gorgeous woman and ask her out, and she's going to take one look at that POS and run the other way."

"I wouldn't date a woman who'd run the other way. If she cares that much about my car, what's the point?" He wasn't sure what made him say the next part; the words seemed to come from some part of his brain he had little control over. "Besides, you're a gorgeous woman, and you're not running away."

For one brief moment, he'd left her speechless, and it was impossible to tell in the dim light, but he thought she might have blushed just a little. Her only response, though, was to punch his arm before starting across the lot.

There was no particular style to Sweet Baby Greens: booths, tables, counters. Colors matching and clashing.

Some seats older than him, some so brand new he could still smell the vinyl beneath the aromas coming from every part of the dining room. There were long picnic tables down the center of the room, shared by families, friends, and strangers. His gut twinged a moment at the thought of sitting there, people passing behind him, leaning around him, but it eased when the host, a none-too-cheerful elderly man, led them to a booth at the back.

"You keep frowning like that, Mr. Arnold, your face is going to freeze that way," Bennie said as she slipped off her coat before sliding onto the bench.

"What frown?" Arnold asked, intentionally looking grumpier. "This is my best smile that's reserved for the prettiest girls."

His grimace looked a lot like the closest Calvin had gotten to a smile for a lot of months. But the old man proved he was able to laugh by doing so as soon as his last words were out. Back then, it would have killed Calvin if he'd tried.

"Mr. Arnold is Melia's grandfather," Bennie said after he left them to study the menus, twisting to look around the room. "That's her over there, in the red. Isn't she stunning?"

Calvin found the woman in red: tall, willowy, a pair of legs that went on forever, and heels that defied good sense; black hair, golden-shaded bronzed skin, an exotic tilt to her dark eyes. She chatted with guests while holding a wriggly little girl with the same warm skin, curly dark blond hair, and green eyes. Daughter was adorable, and mom was stunning, but she didn't take his breath away. She didn't make his hand tremble at the thought of touching her. She wouldn't inspire in him dreams of touching and kissing and a lot more.

Bennie did.

Bennie, his ex–best friend.

His other ex–best friend's widow.

Was this how J'Myel had felt when he'd realized after that leave home that he was falling for their buddy? It was damn sure how Calvin had felt when he'd heard about it, like it couldn't be real. It was like falling for your cousin. Cousins could be really close and know everything about each other and the best friends ever, but there wasn't supposed to be any romance between them.

But he'd had time since then to think of Bennie not as their buddy, not as a friend close enough to be family, but as a woman. There was a lot between them, both good and bad, but being blood relations wasn't part of it. She was just a beautiful, tender-hearted woman whose laugh made him happy and whose smile gave him hope. A man could forget how important those things were.

And a woman who didn't have a clue what he was doing here in Tallgrass. That he had "issues." That the Army didn't want him anymore. That while so many people had fought to live, including her husband, he'd chosen, like a weak-spined coward, to die. The families of every single combat casualty would be thrilled to have their loved one back, and Calvin had disrespected every one of them by trying to kill himself.

Tell her, Jessy had said. *Trust her.*

How could he? He couldn't discuss it with his own family. It was difficult, but they were waiting until he was ready to discuss it with them. Bennie wouldn't wait.

When she wanted answers, she would get them one way or another, whether she had to sit in silence and wear down his resistance like water dripping relentlessly on a rock or pestered him until telling her was the only way to maintain his sanity.

She would want every detail, and it would change the way she looked at him. It would change the way she felt about him. Friendship and affection would become disappointment, pity, fear. Maybe loathing.

He wasn't strong enough to bear that. Not yet.

"Yoohoo." Slender fingers waved in front of his eyes, pulling him from his thoughts. Bennie was looking at him, the menu open in her free hand. "My stomach's starting to growl in anticipation of all the wonderful choices to make, and you're off in Calvin's World. Food now. Mind wandering later."

He forced his attention to the menu. Reading it created visual images of every holiday Gran's family had ever shared. There were a few attempts at healthy offerings, but seriously, what were green beans without ham shanks and bacon fat? Fried chicken meant *fried*, not baked until crispy in the oven, and gravy without drippin's was just paste.

They both ordered, then she asked, "Where is Thanksgiving this year?"

"Auntie Mae's. What about you?"

"Our house. Mama doesn't like to travel, so Aunt Cheryl and Uncle Roland bring their families here. Poor Diez...he's in for an experience."

"He grew up with two brothers, two sisters, an unfit mother, and various men coming in and out. I think he's used to chaos."

"Yes, but loving chaos, where he gets to be treated like the kid he is...that'll be new for him."

All of Calvin's aunties and the older female cousins would fawn over Diez, feeding him, pampering him, pinching his cheeks until they hurt. The uncles and older male cousins would draw him into the no-holds-barred football game after dinner, and if there were girls his own age, he was in for a hell of a lot of fluttering eyelashes.

Just the thought of all that fun made Calvin grin.

That would teach the kid to run away from home and join Calvin's family.

Chapter 13

"Does ol' Harley still keep a bull in the pasture here?"

Hunger sated and feeling content, Bennie gazed across Calvin to the field they were passing. "He does. A big ol' black-and-white one that looks like an Oreo cookie. I can't remember its breed, but Jessy'll know. Dalton raises them on his ranch."

"Remember when we told you the pasture was empty and bet we could outrun you to the fence on the other side?"

She swatted his arm. "You were even so kind as to give me a head start."

"We didn't know that (a) you could run so fast, or (b) that in a few years the track and field coaches would be recruiting you for the long jump." Calvin chuckled. "Instead of being pissed or scared, you climbed on the fence to do a victory dance."

"When you've outrun charging bulls, victory dances are most definitely required." She sighed as she turned her head to watch the old Ford house pass. "Before I came here, I was the best behaved kid. Seriously. Daddy was going through a tough time, with my mother leaving and him trying to work and go to school and doing the single-parent thing. I made myself as helpful and as less a chore as I possibly could. Then I came here, and..."

"And Mama didn't need your help. She had that whole single-parent thing down pat. She just wanted you to be a kid."

She did, Bennie thought with an affectionate smile. "Even if that meant hauling my butt out of trouble—and spanking it half the time."

Calvin slowed to pass the Sweet house. Only a porch light was on at Gran's, while the living room and kitchen lights were on in his folks' house. "Gran's in bed early," Bennie remarked. She and Calvin had stayed at Sweet Baby Greens until the staff began cleaning around them. Still, ten thirty was a late bedtime for Mama and a few hours early for Gran.

"She stays later at the house these days. She and Diez watch movies, play poker, whatever, then he walks her home when she's ready to go."

The tires crunched a few acorns that had fallen onto the pavement, then Calvin was turning into her driveway. Mama had left two porch lights on, plus the lamp beside her recliner in the living room and probably the light over the kitchen sink. She wasn't scared of the dark, but she sure didn't want her granddaughter walking into an un-welcoming house.

"Want to come in? Mama has an amazing collection of gourmet coffees from around the world."

Calvin shifted into park, the dash lights casting shadows across his face. "Mama, who couldn't start her day without two cups of Maxwell House coffee?"

"What can I say? The Internet has expanded her horizons." Bennie waited, her breath caught just a little in her chest. She wasn't quite ready to say good night to him. She didn't even know why. He wasn't home on leave. This wasn't a quick visit on his way to someplace else. The Army had assigned him here, and he would be here tomorrow and next week and next year. She could thank him for dinner tonight and spend more time with him tomorrow.

Or lure him inside tonight. Or both.

"Does she still sleep like a rock?"

"It's like all switches are off. She doesn't hear anything, see anything, feel anything."

"Then coffee sounds good."

Whew. Relief. Bennie climbed out and closed the door as carefully as she had at the restaurant. She half expected parts to fall off it the moment she exerted any real force on it, and Calvin would never let her forget that she'd damaged his ride.

Just like she would never let him forget that it was a public health nuisance and should be put out of its misery immediately.

They went inside quietly. She kicked off her shoes and went barefoot into the kitchen, flipping on the overhead light and taking three large metal baskets from the countertop. "They're divided by continent," she said quietly. "Central and South America are what we typically associate with coffee, the African beans are a little more exotic, and the Asian beans have the most complex flavors."

"I'll try something Asian." Calvin stepped back to glance around the room. "Nothing's changed in here."

Bennie selected an African blend for herself, then measured water from a bottle in the fridge to pour into the machine. "Uh, yeah, one thing has. She traded her black dishwasher for a stainless one."

His brow wrinkled. "I don't remember her having a black dishwasher—" At the appearance of her grin, he rolled his eyes. "Yeah, that old model used to whine a lot."

After a moment, a heavenly rich flavor began rising from the coffeemaker. "'The best part of waking up,'" Calvin sang off-tune.

"That's Gran's Folgers. And Maxwell House was always—"

"'Good to the last drop,'" they said in unison before laughing, then abruptly shushing themselves.

Bennie didn't know what prompted her. Maybe it was all the memories she and Calvin shared. Maybe it was something about the complications between them that wanted to be made simple. Maybe it was nothing more than the fact that it was Friday and she was on a date and the hunger in her belly had been satisfied and she was feeling more like her old self than she had in a very long while.

Whatever the reason, when she turned to get the sugar and found herself standing only a few tiny inches from Calvin, she just naturally closed that distance and lifted her mouth to his.

She kissed him. Oh, God, she was *kissing* him, and he was kissing her back. Never in her whole life had she even imagined locking lips with her best old bud. Never in her whole life could she have imagined it would feel so incredibly right. Perfect. As if nothing stood between them—no past, no disagreements, no J'Myel. As if they existed, had always existed, only for this moment.

Calvin laid his hands on her shoulders, his fingers kneading for a moment before settling firmly, lifting his head, and pushing her back a few inches. His gaze was shadowed, troubled. "You can't...I shouldn't..." Briefly he squeezed his eyes shut, his mouth thinning in frustration, then he looked at her again just for the time it took to bring his mouth to hers.

Bennie had had too many kisses to wax poetic about them. She'd dated one guy whose kisses had been legendary, the sort she wanted to get lost in for hours, but turned out, they were all he brought to the game. She'd known guys who'd mastered the skills of lovemaking, but their kisses were as exciting as watching paint dry. Most of the men she'd known were squarely in the middle: kisses so-so to good, sex so-so to good, attention to foreplay so-so to middlin'.

But these kisses from Calvin...they were sweet and greedy and made her feel like the only person in his universe, like her pleasure was at least as important as his. He understood a kiss was just a kiss but knew it could also be the reason for a person's entire existence.

A sound came from behind her, almost like the *whisk-whisk* of Mama's house slippers on the wood floors, but Mama waking up in the middle of the night was about as likely as a total eclipse of the moon on the thirty-first of November. Probably it was just the hiss of water as the last of it drained from the coffeemaker.

Bennie smiled when the kiss ended. She wrapped her arms around Calvin's neck and rested her cheek gently against his chest. His heart thudded, strong and steady.

It took him a moment to mentally recover, she suspected, from the fact that he'd kissed J'Myel's wife—and he would think wife rather than widow. He was funny that way. And though she would always be J'Myel's widow, though she would always love him, was it selfish of her that right now she didn't want to be anything but Bennie, a woman whose heart was free and whose life needed filling?

Not selfish, she decided. Normal. Natural. She couldn't grieve forever. Nobody expected that of her, including herself.

Coffee and cologne, both hers and his, scented the air she breathed as very slowly, he brought his arms around her. Not tightly, not the sort of embrace she missed like crazy, but he held her, and for now that was enough. Would he enjoy the good feelings for a moment, then pretend it had never happened—yeah, like she'd let him do that—or worse, that it had been a mistake?

She would snatch his hair from his scalp if he did.

The embrace slowly, naturally, fell away. She set the two mugs of coffee in front of him, next to sugar and creamer, then began fixing hers to taste. He silently followed suit.

"Are you hungry?" she asked. They'd eaten like bears preparing for hibernation, but that meant nothing. Their parents had called them the bottomless pit and the hollow leg because of the enormous amounts of food they could put away. Besides, Calvin had been on the peaked side when he returned. He had a few pounds to go to get back to fighting weight.

"I could eat," he allowed.

She grabbed a cookie jar in the shape of a teapot, a

couple of napkins, and her coffee and led the way into the living room. After emptying her load on the coffee table, she sat at one end of the couch, turning to face him at the other. Giving him a chance to ignore what had happened wasn't an option, so she carefully sipped her coffee, then remarked, "Nice kiss."

His hand trembled just a bit as he lifted his own coffee. The shadows were back in his eyes, but they faded before taking up permanent residence. "You've gotten some practice since you were fifteen and trying to kiss around your braces."

"So have you. I believe after the first time you kissed Mary Watashe, she said never again, not even if you paid her."

He snorted. "Kissing her was like kissing an evil life-force-sucking monster."

"I've heard that. She moved away after high school." Bennie casually added, "Last I heard, she was a lip model for some cosmetics company."

That made his eyes pop, as she'd known it would. "A *lip* model? You mean, people pay to take pictures of her mouth?"

"Scary thought, isn't it?" She gestured. "How's your coffee?"

"Good. But it's more like the good-you-should-take-the-time-to-savor-it than the it's-morning-I-need-caffeine sort." He took a cookie from the jar, the scents of raisins and oatmeal wafting between them, took a bite, then tilted his head to one side and studied her.

Serious talk ahead? she wondered. Or memories he didn't want to discuss?

She'd been right the first time.

"How did you and J'Myel end up together? When we left home, you were still our best bud, the younger sister neither of us had, and then one day, I heard you and him hooked up."

Was she imagining that extra emphasis on *heard*, to remind her that she'd never told him they were dating, or was that her own guilt? She'd wanted to tell him, but by then it was impossible to discuss one with the other, and she'd felt sad and conflicted and disloyal. As her boyfriend, J'Myel had claimed, her first priority was him, but she'd been friends with Calvin every bit as long and maybe a little bit better.

She tucked her feet on the seat, wishing she'd built a fire to chase away the chill inside her. But the room would have overheated too quickly, and external temperature had nothing to do with the shame she'd felt so long for the way she'd let Calvin down.

"He'd come home on leave," she began slowly. "He'd just finished a tour in Helmand Province, and he'd been happy to get away from the war and the Army and to have no worries beyond having fun, chilling out, drinking a lot of cold beer, and kissing some pretty women."

"And the first one he kissed was you, and after that there weren't any others."

She shrugged with a tight smile. "I never did learn to share graciously." After another sip of coffee, she wrapped her fingers around the cup. "He was the same J'Myel he'd always been, just grown-up. All those years I thought I was immune to his charm, but his first night here, he looked at me with those brown eyes and that ear-to-ear grin of his, and I…"

She'd done what girls had always done with J'Myel:

fallen hard and fast. It was never permanent; he always moved on before the girls could start bringing up marriage and babies, and she'd known that. She hadn't been totally sure it was permanent for her, either. She wasn't about to let him break her heart, not until he showed some serious commitment. That was why it had taken them three years to get married.

"We spent as much of his leave together as we could. He was stationed at Fort Irwin, and we flew back and forth for long weekends. It was all kind of surreal. I never, ever dreamed I'd grow up and fall in love with the mouthy kid I'd pushed around all those years, but it happened. We got married, had a sweet honeymoon, then went back to living apart. He was deploying again soon after, so we never actually lived together." She stared into her coffee, remembering the last time she'd spent with him. He'd talked about the future, coming home again, getting out of the Army, finally living as a couple and doing all the things couples did, like sleep in the same bed every night.

Neither of them had had a clue that it *was* the last time they'd spend together.

What would the future have held for them? she wondered wistfully. Would he have been happy living the rest of his days in Tallgrass, or had he wanted to move away, like Calvin said? If he'd chosen to leave for good, would she have gone with him? Would she have left Mama here to pass her final years alone?

Would she and J'Myel have loved each other forever?

No one was guaranteed forever. With the divorce rate somewhere around fifty percent, though, she liked to think they would have been one of the lucky couples whose marriage succeeded.

Shifting her cup to one hand, she rested her other arm on the back of the couch and twirled one of her curls around her index finger. "Any more questions?"

"Just one." He hesitated before meeting her gaze. "Did you ever dream you might grow up and...get involved with me?"

She'd said *fall in love with*, not *get involved*. His change of words made her smile faintly. She stretched out her hand to touch his, also resting on the back of the sofa, and gave it a gentle squeeze. "Life is a wonderful surprise, isn't it?"

* * *

"I need a magic wand."

It was Saturday evening, Lucy's bake orders for the following day had doubled from the week before, and she and Joe were now facing a mountain of dishes to wash. Even though she'd cleaned as they went along—mostly—the time constraints and lack of help besides Joe's had combined to overwhelm her. Add aching feet, legs, back, and one shoulder, and she was pooped.

"I have a magic wand." The response came from Joe, teasing and lascivious and naughty, and it made her stop for a moment and just look at him. Not a lot had changed since their big kisses last Monday night. He still got her up at dawn to walk; he still showed up at her house soon after she got home from work; he still lifted, carried, and pitched in without complaints; and he still ate most of his meals with her. But now he touched her, and not the old arm punches or chokeholds they'd been used to. Sometimes he curled his arm around her when they were sitting close enough, and there were times when he held her hand just because. And he was as generous with his kisses as he was with everything else.

Happy mercy, *everything* had changed, and it made her feel fifteen years younger and like she was falling in love for the first time. *You sound giddy,* her mom had said when they had their weekly chat a few days ago, and Lucy's response in the privacy of her bedroom was to pump her fist and silently shriek, *I am!* Who could be blessed with the miracle of a second love and not get giddy about it?

He walked around the huge worktable and pressed a kiss to her forehead. Nearly a week, and it still shivered through her. "Is any of the debris in the dining room maybe hiding a chair?"

"Nope. Just garbage the construction workers didn't haul off."

Joe held up one finger, signaling her to wait, then disappeared through the store room and outside. It took him a few minutes to return, a lawn chair under one arm. He unfolded it in a corner out of the way, gave her a bottle of water from the fridge, a protein bar from his hip pocket, and gestured as if it were a throne.

"Why do you carry a lawn chair in your trunk?"

"I'm a coach. I never know when I'll need to sit down."

"You're a coach. You don't *get* to sit down." She pressed her hands to the small of her back. "Joe, I can't sit here and be lazy while you do all the cleanup." Even as she was protesting, he lowered her into the chair, pulled out a box to support her feet, and tore open the protein wrapper for her.

"I'm just tired," she went on. "Coming down here every night, working all afternoon and evening today, still walking twice a day, and going to work..." She took a bite of the protein bar, and her eyebrows rose. "Hey, that's pretty good. I bet I could learn to make this."

Shaking his head and grinning, he turned to the sinks. He'd already started the dishwashers, but there was plenty to wash by hand. Then the table had to be cleaned—she couldn't even reach the middle of it to scrub—and then they had dozens of sweets in the cake refrigerator waiting to be snuggled into their wrappers or boxes. A couple more hours, she could go home, beg off the evening walk, take some Motrin, and dislodge Norton and Sebastian from the couch so she could lie there and recuperate. Possibly until work called Monday morning. Preferably with Joe at her side.

She polished off the protein bar, drank half the water in one swallow, and breathed heavily. She was recovering her second wind. Sliding to the edge of the seat, she braced her hands on the arms and started to push up. A stab of pain through her right shoulder made her gasp and sink back down.

"What's wrong?" Joe asked.

Gingerly she rubbed her shoulder. "I think I overdid it trying to prove that I could whip cream without a mixer. Just give me a minute, though, and I'll help you."

He gave her a long look before dipping his hands back into the soapy water. "Do you know how much my mom would pay to see me washing dishes all on my own, without anyone twisting my arm? This is a rare sight here, Luce. You might even want to take a picture for posterity."

Trust him to make her laugh even when she felt like crap. Pulling out her cell, she snapped a couple of shots, and then, since watching him do anything was pretty much a pleasure, she tried to resettle in the chair, though the ache in her back just wouldn't let her get comfortable. Lord, was she so feeble that she couldn't handle long hours in the shop? Her feet hurt, her neck was stiff, her shoulder throbbed, her back hurt. She had gotten so disgustingly out of shape over the last seven years. Instead of canceling tonight's walk, maybe she should ask Joe to double it, and she should probably give in to his regular requests that she work out at the gym with him. Rock-hard muscles looked fine on him, she'd told him, but she liked being soft. She didn't want to look ripped.

"So soft that you can't even bake eight dozen cookies and a few trays of muffins and rolls without wearing out," she muttered beneath her breath.

Voices at the back door startled her into looking that way, and when Patricia, Marti, and Carly walked into the kitchen, Lucy's brows arched high. "What are you guys doing—" Dismay turned her toward Joe. "You asked them to come clean up after me?"

Patricia tucked her purse out of the way, then hugged Lucy. "We've all offered repeatedly. Joe just took us up on it. You feeling okay?"

"Yeah, I'm fine. Just tired."

Watching them, Lucy did a mental scan of her symptoms. Shoulder—better. Back—still aching. Feet—thoroughly protesting the remaining extra pounds on her body. Neck—stiff, but she'd endured worse. Chest—not hurting exactly, just kind of fluttering in disapproval at the rest of her. Oh, and a bit of a burn right in the middle of her breastbone, like the beginning of a case of heartburn. Everything else checked out fi—

Chest? When did her chest get involved in this? She grabbed at the likeliest explanation: heartburn, too much hot salsa at lunch, topped off with tastings of too much ultra-rich frosting. That was all it was. All it could possibly be.

"What are we doing here?" Marti asked as she circled to the sink with Carly on her heels.

Lucy heard Joe running through the list of chores but only distantly. Her skin had grown clammy, and her heart was thundering, as if it were trying to escape her body. She didn't blame it. She'd want out, too, if all her other systems were going haywire.

Nona's voice—the grandmother who'd always looked out for her favorite granddaughter—spoke sternly in her head. *You're having a heart attack, child. Go to the hospital.*

A *heart attack*? That wasn't possible. Heart attacks were for elderly people, frail people, people who'd already lived full lives and had health issues. She was only thirty-four. Other than her blood sugar and cholesterol being a little high, and her weight being more than a little high, she was in good health. Despite her own minor problems, she had no family history of heart disease. She was active. She was *young*. She had years to go before she could conceivably have a heart attack.

But deep inside she knew it was true. She'd had acid indigestion before that could have eaten through cast iron, and it had felt nothing like this. She'd suffered panic attacks before, too, in the months following Mike's death, and they'd been nothing like this. She'd had her heart *broken* before, shattered into tiny pieces that had never fit back together right. Not. Like. This.

But what if she was just overreacting? After all, she was listening to her dead Nona's voice. And there was no rule that said every case of indigestion, every panic attack, had to feel exactly the same way. Maybe she was just trying to do too much. Maybe subconsciously she was more worried about this business venture than she realized. And what if she said, *Guys, I'm having a heart attack,* and they called 911, and the paramedics took her to the ER, and everyone got worried and scared, and it turned out not to be a heart attack at all? How foolish would she feel then?

Nona snorted. *How foolish will you feel dead?*

Good point. Pressing her hand to her chest, Lucy leaned forward again but didn't try to stand. "Joe." He was laughing at something Carly said and didn't hear her. *"Joe."*

When he turned to face her, all handsome and charming and so damn happy, something else in her subconscious rushed from the back of her mind to the front: She loved him. Was in love with him. He wasn't her best bud anymore, wasn't the pest of a little brother. She *loved* him.

Oh, God, she'd prayed to fall in love again, to marry and have babies and someone to grow old with, but sometime around her thirtieth birthday, she'd began to wonder if it would ever happen. Even if it had, she'd thought it could never be the same as before. Mike had been so important: her first boyfriend, her first love, her first husband. He was the man she'd been destined to spend the rest of her life with. Even another true love wouldn't be able to measure up to him.

But she'd been blessed with a second chance. She

loved Joe, in different ways maybe but every bit as much as she'd loved Mike. If her chest wasn't hurting, her heart would be dancing with joy.

Blast it, it wasn't fair. She needed time to do something about that.

The amusement slid from his face, and he got really serious really fast. Drying his hands, he came to her, crouching in front of her. He picked up her wrist, held it a moment—counting her pulse, she realized—then grimly asked, "What is it, Luce?"

She glanced at her friends, gathered behind him, and a tear or two seeped into her eyes. "I love you guys, you know?" She wouldn't die or even come close to it, damn it, without saying that. Her voice caught as the pain intensified, making breaths harder to come by. "You don't know how much I hate saying this, but... my chest hurts."

Fingers gripping Joe's like a lifeline, gaze locking on to his stricken face, she whispered, "I think I'm having a heart attack."

*   *   *

Joe hadn't known Marti could whip her phone out of her skin tight jeans so quickly, or that Carly needed only a second longer. Marti dialed 911, and for the first time ever that he'd known her, her voice was wobbly and shaking as she asked for paramedics. Carly had moved away to the end of the table and was talking in a low, urgent voice to Therese, and Patricia stood behind Lucy, hands on her shoulders.

His own chest ached, all the way down into his gut.

He'd heard of sympathetic labor pains. Was there such a thing as a sympathetic heart attack, because his chest was so constricted he could hardly breathe. Muscles in his thighs tight, he lowered to his knees on the thick mat and cupped Lucy's hands in both of his. He couldn't keep a smile steady, or his hands, but he tried. "Aw, my heart gets kind of fluttery around you, too," he teased gently. "This isn't just a ploy to get more pictures of me doing kitchen work to send to my mom, is it?"

An unsteady smile curved her lips. "I am definitely sending the ones I got to all the Cadore women just as soon as I get a chance." Her voice was airy, her breathing shallow, her grip cutting off circulation to his fingers.

"You do that, you might as well post them on Facebook and every other social media platform out there. I don't know if it's genetic, but Cadore women can't keep anything to themselves."

The wail of a siren came sooner than he expected. He found relief in its approach, but it also acted like a spark to the fire of anxiety inside him. As long as it was just them and their friends in the room, it *could* be no big deal, a little scare, a case of better-safe-than-sorry. Once the paramedics arrived, it would be real. Real pain. Real risk. Real danger.

He'd never been a fan of institutionalized religion, but his parents had taught them all the power of prayer. Even as he grinned at Lucy and said, "You'd better not flirt with the paramedics," inside a scared little voice was jabbering, *Please don't let this be serious. Please don't let her die. Please, God...*

The siren grew ear-splittingly loud, then abruptly stopped. Joe glanced around, and Patricia opened her eyes from prayers of her own. "Carly and Marti went outside to meet them."

There was a rustle of noise, the thumping of wheels, as two female paramedics came into the kitchen with a gurney. Lucy, her face pale and damp, looked from them to Joe and managed a grin. "No flirting, right?"

He kept his gaze on her. "With who?"

Pretending earned him a smile before she reluctantly released his hands so the paramedics could take his place. They introduced themselves as Samantha and Jessica and broke out their gear as efficiently and capably as Lucy did—well, everything. Their manner was casual, putting Lucy at ease, doing absolutely nothing for Joe. When Patricia sidled up next to him and slid her arm around his waist, he held on to her tightly.

Samantha and Jessica checked her vitals, ran an EKG, and filled out a medical history. After a moment, one of them glanced up at Joe. "Mr. Hart?"

"Cadore."

"Are you her husband?"

"Not yet." The words slipped out without any thought, and they made Lucy look at him. This time, the widening of her eyes had nothing to do with discomfort. She looked all gentle and sweet and...yeah, that was a bit of wonder there. His chest tightened even more. *Please, God, we need Lucy too much to let her go.* I *need her.*

"He's her significant other," Patricia said, then gestured to include Carly and Marti. "We all are."

"You're a lucky woman, Lucy," Jessica said. "Can you move over here to the gurney? Just take your time, and Sam and I will help you."

Joe had to fight the urge to pick her up and lift her onto

the gurney. Instead, he watched as intently as he did when one of his players got up off the field after a hard hit, looking for signs of pain or injury. She actually looked about the same as she had the first day they'd started exercising together: pale, sweaty, disgruntled. That day, though, it hadn't been the workout so much as the 6 a.m. start time.

"How's your pain on a scale of one to ten?" Samantha asked.

Lucy's fingers fluttered over the middle of her chest. "About a six. Maybe a five?"

"It's a six. Lucy's a minimizer," Marti said from across the room. "She hates to put anyone out."

"We women tend to do that, don't we?" Samantha fastened the straps across Lucy's legs, then glanced at all of them before settling her gaze on Joe. "We're going to take her to St. Anthony's. As soon as we get her loaded into the ambulance, we'll give her some nitro, which should help with the pain."

If it was a heart attack. Joe remembered the tiny pills Grandpa Cadore had never been without. If it wasn't a heart attack, the medication wouldn't do more than maybe cause a headache. And since the paramedics with their EKG thought the nitro would help...

God help them, it *was* real.

Fear spread through him.

Before the paramedics could roll her away, Lucy shoved her phone at him. "Call my mom when you have something to tell her."

He wrapped his fingers around the phone and her hand. "I will."

"Don't scare her, okay?"

He forced a grin. "I won't," he assured her, while thinking that no matter how gently he broke the news, Robbie Cutler would have a heart attack herself. Lucy was her only daughter, her baby.

The paramedics took Lucy away then, and Patricia hugged Joe close. As far as comfort went, it was the next best thing to being held by his mother. He had an absurd desire to hide his face against her shoulder and cry, something he hadn't done since he was fourteen at Grandpa Cadore's funeral.

"She'll be all right," Patricia murmured.

"Yeah." The word was little more than a croak. Straightening, still gripping the phone, he ran the back of his hand across his eyes. "I, uh…I have to…"

"I know. Do you have a key?" she asked.

He fumbled in his pocket for his keys, singling out the one to the shop's back door.

"Marti, why don't you give him a ride to the hospital?" Carly's voice was as calm as always. "Patricia and I will lock up and meet you there. Once we know she's okay, then we'll come back here and take care of everything so she won't find a mess next time she's in."

"Great idea." Marti pushed Joe toward the door, and he let her, moving on autopilot. With every step, Carly's words echoed in his head: *Once we know she's okay…*

She *was* okay. Would be. Had to be. Because he'd waited a hell of a long time to be more than just friends with her, and now that they had finally gotten to that point, he needed sixty years or so to show her just how much he loved her.

Dear God, he prayed, *please let her be okay.*

Chapter 14

Saturday had been a good day, Calvin reflected as he stood at the sink in his mother's kitchen. The table had been full for dinner: him, his parents, Gran and Diez, Bennie and Mama. The food had been great, the company easy to take, and Bennie had offered to let him walk her home with a sly smile and a look that made him feel weak inside, but in a good way. An alive-and-aware-of-a-beautiful-woman-he'd-loved-for-more-than-half-his-life way.

Darkness had settled, coming early on the cold day. His breath had frosted in the air when he'd walked the few yards from his car to the house, reminding him of months in the desert heat. A uniform, boots, and gear could get damn near unbearable when the sun relentlessly baked everything caught in its glare, and he'd often gone to sleep dreaming of winter, cold, snow, days when the simplest exertion wouldn't drench him in sweat. Of course, desert winters could get bitterly cold. Then the blistering summers sounded pretty damn good.

He'd dreamed of so much those years he was gone. Peace. Safety. Life. The comfort of knowing no one was trying to kill him. Not having to kill anyone himself. No more loss, no more sorrow, no more horror at the things people were capable of. The things he was capable of.

Ducking his head, he pressed the heels of his palms to his eyes and sighed. He was proud of his country. He was proud of his service. He just couldn't reconcile the person he had been with the person he'd become. He'd had a strong upbringing, parents who loved him, religious values, moral values, faith in all the right people and things. He should have survived better. He shouldn't have broken the way he had. He shouldn't have—

"You forget how to turn on the water?"

Bennie's teasing voice startled him, causing his hands to fall to his sides, making him spin to face her. His reaction, in turn, startled her. It showed briefly in her eyes, in the fading of her smile before she fixed it back in place. He exhaled deeply and fixed a smile of his own. "I was just thinking."

"Life is too short to think too hard." She nudged him aside, turned on the faucet, and slid a glass underneath the flow. "Gran is the only person I know who doesn't like bottled water. Says it doesn't taste like water. Water's not supposed to *have* a taste."

Calvin inhaled the lingering aromas—dinner, the lemon cleaner Elizabeth used on the counters, coffee, and Bennie—and a little of that peace he'd just been yearning for settled over him. He didn't know what fragrance she wore, couldn't recognize any of the individual components that went into it. He just knew it smelled clean and a little sweet and a little spicy and a whole lot appealing. It was the scent he would like to fall asleep to, wake up to, the scent he would associate with good things the rest of his life.

"What were you thinking about?" Bennie asked quietly.

Talking was good, his therapists said. Remembering was good. The more a person hid from painful or traumatic memories, the more power those memories held. In both individual sessions and group therapy, reliving experiences was a big step forward. Though it had been impossible in the beginning—he'd sat through entire sessions without saying a word to the psychologist or therapist—he was learning.

To talk to them, at least. To other soldiers who had been there. Who were getting better themselves. But talking to family and friends—with Bennie at the top of that list—still seemed impossible. And she needed to know, sooner rather than later. There was something serious between them, and before it went too far, she needed to know that the Army considered him a psychiatric casualty of war, that he considered himself...whatever he was.

He took a breath, filling his lungs with determination, but someone was watching over him because her cell rang at that exact moment. She rarely answered calls when she was busy with someone in face-to-face interaction, but she glanced at the screen, her forehead knitted in a frown, and she raised the phone to her ear.

Calvin couldn't hear the other voice, but whatever she had to say, it drained the life from Bennie's face. Her hands went nerveless, and the glass of water she'd gotten for Gran slid to the floor with a thud, splashing water across the floor and up the bottom cabinets. "Oh, sweet Jesus," she whispered. "I'll be right there."

"Bennie, what's wrong?" he asked, reaching for her, but her fluttering hands evaded his as she looked anxiously around the room.

"I've got to—I've got to go." She hurried to the hall closet, opened the door, and stared inside a few seconds before looking at him. "My coat. Where did I put my coat? And my purse? My keys?"

"Your coat's in the living room, and your keys, I imagine, are in your pocket. You didn't bring your purse." Worried, he followed her into the front room, where Gran gave them a critical look.

"See, I told you that thud was too loud for clothes hitting the floor," she said, elbowing Mama while Elizabeth clapped her hands over Diez's ears. "Mom!" she scolded.

"What's wrong?" Justice asked.

Bennie snatched her coat from the rack in the corner nearest the door, shrugged into it, and anxiously patted the pockets. "Therese called and said paramedics had taken Lucy to St. Tony's. They think she had a heart attack." Her gaze met Calvin's. "I can't find my keys!"

He reached past her for his own coat. "I'll take you. Mom and Dad can find them later. Oh, and there's water spilled in the kitchen."

"Don't worry," Justice said. "We'll take care of everything. Lucy . . . is she the pretty little round one that cooks like an angel?"

Calvin nodded as he guided Bennie to the door.

"Aw, poor thing. We'll pray for her right now." Mama lowered her head and began her prayer in a strong, sure voice.

Diez slid noiselessly to his feet and passed Calvin, murmuring, "I'll clean up the water."

"Thanks."

Despite her shorter legs, Bennie beat Calvin to the car, hugging her jacket to her, shifting restlessly as she waited for him to unlock the doors. "I can't believe... She's been exercising and losing weight and eating healthier..." The instant he opened the passenger door, she slid in and fastened the seat belt. He was a few seconds slower, but within another few seconds, they were on the street and heading toward the hospital.

"She's just the sweetest thing," Bennie went on. "We all love her to death—" Her eyes widened, and her face crumpled. "I didn't mean that, Lord. We all have our qualities. Patricia's the mothering type, Therese is the serene one, Jessy's the bold one, Marti's the cool one, Ilena's the happy one, Fia's the one who needs the mothering." A smile nervously crossed her face. "I'm the mouthy one. I don't know why—and you don't need to explain it."

Calvin reached across the seat and took her hand tightly in his. Some of her tension seeped into his fingers, as if holding on to him made things easier. He hoped so.

It took just minutes to reach St. Anthony's, to follow the winding drive to the bright red and white Emergency Room sign, and find a parking space. Bennie was out of the car before he'd turned the engine off. He jogged a few yards to catch up with her.

He hated ERs. Especially hated them on busy weekend nights. The beginning of the end of his Army career had started in a civilian ER in Tacoma very much like this: check-in desks, a sign directing the way to triage rooms, another leading to locked doors and the treatment rooms behind them, televisions turned to competing channels, and people everywhere. Every age, every race, all with some complaint, real or imagined. Though the evening was still young, there were already the victims of bar brawls. There were parents using the emergency room for routine sick call for their kids, addicts concocting stories of nonexistent injuries to get painkillers, and people with genuine emergencies.

There was also a group who'd claimed one corner of the waiting room for themselves, the margarita girls, some of them sitting quietly, others pacing. Bennie headed straight for them, and everyone enveloped her in a group hug. Calvin stood back awkwardly until he saw Dane Clark on the periphery of their staked-out area. He joined him, hands shoved in his coat pockets, still cold despite the crowd in the room. "She gonna be okay?"

Dane shrugged. "Don't know yet. They did confirm that it was a heart attack. Joe's been texting stuff to Marti—he's the only one they've let go back there. He's the football coach, her neighbor, and I guess her new boyfriend." He glanced over as the hug broke up. "Dalton's over at Ilena's house, taking care of her baby. She didn't want to expose John to all these sick people."

Calvin imagined the big cowboy, who looked like he could wrestle a steer to the ground one-handed, cuddling with the fat little dark-eyed baby he'd seen Bennie with last Monday. It seemed an even stranger picture than himself cuddling the boy.

"You want to get some coffee?" Dane asked. "I imagine we're going to be awhile."

"Sure." Calvin told Bennie where he was headed, and she nodded, pointing toward the sign down the hall that read "Cafeteria."

Dane walked with a slight limp as if his leg hurt, and Calvin figured it probably did. He'd had more friends than he wanted to count who'd lost hands or arms, feet or legs, to the enemy's improvised explosives. They'd been shipped back to the United States to receive treatment usually at Walter Reed National Military Medical Center, the 5C program at Naval Medical Center San Diego, or the Center for the Intrepid at Brooke Army Medical Center. Visits with them had been rare, only when he'd been back in the States and close enough for the trip to their treatment facility.

Sometimes back in Washington, when Calvin had been really down, he'd wished he had a real, physical injury that he could point to and say, *This is why I'm having a tough time.* There was no place he could single out on his uninjured body and say those words and get the same nonjudgmental response.

But Calvin could learn to cope with his issues. He was doing desensitization therapy to take away the impact of the bad memories, learning to avoid his triggers and to control his responses. He could be close to normal again. The doctors and therapists had confidence to spare when his was lacking.

But Dane couldn't grow back his leg.

It was too early for the hospital staff to be taking their

dinner breaks, so the cafeteria was relatively empty. They got large coffees in paper cups and sat at a small table near the exit.

"You known Justin long?" Dane asked.

"Just since I came here the end of October."

"He's a good kid. Had some tough breaks." He smiled wryly. "I guess we've all had some, haven't we?"

"Some tougher than others." He didn't need to look in the direction of Dane's missing leg. It was understood.

"How many rotations did you do?"

"Four."

"Me, too. If I never set foot in that part of the world again, I'll be happy."

Calvin echoed his words. "Me, too."

After a moment's silence, Dane leaned back and stretched out his left leg on the empty chair between them, rubbing a spot about halfway down his thigh. "I had a hell of a time dealing with losing my leg. Maybe it wouldn't have been so bad if it had happened all at once, but only my foot was blown off in the blast. Then I got an infection, and they took it to the knee, and then I got another infection, and they had to go above the knee. It was spread out over nearly a year, so every time I was starting to accept what was gone, they removed more."

He rubbed the stubble on his jaw. "When I first came here, I kept it covered all the time. I wouldn't tell anyone what had happened, not even Carly. Believe me, it's hard to have much of a relationship when you can't take your clothes off in front of your girlfriend. She almost dumped me over it. Not because I'd lost my leg, but because I hadn't trusted her enough to tell her. There's a time and a place for secrets, but she let me know that with your girl isn't it."

Calvin's gaze was steady and flat. "Did Justin tell you I'm a patient at the WTU?"

"Nope. He wouldn't do that. But I spent a lot of years in combat and watching my buddies die and then, after the blast, feeling like I was less than I used to be. I recognize scared when I see it." He waited a beat, then asked, "PTSD?"

It took effort for Calvin to release some of the pressure he held on his coffee cup so it wouldn't explode in his hand. *Talking is good. Get used to the bad memories, and they lose their power. The more you talk, the easier it becomes.* Hadn't he thought just this evening that he had to tell Bennie the truth? Practice always helped when saying something hard. Dane could be his practice, couldn't he?

But it was hard, damn it. His muscles knotted, his stomach turning queasy. Nodding took as much effort as running five miles with a pack, as much courage as racing into gunfire to pull a wounded buddy back.

His gaze locked on the coffee swirling from the vibrations of his grip on the cup. "Bennie and her husband, J'Myel—they were my best friends forever. He and I enlisted together, shipped over together. Things went wrong between us, and by the end of my second tour, I was having some problems coping with...stuff."

Dane nodded. It was one of the good points of confiding in someone with the same experiences. He didn't ask what Calvin meant by *stuff* because his definition was pretty much the same as Calvin's.

Calvin took a slow, controlled breath. The tumbling in his gut was easing, not enough yet to trust that he could keep the coffee down if he drank any, and a vein in his temple throbbed with a matching throb behind his eyes. "On the third tour, J'Myel died. A lot of people died. I couldn't sleep, had nightmares. It changed from day to day whether I was afraid I would get killed or afraid I wouldn't. I made it through that deployment, and one more, but by then, I was in a pretty dark place."

It was a perfect description of the past few years: the darkest place he'd never imagined. Pure despair and utter hopelessness.

"You didn't get help."

The rueful chuckle that escaped Calvin surprised him. "Oh, hell, no. The U.S. Army doesn't like it when their captains can't hold themselves together." He paused a moment, thinking he could count on one hand the number of times he'd volunteered these next words: none. They'd been dragged out of him by doctors, police officers, and Chaplain Reed up there at JBLM, but he'd never offered them of his own volition. "Back in September I took me and my trusty .45 to a remote area in Tacoma and tried to kill myself."

Dane's expression didn't change. Either he wasn't surprised, or he hid his emotions well. Calvin would put his money on the former. Every soldier knew someone who'd attempted suicide. Probably everyone knew someone who'd succeeded. "Did you change your mind?"

Calvin shook his head grimly. He wished he had, he really did, but that night he hadn't found a single reason to go on living. "This kid, fourteen years old, a runaway from a group home, living on the streets, was in the park that night. He saw what I was about to do, tackled me, knocked the gun from my hand, and broke my elbow.

He even took me to the hospital, where he made sure to tell everyone exactly what I was doing when I got hurt. Hospital called the police, police called the Army, and..." He shrugged. Here he was, two months later, home with his family, falling in love with Bennie, finding hope and encouragement and, yeah, plenty of reasons to live.

"You were lucky he was there."

Calvin considered how much he'd hated Diez that night, how furious he was. He'd had pretty much the same reaction the day the kid showed up at his parents' house. But he *was* lucky Diez had been there—lucky he'd had enough decency to intervene. He could have just waited until the deed was done, stolen everything Calvin had, and left him there to rot.

"Yeah, I was lucky," he admitted, then amended it. "Am lucky. You want to hear the rest?"

Dane's nod was patient, measured.

"After taking me to the hospital and ratting me out, the kid stole my wallet, my keys, and my car." They shared a laugh over that, and finally Calvin risked a long swig of coffee. It went down just fine and would stay down. "A few weeks ago, he brought it all back. Now he's temporarily living with my parents and making himself the second grandson my grandmother had always wanted."

Silence settled for a while, Calvin contemplating that old saying, "Confession is good for the soul." His soul felt better. He still had a long way to go and a lot of fears to overcome, but telling his story to Dane—and Dane's acceptance of it—had loosened something inside him. His breaths came a little easier, his burden a little lighter...as long as he didn't think about having to tell Bennie.

Finally he met Dane's gaze again. "How did you finally tell Carly?"

Dane exhaled, then smiled faintly. "I didn't have to say a word. She dropped by unexpectedly. I opened the door on crutches, my pant leg flapping, my bionic leg sitting on the chair."

"Damn."

"Yeah."

"I can't put my nightmares, insomnia, and bad memories out on a chair for Bennie to discover."

"No," Dane agreed. "You'll have to talk to her, and soon. Keeping secrets from your girl isn't healthy."

* * *

It was close to eleven when Joe finally returned to the lobby. Bennie's gaze darted to his face. She'd never seen him looking so somber, not even during the playoffs last year when his star quarterback had been injured. There was exhaustion in his eyes but relief, too, and other emotions she couldn't quite separate. Avi Grant had called it right a few months ago when she'd said Joe had a thing for Lucy. A virtual stranger had noticed while Lucy's best friends had totally overlooked it. Too taken with his boyish charm, she supposed.

"She's okay," he said, and murmurs of relief swept the group. "In the morning, they're going to do a coronary angiogram, see what's going on, whether there's a blockage or she needs stents or whatever, then they'll send her to the cardiac floor and in a few days she'll go home."

"She's so young. Why did this happen?" Fia asked.

That pesky little question that hardly ever had an answer. When Bennie was little and pestering her mother for something, Lilly ended the conversations with one word: *Because.* It wasn't satisfying, and she'd sworn when she was a mother, she would never fall back on it, but sometimes it was the only answer you had. Because things just happened.

Joe shrugged. "No idea. Now she works on keeping it from happening again."

Bennie glanced at Calvin, sitting between her and Dane, while the others talked. He'd been quiet since they'd returned from the cafeteria. Probably just thinking again. A little smile curved her lips. He was handsome when he thought. Lord, he was handsome no matter what he was doing. Even angry, there was a spark in his dark eyes and little wrinkly lines across his forehead that looked so unnatural, she wanted to laugh when she saw them. When they were kids, she usually had laughed, hardly ever failing to coax him back into a good mood.

They weren't kids anymore.

And she wouldn't wish to be. It was frowned upon, kids doing the things she'd like do with him.

After a moment of chatter, Carly said, "I'd suggest we get out of here. Patricia, Marti, you still up to doing the boxing and cleaning at the bakery?"

"Sure," they answered simultaneously.

"What boxing and cleaning?" Therese and Bennie asked simultaneously.

"Just washing a few pans and getting Lucy's baked goods for tomorrow boxed up and ready to deliver," Carly replied.

Choruses of *I can help* joined Bennie's, and Patricia hugged them all around. "There's not that much to do or that much extra space in the kitchen. The rest of you go home and get a good night's rest so you can see Lucy tomorrow. She'll need some loving before her mom gets here around noon." She winked. "We'll all get chances to help until she's back on her feet."

Bennie said her good-byes, then caught Calvin's hand as they strolled toward the exit. "I appreciate you coming and staying."

His only response was a squeeze of her fingers. They walked into the cold night, the air fresh and sweet after the recycled hospital air. About the time they reached the car, he finally spoke. "I like your friends."

"They're the best people in the world." But underneath her light words, she couldn't stop the faint little question of whether J'Myel would have liked them. Would he have appreciated her definitely-light-skinned besties? Would he have appreciated *her*? After all, she was doing the same thing Calvin had done when J'Myel accused him of trying too hard to be white: going to school for a better job, improving her life, being ambitious. Would J'Myel have had problems with her, too?

It was a fact of life that people changed. It was also a fact that she and J'Myel had been apart far more often than together after high school. He very well might have decided he wanted to be a different kind of man—not the small-town life and small-town wife kind—and thought because she loved him, she would automatically have gone along with him.

Maybe she would have. After all, she'd changed, too. Though it was hard to imagine.

Calvin opened the passenger door, but instead of sliding in, she wrapped her arms around his middle. "Do you know how much we take for granted? Mama says she wakes up every morning and thanks God that she's still alive. I figured when I was her age, I would do the same, but in the meantime...it's like I'm entitled to life. Like I don't have to be thankful for each day. I bet Lucy woke up this morning, thinking it was just another Saturday. She would run errands, clean house, work at the bakery. She never dreamed that before the evening was over, she would be facing a life-altering—potentially life-*ending*—event. It just makes me feel so much more thankful that I'm here and healthy and happy and strong. You know what I mean?"

For a long, long time he gazed down at her, his eyes shadowed, the emotions radiating off him intense enough to send heat through their clothing and into her. When he answered at last, his voice was husky, as if the words were squeezing their way out. "I do. And I'm getting there myself."

She didn't ask why he felt the need to get healthier, happier, and stronger. Lord knew, he had plenty of reasons to have lost his way. Tonight, right this minute, she didn't want to know more than that. She didn't want to talk about things that had happened, whether wonderful or too ugly to relive. She wanted to forget the past, focus on the present, and hope for the future. She wanted to stay in his arms, long after the sun had risen on Sunday, long enough that she would have to scramble to get to church on time.

Her head rested against his chest, and she fancied for a moment she could hear the steady beat of his heart. The cold didn't bother her. Even a whistle from a passing pickup—only Jessy among the margarita girls could whistle like that—didn't do more than curve her lips into a smile. His arms held her with gentle pressure, his hands moving slowly along her spine, tempting her to stretch and arch her back, wanting to do that and much more as soon as they got someplace private.

Finally, with her extremities on the verge of numbness, she tilted her head back to smile at him. "Want to go home with me and do things on the couch that would make Mama blush if she found out?"

Calvin snickered. "Mama doesn't blush. She grabs a wooden cooking spoon and makes other people turn red."

Bennie hesitated before suggesting, "We could go to your place." Her smile was flirtatious, her tone sly, but inside every nerve was quivering. Was she ready for this? For sex with Calvin, the man who'd been like a brother to her most of their lives? The man her husband had loved, then hated till the end of *his* life?

There might have been a voice in the rational part of her brain saying, *Let's think about this,* but all the irrational, emotional, womanly parts were dissenting loud enough to drown it out. Yes, the boy he used to be had been like a brother to her, but as she'd thought earlier, they weren't kids anymore. And yes, J'Myel had ended their friendship, but she'd thought he'd been wrong at the time, and she was sure of it now.

And J'Myel was dead. She was alive, and she'd never stopped loving Calvin in one way, and she wanted to try the way that included all the fun, naughty things. She wanted to be with him, physically, emotionally, sexually.

But it wasn't going to happen tonight. She could feel the regret seeping through him before she saw it in his face or heard it in his voice. Disappointment rose inside her, but she tamped it down, keeping her smile in place through sheer will.

"I— You know— The timing..." His hands stopped that lovely stroking of her back to move to her shoulders, and though he faced her, he kept his gaze locked somewhere around her chin. "I'm sorry, Bennie. I just can't—"

She pressed her fingers to his mouth to silence him. "It's all right, Calvin. Really. You, me, J'Myel... I know. It complicates things."

His eyes fluttered shut, and he pressed a kiss to her fingertips, slow, erotic, quivery, and intent, before moving a few steps away. "It's cold out here. We should go."

She had to command her feet to move, her body to slide onto the car seat. She settled on the old quilt, fastened the seat belt, held her tingly, shivery hand with her other hand, then gave him another grin. "Yeah, we should. Wouldn't want you to freeze off anything important." *Because I have plans for you, Calvin Clyde Sweet.*

Plans that required every single part of him.

* * *

The Sweet house could have been mistaken on smells alone for a fine restaurant Sunday afternoon. Calvin arrived before his family and let himself in, stopping in the hallway, and simply inhaled for a long moment before finally shucking his jacket and moving toward the kitchen. The pastor must have thrown in a few extra prayers. It was a good thing Gran had no plans for going out to eat, or the Mount Zioners might get there first and scarf down all the food.

Three slow cookers on the counter held their dinner: pot roast with potatoes and carrots; pinto beans and ham in the second; and collards soaking in a ham-vinegar-chili pepper-infused liquor. On another counter waiting to reheat was a dish of corn bread and a dozen sweet rolls from CaraCakes Bakery. "Never let it be said that the Sweets skimp on calories," he murmured.

A voice came from the kitchen table, startling him. "Huh. You should eat here on weeknights sometimes," Diez said. "Miss Elizabeth fixes a lot of salad and grilled chicken and baked fish that Mr. Justice complains about but eats plenty of anyway. She says she's watching his cholesterol. This kind of food is weekend treats mostly."

Calvin faced him. "Why aren't you at church?"

"I went to Sunday school. Miss Elizabeth let me come home when the church service started because I didn't sleep much last night."

"Huh. Lack of sleep never got me out of sitting through a sermon." Calvin studied the kid a moment, Dane Clark's words echoing: *You were lucky he was there.* It might not have seemed lucky at the time, but he'd come to his senses since then. And Justice's words on the subject: *Suicide is a permanent solution to a temporary problem.* Calvin owed Diez for stopping him from taking that permanent solution.

He just hadn't found a way to tell him so. *You boys,* Mrs. Ford used to say, *you think it'll kill you to be the first one to make amends, but trust me, it won't.* And then she would flash them a bright smile. *Because if you don't stop fussing, I'm gonna kill you both.*

Instead of stepping up like a man, Calvin asked, "You like grilled chicken and baked fish?"

Diez shrugged. The T-shirt he wore was an old one of Calvin's. Where it had been loose a few weeks ago, now it was almost snug. "When you're used to eating one meal a day, you learn to eat anything. And I do like fish. The only kind I'd ever had before coming here was the fish sandwich at McDonald's. They don't deserve the same name."

"No, they don't." Calvin got himself a bottle of water from the refrigerator and offered one to Diez before taking a seat across from him. It hurt his gut to hear the kid talking so naturally about going hungry. It was a sin, in a country where there was so much food that obesity ran rampant, that some people couldn't scrape together even a decent meal a day. "You won't ever go hungry here."

Discomfort flashed across the boy's face, accompanied by longing and distance in his eyes. "Yeah. One last feast for Thanksgiving, and then..."

Calvin felt every bit as uncomfortable. Normally, when he felt that way, he clamped his mouth shut and just refused to go where the conversation went. He could do that now. He was good at it. But avoidance never helped solve any problems. Avoidance wouldn't tell Bennie what she needed to know, or Diez, either. "And then what?"

Diez sniffed, swiped his arm across his nose, and shrugged. With the return of his smug attitude, Calvin realized it had been missing the past couple weeks. He'd behaved like any kid under Elizabeth's, Justice's, and Gran's influence. "Dude, I told you, I'm headin' south. I'm gonna find me a beach to live on."

"And you're going to get there by...what was it? Hitchhiking?"

"Yeah. You'll be up here freezing your as—self, and I'll be kicking back in the sunshine," he boasted. The kid could control his physical responses—the smirk, the body language—but he couldn't keep the fear completely out of his eyes. He knew he'd struck gold here. Did he think it was temporary? That the Sweets' gratitude would wear off and they would push him out the door? Was that why he planned to leave before they could ask him to?

It wasn't temporary, and their gratitude would never wear off, and they'd already formed a bond with Diez. They wouldn't let go as easily as he seemed to think.

Instead of warning him of that, Calvin asked, "When was the last time you hitched a ride?"

"I dunno. Five, six years ago."

"Oh. When you were...what? Eight, maybe nine? And you were with your sort-of father. And you went...to the grocery store? The liquor store? Maybe to hang out at a bar for a few hours, hiding you in a back room or in the alley out back?"

Diez didn't answer, but his deep scowl and the growl that came from his mouth were answer enough.

"Hitching cross-country's not quite the same. Putting yourself in a situation where nobody knows where you are or who you're with...Could be a nice mom and pop on the way home from church. Could be a thug who likes hurting people for fun, or it could be a raping, murdering pedophile with a penchant for fourteen-year-old Latino boys." Calvin matched his scowl. "Hitchhiking is the single stupidest and most dangerous way to travel."

Heat and anger flooded Diez's face. "I'm not stupid. I'm broke. There's a difference. It ain't like I can walk into the bus station and buy a ticket with money I don't have."

Calvin glanced at the clock. If the pastor hadn't started

to wind things up by now, Gran would do it for him. An old lady needed a regular schedule, and eating on time occupied prime spots on that schedule. The cold wind would cut down on churchyard chatter, so he figured ten minutes or less after the final *Amen*, the family would be walking in the door.

"So you're just sticking around for one last big meal before you take off."

"I've got places to go, things to do, people to meet," Diez said breezily, but he couldn't meet Calvin's gaze.

"You don't like it here?"

He resorted to a shrug, as if the answer could go either way.

"Aw, come on. You've got a room of your own, plenty of food, clean clothes, someone to look out for you."

With a snort, Diez jerked his gaze upward. "Who was the one sitting in the dark with a gun to his head? Oh, yeah, that was *you*. *I* look out for myself."

The words echoed in Calvin's head. *Sitting in the dark with a gun to his head.* All these weeks later, he had trouble forming the image. He remembered the details: the drive to the abandoned park, the walk from his car to the concrete table. Water had soaked his shoes and the hems of his jeans, and the table had been damp beneath him. He'd pulled out the pistol, had found himself at peace for the first time in years because he'd finally found the courage to end it. He could remember all that, lifting the gun to his temple, the impact of Diez's tackle knocking him from the table to the ground, the sharp ache of his arm breaking.

But he couldn't put images to it. It was hazy, unreal, such a shameful final act that he'd planned.

Calvin was distantly aware of sounds outside: engines shutting off, car doors closing, first two, then three others. Gran must have gotten a ride home with Mama and Bennie. He unfolded from his chair and stuck out his hand. "You're right, Diez. You did look out for me, and I haven't thanked you for that yet."

After staring at his hand a moment, Diez stood and accepted it. Once again, his face was hot and red, and his only response was a jerky shrug.

As the front door opened, Justice's voice booming as he invited the ladies in, Calvin released Diez's hand, then leaned close. "Don't take it on yourself to decide when it's time to head south and break my mom's and Gran's hearts. You do that, I will track your skinny butt all the way to the Gulf Coast and take great pleasure in kicking it all the way back home."

Savoring the wide-eyed shock that crossed Diez's face, Calvin turned just in time to see Bennie stroll in the door, bringing up the rear. She gave Justice one of her usual smiles, all bright and happy, and thanked him for holding the door, then shrugged out of her coat to reveal a sapphire blue curve-hugging dress that was somehow perfectly appropriate for church and still made it hard for him to swallow.

Man, it had been hard to turn down her offer of going to his place last night. Standing there with her arms around him and her cheek pressed to his chest had been the best, happiest few minutes of the past five years of his life. He'd felt like he *belonged* there, like no one, no memories, nothing, could possibly interfere with such an incredible moment.

He'd been wrong, of course. He couldn't take her to

his apartment without telling her everything. One look at the sign outside his building, she would know he hadn't been honest with her. One good look at him, and she would guess what he'd hidden. She thought things were already complicated between them? Wait until he threw PTSD and a suicide attempt into the mix. Until he told her that while thousands of other troops had struggled with their last breaths to survive, he'd done the opposite and tried to throw his life away. It was a slap in the face to J'Myel and every other casualty.

And it would always be a problem. It wasn't something that healed and went away, leaving only a few bad memories in its place. The shrinks had warned him that PTSD could manifest at any time. It could improve or get worse without warning. It could become harder to cope with, the depression harder to control. It could disappear for weeks, months, even years at a time, only to return stronger than ever.

It did a lot of things, but what it did not do was go away once and for all.

Bennie had a right to know before she got any further involved with him. Before she might fall in love with him, consider marrying him and having kids with him. If she was signing up for the long haul, she deserved to know about all the possible bumps and detours in the road ahead.

And with Bennie, under normal circumstances, she would always sign up for the long haul.

God, he wished he could be normal for her.

Chapter 15

Even more than Christmas, Thanksgiving had always been Bennie's favorite holiday. Maybe it was the lack of pressure to provide gifts or the tighter focus on family itself; she wasn't sure, but she'd always loved the day, and this one had been no different.

Before the family had arrived, she and Mama had visited Lucy, home from the hospital. Her color was good, her mood maybe a tad less cheerful than usual though she tried to hide it, and she'd basked in the pleasure of all the pampering being done by Joe and her mother. The heart attack had been a fluke, she said, payoff for seven years of not caring for her body, but the cardiologist declared she was as healthy as a brand-new heart attack patient could be. She was going to be okay, she'd insisted.

Of course you are, Mama had agreed with a smile filled with grace. *The Lord and I have discussed this.*

Then it had been back home to meet Aunt Cheryl and her boyfriend, an engineering professor at OSU. They'd been together longer than most people stayed married, though Mama hadn't yet quit hoping for a wedding ceremony someday. Uncle Roland, his wife, his sons, and their families had arrived soon after, caravanning up from Ada. They had all eaten too much, talked too much, and sat in the living room for too long, but after darkness settled, they'd piled into their cars and returned home.

Now it was just Bennie and Mama. The house was spotless—Pickerings were good about cleaning up after themselves—and quiet and just the tiniest bit lonely.

Settled into her chair, Mama gave a heavy, satisfied sigh. "On days like this, I miss my family like crazy. And on days not like this, too."

"I know you do." Mama had taken a huge step, leaving South Carolina with three young children and settling in a place where she didn't know anyone and didn't have the support her family was so good at providing. She'd done it because she'd felt a need for a new start, she said, and because divorce hadn't freed her completely from the irritation of her ex-husband.

That was how Bennie thought of him when she bothered: not as her grandfather but as Mama's ex. Mama rarely spoke of him, and it was even rarer when she said anything negative about him. Though Bennie had never met him, in her opinion, it said more than enough that he'd refused to pay child support, hadn't come to any graduations or weddings or to her daddy's funeral, had never acknowledged his grandchildren or great-grandchildren.

"I've been blessed, though."

"Hmm." Bennie sipped her coffee. Tonight it was an Italian blend, soothing and familiar.

"I've got my health, my family and friends, my church, and renewed hope for getting more great-grandbabies while I'm still young enough to play with them." Mama gave her a sly smile. "My eyesight may not be what it was twenty years ago, but I've seen the way you and Calvin look at each other."

The last drop of coffee went down the wrong way, making Bennie cough as she set the cup aside. She knew better than to deny there was anything between her and Calvin. Mama really did see everything. She didn't sound displeased or worried by it, though. That was good.

Then Mama snorted. "Even Emmeline can see it, and she's practically blind."

"Oh, she is not."

Mama shook her finger. "Just because she's not here doesn't mean you have to do her arguing for her."

"No one can argue like her, that's for sure." Bennie wondered how Calvin's Thanksgiving Day had gone. They'd met at his aunt Mae's house, no doubt with chaos abounding. If the whole family showed up, there would have been easily sixty, maybe seventy, people. And they were loud, boisterous, emotional people—like Bennie's South Carolina family without the Southern drawl.

It would have been the first time he'd been together with all of them in years—the first time for Diez, too. It would have been fun to get a peek at the boy's face about ten minutes after they'd walked in, before he'd had a chance to adjust to the abundance of noise and love.

"So how do things stand with you and Calvin?"

Bennie risked picking up her coffee again. "It's complicated."

A great laugh burst from Mama. "Of course it's complicated. It involves a man *and* a woman." After a moment, she sobered. "Love's not complicated, Benita. It's as simple and as natural as breathing. It's the logistics of it that can get out of hand. I used to look at Montgomery sometimes, and my heart would just swell with all the love I felt for him, and then sometimes he'd make me so mad that I'd look at him in his sleep and think, 'I could kill him and hide his body and nobody would ever be the wiser.'"

Bennie chuckled at the thought of her round, gentle grandmother bringing harm to anyone. It was about as likely as Ilena actually becoming the 800-pound gorilla she thought she was. "Aw, you wouldn't have killed him."

"No," Mama agreed. "Though I probably should've whacked him a few times with my wooden spoon."

Outside the window behind Bennie, the wind rustled through the trees, squeaking the chains holding the porch swing a few times. It had been a gorgeous day, the sun bright, just a bit of a chill in the air. She'd taken Uncle Roland's five grandkids exploring, wandering through a wooded lot, jumping over ditches, standing at the fence watching Mr. Harley's bull graze, but the temperature had dropped as quickly as the sun had. The only downside of Thanksgiving for her sun-and-heat-loving body was that it made winter official.

"Is it J'Myel?" Mama asked.

Bennie kicked off her slippers and drew her feet onto the seat. "Do you think it's odd, me being interested in my dead husband's best friend?"

"You being interested in your live husband's best friend…that'd be odd. Besides, they weren't friends when J'Myel died." Mama pulled her quilt higher around her and the habit made Bennie smile. Mama had lived through a lot of years where frugality wasn't a choice. Times were much better now, but she kept them that way in part by holding on to most of those penny-pinching habits. If Bennie offered to raise the thermostat, she'd say, *Why turn up the heat, sugar doll, when I'm cozy under my granny's quilt?*

"Did you ever find out what happened between them?" Mama went on. "Because I've got a thought or two on the matter."

That caught Bennie off guard. "And how did you come by these thoughts?"

Mama tapped one thick fingertip against her temple. "Pulled them right out of my brain. I store all kinds of tidbits away until I need them again someday. 'Course, most of 'em I don't ever need again, so my head's so full to overwhelming of useless bits that I hardly have room for the necessary stuff."

"That's why you always win at *Jeopardy*."

"Yes, ma'am. And because Alex Trebek is still so pleasing to the eye." Mama reached into the basket beside her chair and pulled out three skeins of yarn: cream-colored, dusky blue, and barn red. She'd started the piece the night before, the yarns baby soft, the needles thinner and more delicate than she normally used. Her gaze stayed on the yarn as she worked a row. "One time, back in the beginning, when J'Myel came home for a long weekend, he said Calvin couldn't come because he had finals coming up. Him and I, we were talking while he waited for you to get ready to go wherever you two were going, and I told him I hoped he would follow Calvin's lead and get his degree while he was in the Army. He gave me one of those looks his mama used to smack him for and told me in grammatically incorrect and obscenity-laced language that he had no intentions of ever getting a college degree."

Bennie cringed. One of their families' golden rules had been you didn't disrespect an adult, and you certainly didn't cuss at one, Mama and Gran above all. If Golda Ford had heard that, tough soldier or not, she would have dragged him home for a butt-chewing. If Bennie had heard it, she probably would have wrestled him to the ground, twisted his arm behind his back, and made him apologize before turning him over to Golda.

"The other thought that comes to mind was on your wedding day. We were making small talk about the future, and he told me he wasn't going to live a loser life in Tallgrass. He said that once his enlistment was up, he was taking you away from here. His daddy was in Seattle, and he had friends in Chicago, and you could live with one or the other until he got on his feet." Mama's gaze turned shadowy, gazing at the fireplace though no fire burned there. "I told him he might want to discuss that with you because you would likely have a lot to say on the subject, and he said there was no need. The decision had been made."

Butterflies tumbled in Bennie's stomach. She felt foolish that other people had known her husband's plans for their future when he'd never breathed a hint of them to her. Her lack of desire to move aside, his arrogance in believing the decision was his and his alone, would have surely caused a blowup.

Though it had been his decision alone for the two of

them to end their friendship with Calvin, and she'd gone along with that.

"Mama, why didn't you tell me this back then?"

"Because you were in love," she said simply. "He wasn't the one I would have chosen for you, but it wasn't my place to choose. He'd changed his mind about a few things since leaving home, and I figured if you were determined, you could change it back. Besides, how could I know that you weren't secretly pining to escape this town just like him?"

"Never. This is my home," Bennie answered. She stared at the fireplace for a moment, too, remembering their wedding day and how happy she'd been. How hopeful. "He never said a word to me about moving away or getting out of the Army. I knew we'd have to move away for a while once he came back from Afghanistan, until he could retire, but I could manage that. But to stay away?" She shook her head so emphatically that her curls bounced around her face. "That never would have happened."

Mama nodded as she knitted, loops forming and sliding along the needles. It would be a perfect time for Bennie to ask for her first lesson, but she was satisfied at the moment to just watch.

"You asked if I thought it was odd, you being sweet on Calvin," Mama said after a while, "and I told you J'Myel wasn't the one I would've chosen for you. I could see you with Calvin—not just now but back then. Golda and her ex and Justice and Elizabeth set the best examples they could for their boys, the same way I did for you. We taught you right from wrong, to be respectful and courteous and compassionate, to accept responsibility for yourselves, to always strive to be a better person. It's not my place to judge, but I'm only human, so I'm going to give my opinion anyway."

When she paused, Bennie's nerves tightened all over her body. She knew J'Myel had had his flaws. They all did. But she'd loved him in spite of them, and it disquieted her a bit that the other person she'd loved so much hadn't quite approved of him.

Mama let the knitting rest in her lap as she met Bennie's gaze. "J'Myel fell short of the man he should have been. He needed more loyalty, more maturity, less arrogance, less fun-seeking, and more responsibility-taking."

Bennie couldn't argue even one point. The arrogance had been charming in its way, all bold and forward and right up front for everyone to see. He'd been, oh, so confident in himself, but once they'd begun living together, once they'd had children and obligations and responsibilities, would that arrogance have gotten old?

And he *had* been all about the fun, live for today, let the future take care of itself. It wasn't a bad attitude for a single man, but once he added someone else to the mix, that attitude would wear thin, too. Heavens, he'd actually intended to move her to Seattle to live with his father or to Chicago to live with his buddies. Anyone even mildly acquainted with her would have realized that was never going to happen. How had her husband managed to convince himself otherwise?

Because he'd needed more loyalty, maturity, and responsibility-taking.

"You've got all those qualities, Bennie. You're exactly the woman your daddy wanted you to become."

Tears pricked at Bennie's eyelids at the unexpected praise. Her heart warmed to Mama's next comment.

"And Calvin has those qualities in spades."

* * *

Calvin didn't know how long he'd been sitting on Mama Maudene's porch swing when a dim figure stepped out of the shadows on the street and turned up the sidewalk. Diez still looked a little shell-shocked from his long day with Gran's four children, ten grandchildren, and her herd of great-grandchildren who wouldn't stand still long enough to be counted.

"What are you doing here?" Calvin asked quietly. Mama and Bennie were likely in the living room, enjoying coffee and one last serving of dessert. He'd been quiet when he'd come up the steps, and he'd stayed quiet, not sure whether he wanted to ring the bell or just enjoy the solitude for a time, because he was feeling a little shell-shocked himself.

"Miss Elizabeth was worried. She thought maybe you'd tripped and broken something. I told her I needed the air so I'd walk back toward your aunt's." The down-filled jacket Diez wore was new and rustled with every movement he made.

Calvin's smile was grim. He appreciated his family, he really did, and all the attention and affection they'd shown him had been overwhelming, but after six hours of it, he'd needed a break. Everyone had tried to give him a ride back to his parents' to pick up his car, but he'd insisted on walking. Like Diez, he'd needed the air. The quiet. The time to breathe and think and be the only one in his world for a while.

Somewhere along the way, his need to be alone had morphed into a need to be with Bennie, leading him straight to her house, right up the steps, and to a seat on the porch swing. Not leading him to the courage to ring the bell.

"You try to kill yourself one time," he said dryly, "and every time you're late, people start to worry." It wasn't a comment he could have made to just anyone. The guys at WTU maybe. Dane Clark. Definitely not to his parents or Gran or Bennie.

"You made your bed, now you lay in it." Underneath Diez's flippancy was some sympathy. Calvin wondered if the kid was feeling responsible for him—*save a life, it's yours forever*—or if Calvin feeling responsible for *him* would be enough.

"You've been listening to Gran."

"I told her of course I'm gonna lay in my bed if I make it. She just laughed." Diez's gaze went to the door. "Either Mama or Bennie own a gun?"

"No, but Mama swings a mean cast-iron skillet, and Bennie can flip a wet towel and make it burn like fire. She pinches, too. And she'll pretend to be all sweet and apologetic to get you off guard, then grind your face into the dirt."

"I was just wondering 'cause you sitting out here like some kind of stalker might freak 'em out."

"Nah, they'd just kick my butt and tell my mom." Calvin smiled. "Do me a favor. Tell Mom I'm over here and I'll come in and say good night before I head home."

"Yeah, I don't do favors without getting something in return."

"Like what?"   •

"Talk to the girl instead of hiding in the dark." Diez took two long strides forward, pressed the doorbell, then leaped, clearing the porch, steps, and a good portion of the sidewalk before disappearing into the shadows again.

Calvin had long legs and had learned to move damn fast when the situation called for it. He could dive over the swing and take cover in the bushes that grew between the porch and the driveway. He could run like Diez had and disappear into the shadows. He didn't do either. He stayed where he was, palms growing damp, chest tightening, waiting for the porch light to come on, for the click of the lock being undone, for Bennie's sweet face to appear in the doorway.

It didn't take long. The light fixture beside the door cast pale light across the porch, and the lock sounded, and then she stood there, hugging herself, smiling as if she'd been waiting for him. "Hey," she said.

"Hey."

"You want to come in?"

"Is it too cold for you to come out?"

"Just a minute." She closed the door, then returned almost immediately, a heavy quilt bundled in her arms. "We'll have to sit close. Stand up."

He obeyed, and she wrapped the quilt around their shoulders. With her fingers clutching the left side and his gripping the right side, they sat down again and pulled the extra fabric across to cocoon them. Its scent took him back fifteen years, as if it had come straight from the clothesline on a sunny spring day.

Her scent took him back, too, to better times. Innocent times. Though his innocence was long lost and never to be regained, *better* was a possibility. It was within his reach.

It was cuddling under the blanket with him.

"How was your day?" she asked after a while.

"Noisy. How about yours?"

"The same. I'd ask if you knew how much noise five kids under the age of six can make, but I figure you experienced probably double that today." She pushed with her feet to put the swing in motion, giving him a glimpse of her house shoes. When she caught his smirk, she extended both legs to admire them. "What do you think?"

They were soft, shearling-lined fabric, sewn in the style of cowboy boots: light green with elaborate yellow and turquoise flowers stitched on. "They're exactly what I'd expect."

"When the margarita girls did an overnight trip, I won the prize for best house shoes," she bragged. "My jammies were unbearably cute, too, but Ilena beat me there."

Calvin had seen her in her jammies dozens of times at sleepovers or lazy Saturday breakfasts. He would give an awful lot to see her in them again.

Even more to see her out of them.

Another silence settled for a few minutes, and again it was Bennie who broke it. "How did Diez do with your family?"

"They welcomed him like he was their own. He's still recovering. I heard Mom tell Auntie Sarah that she and Dad have an appointment with a lawyer about him next week."

"They want to keep him."

"Yeah."

"Are you okay with that?"

He considered it for a moment, though he didn't really need to. His parents were responsible adults. If they wanted to take on the challenges of a fourteen-year-old runaway, they didn't need Calvin's permission. "Yeah, I am. God knows, he can use a family who cares enough to have him."

"Don't they all."

Her sigh was fervent, bringing to mind her comment about working with kids when she finished her degree. What kinds of things would she see? What had she already seen?

"In a perfect world," she went on, "all kids would be treasured, all adults would be responsible, and all war would end."

Amen to that. "But it's not a perfect world."

She cocked her head to one side, gazing up at him. "Would you change any of it? Your life, I mean. If you could go back to eighteen, would you do anything differently?"

To give himself a moment before answering, he chuckled. "Leave it to you to ask the hard questions."

"I like hard questions. They make you think."

"Just the other day, you said life is too short to think too hard."

She shrugged off the reminder, her action pulling the quilt tighter around them. "That was the other day. Tonight I'm feeling thoughtful. So . . . would you?"

He'd called it a hard question, but it wasn't. Joining the Army had been a lifelong dream. He'd known he would go to war, and though he'd thought he was prepared for it, he hadn't had a clue. But it was something he'd needed to do. It had given him a chance to grow up, to grow strong, and to learn what sacrifice and service truly meant.

Had *he* sacrificed? Hell, yes. He'd learned he wasn't as strong as he'd thought, and for too long he'd seen that as a failure in his character. Sometimes he still did. But as long as he breathed, growing stronger, getting strong enough, was an option.

He'd lost friends, including the most important one of all, and then he'd lost himself. But he was finding himself again. And the friends...he was richer for having had them. He would never forget them, never forget all that *they* had lost. He would do his best to live a life that would honor them.

"If it's too hard, you don't have to answer," Bennie said, her voice quiet in the night, the bump of her shoulder against his gentle and reassuring.

"No," he answered just as quietly. "I'm learning to like hard questions." He took a deep breath. "There are things I would change if it was in my power. J'Myel wouldn't have died. Nobody would have suffered or died, not Americans, coalition forces, insurgents, civilians." And he would have wished that his own lessons hadn't been so difficult.

"But would I still have enlisted? Yes. Would I have fought as hard? Yes. Would I do it all again?" He stared down at her, her face still tilted up to his, her eyes dark, her lips parted just a bit. "Pretty much, yeah."

Then, as a reward for answering the question, he closed the distance between them and kissed her. Her mouth opened as naturally as if they'd done this a hundred times, and he slid his tongue inside. What had he been thinking when he was fourteen, sixteen, eighteen, spending all day and every weekend with Bennie without once doing this? He'd seen the guys at school and the younger soldiers in town look at her like they were aching to get a chance alone with her, and he'd never once thought he should feel that way, too. It had taken him way too long to realize that his best bud was the prettiest girl in town.

Her cool fingers slid up his neck, stroking his jaw, heating his skin to simmering. She maneuvered around until she sat astride his lap, leaving him to hold on to the quilt edges so she could twine her arms around his neck. Every cell in his body went on alert, warming his blood, spreading heat through him, making tension crackle, his breathing get shallow, his erection get hard.

His nerves went on alert, too. The natural progression of what they were doing was pretty obvious: kisses leading to touches leading to an invitation inside or a request to go to his apartment leading to sex leading to...

She ended the kiss halfheartedly—pulling back, nipping his lower lip, withdrawing again, brushing her mouth across his—then finally broke contact, at least, with his mouth. Her breasts were still pressed against his chest, her hips spread wide to cradle his. He wished they could stay like that forever, snuggled warm inside their blanket, taking their time and exploring every way to kiss, every way to touch, everything a man and a woman could do without actually doing everything.

Not that that was any better an idea than having sex with her. Not until he told her everything.

"Wow." Moving carefully, Bennie lifted herself off his lap and sat on the bench beside him again, reclaiming her share of the quilt. "Since our privacy issues remain unresolved and it's far too cold to for public exposure, that kiss is all you're gonna get tonight, Squeaky, unless you have a better idea."

Though her voice sounded normal, there was hope in her eyes. Hell, there was hope in him, and he knew better.

When he didn't answer, she shifted onto her right hip to face him. "I was going to ask if you *wanted* to have sex with me, but considering what I was, um, sitting on, I'd say the answer's a firm yes."

His face flushed. "Of course I do. It's just…"

When he shook his head without finishing, she bent forward to squeeze both of his calves, muttering, "Okay." The action would have puzzled him before hearing Dane Clark's story about hiding his amputated leg from his girlfriend.

"Bennie…"

She waved one hand dismissively. "I'm a patient woman, Calvin," she said, and the anxiety in him eased a little of its grip.

Then she softly finished with a teasing smile and an admonishing finger. "To a point." She leaned close enough that her mouth brushed his ear, sending shivers through him. "Consider yourself warned."

*   *   *

When a margarita call went out for assistance at Prairie Harts on Saturday morning, Bennie was happy to volunteer. She dressed in her comfiest jeans—a pair with plenty of stretch fibers to make up for the sins of Thanksgiving—plus a T-shirt and the thick-soled shoes she wore at work. The others included Patricia, in charge since she knew the kitchen better *and* could bake; Therese, Ilena, and Jessy, wearing a crisp white T-shirt that showed a voluptuous cartoon blonde holding a tray of tiny baked pies. It was captioned "Queen of Tarts."

"Where are our T-shirts?" Therese asked, feigning a pout as she picked up a heart-shaped cookie cutter. "I want one that says 'Queen of Hearts.' Patricia can have one that says 'Queen Mother.'"

"Mine would be 'Queen of the Beasts,'" Ilena said before mimicking a fearsome lion's roar...if lions were kittens.

Bennie leaned one hip against the counter. "I want one that says 'Queen of Everything.'"

After a chuckle, Jessy asked Patricia, "How is Lucy?"

"She's fine. She starts cardiac rehab in another week or two, and that'll last three months." Patricia studied the order sheet Lucy had given her. "You know, her mother, Robbie, is a lovely woman, but somewhere she got this idea that Lucy is hers to cuddle and fuss over."

"Silly woman. Lucy belongs to us, too," Therese said.

"I think we've all slipped a rung on the ladder of her priorities," Bennie said. "We've been displaced by a gorgeous, sweet, hot-damn football coach."

Patricia began instructing them on their projects and the supplies they needed. As Jessy hefted a twenty-five-pound bag of flour past Bennie, she elbowed her. "I don't think Lucy's the only one doing some displacement."

"Ooh, tell us about Calvin," Therese invited in a singsong voice.

Bennie made a point of keeping her back to the others as she gathered a bowl filled with eggs and pounds of butter from the refrigerator. "He's an old friend. I've known him forever."

When she turned back, they were all looking at her.

"Isn't that cute?" Ilena said. "She thinks we'll be satisfied with that answer."

Bennie gave them a longer version, knowing it wouldn't be enough, either. Maybe because they'd shared such sorrow, when one of them found herself in a new relationship, they wanted to share in the joy—and the details. She couldn't even tell them to mind their own business because she'd been right there with them, questioning Carly, Therese, and Jessy.

"His smile is awfully sweet," Ilena said, "and he looks pretty capable."

"I bet he's a great kisser." That came from Jessy, followed by Therese's retort. "When you haven't been kissed in way too long, they're all great kissers, at least the first time."

Oh, yeah, Calvin was good at that, Bennie thought, measuring her ingredients as they continued to debate kisses. She'd been assigned cupcakes since they were as close to a baked specialty as she got. While Calvin was the topic of conversation, she had to pay attention that she didn't put a cup of salt into the batter instead of sugar.

Finished, she double-checked the recipe before she started cracking eggs into the mixer bowl. She was about to flip on the switch when Jessy's small hand stopped her. "So?"

Bennie pretended innocence, shifting her expression to puzzled.

"You and Calvin," Ilena prodded. "Is it serious? Did absence make your heart grow fonder? Have you gotten physical?"

"You guys get your jollies someplace else," Bennie teased. "Therese, you've got Keegan. Jessy has Dalton."

"And Ilena and I are living vicariously through you and Lucy." Patricia flashed a smile. "We might be persuaded to delay our questioning if you promise to tell all later."

"Sounds like a deal." When there was something to tell. Hopefully soon.

There was nothing like extra hands and lots of laughter to make work easy. Following Lucy's recipes, Bennie made more miniature cupcakes than she could keep track of—chocolate, yellow, carrot cake, and butter pecan—and batches of butter cream frosting to go with them. Ilena, seated on a tall stool at one end of the counter, was in charge of icing them, piping tall swirls of frosting that were as big as the two-bite cakes themselves. Therese was focused on cookies, Patricia on tarts, and Jessy—a self-admitted stranger to the ways of baking—kept busy measuring ingredients and tracking timers for them.

By two o'clock, Bennie was worn out. Her back ached, her feet protested, and her stomach was growling for something that didn't contain massive amounts of butter or sugar. The kitchen was clean, everything was packaged up in adorable boxes or bags, and she was contemplating an afternoon nap when conversation was interrupted by a small voice squealing with delight.

It was Therese's soon-to-be-daughter, Mariah, dashing across the floor as fast as her chubby legs could carry her. "Trace, Trace!" she shrieked as she jumped into her arms. "Look what we found! His name is Calbin, and he—" The flow of words stopped, and Mariah's nose twitched before her gaze darted around the room. "I smell cookies! Where are they? Can I have one?"

Patricia silently checked with Therese, waiting for her

nod before handing over a paper sleeve with a chocolate chip cookie in it. Bennie watched pure pleasure spread across Mariah's face before shifting her gaze to the doorway where Mariah's father, Keegan, stood with Calvin, and the same pleasure spread all the way down to her toes.

He wore khaki shorts and a T-shirt advertising Eskimo Joe's, Stillwater's world-famous bar, and he looked...aw, man, better than all the fabulous baked goods she'd been handling. His smile as he returned the girls' greetings came more easily than it had in his first weeks back, but it didn't quite dislodge the solemnity in his eyes. It twinged a bit around her heart. The boy she'd loved who didn't have a care in the world had a whole world of cares now.

She rubbed a dollop of vanilla-scented lotion into her hands as she slipped past Jessy and Ilena to get to the door. She said hello to Keegan, then bumped shoulders with Calvin. "Hey, Calbin. What are you doing wandering the streets and charming little curly-haired girls?"

"Actually, Mariah found me in the parking lot out front looking for a grown curly-haired girl."

"And what do you want with our grown curly-haired girl?" Ilena asked primly, arms folded across her chest, doing her best stern-mother look.

"Since it's such a nice day, I came to tempt her into a picnic."

Around a mouthful of cookie, Mariah announced, "Calbin's got a dog and Daddy's gonna get me a dog. Maybe five. All girls." She grinned ear to ear, bearing a striking resemblance to her half sister, Abby, and punched one fist in the air. "Girl power!"

In concert with Therese's groan, Bennie arched her brows. "You've got a dog?"

"Nita's not mine. She's a shelter dog, and I'm just giving her some time away. Kind of a doggy day out." He glanced at Jessy, then back at Bennie. "I help out there sometimes."

She was surprised, not because he would volunteer but because he'd never been much of a pet person. Raising money for a charity with a 5K run or building something—that seemed more his style.

Then something registered that had floated past: the dog's name. She gave Jessy a narrow-eyed look. "Nita? Like Be*nita*? You just happen to have a dog named Nita?"

"I wondered when you'd catch that." Jessy's smile was her biggest and brightest. "I didn't name her." While declaring her innocence, she jabbed an accusing finger in Calvin's direction.

Though his ebony skin hid the signs of a flush, Bennie knew him well enough to know his face was hot. She decided to give him a break, retrieving a sleeve of white chocolate macadamia nut cookies to reward him. "You named your beautiful, intelligent dog—or the shelter's beautiful, intelligent dog—after me. That's sweet."

"Wait till you meet her. You might change your mind," Calvin joked.

"Where is she?"

"Probably tearing up my car."

Bennie rolled her eyes. "What damage could an innocent dog do to your POS car?"

From across the room, Mariah piped up again. "What is that? Do we have a POS car, Trace? Can we get one?"

Keegan gave Bennie a faux chastising look. "Thank

you. We have a long trip back to Fort Polk tomorrow, and she'll probably ask if every car we see is a POS car."

"Oops. I think I'll make my escape before I put my other foot in my mouth. Are we all done here?"

Everyone looked to Patricia, who nodded. She hugged Bennie's neck. "Thanks for coming. It means a lot to Lucy."

"Being asked means a lot to me. Give her my love." Bennie located her purse on a storeroom shelf, slung the strap over her shoulder, and said, "All right, Calvin. Show me this incredibly smart gorgeous dog who shares my name with me."

Chapter 16

Calvin had been restless when he got up this morning. Bennie had texted that she was helping out at her friend's, and his parents had taken Gran and Diez to Tulsa for shopping and a movie. Since it was likely one of the last mild days they would see for a while, Calvin had wanted out of the apartment, and after breakfast, it had just seemed normal to head to the animal shelter. When he'd mentioned the idea of a picnic to Angela, she'd asked if he'd be willing to take Nita along. The more exposure she got to people and to different aspects of life, hopefully the sooner she'd be ready for adoption.

She'd said the last with a hopeful look at him. *I can't have a pet,* he'd warned, and she'd acknowledged him with a bob of her head before helpfully pointing out, *But you're not going to be there a whole lot longer.*

He wasn't. Once his team declared him fit to resume life, his medical board would be completed and his final transition from the Army would take place. Two months ago, even a month ago, the idea had scared him spitless. What would he be if he was no longer a soldier?

Truthfully, he wouldn't be much worse off than a lot of people his age who'd never been soldiers. He had a college degree he could use, only he'd gotten his without going eyeball-deep in debt. The Veterans Administration would pay most of the cost of getting another one if he wanted. He could go to work in his father's tile business.

He could be a husband, a father, a son, a grandson, a sorta brother.

He could do or be anything—almost—because he was a survivor.

Could he survive the next few hours with Bennie?

They walked around the building in silence. When he'd arrived, there'd been no sign to indicate he was at the right place, but finding the employee lot of an apparently abandoned building full of cars, he'd guessed he was, then Mariah had confirmed that this was *the place cakes are born.*

Bennie stopped short, a startled laugh coming from her. "She's definitely an improvement to your clunker."

Nita stood in the driver's seat, her front paws on the steering wheel, staring at them, her tail up and quivering. In the time Calvin had been spending with her, she'd made some big strides, but her confidence came and went. As long as it was just the two of them, she was fine, but when anyone else came around, she took cover behind Calvin.

"Why don't you wait here? I'll get her out so she can meet you in the open."

Bennie stopped, lowering herself to the curb. Calvin opened the driver's door, scooping up the leash as Nita jumped to the ground. At first she ignored Bennie, sniffing a trail across the lot to the sidewalk that ran the length of the bakery, then with an air of nonchalance, she walked back to circle Bennie cautiously.

"If I'd known I would have to charm a dog, I would have sneaked a cupcake out in my pocket," she said dryly.

Nita completed her circle, tail wagging, and propped her front feet on Bennie's knees, then stretched out to give her a thorough check. After a moment, she pulled Calvin back to the car, jumped inside, and planted herself firmly in the passenger seat. He closed the door, then returned to offer Bennie a hand. "No signs of aggression," he said.

Bennie bared her teeth at him. "Am I going to have to wrestle that dog over the right to sit in the front seat?"

"I don't know. But I think you could win."

"When we get those T-shirts, Nita, we need to get you one that says, 'QBit. Queen Bitch-in-Training,'" Bennie murmured as she let him pull her up. Her fingers tightened around his for an instant, and her gaze, all soft and sweet, met his.

"Are you saying bad things about your namesake?"

"Of course not. I can see we share things in common. We're smart, pretty, and we both like being the alpha." Still holding his hand, she tugged him to the passenger door. "Where are we going for this picnic?"

"I've got a place in mind."

When he opened the door, Bennie shooed Nita away. The dog stood her ground for a moment, eyeing Bennie with a challenge, before hopping into the backseat and stretching out as if she preferred having the large space.

As he pulled out of the parking lot, Bennie talked about how well Lucy's bakery was doing, given that there hadn't been a formal opening yet, and she discussed all the incredible food they'd made that day. One whiff of the air around her confirmed that if the food tasted half as good as it smelled, it would be outstanding.

When he turned into Gran's driveway, a smile stretched across Bennie's face. "Aw, I haven't been to the pond in ages. It's a perfect day for it."

"That's what I thought."

Calvin shut off the engine, took Nita's leash in one hand, then went to the trunk to get the food and a quilt. Bennie came alongside him. "Want me to take QBit?"

"Nita," he corrected. He handed the leash to her, balanced the basket of food and the quilt, and closed the trunk. It popped back up, requiring another forceful slam before the latch caught. A great burst of laughter came from Bennie, but she didn't say anything, just laughed and shook her head.

The path to the pond entered the woods behind Gran's cabin and meandered through thick growth of blackjack oaks, red cedars, and sumac bushes. It came out on the other side into a clearing, the pond in the center and wide swaths of neatly mowed grass all around. The dock that had been platform to their dives and bellybusters, home base for games of water tag and baseball, and generally a safe spot to rest had been replaced over the years, rickety boards gone, now wide planks sealed to prevent warping and fading.

Two Adirondack chairs sat on the dock, a recent coat of white paint spiffying them up, and neat beds of flowers extended from the dock on both sides.

"When it was just us kids coming out here, the only place to sit was the ground," Bennie commented, "and we were always getting splinters from the dock. Now that Miss Elizabeth comes out every pretty morning to read her Bible, it's got comfy chairs and flowers and looks like a picture from a book."

"What can I say? My dad is way more interested in providing creature comforts for my mom than for us wild kids."

"As he should be." Keeping an eye on Nita, Bennie walked onto the dock, gave one chair seat a halfhearted swipe, then sat down, tilted her face to the sun, and closed her eyes. "What a wonderful place for Bible study. So peaceful and beautiful."

Peaceful and beautiful. The words applied to Bennie even more than their location. Her face was softened, her curls gently framing it. She didn't mind pointing out that she was round, but any weight she'd gained since high school had gone to all the right places. She didn't seem aware that she was gorgeous enough to take men's breath away. She didn't seem to think of herself much at all. She was too busy with life and appreciation and the people she loved who loved her back.

Nita ventured to the edge of the dock, feet spread wide apart, and looked over into the water, her nose twitching. After a moment, she retreated, curled up on the sun-warmed boards near Bennie but not too close, and closed her eyes.

Calvin set down his load, stepped past them, settled in the second chair, and cleared the emotion from his throat. "I thought Mom still did her Bible study at the kitchen table." How many thousands of mornings had he gotten up sleepy-eyed and stumbled into the kitchen in his pajamas to find her there with a cup of coffee, her worn old Bible, and her prayer list?

"She does when it's cold or rainy. The rest of the time, she likes to read and say her prayers amidst the beauty God provided."

That sounded like his mom. And God knew, Calvin had given her plenty to pray about in his lifetime. He wished he'd asked her to say an extra prayer for him today. The way his insides were knotted, he would need it just to get the words out. He was trying to think of a way to start when Bennie unexpectedly gave him another of her dazzling smiles.

"Let's spread that quilt out, sit on the ground as proper picnic etiquette requires, and eat. All I've had today is carbs, and my body is demanding protein like a whiny child three hours past her naptime."

Relief went through him. It was a temporary reprieve; he knew that. But right now, he would take what he could get.

* * *

Lucy's house was quiet. Wearing yoga pants and a T-shirt, she lay on her side on the sofa, face pressed into the pillow, throw pulled to her chin, breathing evenly. She hadn't tried faking sleep with her mother in years and had never been very good at it, but this time it seemed to be working.

"I'm going to run some errands," her mother murmured to Joe in the kitchen doorway. "Walmart, the drugstore, Whole Foods, oh, and Java Dave's. If I go home without their coffee beans, Lucy's dad will pout for a week."

Lucy imagined that conversation: *Our only daughter's had a heart attack.* And her dad: *Would you bring back some Java Dave's coffee?* The grin almost ruined her sleep pretense.

"She had a good lunch, and there's nothing she should be doing but rest." Her mother paused, and Lucy peered just enough to see her hug Joe. "I can't tell you how grateful I am that you're here with her. It's such a relief to the whole family." She dabbed her eyes and stepped back. "I'll have my cell, so if you need anything at all, call me. I can be back in five minutes."

"We'll be fine, Robbie. Just go, enjoy the weather, and take your time."

It took a few moments for Mom to get out the door. Once the car door slammed, then the engine revved to life, Lucy let her muscles relax. She was waiting for the motor noise to fade completely when Joe said, "Okay, possum, she's gone."

Chagrined, she pushed the throw aside and gave him a crooked grin. "I love her dearly."

"But she's driving you nuts."

Sitting up, she propped her feet on the coffee table and combed her hair with her fingers. "She makes me shower with the bathroom door open while she hovers just outside. My second day home, I had to beg to go pee by myself, and she insisted on putting my shoes on for me until this morning."

Joe slid over the back of the couch, bouncing Lucy a bit as he settled in beside her. "You're her baby."

"I know."

"And you had a heart attack."

Lifting her hand, she held her thumb and forefinger a half-inch apart. "A baby heart attack." The cardiologist had said it was an uncommon event. Everyone at the hospital called it *an event*, as if it were somehow a milestone she'd marked or something to celebrate, though a tear in the plaque in the left anterior descending aorta was neither a milestone nor a celebration, even if it had already begun to resolve itself by the time they took her to the cath lab.

Before she'd managed a huge sigh of relief that it was just a fluke, the doctor had added the fact that she'd had this uncommon event meant she was susceptible to it. They'd be trying to prevent a recurrence the rest of her life.

Thank God she *had* a "rest of her life."

"It was a small one because you were smart enough to tell us before it became a big one. You scared her, Luce." He slid his arm around her shoulders, hugging her tightly. "You scared all of us."

Her head rested against his shoulder, sending pure satisfaction through her. There was no other place she wanted to be right now, no other person she wanted to be with. As long as Joe was there, she was okay. He would always make her okay.

After a moment, she asked, "How long do you think she'll be gone?"

"Walmart? On a Saturday? Almost the first of the month? At least a couple hours." His blue eyes narrowed. "Why?"

"Take me for a walk. Walking's good—the cardiologist said so—but Mom only lets me walk in the house. Please, I just want to go around the block a time or two. I want to feel the sun and smell the fresh air." She gave him her best pout. "Please don't make me whine and beg like Norton."

"She'll be pissed if she finds out."

"But I'll be unhappy if you don't."

"Yeah, but you don't scare me. Your mom does."

She frowned. "Then I must be doing something wrong. Mike was always afraid of me when my eyes turned red and my hair caught fire."

"Aw, I've never seen you even mildly ticked off." He grinned. "It gives me something to look forward to."

He leaned forward, and Lucy thought for a moment that he was getting up to leave her on the couch. Instead, he handed her first one shoe, then the other. "Lace those up and let's get going so the flush in your cheeks and the fresh-air scent have time to fade before your mom comes back."

She shoved her feet into the shoes and tied quick, sloppy bows before wrapping her arms around his neck. "Thank you, Joe." The romantic aspect of their relationship was still new enough that in the instant he took to hug her back, insecurity bubbled in her stomach. With his arms holding her close, his scent fragrant and comforting, the bubble burst and the nerves slunk away, leaving a tingly, giddy, girly sensation in their place.

As they headed for the door, Norton looked up from his snoozy spot beneath the coffee table, a yawn crinkling his eyes into narrow slits. He moved as if he was thinking about joining them, but Sebastian, curled against him, protested, and Norton sank back down.

"Lazy dog," Lucy muttered, walking out the door ahead of Joe.

"I take him for two runs a day," Joe protested. "Be-sides, he keeps Sebastian so happy that it's not really like you have a second pet."

Joe was right about that. The two of them were Nor-ton's humans; Norton was Sebastian's. If the dog could learn to operate the can opener, the kitten would have no use for anyone else.

At the top of the steps, Lucy stretched her arms to the sky, breathing deeply. She'd been a prisoner for the last week, first of the hospital, then of her mom. Like she'd said, she loved her mother dearly and appreciated that she'd dropped everything, including Thanksgiving with the family, to come and be with Lucy, but Robbie was *so* cautious, and Joe hadn't been much help reining her in. He'd spent all his free time at the house, helping Robbie, taking care of the animals, and pampering Lucy way be-yond reasonable.

Though the definition of *reasonable* was certainly sub-jective. If their places were switched and it had been Joe who'd suffered a heart attack—as if his heart would ever betray his gorgeously healthy, fit body—she would be hovering in constant panic mode. But there were little voices inside her that wanted to shriek, *I'm okay!*

"This is just a stroll," Joe reminded her, catching her hand and tugging her back to his side. "You don't want to overdo it before rehab. Wait until you're hooked up to the monitors and under supervision before you try to show them how far you've bounced back."

"What do you know about cardiac rehab?" she asked, hands shoved in her pockets. They really were just strolling. She'd been outstripping this pace for all but the first week of their exercise program.

"I used to take my grandfather to rehab after school. And I talked to the nurse who came by your room to tell you about it."

Lucy had listened to the nurse, a sweet woman named Debbie, but she'd still been in worried mode. How the heck could she have had a heart attack? How would it affect all the plans she'd made for life? Would she have to give up Prairie Harts? Was she going to die younger than all her family and friends? Could she have children? Could she live long enough to see them graduate and get married? Could she have *sex*?

She hadn't learned much about rehab.

"You'll go in a week from Tuesday for an evaluation," Joe went on. "Your mom wanted to stay to go with you for that first appointment, but I persuaded her I could be trusted to get you there and back."

Saved from another week and a half of her mom's worry. "I owe you."

Joe squeezed her fingers lightly. "I intend to collect." At the end of the block, he steered her to the right and across the street. "The rehab staff has two RNs, Debbie and Tina, and Jill is an exercise physiologist. You'll have classes on medications, nutrition, weight training, diabetes, reading food labels, good stuff like that. You'll go Monday, Wednesday, and Friday for twelve weeks, and when you finish, you get a cool T-shirt."

So far, nothing he'd said had made Lucy's ears perk up. Of course she would complete the course of rehab. She would work out and learn even better eating habits and everything else. She would do her best to keep the very scary heart attack thing from ever happening again.

But the idea of being rewarded with a cool T-shirt

made her grin. "I will work for cool T-shirts," she announced.

"And if a longer, happier, healthier life is a benefit of getting cool T-shirts, so be it," he added dryly.

After a moment, they turned to the right at the next corner. A few blocks straight ahead, and they would be standing across the street from Prairie Harts. She hadn't asked if they could walk that far—she was just thrilled to be outside and moving—and she wouldn't. If she had to give up the shop after all her dreaming, if it was the stress factor that had pushed her into the event, maybe it was better that she start getting used to the idea now before the doctors came right out and said so.

But Joe didn't turn around at the next intersection, or the next. He kept heading east, and then there it was, looking exactly the way it had the first time she'd seen it. The front windows were still grimy, the parking lot still rutted. She'd thought it a wonderful place that first time and still thought so now. Her mind could so clearly see the bright paint and the cozy chairs, could smell the fresh baked goods and the rich coffee, and could hear the crowds waiting in line for breakfast pastries and after-dinner treats.

A lump formed in her throat as she tried to surreptitiously swipe her eyes. "What if I have to give it up, Joe?"

He bent to see her face. "Why would you have to do that?"

"Hello? MI?" She fluttered her hand over her chest.

He pulled her tight against him. "The docs don't know what caused it. They certainly didn't single out the bakery. But I can tell you as your coach, what you've got to do is work smarter, not harder. You might have to cut back on your hours at your regular job, or you might have to hire a few people sooner than you expected. I know one, in fact, who's determined to be first in line to put her application in."

"Who?" Lucy's forehead wrinkled. Her friends had helped her out tremendously, but most of them had jobs and weren't looking for a career change.

"Patricia. Whenever you're up to talking business, she wants to come over and discuss it with you. I'm thinking that means after your mom goes home tomorrow. And I'll still help out, and I know a couple of kids from school who are dependable and like to earn their own spending money."

Patricia. He couldn't have said a name that could have brightened her as much. Lucy and the older woman were the best of friends, and Patricia was a fabulous baker herself. They got along well, and Patricia had a way of making everyone around her feel better about themselves. She would be perfect. And any kids Joe sent over would be exactly as he described. He had no patience for slackers.

Her day suddenly lighter and sunnier, Lucy smiled up at Joe and asked a question she knew he'd heard a lot, especially from the margarita girls. "You're about as close to perfect as a man can get. Why aren't you married?"

His grin faded as he raised his hand to her face, brushing her cheek, touching her as if she were gentle and fragile and precious, then he did it again with his mouth. It started as just a touch, lips to skin, but in a heartbeat— yep, her heart was beating steady and strong—he'd kissed his way to her mouth and was doing some interesting nibbling at the corner. "I've been waiting for you, Luce."

His husky voice sent shivers through her, and the kiss that followed spread heat, made her feel weak and strong and excited. It also made her wish she'd paid more attention to her doctor during the discharge meeting. *Do you have any questions about activities?* he'd asked, and one had instantly danced into her mind: *Can I have sex?* She'd kept it in, though, because her mother was there, and Joe was there, and after all, she hadn't had sex in seven years. Waiting a week until her follow-up appointment was no big deal.

Right this moment, standing on the sidewalk across from her shop, resting her hands on Joe's waist and getting her toes curled by his kiss, she decided for future reference that she *really* needed to redefine *no big deal*.

*   *   *

"Remember when we went skinny-dipping here?"

Bennie lay on her side on the quilt, her head pillowed on her bent arm, feeling as full, fat, and lazy as the pooch snoring next to Calvin, who mimicked Bennie's position. The remains of their lunch were scattered between them: fried chicken, potato salad, tabouli, and a foil pan of frosted brownies topped with giant walnut halves. Perfect picnic food.

"I didn't go skinny-dipping here," she disagreed. "The only naked bodies in that water belonged to you and J'Myel. I kept my T-shirt and shorts on."

"Yeah, but we could see right through your shirt."

She feigned a scandalized look, then laughed. "We were so afraid of getting caught. Not that I did anything wrong. I didn't even sneak a peek at your scrawny selves." They'd been eleven, maybe twelve years old. She'd been learning from her friends that boys might be good for something other than outrunning, outfishing, and outsmarting. Of course she'd sneaked peeks. "Oh, we thought we were something back then," she said with a sigh.

The humor faded from Calvin's eyes, and his mouth thinned as he stared off into the distance. Was he seeing J'Myel instead of their setting? Or maybe his innocent naïve self with his innocent naïve view of the future?

She wished he didn't have so many sorrows in his life. Their pastor said they needed the bad times to appreciate the good ones, but Bennie was pretty sure she could be totally appreciative of the good without the adversity. She would at least like to give it a try.

"What are you thinking about, Squeaky?"

For a long time he didn't acknowledge even hearing her. He reached out one unsteady hand and scooted QBit—sorry, Nita—closer so he could rub her spine and shoulders. The dog had been fun to watch, fierce one moment, timid the next. She clearly knew she was Calvin's girl, showing an occasional interest in Bennie but mostly ignoring her. Whether he knew it yet, Calvin had himself a dog. Someone might have to house her until he moved out of the barracks—Gran would surely volunteer—but Bennie doubted Nita would deign to a home longer than very short-term with anyone other than Calvin.

Good thing Bennie liked dogs.

A low sigh came from the other side of the quilt, drawing Bennie's gaze from the puppy to Calvin. His expression was haunted, tightening his face, his muscles, his nerves, as he stared bleakly at her. "Before I came here, I tried to kill myself."

Bennie blinked, confused. There was no doubt she'd heard the words, that they'd come, broken and guttural, from him. There was no doubt she understood what each of them meant. They just didn't—couldn't—register in her brain. "You—you what?" She tried to laugh at the ludicrousness of it, but the laugh was a failure. With her chest suddenly tight and her hands clenching into fists, with fear washing through her and blocking the sun's heat, she was pretty sure not so much as a choked giggle was hiding anywhere inside her.

"God, that's not how I intended to do this." He sat up, covering his face with both hands, scrubbing at his eyes. The blood veins in the backs of his hands stood out with the movement, and a sudden, sob-like breath shook his shoulders. Shame darkened his eyes when he lowered his hands, but she caught only a glimpse as he pushed to his feet. He collected Nita's leash in one hand, then extended the other to Bennie. "Can we walk?"

She reached through the anguish and despair hovering suffocatingly thick around him, swore it was clammy against her skin before she found his hand. Under other circumstances, she would have teased about whether he was capable of pulling her rounded curves up from the ground, but instead all she did was cling tightly to his hand, even after she was on her feet, even when it would have been polite to let go or to at least ease her grip.

With Nita exploring as far ahead as her leash allowed, they started along the neatly mowed bank of the pond. There were little soothing sounds: fish splashing, a frog ribbeting on a rock, a light breeze, Nita's snuffle when she found a particularly interesting scent. There weren't any sounds from Bennie or Calvin. She didn't know what to say or how to say it. Did she need to be gentler, warier, in the way she couched things to him? Was his suicide attempt a one-time thing, a heat-of-the-moment-things-are-bad-so-screw-life action? Or was it something he still wanted, that he would keep trying until he succeeded?

The possibility of Calvin dying, of not being there for her and his parents and Gran and Mama, absolutely broke Bennie's heart. It was so ugly a thought, so hurtful, that her knees buckled, sending her stumbling a few feet across the yellowed grass before his grip brought back her balance. If he let go, she would sink to the ground and sob the way she sobbed only twice in her life: when her daddy died and when J'Myel died.

Would he cry with her?

With her free hand, she swiped away tears seeping down her cheeks. It took a huge effort to make her voice work, to get the words out in a somewhat coherent stream. "Calvin Clyde Sweet, you know I love you, but I'm going to beat you senseless if you don't start talking fast." She waggled her index finger. "And before you pull any of that I'm-a-boy-you're-a-girl crap, just remember that I've done it before."

His mouth tried to smile, tilting up the tiniest bit at one corner, but the light moment faded into the darkness around him as if it had never been there. He took a breath, fixed his gaze on Nita, and slid quick glances Bennie's way as he began talking. His voice was heavy, empty of emotion because, she knew, he was overwhelmed by emotion. "The Army's getting rid of me. After the suicide attempt, I was diagnosed with PTSD. They sent me to the Warrior Transition Unit here so I can get treatment before they boot me out."

Then his voice broke. "They say I'm too unstable to wear the uniform anymore. And they're right."

It was the most surreal situation she had ever found herself in—a place where she'd spent a thousand happy hours growing up, a boy she'd relied on and trusted and looked up to all those years, a beautiful fall day, a happy puppy, and words that made perfect sense and absolutely no sense at all. Yes, people attempted suicide, but not Calvin. People suffered psychiatric problems, but not him. He was too strong. Too centered. Too spiritual. Too normal. Too—

Haunted, the voice in her head whispered. *Broken.* She'd thought it was weariness from the war, grief about J'Myel, guilt for missing his funeral. She'd thought it would pass, a phase people went through, tough times that they dealt with, that made them stronger.

But post-traumatic stress disorder...suicide. Having to leave the Army that was all he'd ever wanted to do with his life. Those things didn't sound like phases. Tough? Oh, yell, yes. Making him stronger?

He'd considered suicide. Justice and Elizabeth's boy, the light of Gran's life, had wanted to die so badly that he'd tried to make it happen.

And J'Myel had wanted to live just as badly. Carly's husband, Ilena's, Therese's, Lucy's, Marti's, Fia's, Jessy's, Patricia's—all their husbands had fought to live, to come home to the people they loved.

That last thought stirred a twinge of anger underneath her shock and disbelief and fear, but she burrowed it in deeper. It was one more emotion she couldn't deal with at the moment.

A shudder vibrated through him, transferring into his

fingers that still clenched hers. "That's how I met Diez—
the night I tried to…He tackled me, got the gun, and
threw it away—threw it onto a damn train passing by.
That's when he stole my car and wallet, and that's how
he ended up here. That's how *I* ended up here, Bennie,
because the Army doesn't want me anymore. Because I
was stupid and depressed, and no one knows how long the
patches keeping me together will hold or even if they will
hold, and I'm not fit for duty anymore." His next words
were little more than a whisper. "Some days I don't think
I'm fit for anything."

She recalled the angry scene when they'd first come
upon Diez in the Sweet driveway, how volatile Calvin had
been. Had it been because the kid saved his life when he'd
wanted to die—dear God, even thinking that made her
hurt—or because he didn't trust Diez to keep his mouth
shut about it?

"Your parents know." *This is the boy that helped you
out,* Justice had said that day before welcoming Diez into
their house and hearts.

"Mom and Dad. Gran." Calvin gazed across the pond
to the chairs on the other side. "Dane Clark. Jessy knows
part of it."

Her mouth dropped open in automatic protest. He'd
confided his secret in Dane, whom he'd met all of two
times, and Jessy Lawrence, while not admitting a hint of
it to Bennie?

Then common sense clamped her jaw shut again. Dane
was a soldier, too, whose injuries in Afghanistan had put
an end to his career. He would understand in ways she
couldn't.

But Jessy?

As if reading her mind, Calvin gestured toward Nita. "The shelter. It's part of my therapy. I'm pretty sure she doesn't know what happened in Tacoma, but all the patients in the program have PTSD. She couldn't have told you anything even if she wanted."

"Of course she couldn't." Being a nurse's aide, Bennie understood the concept of patient confidentiality all too well.

"I suspect Mama knows, too. She hasn't said anything, but..." He shrugged. "Have you ever known Gran to keep a secret from her best friend?"

"No." The idea would be laughable if Bennie could laugh. Mama and Gran told each other *everything*, and neither of them had ever broken a confidence in forty-plus years. The CIA and NSA could learn lessons from them.

After walking another quarter of the distance around the pond, Calvin glanced her way. "So that's it, Bennie. That's what's going on with me. I'm working to get past it, but no one knows what'll happen, whether I'm ever gonna be normal again or—or if I'll do something stupid again. I take my meds, and I talk to the doctors and the therapists and the guys who have been there and gotten better, and most days I feel hopeful, but some days...I just don't know. And you have a right to know that. You had a right to know it before we spent any time at all together, but I was ashamed. I'm working on that, too. I didn't want you to look at me and worry or wonder. I just wanted to feel like...like maybe I can be the one that gets over it."

Dear God, she hoped he could be one of the lucky ones to get over it. If he couldn't, if he tried again, if he succeeded...

With a lump in her throat and her eyes growing damp again, she searched deep inside herself for words. He was stealing looks at her, waiting for her to say something, to do something, and she wanted to, but she desperately needed it to be the *right* thing. She wanted to throw her arms around his neck and hug him so tight that he could never get free. She wanted to smack him on the back of the head, give him a good shake, and demand to know what in sweet heaven had he been thinking. She wanted to assure him that it didn't make a difference, that he would be okay, that they would be okay. But there was so much shock, so much fear, and so damn much hurt—for him. For herself and her dreams. For J'Myel.

They reached the dock again, and Calvin stopped, releasing her hand, turning to face her. She forced herself to meet his gaze, to study his familiar brown eyes, as if she could find something there, hope or a promise she could believe in. All she saw was misery and pain.

"Calvin..." Her voice quavered, and she took a swipe at her eyes while waiting for magic words to pop into her mind. When they didn't come, she turned onto the dock and sat in one of the chairs. After a moment, he sat in the other, and Nita immediately climbed into his lap. He had certainly formed a bond with the puppy, and she with him. Two lost souls connecting in a way that might save each other's lives.

A sob rose inside her, struggling to find its voice. Why hadn't Miss Elizabeth told her this, or Gran or Mama, so she could prepare herself? Why hadn't she realized on her own that something was wrong? Why hadn't she pressed him for answers about Diez and how they'd met and why the boy coming to Tallgrass had made him so angry?

Because she'd been falling in love. She'd been opening up her heart for the first time since J'Myel and loving that giddy feeling, the flush of sexual attraction, the possibility that being a well-loved wife and mom was once again within her reach.

Was still within her reach.

If she could deal with this news.

"I don't know what to say, Calvin," she managed at last. "I never imagined…" She was having trouble with it even now. Suicide was a sacrilege, life far too precious to waste like that.

But he'd had reasons she couldn't begin to understand for the actions he'd taken. It wasn't a decision he'd come to lightly. He'd felt he had no other option.

And that broke her heart.

Chapter 17

Despite Bennie's silence and her obvious distress, Calvin felt something very much like relief seeping through him. He'd done it. It hadn't been pretty or elegant, but he'd bared his secrets to her. What happened next was entirely up to her.

He didn't beg her to understand. How could he when he hardly understood himself? He didn't push her for more of a response. When Bennie had something to say, she said it. Right now, he imagined, she'd told the absolute truth: She didn't know what to say. He'd hit her with a lot. Of course she was stunned. Of course she needed time.

Time to make some decisions. Would she want to spend the rest of her life with someone like him, always looking for chinks in his recovery, always evaluating? *Is this normal behavior? Is he having trouble coping? Does this outburst mean a relapse?* How could he blame her when she did wonder, since his own doubts could be overwhelming?

Would she want to marry someone like him, have children with someone like him, knowing there would never be a promise that he would always be there, calm and capable and rational and able to act as a husband and father?

Or would she reject anything but friendship from him, nothing more complicated, no way he could break her heart? Would she break his heart?

He understood if she didn't want to be with him because he didn't want to *be* him.

Nita trembled in his lap, a tiny whimper escaping her, and he laid his hand gently over her rib cage. Her legs twitched a time or two, along with another whimper, then she stilled again, her deep breathing resuming. When she'd first come to the shelter, she hadn't wanted anyone to touch her. Now she slept like a baby on his legs. She didn't hold his mistakes against him.

The knowledge sparked a bit of a smile. He might still be finding his way. His future might be one giant blank. The woman he loved might decide life was better without him. But Nita was on his side.

The breeze picked up, rustling leaves still clinging to the mostly bare branches. The grass out here was already dormant for the winter, but the flowers—pansies, his mother's favorite in part because they tolerated cold— would hold on to their color. Before long, she wouldn't be able to sit out here for Bible study. She would complain about the lower temperatures and the wind that seemed to blow straight in from the North Pole and the sun that hid behind the clouds. Then one day buds would appear, bits of green here and there, blossoms on the redbuds and dogwoods and Bartlett pears, and Elizabeth's mood would turn sunny again.

Sunny was too girly a word to use to describe himself, but he would be happy to see spring again.

Bennie shivered, hugging her arms across her chest. "What time do you need to get Nita back to the shelter?"

He swallowed hard, wishing her question had been something more personal or hadn't been a question at all but something to give him a hint of what she was thinking or feeling. "Meredith and Angela will be feeding the animals and getting them settled for the night between five and seven."

"You should see about adopting—" She broke off, her gaze flickering away, and she shifted in the chair as if she was anxious to get up and move.

What had stopped her from completing the suggestion? Did she wonder whether he was fit to adopt a puppy? The possibility stirred an ache in his gut. She *knew* him…

But he'd changed.

Abruptly she pushed to her feet, gathered the leftovers into the basket, and gave the quilt a shake. "We should probably go," she said, trying to fold the quilt neatly into quarters, failing, and trying again. Her hands trembled, and so did her voice when she went on. "I imagine the sooner they have all their fur babies accounted for, the sooner they can get home."

Calvin shook Nita awake, set her on the dock, and looped her leash around a chair leg, then went to Bennie, tugging at the quilt, intending to fold it for her. Instead, he wrapped his arms around both her and the cover. With a soft, strangled cry, she buried her face against his chest, her hands clenched so tightly that he felt the tension all through her body, shudders rocketing like little earthquakes.

Wishing he had comfort to give her, he held her, stroking her back, breathing deeply of the scent of her hair, her clothes, her perfume. He wanted to say, *We'll work this out,* because one way or another, they would. It just might not be the way either of them wanted. Because he couldn't face the possibility of losing her again right now, he settled for a less personal assurance.

"It'll work out, Shorty," he murmured.

She freed one arm to punch him in the shoulder for the nickname, but there was no force behind it. "I know that. It's just hard." Her voice broke on the last word, and a fresh wave of tears started.

Yeah, he recognized *hard.* He'd lived with it so damn long that he'd thought there was no other option for him.

But he'd just finished the hardest thing he'd ever had to do, besides dealing with J'Myel's death, and he was okay. Worried. Hurting for Bennie. Scared. But not despairing. Not thinking that whatever life might have to offer couldn't possibly be better than the nothingness of death.

He was making progress.

Finally Bennie swiped her eyes before giving him a weak smile. "We should go."

He glanced at Nita, listened to the breeze, looked at the sun, which wasn't far from setting. It had been a lot of years since he'd watched the sun set over the pond, back when they'd had folding lawn chairs and a fire pit and thought roasted wieners on cold buns and s'mores were the perfect meal.

A glance at his watch showed that he still had plenty of time to get to the shelter. "Why don't you head on back, and Nita and I will—"

The expression that darted across her face, surprise tinged with panic, cut off the words in his throat. He knew that look. He'd seen it to different degrees on other faces the past few months. She was afraid to leave him here alone. She didn't trust that if she walked out of the woods by herself, he would soon follow.

Feeling about two feet tall, he smiled at her. "Never mind. I'll take you home."

Relief flooded her eyes even as her caramel-toned skin took on a reddish tinge. "I'm sorry, Calvin."

"It's okay." He didn't like that her natural response was to worry about his mental health, but he had taken the actions; he had to live with the consequences.

They walked silently back to the car. She offered to walk home, and he reminded her that her car was at the bakery. That trip passed quietly, too. Before opening the car door, she faced him. "Will you be at Sunday dinner?"

"Will you worry if I'm not?"

"I've worried about you for the better part of my life, Calvin. Worried you and J'Myel would get me in trouble as kids, worried about you both every single day you were gone. I don't think the worrying is ever gonna go away."

He took her hand. "I'll be there."

"Good." Then she did the thing that gave him the most hope. She leaned across the seat and kissed him, not as long and hard as he would have liked but not just a brush of mouths, either.

She got out, closed the door, and bent to look through the open window as Nita jumped into the seat she'd just vacated. "Miss Nita, it's been a pleasure meeting you. I'm sure we're gonna be seeing a whole lot more of each other, though, so you should get used to that backseat."

The dog stretched and turned her back on Bennie.

"Queen Bitch-in-Training," Bennie murmured before shifting her gaze to Calvin. "Thank you," she said solemnly. "For the picnic, the company, the talk. For trusting me. For giving me some time."

He acknowledged her with a nod, shifting into reverse as she took a few steps away. Abruptly, she came back. "I've always loved you, Calvin. I always will." With an emphatic nod, she spun around and went to her own car.

There were all kinds of love. Though Gran said a person could never have too much, this was one time he might disagree with her. Bennie had always loved him like a best friend, like a brother. After she untangled all the thoughts in her head, that might be the only way she could continue to love him.

God help him, he wanted so damn much more than that.

It was a short drive to the shelter. The only car in the parking lot belonged to Angela. Calvin figured Meredith had ridden with her—they lived together, after all—but when he went inside, he found just the shelter manager.

She greeted him with a smile, then crouched to Nita's level. "How'd you do on your picnic, sweetie?"

Nita sat down beside Calvin and eyed Angela, not suspiciously, just without any real interest. Angela laughed and stood again, directing her question to him.

"She was great. No aggression, no running wild. She played a bit, walked a bit, slept a bit."

"How was she with your girlfriend?"

The last word twinged inside him—would Bennie still be his girlfriend tomorrow or next week?—but he grinned at the memory of Nita claiming the front seat in the car at the bakery before reluctantly surrendering it to Bennie. "They're not best friends forever, but neither of them snapped or snarled at the other, so that's good. Where's Meredith?"

"She had an emergency at the clinic. If we both get done in time, we have a date in Tulsa. We're going to dinner, then to a new club in Midtown."

He followed her back into the kennel, where he unleashed Nita into a small crate. "I bet every heart in the room breaks when you two walk into a club and people realize you're together."

Angela smiled. "Depends on the club. There are a few we wouldn't dare walk into. Not everyone is as accepting as we'd like."

Acceptance was a big thing, he acknowledged as they began dishing up food. He'd had it most of the time, had had friends of every ethnicity both here in Tallgrass and in the Army. J'Myel hadn't rejected him because of his race or sexual orientation but his ambition. Bennie didn't care about race and shared his ambition, but she might not accept his psychiatric issues.

Life was never easy, but the struggle, Gran claimed, made it all the sweeter.

Given the struggle, his life should be sweeter than honey melting over ice cream, but he'd settle for Bennie's kisses.

If she ever gave him another one.

* * *

Lucy gazed out the passenger window of Joe's car, the day a pretty accurate reflection of her mood. The Sunday afternoon sun kept slipping behind clouds that darkened the sky, and rain would spit just long enough to require the wipers, then stop again. While the sun shone, it looked like a perfectly lovely day, but when the clouds took over, the temperature dropped thirty degrees, at least in her mind.

She and Joe had dropped her mom off at the airport in Tulsa and were on their way back to Tallgrass. She was happy that life was going to start getting back to normal, but it always made her homesick to say good-bye to someone she loved.

"You okay?"

She glanced at Joe. "I'm a little relieved she's gone. Does that make me a bad daughter?"

"Of course not. Admitting it, though…"

Her mouth dropped open before she saw his grin. "Don't tease me, Joe. I'm fragile. I had an event."

He snorted, the same way they both had in the hospital when they'd realized the event the staff was referring to was her heart attack. "They make it sound like some high-class party or something. Can't they just say *heart attack* like the rest of the world?"

"Maybe they get paid more for handling events rather than heart attacks. It does sound a little more complicated. Thank heavens I've got great insurance." *Thank Mike.* As a widow who hadn't remarried, she was still eligible for care through the military health system—a huge relief when her hospitalization and upcoming rehabilitation could easily cost more than her house was worth.

They passed the Tallgrass city limits sign two miles

before they reached the turnoff to Fort Murphy's main gate. A little flutter of homecoming flitted through Lucy. She'd lived her first eighteen years in California, but Tallgrass was top of the list for the title of home. She'd never dreamed when she'd come here with Mike that she would lose him here, that she would live alone in their little house and make a place for herself here, that she would start a business here, but it had happened. She couldn't imagine trading the love and support and roots of this place for anywhere else.

Wait, that wasn't quite true…Her gaze slipped sideways to catch a glimpse of Joe, sunglasses hiding his eyes, his attention on the street ahead as traffic picked up. A young football coach with big aspirations and a winning record was always being lured from one school to another. Joe had already been approached a couple of times, and there was no doubt more recruiters would come knocking on his door. Love of a man had brought her to Tallgrass. Could love of a man take her away again?

Of course, she knew the answer without even considering it. Given the choice between being with Joe in a new town or being lonely in Tallgrass…that was no choice at all.

At the intersection of Main and First, Joe turned north. Warmth bubbled inside her because she knew where he was going, even though she hadn't asked. Her mom had made it clear from the day of her arrival that she thought Lucy had taken on much too big a challenge, which was probably the reason for the heart attack. To Robbie, it had been a foregone conclusion that Lucy would get rid of the shop and thereby lessen the stress in her life.

Her mom had been too worried to understand that getting rid of it now, before it had even had a chance to bloom, would break Lucy's heart.

When Joe turned into the parking lot, shut off the engine, and walked around to open her door, she was grinning. "Oh, Prairie Harts, I've missed you." She let him help her from the car—because she liked the chivalry and the physical contact, not because she needed help—then followed him to the front door, where she briefly laid her hand flat against the grimy plate glass before walking inside. "I should finish rehab just in time to get this place all fixed up for spring."

"Yeah, I hear your logo designer has some ideas about that. She was talking to one of my boys about using his dad's welding equipment to make some heart-shaped flowers like the ones on your packaging. She plans to talk to you when she's got something to show."

"Aw, that's so sweet of her." Last spring, the idea of Abby Matheson with a welding torch in her hands would have sparked fear in the margarita girls' hearts. With a little love, the Princess of Whine had made an amazing turnabout. Nope, make that a whole lot of love. And prayers. Patience. Understanding.

Though the front area was dusty and needed plenty of work, when Lucy looked around, she could so easily imagine tables and chairs, display counters filled with goodies, and Abby's super-cool metal bouquets. Customers, too, of course, and Lucy herself, wearing an apron and feeling supremely contented. *That* was the kind of "event" she could look forward to.

Twenty-four hours after yesterday's marathon baking session, wonderful aromas still drifted on the air. They made Lucy's mouth water, not with hunger for sugar and spice and everything nice. It was food for her soul, that the church orders had gone out on time, thanks to her margarita girls; that the heart attack wasn't going to shut her down before she got started; that she had this incredible chance to do something with her life that made her so darn happy; that she had an incredible guy backing her a hundred percent.

The kitchen was spotless, with only a small bakery box in the middle of the worktable. *For Lucy and Joe* was swirled in black ink across the top—how had Patricia been so sure she and Joe would come by as soon as Robbie left?—and inside nestled four two-bite cupcakes and a stack of cookies tied with a ribbon. Lucy sighed. "I have to watch my sugar and fat intake."

"And yet the cardiac diet in the hospital included dessert with every meal." Joe broke off a quarter of a cookie and popped it in his mouth. "You've been watching your sugar and fat intake for the last six months, Luce. Now you add sodium and cholesterol to that, and you balance your proteins and carbs. Everything in moderation." Then he grinned. "Except me."

She rolled her eyes. In addition to the exercise physiologist and the nurses at rehab, she would have classes taught by a dietitian, a pharmacist, and other professionals, plus she had her own personal trainer, coach, and nutritionist. If she didn't come out of this event healthier than ever, it wouldn't be for lack of trying.

Joe polished off the cookie, closed the box, and slid his arms around her from behind. She let herself lean back against him, the way she'd been leaning on him for years, and gripped his forearm with both hands. He nuzzled her hair back from her ear and murmured, "You wanna go home and see what fun we can have now that your mom's not there?"

Letting her eyes drift shut, she tilted her head to give him better access to the sensitive skin around her ear and along her jaw. Shivers swept over her, raising tiny goose bumps on her arms despite the heat pumping through her veins. She'd waited so long to feel this way again—had sometimes given up hope of it ever happening. The pleasure of Joe's embrace and his little intimate kisses was so incredible that anything more just might kill her. But, oh, what a way to go.

She turned in his embrace, wrapped her arms around him, and just pretty much melted inside at the feel of his arousal against her. A blush heating her face, she lifted her gaze to his. "You know, the doctor didn't say I could have sex yet."

Joe's grin was quick and boyish and far too charming. "He didn't say you couldn't." Then his blue eyes went serious as he freed one hand to touch her face, and his voice turned husky. "I've waited all my life for you, Lucy. I can wait awhile longer."

Then he let her go, picked up the dessert box in one hand, and took her hand in his other. As he pulled her toward the door, he glanced back over his shoulder, and the grin reappeared. "Besides, Luce, we can have all kinds of fun without actually having sex." His brows arched, making the blue of his eyes pop. "I'll show you."

Lucy flipped off the light switch as they passed it, then they made their way through the dining room with only the sun shining through the windows. With the exception of Mike, she had never been this happy. She could take the time to list all her treasures in her head: Joe loved her—incredible. She loved him back—naturally. She had the best family and friends—wonderful. Despite the heart attack, she was happy and surprisingly healthy. She had her baking business.

And the man she loved was looking at her, reaching for her as if he couldn't live without a cozier touch than just holding hands.

Her heart was about to burst in her chest with pure happiness.

*   *   *

Sunday and Monday passed in a blur for Bennie, her mind stuck on a never-ending loop of Calvin's words: *I tried to kill myself...I was diagnosed with PTSD...I'm not fit for duty anymore...I don't think I'm fit for anything.*

It broke her heart that he'd been suffering so much and she'd done nothing to help. Other than an odd behavior here or there, she hadn't guessed a thing, and she should have. The better part of their lives, she'd known what he was thinking and feeling just by looking at him, but she'd seriously failed him this time.

She knew she'd been distant at Sunday dinner and hated it, but she needed reassurance. Faith—or was it trust? She couldn't pretend that Saturday's conversation hadn't been a shock, that it hadn't changed things. She had emotions to deal with, questions to answer, decisions to make.

She'd spent every free minute since online, reading about PTSD, and had found hope and despair on every page. Troops were receiving better care than ever; the stigma was loosening its hold; but patients were still committing suicide in alarming numbers.

She wanted the stories to end: *And they lived happily ever after.* Not very many of them did. "You're not a child in a fairy tale," she muttered as she walked down the hall at the end of her shift Monday afternoon. "We don't all get happy endings. Everyone you know is proof of that."

"Talking to yourself, sweetie?" Trinity caught up, bumping shoulders with her as they turned into the staff lounge, each heading for her locker against the wall.

"Just thinking out loud."

"You've been someplace else all day, and it doesn't seem like a happy place." Trinity yanked out the clamp that kept her blond hair under control while working and shook her head, long waves falling halfway down her back. "Crap's all around, Bennie. No need to let it into your head, too."

Bennie forced a smile. "I'm just trying to get a handle on a few things."

"Any of them have to do with Calvin Sweet?" Trinity shrugged one shoulder through her backpack strap and gave a dreamy sigh. "He was always so cute once he got past that doofus geek stage."

"I didn't know he got past the doofus geek stage." The remark came out before Bennie could stop it. Calvin was many things these days, but neither doofus nor geek was on the list.

"He's in the grown-into-a-mighty-fine-man stage. If you decide to set him free, give him a shove in my direction, would you?"

"I'll keep that in mind," Bennie said with a phony smile as she took her lunch cooler from the locker. With all the wonderful cooking Mama did at home, Bennie wasn't about to pay good money for bad cafeteria food.

"You ready to walk out?"

"Sure." She gave the combination lock on her locker a spin, then left with Trinity. They didn't get far, though, when a sign on a lobby door caught her attention. "Hey, there's something I need to take care of, Trinity. Go ahead without me. I'll see you tomorrow."

She waited a moment for her friend to walk out of sight, then she crossed the crowded lobby to a plain wooden door fifteen feet down the hall from the stained glass door of the chapel. Her knock was answered with an invitation to enter, and she opened the door with some hesitation.

"I don't bite." The voice came from out of sight, female, the accent New England, the tone droll.

Bennie hesitated, thinking better of her decision, but before she could back out of the room, the woman popped around the door that had hidden her and took her hand. "I'm Chaplain Roberts. You can call me Andi if you prefer."

Bennie shook hands and let go of the knob, nudging it shut with her foot. "I've gone to church my whole life, and I can't think of a single time my grandmother would have let me get away with calling a man—or woman—of God by his or her first name."

The chaplain laughed. "Whatever you're comfortable with, Bennie."

How did she—Bennie realized she still wore her name tag on a lanyard around her neck. It wouldn't have surprised her, though, if Chaplain Andi had just somehow known. God worked in mysterious ways.

"Have a seat. Would you like some coffee? Diet Coke?"

"No, thank you."

The chaplain sat down behind her desk and folded her hands together. "What can I do for you, Bennie?"

She'd thought of talking to her own pastor, but the fact that he knew the Sweets had stopped her. She'd considered an appointment with an Army chaplain or a call to Loretta Baxter, the casualty assistance officer who'd helped her tremendously after J'Myel's death, but the Army connection made her wary, not without clearing it through Calvin first.

When she didn't speak right away, Chaplain Roberts said, "Anything you say to me is held in strictest confidence."

Bennie nodded, then studied the woman. At first glance, she'd figured her in her fifties or sixties, thanks to the short cap of startlingly white hair. A closer look, though, revealed much younger skin, blue eyes, and smile wrinkles at the corners of her eyes and mouth. The very best kind of wrinkles to have, Mama insisted. Despite the white hair, she was probably only ten years or so older than Bennie.

With a deep breath, Bennie blurted out, "Do you know anything about post-traumatic stress disorder?"

For just an instant, the chaplain's eyes widened, then the skin smoothed again. Her voice was smooth, too. "More than I want to. Is it you or someone close to you?"

"Someone close." Someone she wanted to keep very close for a very long time. Not just because she loved him but because since Saturday, she'd been afraid for him. She wanted to wrap him up tight and make him stay at her side to make sure nothing bad happened.

"I know it can be devastating to a patient and a family. I know there are times when everything seems hopeless. They require counseling and medication, and they have good days and bad days, and if they're lucky, their good days outweigh the bad." She paused. "I know it can be a difficult condition to treat. Treatment can last weeks, months, or years; sometimes it takes years for the symptoms to even appear. I know there's no cure in the traditional sense, and the saddest thing I know is that it has a high mortality rate."

All things Bennie had read online. Hearing them in the chaplain's matter-of-fact manner made her feel like a balloon subjected to a tiny pinprick. It didn't go racing wildly around the room but instead drooped slowly but surely as its air leaked out.

As if sensing the disappointment, the chaplain continued in a more encouraging tone. "But there are varying degrees, Bennie, and there's always, always hope. A patient whose treatment is well managed can do anything anyone else can do. They can hold jobs, get married, have kids, be great parents and spouses. They may have to try harder sometimes—don't we all?—but they can do it."

Calvin felt that he'd already expended tremendous amounts of energy just trying to survive until now. Did he have the strength to keep going? Even surrounded by his parents, Gran, Bennie, and Mama, could he dig deep enough on those bad days to hold on, even if it was by his fingernails, until the dawn of the next, hopefully better day?

"How long have you known him?" the chaplain asked quietly.

"Since we were nine."

"He went to war?"

She nodded.

"What's his status?"

"He's separating from the Army. Not his choice."

There was a pause. "Are you in love with him?"

Tears welled in Bennie's eyes, surprising her. She'd done her crying on Saturday, getting it out of her system. Since then, she'd focused on reaching a place of peace and acceptance, but apparently she wasn't there yet. "Like a crazy woman," she replied, her chuckle turning into a hiccup. "But it's…"

"Complicated." Chaplain Roberts smiled as if she'd heard that a thousand times before. "Why is it complicated?"

Bennie told her their history: the Three Stooges, the Three Musketeers, her and J'Myel's marriage, his death. "I just found out this weekend that Calvin attempted suicide a few months ago. I was surprised and shocked and scared and—and angry." It even made her angry to admit the last. What kind of woman reacted to such horrifying news that way?

"Why the anger?"

She blew out her breath. "My husband wanted more than anything to come home from the damned war, and Calvin came home and did his best to throw it all away." Her voice vibrated with the last words. She could keep that thought at bay most of the time, but every time it sneaked into her head, it stirred her sense of unfairness to the max.

"That's a fair reaction," the chaplain said. "But you have to realize that Calvin was coming from a place that you've never been. You've never been to war. You've never watched your friends die. You've never killed people to stay alive. You've never felt guilty for being the one to survive. You've never been buried in despair."

No, thank the sweet heavens, she had not. She couldn't imagine torment so unending that death would seem preferable.

"You know, when troops are killed, there's no doubt that they made the ultimate sacrifice in the war," Chaplain Roberts said quietly. "The proof is painfully obvious in the lifelessness of their bodies. When people lose limbs or suffer horrific burns or head injuries, their sacrifice is usually pretty obvious, too. But when you get patients like Calvin, whose wounds are unseen, whose bodies survived intact, it's easy to dismiss or overlook their problems. They look okay. Most of the time they seem to function okay. The insomnia, the mood changes, the drinking or drugs, the hyperarousal, the nightmares, the paranoia... Most of that can be hidden or attributed to other causes. It's harder to identify casualties of the mind, especially when a lot of them don't want to be identified because it can mean the end of their military careers.

"But make no mistake, Bennie: The injuries that Calvin suffers are every bit as real and critical as the injuries that killed your husband. They're as real as the amputations and the third-degree burns and the gunshots, and they can be harder to treat. You look at a broken bone, you put a plate here and screws there and splint or cast it and do physical therapy, and when you're done, you have a pretty good bone. You can't just look at the brain and say, 'Oh, here's the survivor's guilt; let's do a quick nip and tuck. And over here we need a few stitches to stem the hyperarousal, and as long as we're in here, let's do a happiness transplant to get rid of that pesky depression.'"

The chaplain sadly shook her head. "I'm sorry, Bennie. It just doesn't work that way."

Chapter 18

The ring of a cell phone interrupted the quiet that had settled. Bennie watched the chaplain check the screen, smile a tiny private smile, then mute the sound and slide it into her pocket. "Sorry about that."

Her voice small and quavery, Bennie said, "I want promises, Chaplain." She was well aware she sounded like a whiny child, but if she couldn't whine once in a while, she might explode.

"Me, too." Chaplain Roberts's smile was faint and tinged with wryness. "Wouldn't it be lovely if we could have them? If the promise fairy waved her wand and said, 'I promise that Calvin will heal and recover one hundred percent and will be a man worthy of your commitment'? But if that happened, a commitment wouldn't really be a commitment, would it? You wouldn't be taking any risks. You'd have a promise in writing of sunshine and roses, and someone to hold accountable for it."

After a moment, she went on. "If the situation were reversed and Calvin had come home in J'Myel's place, and J'Myel had come home with Calvin's diagnosis—"

Bennie's gut clenched.

"You were married to J'Myel. You'd already made promises to him. For better or worse, in sickness and in health. Would those promises have been enough for you?"

"Of course." Bennie had been raised to take vows seriously. She'd intended one marriage, like Mama, like her daddy, like most of the people in her family.

"You wouldn't have said, 'Eh, sorry, I didn't sign up for this hassle. I'm outta here'?"

"Never. He was my husband. I loved him."

"So if you could honor old promises to your husband, what's stopping you from making and honoring new promises to Calvin? Your eyes are open. You know what he faces. You'd be making an informed decision."

Bennie gazed out the window to the parking lot, the shift change traffic mostly cleared out now. Instead of waiting to be the fiftieth vehicle out of the garage, she would just sail out and still make it home within a few minutes of her regular time. Hopefully feeling a little better. A little more determined.

"You want to know that Calvin will recover, that he'll get stronger every day. That he can hold a job and be a productive member of society, that he'll be a good husband and a better father, and that the idea of suicide will never, ever cross his mind again. But you can't get that, Bennie. None of us can. Things change, sometimes for the better, sometimes for the worse, but life isn't static. It's always changing."

Bennie's sigh felt as if it heaved up all the way from her toes, expelling out of her with dismay and dissatisfaction and, yes, a little acceptance. "I know. My mother abandoned me, my father died, my husband died. I just think…" Here came the whiny child again. "I'd just like to think I'm due for a break, that it's my turn to be young and carefree." She snickered over the last word, and the chaplain joined her. "My grandmother says anyone who's truly carefree lacks the capacity to understand what's going on."

"Wise woman." The chaplain toyed with her name tag, sliding it along a deep purple lanyard, as if considering her next words. After a moment, she picked up a framed photo on the shelf behind her desk and offered it to Bennie. "I'm going to set aside my chaplain's hat for a moment and talk to you as a wife—the wife of a survivor. My husband is a Marine. A retired gunnery sergeant. He also has PTSD."

Bennie studied the photo: a tall muscular man with dark brown hair—still worn in a high-and-tight regardless of his retired status—brown eyes, and a crooked smile that must have melted more than a few hearts. With his right arm he held his wife close, and his left arm braced a little girl on his hip, maybe three years old, with the same hair and eyes and adorable smile. Another girl, looking much the same, just a few years older, stood on his feet, arms flung back and around his knees for stability.

"You look happy."

"We are. Most of the time. We have our moments, of course." Taking the frame back, the chaplain smiled tenderly at her family before returning it to the shelf. "I knew

Zack's diagnosis before I started dating him. I knew it wasn't going to be the easiest path. There would be bad times and sad times and times when I might feel more like his guardian or his medical advocate than his wife. But I loved him. What else could I do?"

She'd believed him worthy of commitment, Bennie thought. Just as *she* knew Calvin was worthy of the same.

"Zack is a leader, your typical gung-ho Marine. He would charge a thousand enemy troops by himself if it meant giving his men a chance to survive. He would throw himself in front of a speeding train to save a stranger, and there is *nothing* he wouldn't do to protect the girls and me. Life is precious to him...but he attempted suicide twice before he got a diagnosis and began treatment. Trust me when I tell you that psychologically, morally, ethically, he's the strongest man I know. But men who live hard and fight hard and love hard also hurt hard."

Bennie nodded in agreement. Calvin had always been the most responsible of them. He'd been the planner, the leader, the one who found the flaws in their ideas and kept them out of too much trouble. How much more seriously had he taken that responsibility as a soldier? While J'Myel had been letting everything roll off his back, the way he'd always done, Calvin had been internalizing everything, holding himself responsible for everything. Was it any wonder it got to be too much for him?

"Zack and I have been married seven years. Sometimes it's a little harder than I'd like. But there's a character in an old movie who says she'd rather have thirty minutes of wonderful than a lifetime of nothing special. That's my golden rule. I could have kept looking, maybe found a guy without Zack's medical history, maybe even learned to love him, but it wouldn't have been dazzling, heart-stopping love. It wouldn't have given me my babies, and the freedom from worry wouldn't have been worth settling for a lifetime of nothing special."

Bennie loved *wonderful*. She loved the way her heart skipped a beat when she saw Calvin, the way she craved his kisses more with each one she got. She loved that he cared so damn much about the people in his life and the way he was gentle and kind with a stray dog that had never known tenderness. She loved the idea of spending the rest of her life with him, of having babies with him, of giving to him when he'd already given so much of himself.

"It's okay to be a little scared," Chaplain Roberts said. "Love and marriage and babies are a huge deal no matter what else is going on in your life. It's all about commitment and sacrifice and promises and compromises."

Bennie's fingers knotted tightly together as she summoned a faint smile. "I thought the promise fairy didn't exist."

"It's the promises you make to Calvin and to yourself that matter. Zach and I—our promise is to do the best we can. That's it. Nothing fancy or complicated. Whether we're having a good day or a bad one, and we both have those bad days, we promise to try our best." Chaplain Roberts left her chair to sit in the one next to Bennie, taking Bennie's hand in both of her own. "That's all you can ask of Calvin, Bennie, and that's all anyone can ask of you. Try your best."

* * *

Calvin leaned against the wall outside his apartment door, unlacing his work boots, using the toe of one to pry off the first, then carefully nudging off the second. He'd just come from the shelter, and the thick treads were caked with dirt, gravel, mud, and something much more pungent. It was amazing how much crap—poo—small animals could generate.

He'd talked with Meredith this afternoon, and as soon as she decided Nita was ready, the pup was moving into Gran's house until he had a place of his own. It was a good thing Nita, small as she was, wasn't a big producer of stinky stuff since if there was one thing Gran didn't like, it was cleaning up after critters, regardless of how many legs they had.

But at least he'd have one pretty girl sharing his life with him.

Leaving his boots, he went inside, tossed his keys on the counter, and headed down the hall to turn the shower to hot. He dropped his clothes on the bedroom floor, gave the unmade bed a look, then left it unmade. After all, he'd be getting back in it in five hours or so.

Music came through the wall from next door, Garth Brooks, Oklahoma's favorite hometown-boy-made-good. Calvin wasn't a country music fan himself, but it was better than the classical music the soldier on the other side preferred.

He made his shower quick, dressed in PT shorts and a T-shirt, and rooted through the kitchen for a snack. After tossing a foil pan of frozen lasagna in the oven and setting the timer, he located the cookies Elizabeth had sent home with him yesterday, took two of those, poured himself a glass of milk, and wandered into the living room to stare out the window.

The sky was darker than normal for this time of day, and tiny whirlwinds of dust and leaves skipped across the grass separating the barracks from the WTU. He hadn't listened to the forecast—not much point as changeable as the local weather was—but the chill radiating from the window glass showed the temperature had dropped significantly since he'd come home. Maybe they would have a really good, loud thunderstorm, the kind that rushed across the prairie, drenched the ground, and rattled the windows in their frames. Or maybe a nice, gentle snow, no sleet, no ice, just thick fat flakes to turn everything white and make the world a quieter place for a while.

Maybe, he thought with a grin, they'd get thundersnow, J'Myel's favorite: rumbling thunder and lightning muffled by heavy snowfall.

With his free hand, he rubbed absently at his chest, not at the gut-wrenching ache that had always accompanied thoughts of J'Myel but at the absence of it. It still hurt—it always would—but it wasn't the despairing never-gonna-stop throb that had convinced him he would be better off dead. This was a natural kind of hurt, full of regret and missing but nothing insurmountable. This was a hurt he would survive.

He would survive the hurt with Bennie, too. He wanted like hell for her to decide he was worth taking a risk on, but if she didn't…He swallowed hard, and his fingers pressed a little harder on his chest.

If she didn't, it would break his heart. It would mean

the end of a lot of hopes and dreams. It would be one of the worst things in his life.

But it wouldn't kill him. It wouldn't make him backslide into the bleakness where he'd lived so long. Every day he made it through was a victory. He intended to reach the point where he didn't count days but weeks, months, years. He intended to be whole and healthy and happy.

Though right now it was hard to imagine happiness without Bennie.

He reached for the milk he'd set on the windowsill and realized the glass was empty. The cookies were gone, too, though he didn't remember more than the first few sips, the first few bites. Mindless eating, Elizabeth called it, patting her rounded curves with a laugh. *It's one of the things I excel at.*

The thought of her made him smile, and the glass reflected it back at him. He stared at the image for a long time until a steady tapping caught his attention. He glanced at the door, then back at the window, where his view was distorted by raindrops hitting the glass. They were fat and ran into rivulets to the bottom before streaking out of sight. Rain, storm, snow—he didn't care what the skies delivered. He was home, and he was comfortable. He didn't feel the need to go anywhere, do anything. He didn't need to dwell on ugly memories, but he didn't need to hide from them, either. He could watch TV, get online, read a book, and just *be*.

God, he had waited a long time to just *be*.

The tapping grew louder, more insistent, but not at the window this time. When he'd first come here, a knock at the door would have made his gut clench, but all he felt as he crossed the room was mild curiosity. Other than the one time with his family, his only visitor was Justin, either bringing food or wanting to go out and get some, both of which, Calvin had finally realized, were his way of taking care of the new guy. Maybe, given the weather, Justin would like some of Elizabeth's lasagna and the garlic bread she'd sent with it. Homemade meals like that—

Calvin opened the door, wind whistling between the two halves of the building, and stopped cold. Stopped breathing. Stopped thinking. Stopped everything except feeling, and all he could feel was, *Damn*, he was lucky.

Bennie stood on the landing, a deep purple parka covering her to her knees, her curls glistening under the hood, her fingers hidden in black gloves, and black pants showing beneath the coat's hem. Instead of her ready smile, she wore a look of intense seriousness, though a flash of pleasure passed through when she saw him.

The silence dragged out a long time, him looking at her, her looking back at him. He searched her eyes and face for any hint to what she was thinking, feeling, and found uncertainty, hesitancy, and—the best thing he could have found—hope.

A gust of wind made her hug her arms across her middle and loosened her tongue. "I meant to come bearing gifts, but the cold front moved in, and I couldn't bring myself to make any unnecessary stops. Can I come in anyway?"

He gazed at her—the soft round lines of her face, the exotic tilt of her eyes, the smooth mocha shade of her face, the lush body hidden beneath the dripping coat, the black boots that made her seem three inches taller and hopefully kept her feet dry if not warm. Then another blast of wind came down the passageway, and he stepped back, opening the door wide. She hustled inside.

"I swear, the temperature has dropped forty degrees since I left Mama's. The weather guys are saying snow, but you know how that goes. The more certain they are, the less likely it is to happen. Whatever, it's definitely cold and wet out there." She lowered the hood, unzipped the parka, and shrugged out of it. Calvin watched the sensuous movements of her shoulders, arms, spine, then wordlessly took it and hung it on the coat rack in the corner next to his PT jacket and hoodies.

Her sweater was blue, the same shade of sapphire that was in the mother's ring Gran wore. It was designed more for looking good than staying warm, the fine silky knit clinging to her curves, the rounded neck dipping to reveal a patch of creamy skin where her breasts began to mound.

He should be worrying about her reason for visiting unannounced. His stomach should be tied in knots, his heart skipping every other beat, his familiar old friend doubt settling around him.

But he wasn't worried. Somewhere deep inside, where his darkest fears lived, he knew Bennie wasn't here to break his heart. Why bring gifts? Why brave the weather? Why dress up like she was going somewhere—or seeing someone—special?

She laid her purse, which had been shielded beneath the coat, on the dining table, then folded her hands together and nervously glanced at him. "I like your apartment."

He had to swallow hard before he was able to speak. "You saw enough to tell that in the two seconds you looked around?"

She gave him a chastising look before letting a smile spread across her face. "It's warm, it's dry, it smells good, and it's relatively clean. Your mother would be proud."

"She'd be proud anyway. It's in the mother code."

That made her laugh, one of Calvin's favorite sounds in the world. As long as Bennie could laugh, life couldn't possibly be bad. "I remember a few times when she would have strangled you if she could have gotten her hands on you, mother code be damned."

"Those were all J'Myel's fault." Once again, that deep stab of pain had faded to little more than a twinge. "Would you like to sit down, or would you rather stand by the door all night?"

She gave him another chastening look before taking a seat on the couch. The furniture was nothing fancy, clean, in good shape, sturdy, but it sure looked better with her on it. The vivid blue and black of her clothing, the vibrancy that was just Bennie, and even the fragrance she wore, in the space of a moment, had turned his apartment from home to homey.

"You want some of Mom's cookies?"

She sniffed the air, then snorted. "I'm holding out for some of Miss Elizabeth's lasagna, if you have enough to share."

He sat at the opposite end of the sofa, his bare feet drawn onto the cushions to seek a little warmth. "She always makes enough to share."

"I know." Bennie picked up the heart on the chain around her neck and slid it a few times side to side. It was a gift from J'Myel, he knew, back when they were all still friends. Seeing it on her in the beginning, in the photos J'Myel had flashed to everyone, and knowing what it had represented, had seemed strange. Now it was as much a part of her as the bracelets, rings, and earrings she favored.

The rings...His gaze settled on her hands. The last time he'd seen her, every time he'd seen her since coming home, she'd worn an elaborate wedding set on her left hand. It had cost two months' pay, J'Myel had boasted, pricey considering that that salary had included hostile-fire pay. Now, even though she'd substituted a narrow band with a teardrop-shaped yellow stone, her hand looked naked...or ready for a new ring.

Calvin couldn't decide whether the jitteriness spreading through him was anxiety, anticipation, or all that cool calm bouncing itself to bits. She'd come to see him because she'd reached a decision, logic dictated, and that decision had led her to remove her dead husband's rings.

Damn, he really was lucky.

* * *

Bennie slipped off her boots and lifted her socked feet onto the couch. Pressing her palms together, she thought how strange her hand felt without J'Myel's rings. She'd worn them from the moment he'd placed them there during their wedding, not even taking them off to bathe. They'd rubbed a ring of flattened skin around her finger that the gold band she was wearing didn't quite cover. But the strangeness was good. It was like a final letting-go of the past and the first step to a new future.

"I had grand plans when I left the house," she began. "I was going to get a gallon of sweet tea from Bad Hank's, then pick up dinner at Sweet Baby Greens, including some of Mr. Arnold's to-die-for cobbler. Then I was going to buy a carton of your favorite Bordeaux cherry ice cream from Braum's and offer it all to you with one condition."

"What condition?" His gaze was level with hers. He wasn't smiling, wasn't frowning, wasn't giving away much of anything he was thinking, except...yes, there, a tiny bit of amusement lurking in the corners of his dark eyes.

Bennie wasn't a shy woman. Never had been. It was easier for a person to get what she wanted if she was up front about it. But from nowhere came a whisper of insecurity, confidence lacking at a time when she needed it more than ever. When she touched her tongue to her lips, it came off as nerves, and nerves tempted her to giggle, but she stifled the sound and managed to answer without sounding too over the top.

"That you had to take me to get the food."

He looked at her a moment, and she realized his face was more relaxed—more *Calvin*—than ever before. Ever since he'd come home, there'd been this tension, this dissatisfaction, that seemed to have become a very part of him, but it was gone now. He looked—*thank you, God*—as if he'd found some peace.

"Damn rain. Ruins the best of plans," he said mildly. "So I got no tea, no dinner, no cobbler, and no ice cream. But I got you."

The best of plans. Aw, she had such plans if he was amenable, and the aura of peace about him made her pretty sure he was—once she'd said what she had to say. "But Miss Elizabeth provided her fabulous lasagna, and she never sends that without adding a loaf of garlic bread from CaraCakes, so there's still food, and there's still me." A lump formed in her throat, making her next words hoarse. "But first..."

She watched him closely for some response—fear, anxiety, confidence. Though his muscles tightened briefly, his expression remained even. Calm. He knew, she thought. Knew she loved him. Knew she wouldn't give up on him. Knew she would fight for him. Just like the old Calvin, so sure of himself. Sure of *her*.

"What you told me Saturday... I couldn't believe the boy I'd grown up with, the man I'd fallen in love with, had been through so much and I hadn't had a clue. I was shocked and scared and hurt and—and—"

"Pissed off," he said quietly, "that I'd dishonored J'Myel and everyone else that way."

"Not dishonored..." Honesty forced her to correct that. "Well, a little. At first. But while you were in Iraq and Afghanistan, fighting and losing people, I was right here where I'd practically always been, living with Mama, going to work and to church, seeing all my friends. I was as safe as I had ever been. I heard stories about what it was like to be in combat, and they helped give me some perspective, but in the end they were really just words. I could imagine, but I couldn't *know*. I couldn't put myself in your shoes, or J'Myel's or anyone else's. I couldn't experience what you'd experienced." She paused. "I sure couldn't claim any right to judge you."

"What I did..." His gaze slid away, still tinged with that survivor's guilt that might never go away, then came back to hers. "It's hard to understand. I mean, I was *there*, and for weeks afterward, I still couldn't believe it. It was

like a really vivid, really bad dream. I still can't explain
why…"

That awful little word: *Why?* The nagging little question that could drive a person insane. There were a thousand possible answers. There was usually not one single
good answer. Calvin might never understand why.
Bennie probably wouldn't. But Mama had suggested an
answer she could live with. "Mama thinks it was part
of God's plan to get you back home, to get us back
together, to bring Diez into your family's lives." And
to get Mama some great-grandbabies to cuddle before
she was too old. *I'll try my best to make that happen,*
Bennie had told her.

Try your best, Chaplain Roberts had said. If she
could paint, Bennie would put it on a piece of old barn
wood in flowing script and hang it on the wall where
it was the first thing she saw in the morning and the
last thing at night. If she could cross-stitch, she would
make a fussy little sampler, and if she were into body
art, she would have it tattooed in a place that only she
and Calvin would ever see. *Try your best,* because that
was all anyone could ask, all anyone could offer.

"It would have been easier if God had just smacked me
on the back of the head," Calvin said dryly.

"He did smack you on the back of the head. He just
used Diez to do it."

A wry grin tugged at his mouth. "There are better ways
of getting my attention than having a mouthy kid break
my elbow."

"I don't know. Gran always said you were more hard-
headed than anyone she'd ever known. Coming from the
most hardheaded person *I've* ever known, that says a lot."

After her smile faded, she took a deep breath. "I talked to the chaplain at the hospital today, and to Mama. I thought long and hard about everything you told me, about everything I know about PTSD and about you and me and life, and every train of thought led back to the same place."

The patter of rain had faded, she realized in the silence that followed, and a glance at the window showed that the forecasters had gotten it right this time: Snow was falling in the sort of big, fat flakes that turned the world beautiful and sweet and soft.

Calvin stretched one leg out, nudging her with his foot, bringing her attention back to him. Expectancy lit his face, making it beautiful and sweet and soft.

"I'm not scared of your PTSD, Calvin, or your insomnia, your mood changes, your nightmares, your paranoia, or anything else your guilt can throw at us. By ourselves, we're damn strong people. Together we are unbeatable." It took another deep breath to fill her lungs, and still her voice came out wavery. "I want to spend the rest of my life with you. I want to be there for you when you need me and when you don't. I can't bear the idea of *not* being there for you because I love you, and there's nothing in the world that can change that."

The timer went off in the kitchen, but Calvin ignored it to say in a husky voice, "So you're okay with the Army not wanting me anymore."

"You gave them your best. The rest belongs to you and your family and me."

"You don't care that I don't know what the hell I'm supposed to do for work when I get out? I could need another degree. I could follow my other childhood dream and become a cowboy, or I could to learn to lay tile and be the Son in Sweet and Son Tile."

Trying to ignore the beeping alarm, Bennie's jaw muscles tightened even as she smiled. "Your daddy would be overjoyed. I'd let you tile my house anytime."

"Would you let me live in that house? Cook in the kitchen? Sprawl in the living room with Nita? Soak in long hot baths in the evenings? Sleep—"

Maybe because alarms were such a huge part of her job, they were one thing she couldn't ignore. She shot up from the sofa, asking, "Sweet heaven, how long does this go on before I have to stomp it into the floor?" In the kitchen, a dozen steps away, she snatched up the timer, jabbed the stop button, then bent, breathing in heavenly scents of pasta, cheese, and tomatoes, to turn the oven off.

When she straightened, she saw Calvin had followed her in, eyes glinting as he blocked her way, backing her against the counter and the wall of the pantry. "Where was I? Oh, yeah, soak in long hot baths in the evenings and sleep every night in the smallest bed we can find so I can hold you close every night?"

Her breath caught in her chest. The idea of finding an old house in the Flats, one within easy walking distance of Mama's and the Sweets', stirred an ache around her heart. She wanted a house that needed some work, that would accommodate three or four children—and Mama, when the time came. She wanted an old-fashioned place that suited, not dazzled, filling it first with her stuff, his stuff, family stuff, and Nita, then growing it every year or two, more babies, more dogs, a cat or three.

"I most certainly would welcome you to do all those things there." She raised her left hand, wiggling her fingers to draw his attention to the citrine ring. "But it would involve taking a few vows and putting a ring on my finger."

Catching her hand, he rubbed the tip of his finger over the yellow stone. "On my twenty-first birthday, Gran told me she wanted me to have her wedding ring. It's just a plain gold band, and she didn't think most women would want something so simple, but it had seen her through more than forty years with my grandfather. She thought having it might bring me luck even if my bride didn't wear it."

The words set heat building in the pit of Bennie's stomach, creating currents that somersaulted and warmed her from the inside out. She knew Gran's ring, simple but far too important to ever be considered plain.

"Calvin Clyde Sweet, is that a proposal?" she asked, but before he could answer, she tugged her hand free, wrapped her arms around his neck, and snuggled close so that their bodies touched. He was hard, and she was soft; he was warm, and she was shivery; he was home, really home, and she was so very happy to be there. Rising onto her toes, she touched her mouth to his, and desire surged through her, humming just beneath the surface of her skin. Forget the frigid temperatures outside—she was about to burst into flames. Her heart was melting, and everything else was tingling delightfully.

He took control of the kiss, sliding his tongue into her mouth, sliding his hands over the blue sweater that made her sparkle inside. The clean sexy scent of him made the spicy aroma of the lasagna fade away, and the pressure of his arousal against her gave new meaning, she thought naughtily, to *hyperarousal*.

When her lungs were straining for breath—and her body for so much more—he ended the kiss and gazed down at her with a sweet, lazy grin. "Is that a yes?"

She stopped stroking the soft skin on the back of his neck long enough to deliver a light smack to the back of his head. "Of course it's a yes." She wanted to follow it up with all the *–ly* words she could think of: absolutely, positively, definitely, undoubtedly, happily, immediately. But the only *–ly* words that appealed to her at the moment were simple and to the point. "I love you, Squeaky."

The best anyone possibly could.

With the help of the Tuesday Night Margarita Club, Fia knows she can tackle anything. But sometimes she dreams of a hero who will ride in bigger than life, love and cherish her, and make her life a little easier...just the way her beloved husband did before his death. Lucky for her, Tallgrass is the next stop for ruggedly handsome ex-Army man Elliot Ross...

Please see the next page for a preview of *A Summer to Remember.*

Chapter 1

His neck aching from hours behind the wheel, Elliot Ross gave in to just a bit of relief when lights became visible a few miles ahead. He'd been driving a long time, most of it through spring storms, wind buffeting the truck, rain falling so hard that the windshield wipers couldn't keep up. Every muscle in his body was knotted and sore. If he had the money, this would be a good night to check into a motel, to take a shower as long and as hot as he wanted, to sleep in a real bed with real privacy.

He didn't need to pull out his wallet to know that he didn't have the money. He wasn't broke, but his funds were reaching the level that always made him itch. With any luck—he snorted—he'd be able to find work in Tallgrass, short-term if nothing else. He could build up his safety net, maybe run into some old friends, maybe even find a place to settle. Eight years in the Army had left him with buddies all over the world, and though he was alone by choice, he always appreciated meeting up again with friends.

Rustling from the passenger seat reminded him that he wasn't exactly alone. His companion, fifteen pounds of lazy, shedding tan hair, and giant puppy-dog eyes, uncurled and sat up, tail thumping against the console, then raised her gaze to him. He hadn't known her long enough to read all her cues, but he was pretty sure that look was universal in the canine world for *I need to take a leak.*

"Hang on, Mouse. According to Matilda, we'll be in Tallgrass in a couple minutes." Elliot had given the name to the truck's GPS the first time he'd ever used it and found the previous owner had set it to a woman's voice with an Australian accent. He'd traveled to Perth a few years back, and all it took was one simple *turn left* in that accent to remind him of good times with Aussie girls soft enough, sweet enough, and sexy enough to almost make him think about renouncing his U.S. citizenship and spending the rest of his life learning to be a sandgroper.

Almost.

Mouse stared at him a moment before blinking and looking away. Elliot had found her in eastern Tennessee two days ago. A group of kids had been messing with her in a McDonald's parking lot, offering the starving pup a scrap of burger, then kicking her away before she could get it.

Worthless punk cowards. Elliot flexed his still-tender right hand. He'd made sure they understood they'd picked on the wrong dog before he'd loaded the scrawny pit into his truck and headed for the nearest vet.

Always a white knight, his sister used to tease, but it wasn't anything so noble. He just didn't like seeing anyone mistreated, and luckily he was tough enough and strong enough to put a stop to it most times.

The lights grew brighter despite the heavy cloud cover, and within minutes he was passing the main gate to Fort Murphy. It seemed strange to drive past with no plans to turn down the long drive. He'd spent so much of his life going to work on similar posts, places so familiar that they felt more like home than his real home ever had.

Another couple miles, and a shopping center appeared on the right. With a glance at Mouse, he slowed, then turned into the lot. The only businesses open this late on a Friday night were a Mexican restaurant at the front and a pharmacy at the back. A strip of grass separated the pharmacy from the parking lot, only a few feet wide and maybe twenty feet long, but that was more than enough for Mouse to do her business.

He parked near the median and shut off the engine, then contemplated the rain for a moment. "I don't suppose I could just open the door and you'd jump out and do your thing, then come back?"

Mouse held his gaze with a steadiness he found unsettling. He'd known his share of animals that had been mistreated, but he'd never seen one less skittish than this one. She showed him no fear. She'd trembled and whimpered with the punks, and with the vet and his assistants, but she was steady as a rock with Elliot.

She trusts you, idiot, his sister Emily's voice commented. *Women and girls always trust you.*

The truth of her statement made him grin.

Tugging his jean jacket collar a little closer, he slid out of the truck, jogged to the other side, opened the door, and hooked Mouse's leash on before lifting her to the ground.

She didn't dart off the ten feet to the grass like he'd hoped but instead hunkered underneath the truck, still giving him that long, steady look. "Come on, Mouse, I'm getting soaked here."

She didn't move.

"Come on, you're a pit bull. Big, fierce dog." He growled softly at her. "You can't tell me you'd rather hold it than piss in the rain."

No response.

With water dripping from his hair and trickling down his neck, Elliot gave the leash a tug. When she didn't move, he sighed and reached under the passenger seat. The umbrella he brought out had been in the truck when he bought it. He hadn't used one in . . . well, ever—he was a tough guy, right?—but he'd never bothered to throw it away, figuring someday he might find himself with a pretty female who cared about things like getting wet. Mouse was a good-looking dog, or would be once she'd put on some weight, but she wasn't exactly the kind of female he'd had in mind.

He popped the umbrella, tilting it at an angle that would provide protection for the pup, and Mouse instantly came out from under the truck, walking alongside him to the grass.

"Grown man holding an umbrella for a prissy little dog so she doesn't get wet," he grumbled as the dampness spread over him from the outside in. His jeans were sticking to his legs, and even inside work boots, his feet were getting wet and cold. His hair was soaked, his jacket sodden, and his shirt—

"I think I'd worry more about talking to myself than pampering the baby."

The voice came from behind him, soft and amused, its accent muddled, and very definitely female. Abashed at being caught off guard, he turned to face a slight woman a few inches shorter than him. A neon green slicker covered her clothes, showing bare legs and feet shoved into disreputable sneakers, and its hood kept most of her face in shadow. Not the smile, though. Her smile was wide and filled with good humor.

"She, uh, doesn't like the rain." He gestured toward the dog, who'd turned her back to them before squatting carefully over the wet grass. "I've never done this before. Held an umbrella for a dog, I mean. Hell, I've never held an umbrella for a person, either, except for the time I tried to hit my sister with one, if that counts." Jeez, he was rambling. He hadn't rambled with a pretty girl in his life. His mama called him a natural-born charmer, but his best hope for charm now was his smile.

"Did you succeed?" At his blank look, she pointed to the umbrella. "You said you tried to hit your sister. Did you succeed?"

"No, she outran me. Emily was six feet tall by seventh grade, and I hadn't hit my growth spurt yet." He grinned at the obvious fact that his growth spurt had never come. He reached five-ten only by standing on his toes, but he'd compensated for his lack of height by building strength.

At his feet, Mouse barked, the first sound he'd heard from her that wasn't pain-filled. When he looked down at her, she stared back, her way, he guessed, of saying she'd had enough of the rain.

The woman apparently thought the same thing. "She probably needs her feet dried. I assume you carry a towel for that purpose?" Adjusting the slicker hood, she took a few steps away, then turned back. "I think it's sweet, you holding the umbrella for her."

He grinned again. "That's me. Sweeter than honey."

Once again she smiled, and anticipation crackled around them, like lightning about to strike. He even took a quick look at the sky to make sure they weren't about to get fried, then reconnected gazes with her. If he didn't say something, she was going to make another move to go, and he'd be left standing here in the rain, watching her drive away, full of things to say, just too late. He hated being too late.

"Could Mouse and I interest you in a drink?"

She stood there a long time, as still and steady as Mouse, probably considering the wisdom of going to a bar with a total stranger. She could be married for all he knew—could be a *nun* for all he knew—but he wouldn't recall the invitation if he could. She was pretty and nice and seemed to like his dog, and her voice could make a man weak, and her smile . . .

"I don't drink," she said at last. "But how about a burger? There's a Sonic just down the street, so Mouse wouldn't have to stay alone in the truck."

A drive-in on a rainy night, cool air drifting through the windows, fog steaming the glass, privacy without risk. "Burgers sound great. You want to leave your car here?"

She hesitated again before beeping the door locks of the only car parked nearby. "You can follow me."

He watched until she'd reached the car before giving Mouse a tug and heading back to his truck. After lifting the dog inside and tossing the umbrella into the rear floorboard, he climbed in himself and started the engine.

"Yes, ma'am," he murmured. "We'll be happy to follow you, won't we, Mouse?"

*   *   *

"What are you doing?" Fia Thomas asked aloud as she peered through the rain on her way through the lot to Main Street. "You should be home in your pajamas. You shouldn't be out in the rain. You certainly shouldn't be driving in the rain, and having a hamburger with a stranger... You don't even know his name! That's so far off the top of the scale of shouldn'ts that it doesn't even register."

Shoving her hood back with one hand, she checked her appearance in the rearview mirror and grimaced. "No makeup, you didn't even comb your hair, and... Oh, my God, when did you start talking to yourself like this?!"

A paper bag crinkled in her slicker pocket, the pills she'd picked up at the pharmacy. It was one of the multiple medications her doctor had her on to treat the symptoms of the illness they hadn't yet identified. She could have waited for it until tomorrow morning. She could have called any one of her best friends, and they would have picked it up and brought it to her. Wind and flood wouldn't keep them away when they knew she needed them. That knowledge warmed her heart almost unbearably.

But she'd had a good day. No vision problems, no muscle spasms, no stumbling or headaches or nausea. For the first time in a long time, she was feeling like herself, and she'd grabbed the first excuse to come to mind for rushing out into the rain and driving a car for the first time in months. She'd relished the feel of sitting behind the wheel, hands on the steering wheel, the radio tuned to the loudest and most favorite of her country stations. She'd felt strong. Empowered. Independent.

After more than a year of fearing she would never be any of those things again.

The white pickup followed her through a green light and into the left lane, then into Sonic's driveway. Overhangs protected the cars on both sides from the downpour, and bright lights made it feel like midday.

With a glance in the rearview mirror, she drove to the last spot on the row and shut off the engine. The wipers stopped in mid-swipe with a squeaky-smudgy sound, replaced almost immediately by the powerful engine parking beside her. She pulled the pills from her pocket and tossed them on the passenger seat, combed her fingers through her hair again, patted her other pocket to make sure her tiny purse was there, then reached for the door. Her hand stilled on the handle.

Was she really going to do this? Get in a stranger's truck, eat a hamburger, make small talk, maybe even flirt with him? All because he was sweet to his dog and had a great smile and gorgeous eyes and radiated *nice, sexy guy* with every breath he took, and because she'd had a good day and those times came so rarely that it seemed wrong not to celebrate? And maybe partly because she hadn't sat with a man, sharing a meal or a drink or a laugh, since Scott, and twenty-four was way too young to be so alone?

Her fingers tightened as the defiant voice in her head answered, *Yeah, we're gonna do this. Scott's dead. He's not coming back, little girl, and he'd never want you to live alone like this.*

The words hurt her heart, a tug of pain so powerful

that nausea stirred deep in her gut, but she pushed it back. Scott *was* dead, and she hated that fact with all her soul, but she couldn't change it. And he *would* be pissed if she'd given up without him. Warrior girl, he'd called her, the strongest, the toughest, the baddest-ass woman he knew. The one who could do any damn thing, could survive any damn thing. Hell, yeah, she was gonna do this.

With a deep breath, she opened the car door and slid out. The rubber soles of her sneakers made a sound similar to the wipers as she pivoted through the narrow space to the pickup's passenger door. Mouse's owner leaned across the truck and opened the door a few inches while Mouse sat halfway between the front and the rear seats, still and sniffing the air. Was it Fia's unfamiliar scent that had caught her attention or the burgers-grease-fries aroma that announced *Good food found here*?

Obvious answer. The dog's nose was twitching, and drool was starting to form at the corners of her mouth.

But it was Fia that held the man's interest. A shiver ran deep inside her. Oh, man, it had been so long since she'd felt the tingle brought on by a man's interest—so long since she'd let herself feel it, since she'd wanted to feel it. The sad truth was, she didn't have much to offer a man besides worry and frustration and a whole lot of hassle. But for one night she could pretend that the medical issues didn't exist, that she was a perfectly normal, healthy woman who'd been asked out by a perfectly gorgeous man.

She climbed in the truck, settled in the worn seat, and closed the door before looking his way. *Perfectly gorgeous* was an understatement. He was incredible. His hair was dark brown, falling over his eyes and past his shoulders, sleek and shiny. His features were sharply defined: dark eyes with ridiculously long lashes, strong nose, stubborn jaw, and a mouth that sensuously softened the angles. He wasn't tall, as he'd pointed out, but he was compact, broad shoulders, rock-hard muscles, strength tempered by gentleness. There was an air about him of peace, decency, zen, but also a sense of limits. He was a man who couldn't be pushed too far.

That's a lot to read into one look, she mocked herself. Honestly, he was damn good-looking. The rest was fantasy.

Nothing wrong with a little fantasy, Scott's memory whispered.

"So . . ." The guy's husky voice broke the silence, along with the sound of his window sliding down. "You know what you want?"

An innocent question to conjure so many answers in her head. She stuck with the pertinent one. "A number one combo, no onions, and a cherry limeade."

He pressed the order button, waited for the tinny response, and ordered two of the same. She breathed in the cool air that filled the cab, catching a faint scent of dog and a fainter scent of man. Men had the best smells. Sometimes when she was out and about, she would catch a whiff of someone wearing the same cologne Scott had worn or the same shampoo, and that little bit of aroma would take her back in a flash to happier times. Definitely better ones.

He swiped his fingers through his hair, then took a band dangling from the gear shift and pulled it back into a ponytail. She'd never been a fan of long hair on men, but it worked for this one. After drying his hands the best he could on his wet shirt, he extended the right one. "I'm Elliot Ross."

The introduction reminded her how out of character this was for her. Meeting a man for dinner, even if it was at Sonic, without learning his name first was something the before-Scott Fia would have done, certainly not something widowed, struggling Fia should do. *But now you know his name, and it's a nice one.* Not too common, not too unusual, masculine without sounding too macho.

"And yours is?" His brows rose, and so did the corners of his mouth. She liked a good-natured man. Angst was nice to read about in a novel, and it worked fine for some of her besties and the men in their lives, but Fia was happy with balance, good humor, and well-adjustedness. She tried to be that way herself. It made life easier.

"Fia Thomas," she said, and after an instant, she took his hand. Shaking hands was such a common, ordinary thing. She'd done it a thousand times, and nine-hundred-ninety-five of them had been brief, impersonal, barely worth classifying as contact. But on a few rare occasions, there had been more: a charge, a spark, the recognition of the potential that this person could actually rock her world, good or bad.

Elliot's palm was warm, the skin toughened from years of work. It was twice the size of hers, and it gave her that spark, that warning, that he could shake things up. Trouble was, things were already shaky. Any more shaking, and she could end up like the woman in the old commercial, knocked on her ass and unable to get up.

Though he showed no sign of letting go, when she tugged, he released her hand. She clasped both hands in her lap with an internal sigh of relief, feeling... safer that way.

What had happened to the days when being safe was the last thing on her mind?

"You don't have the typical Oklahoma accent," he remarked.

"I'm from Florida."

"What brought you to Tallgrass?"

"My husband, Scott, was in the Army." The air between them changed, a flutter of discomfort, or maybe disappointment, accompanied by his quick glance at her bare left hand. Good. She appreciated a man who cared whether the object of his flirtation was married. "I was here when he deployed to Afghanistan, and I stayed here when he died."

Elliot's expression turned solemn, his eyes somehow going even darker, his mouth flattening. "I'm sorry."

She'd heard those words a thousand times—said them ten thousand—with little real meaning. *I'm sorry I was late, I'm sorry I missed dinner, I'm sorry to bother you.* But there was genuine emotion in his voice—not just sympathy but empathy, too. It wasn't something he automatically parroted but something he actually felt.

She couldn't bring herself to offer the other bland, automatic response—*Thank you*—so she forced a small smile instead. "What about you? You don't sound like a native, either."

"I'm from West Texas."

Instantly an image of him in Wranglers, cowboy boots, and a Stetson formed in her mind. It warmed her enough inside to require the unzipping of her slicker. "And what brings you to Tallgrass?"

"The highway and my trusty steed." He patted the dashboard with a grin before shrugging. "I'm just looking for a place that feels like home."

"West Texas doesn't anymore?"

A distant look came into his eyes, resisting the casual smile he offered. "Nah. I've been gone too long, and the town where I grew up pretty much shriveled up and blew away. My folks moved to Arizona, my sister to New Mexico, and me...like I said, I'm looking."

"I get that. I was looking for a while, too." For most of her life, she'd been on her own, except for those too-short years with Scott. Absent father, disinterested mother, no family to help her get along...It had made her strong, but damn, that strength had come at a price. There was a part of her that would give it all up in exchange for a normal life, good health, and a man who would protect and keep her safe. She knew what it was like to be fierce and independent. Sometimes, just for a change, she wanted to be pampered and coddled.

Elliot's dark gaze fixed on her, searching, before he asked, "You find what you needed here?"

There was such intensity in his eyes that it seemed almost physical, warming her face, sliding along her skin, tying a knot in her gut. She had to shrug out of the slicker to slow the heat burning through her, had to clear her throat before she could answer, and when she did, the words came out husky. "Yeah. I did." What she needed, what she wanted, and the hope that maybe, someday, what she only dreamed about.

Movement blurred on the sidewalk, a carhop on skates

rolling their way. Elliot's gaze didn't waver, though, not until it softened, not until he quietly, with some satisfaction, said, "Good. That's good."

*　*　*

Elliot liked women. All women. He didn't have a type, no preference in hair color, physical characteristics, sometimes not even personality: He had great memories of a few women who would have driven him crazy if they'd stayed together one minute longer. Women were the best idea God had ever had, soft and funny and smart and difficult and beautiful and sexy and aggravating and intriguing and frustrating and so incredibly sweet.

Fia Thomas—he wondered if that was short for Sofia—was making a great start on being all those things. He wouldn't be surprised if he drove away from her tonight with one of what Emily called his serious casual crushes. He always fell a little bit in love with the women he dated. It never lasted long, and he was okay with that, since he wasn't eager to get his heart broken. He'd volunteered for a lot of dangerous things in his life, but heartache wasn't one of them.

He paid for their dinner, brushing away the five bucks Fia produced from one of her slicker pockets. Handing her a paper bag and a drink, he grinned. "You can buy next time." Since he would be in Tallgrass awhile, he might as well make sure she had a reason to see him again.

"That sounds fair." She unpacked her bag: fries on the dash, hamburger staying warm in foil, ketchup squirted from plastic packets onto an edge of French-fry packaging. "It can even be home-cooked as long as it doesn't have to be my cooking."

"Hey, you provide the kitchen, I can do the cooking. I like to cook."

She studied him a moment before licking a dab of ketchup from her fingertip. "I like a man who knows his way around a kitchen," she said at last.

If she would lick her finger like that again, all innocent and tempting and unself-conscious, he'd gladly do the shopping, the prep, the cooking, the serving, and the cleanup for the best gourmet meal she'd ever had—and breakfast to follow.

Mouse climbed into Elliot's seat as he unwrapped his burger, breaking the tension that surrounded him, making it easier for him to draw a breath. When he tore off a bite, she took it delicately from his fingers, chewed it carefully, then set her butt on the console, and waited, quivering, for the next.

"How long have you had her?" Fia asked around a mouthful of her own burger.

He gave the dog an affectionate nudge with his elbow. "Two days."

"Is she a rescue?"

He didn't need to study Mouse to see what Fia saw: scrawny body, ribs showing through her skin, old injuries to her legs and torso. "Yeah. Some kids were playing soccer with her. She was the ball." He flexed his hand again, taking satisfaction in the aches there—and greater satisfaction that the teenagers were in a lot more pain than either him or Mouse.

"Poor baby. Lucky you and your trusty steed rode to her rescue." She smiled, softening the lines and the thinness of her face. Mouse wasn't the only one who needed a few pounds to fill her out. Though her T-shirt and shorts were loose-fitting, Fia looked as if she hadn't found much interest in food lately. Grieving a husband who'd died so young could do that to a woman.

He thought briefly of Scott Thomas, wishing him peace, respecting his sacrifice. Not every service member saw combat, but every one who signed up during wartime knew it was a serious possibility, and they were willing to accept that. Elliot had been lucky enough to come home, as tough and determined as when he'd left, thanks to his parents, Emily, and his own stubborn determination.

He'd lost a lot of people he'd loved, though, and a lot he'd hardly known. He was glad to be out of it, to be home in the United States, but if the Army needed him to go back, he would. *Live for something rather than die for nothing,* General George S. Patton Jr. had said, a fine sentiment, but Elliot preferred to switch it around: *Die for something rather than live for nothing.*

There had always been passions in his life, so he'd never had to settle for nothing. He never would.

"What kept you in Tallgrass after your husband passed?" He softened the words with a smile. "Remember, I'm looking for a place that feels like home."

She pinched off a piece of her hamburger, including a generous hunk of meat, and offered it to Mouse. The dog hesitated, glanced at Elliot, and he nudged her with his elbow to let her know it was okay. She took it in her mouth, then retreated to the backseat to eat it.

"Well, there was nothing in Florida to go back to. And Oklahoma has the best people. All my friends are here." Fia paused long enough to dip a tater tot in ketchup, then studied it a moment before adding, "Though all of them are transplants except Bennie and Patricia. They're all Army wives. Army widows. They're my family."

He understood the value of family, both the one a person was born into and the one they picked for themselves. He stayed in close contact with his parents and Emily; he talked with his nieces and nephew every week; he'd attended the last two family reunions and felt like a better person for it.

Holding what was left of her burger in one hand, she gestured toward Mouse. "Can she have . . ."

"Sure. I don't want her to get used to people food, but right now, I figure she needs all the calories she can get. She's been hungry too long."

Finishing off his own sandwich, he watched her feed Mouse one bite at a time. When she was done, she crumpled the wrapper, then swiped one hand through her hair. It was brown like his, just a few shades darker, and shorter than his by inches. Even with the dampness in the air, it lay smooth, framing her delicate face and, at first glance, making her look dangerously young. At second glance, though, it was clear she'd passed legal age a good while back. He would guess she was in her mid-twenties, maybe a year or two younger.

At first glance, second, and third, she was beautiful in a fragile, innocent way, though he knew appearances could be deceiving. She might rouse his protective instincts—most women did—but physically she was strong, evidenced by impressive biceps and triceps and long solid muscles in her thighs and calves. Emotionally, she was probably pretty strong, too. Being an Army wife wasn't for the faint of heart.

Despite losing her husband, her smile came quick and easy and found its way from her mouth into her dark eyes. It was something to behold, that smile. "I've never met a pit bull before. She's sweet."

"The breed's gotten a bad rap. Worst damage I ever suffered from a dog was from a miniature poodle with pink bows on her ears. I've still got the scars on my ankle." He moved as if to pull up his jeans leg to show her, earning a laugh from her that was so damn appealing, it made him laugh, too.

Just think, if Mouse hadn't needed to take a leak, he wouldn't have been standing in that parking lot in the pouring rain, he wouldn't have been holding an umbrella for the pup, and he wouldn't have met Fia.

Damned if he didn't owe the dog a T-bone.

Fall in Love with Forever Romance

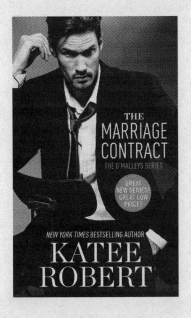

THE MARRIAGE CONTRACT
by Katee Robert

New York Times and *USA Today* bestselling author Katee Robert begins a smoking-hot new series about the O'Malley family—wealthy, powerful, dangerous, and seething with scandal.

Fall in Love with Forever Romance

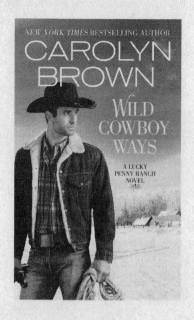

WILD COWBOY WAYS
by Carolyn Brown

New York Times and *USA Today* bestselling author Carolyn Brown begins a hilarious and heartwarming new series with Lucky Penny Ranch, where the wild Dawson brothers might finally be looking to settle down.

Fall in Love with Forever Romance

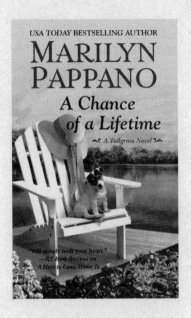

USA TODAY BESTSELLING AUTHOR

MARILYN PAPPANO

A Chance of a Lifetime

A Tallgrass Novel

"Will simply melt your heart."
—RT Book Reviews on
A Hero to Come Home To

A CHANCE OF A LIFETIME
by Marilyn Pappano

In the tradition of *New York Times* bestselling author Robyn Carr comes the fifth book in Marilyn Pappano's Tallgrass, Oklahoma, series. Calvin Sweet is back from the war and Benita Ford's husband has died in combat. Can the two find love and chase away Calvin's demons?